Che Committed Suicide

PETROS MARKARIS

Translated from the Greek
by David Connolly

Arcadia Books Ltd
15–16 Nassau Street
London W1W 7AB

www.arcadiabooks.co.uk

First published in the United Kingdom by Arcadia Books 2009
Original Greek title *O Tse aftokonise*

A catalogue record for this book is available from the British Library.

ISBN 978-1-906413-34-7

Typeset in Garamond by MacGuru Ltd
Printed and bound in Finland by WS Bookwell

Arcadia Books supports English PEN, the fellowship of writers who work together to promote literature and its understanding. English PEN upholds writers' freedoms in Britain and around the world, challenging political and cultural limits on free expression. To find out more, visit www.englishpen.org or contact
English PEN, 6-8 Amwell Street, London EC1R 1UQ

Arcadia Books distributors are as follows:

in the UK and elsewhere in Europe:
Turnaround Publishers Services
Unit 3, Olympia Trading Estate
Coburg Road
London N22 6TZ

in the US and Canada:
Independent Publishers Group
814 N. Franklin Street
Chicago, IL 60610

in Australia:
Tower Books
PO Box 213
Brookvale, NSW 2100

in New Zealand:

Arc

Alles was im Subjekt ist, ist im Objekt, und etwas mehr;
alles was im Objekt ist, ist im Subjekt, und etwas mehr.

What exists in the subject also exists in the object, and something more; what exists in the object also exists in the subject, and something more.

GOETHE

In memory of my mother, Tassoula

1

The cat sat opposite me on the park bench staring at me. I always found it there in the afternoon straddled over the back of the bench. The first few days, it stared at me suspiciously, ready to take to its legs if I made any move towards it. When it was sure that I couldn't care less about it, it stopped paying any attention to me and no longer bothered to disturb itself on my account. In this way, we implemented a policy of good neighbourly relations. It never occupied my bench and, on the few occasions that I was the one to arrive first, I always respected its bench and would leave it free. It was an alley cat, but not the usual orange colour of pedigree alley cats. Its fur was a kind of pinstripe greyish black, like the suits worn at police balls or at funerals. Black ones are invariably reserved for weddings.

Adriani was sitting beside me, knitting away. Since that fatal evening when I had had the bright idea to save Elena Koustas, using my chest to stop the bullet fired by Makis, her adopted son, my life had changed radically. First I had spent eight hours in the operating theatre, then a month and a half in the hospital and now I still had two thirds of my three-month sick leave before me. My dealings with the Homicide Department had been suspended until further notice. I hadn't been in to see them even once since I came home. My two assistants, Vlassopoulos and Dermitzakis, came round every other day at first, then they stopped the visits and limited themselves to phone calls, till in the end they ceased all contact. Ghikas came only once to the hospital, together with the Secretary General from the Ministry, who can't stomach me, but on that day he was all smiles and praise for my bravery. In the end, it was Adriani who took charge of my life, and I confined myself to dragging my steps from the house to the park and from the bedroom to the sitting room, like a Palestinian placed under house arrest by the Israelis.

'What's for dinner tonight?'

Not that I was particularly bothered. I still hadn't got my appetite back and every mouthful stuck in my throat. But I made a thing about it because it helped me to break the monotony.

'I've boiled you a nice bit of chicken and I've made a noodle soup.'

'Chicken again? I had chicken the other day.'

'It's good for you.'

'And why exactly is it good for me, Adriani? I had a perforating wound in the chest, not a punctured stomach.'

'It'll build up your strength. I know what I'm talking about,' she said definitively, without even lifting her eyes from her knitting.

I heaved a sigh and recalled with nostalgia my days in intensive care, when my loved ones came by to pay their respects for one hour in the morning and one hour in the evening and in-between left me in peace. For the nine days I was in there, surrounded by a white ceiling and two white curtains, I experienced the same ritual twice each day. Fist Adriani would come in.

'How are you feeling today, Costas dear?' she would ask with a smile like a flickering candle-flame.

I would try to react to this current of distress that penetrated my cubicle and I pretended to be in better spirits that I actually was. 'Just fine. Waste of their time keeping me in here, there's nothing wrong with me,' I would reply, even though I felt much safer in intensive care.

A restrained sorrowful smile and a slight nod of her head convinced me once again that no one can escape their fate. Then she would sit on the only chair, take my hand and fix her gaze on me. When she went, as soon as the half-hour was up, she left me with my hand numb through lack of movement and with the conviction that I was going to kick the bucket some time in the next twelve hours.

If Adriani led me to make out that I was fine, Katerina, my daughter, had me going in the opposite direction. She would breeze in smiling all over her face. 'Good for you, you'll soon be up and about,' she'd say. 'You're looking better each day.'

'Looking better!' I'd answer her indignantly. 'I'm a wreck. I'm hurting, I'm worn out and all I want to do is sleep.'

Her reply was a warm kiss on the cheek and a tight hug that made my wound hurt even more.

The last to come in was Eleni, my sister-in-law. She'd almost swum from the island where she lived when Adriani had told her that they'd brought me to the hospital half-dead.

Eleni belonged to that category of people who cheer you up by relating the sorry plight of others to you. So she'd begin by counting out one by one all those who were sick in her family, starting with her daughter, who suffered from an allergy and had to be careful of what she ate and how she dressed, then moving on to her husband, who had high blood pressure and who went around with bottles of pills in his pocket. Then there was her mother-in-law, who was confined to bed because she had broken her hip and whom she had to clean and change every day, taking it in turns with her sister-in-law. She even threw in a distant cousin, who had come off his motorbike and had been three months in hospital and it was touch and go whether he'd live. Finally, she came out with the moral of it all: 'So you should be grateful and thank God each day,' she said as she left.

When, however, Adriani's half-hour and Katerina'a and Eleni's quarter of an hour were over, I had all the time to myself until the evening. In the ward, total silence reigned; the nurses were exceedingly discreet and, in general, no one bothered me.

The cat opened its cavernous mouth and yawned majestically. As though it were bored with my presence. I didn't take offence, I'm equally bored with myself.

'Shall we be going?' I said to Adriani, while inside I asked myself why, it would be just as miserable at home.

'Just a bit longer. The fresh air is good for you.'

'I meant in case Fanis comes ...'

'Don't expect him today. From what I recall, he's on duty.'

It wasn't that I was anxious to see the doctor, but quite simply

I get on well with my daughter's boyfriend, Fanis Ouzounidis. My relationship with Fanis was in inverse proportion to the course of the Athens Stock Exchange. Whereas it reached a peak and then began to fall, our relationship first reached a low and then began to climb. I'd met him as the cardiologist on duty when I had ended up one night at the General Infirmary with acute ischaemia. I immediately liked him because he was always smiling and full of wisecracks. Until I discovered that he was seeing my daughter and I was furious. In the end, for Katerina's sake, I reconciled myself more with the idea that he was her boyfriend than with him personally. I felt that he had betrayed my confidence, and when you have come up through the Police Force, the idea of betrayal clings to you like a leech. It was in intensive care that I first felt close to him, and that had nothing to do with medicine. He'd pop in at around twelve, just before lunch, and always with a smile on his face. And every time, he called me something different. From 'And how are we today, Inspector' to 'How's my future father-in-law, then' and the ironically intoned 'Dad!' This was repeated three or four times a day, and also at night, when he was on duty, and it was combined with discreet questions about how I was getting on, whether I needed anything. I found out about this indirectly, from the nurses, who every so often came out with things like 'We have to take good care of you, otherwise we'll have Doctor Ouzounidis after us.'

Things began to turn sour from the moment that they took me out of intensive care. That same day, Adriani moved into my room on a twenty-four basis and began to take charge of everything. Partly the fact that I was a police officer who had been wounded on duty and partly the relationship between my daughter and Fanis meant that the doctors thought they had to give a daily report to her on the course of my recovery, on the medicines that they were administering to me and on the minor problems I faced from the effects of the operation. From the third day, she would stay in the visiting room and strike up a conversation with the doctors on every matter you could think of. If I were to dare venture an opinion of my own, for example, that I was in pain or that I felt the wound tugging, she would cut me short at once. 'Leave it to me, Costas. You don't know about these things.' The doctors kept their anger in check because of Fanis, I was too weak to react, while the nurses hated her but didn't dare to show it. In the end, it was Katerina who got up the courage to talk to her. Adriani burst out sobbing. 'All right, Katerina,' she said through her tears, 'if I'm not the right person to take care of my husband, then hire a private nurse and I'll go home.' Her sobbing took the wind out of Katerina's sails and sealed my fate as a hostage.

'It's chilly, put your cardigan on.' She took the cardigan that she had knitted for me out of her bag and handed it to me.

'I don't need it, I'm not cold.'

'You are cold, Costas dear, I know what I'm talking about.'

The cat got up from its place, stretched and jumped lightly down to the ground. It cast one last look at me, then it turned and went off with its tail erect, like a patrol car aerial.

I have no relationship at all with animals, neither a friendly nor an unfriendly one. But that cat's arrogance got on my nerves.

I took the cardigan and put it on.

2

Fanis proved Adriani wrong. He showed up at around seven, just as I was reading the evening newspaper. This was another novelty of my post-hospital life: in the past it was dictionaries that monopolised my reading interests. Now I had moved on to newspapers, as an antidote for my boredom. I started with the morning paper, brought to me by Adriani, then I thumbed through my dictionaries; when I go out for my afternoon stroll, I buy the evening paper and read once again, in carbon copy, the morning news and, finally, I hear the same news for a third time on television just in case I've missed anything. The doctors kept talking of post-operative side effects, but they were nothing compared to the side effects of convalescence: unbearable boredom and inactivity to the point of paralysis.

Fanis found me reading the minor pieces on the finance pages with the absorption of an autistic. I was still wearing the cardigan that Adriani had had me wear in the park, not because I was feeling cold, but because I had reached such a state of apathy that I could no longer distinguish cold and heat. I was quite capable of going to bed wearing the cardigan if Adriani didn't take it off me.

Fanis stood before me and smiled.

'Are you up for a drive?'

'How come you're not on duty?' I asked him, lifting my eyes from the newspaper.

'I swapped with a colleague. It suited him to do his shift today.'

I put down the newspaper and got to my feet.

'Just don't be late for dinner!' Adriani shouted from the kitchen. 'Costas has to eat at nine.'

'Why, what will to happen to him if he eats at ten?' asked Fanis with a laugh.

Adriani appeared from the kitchen. 'Fanis, you're the doctor. Do you think it's good for him to sleep on a full stomach while he's convalescing?'

'Yes, but you're the one cooking for him. Even if he eats at midnight, he'll still sleep like a baby.'

'Let's be off, it's getting late,' I said to Fanis, because I saw she was about to counter him with all her quack remedies and I'd end up missing my outing.

In the past, whenever she saw Fanis, she'd leave whatever she was doing in order to be sociable. Now she opened the door for him and then disappeared into the kitchen. In general, she didn't look kindly on anyone coming to the house because she thought that it took me away from her complete control. With Fanis, she was reserved and a little suspicious because he was a doctor and she didn't know what it might come to.

'Why are you wearing a cardigan? Are you feeling cold?' Fanis asked me.

'No.'

'Take it off, it's warm outside and it'll make you sweat.'

I took it off. My wife tells me to wear it, my doctor tells me to take it off, I just obey.

'Let's go along the coast road and get a bit of sea air,' Fanis said, turning from Hymettou Avenue into Vouliagmenis Avenue.

The traffic was light and no one was in a rush. Since the airport was moved to Spata, Vouliagmenis Avenue is not so busy. Fanis drove down Alimou Avenue and turned into Poseidonos Avenue. Crowds of people were squashed into the four feet in front of the stone wall overlooking the sea. The rest of the pavement had been taken over by various Indians, Pakistanis, Egyptians and Sudanese, who had spread out tablecloths and were selling women's handbags, wallets, euro converters, purses for the new euro coins, binoculars, watches, alarm clocks and plastic flowers. They themselves were squatting next to the tablecloths and chatting to each other, given that the passers-by didn't seem to care a fig for their merchandise.

It was June. The really hot days hadn't arrived yet and I could feel the breeze from the Saronic Gulf on my face. There were many people still in the sea or playing rackets on the beach, while some of those fake sailboats that keep sinking and then righting themselves were skidding back and forth in the bay of Faliron. I shut my eyes and emptied my mind of the thought of chicken with noodle soup that made me feel sick, of two months more of autism in the form of convalescence, of the cat that would be waiting for me the following evening in the usual place in the park … I tried to think of something else, but I could find nothing.

'You have to get yourself out of that vicious circle of convalescence.'

Fanis's voice woke me up and I opened my eyes. We had left Kalamaki behind and were heading towards Elliniko. Fanis went on talking, with his eyes fixed on the road.

'You know how at first we were always at loggerheads. You had me down as a cold and conceited young doctor and I saw you as a crabby old copper, who thought I had seduced his daughter. Well, I still preferred you even like that to the sop you are now.'

In his attempt to bring me to my senses, Fanis had become distracted and had to swerve suddenly to avoid bumping into the back of a Ford cabriolet with a couple inside. The driver had spiked hair, like almost everyone today, as if they had all just had a run-in with Count Dracula. The young girl had a ring through her nostrils.

The fellow with the spiked hair caught up to us at the next red light. He sped up close to let Fanis have a piece of his mind, but then he caught sight of the doctor's sticker on the windscreen.

'Doctor, eh? I should have known!' he shouted triumphantly. 'With driving like that, you've either got to be a doctor or a woman.'

'Why, what's wrong with women, Yannis?' the young girl next to him chipped in angrily.

'Nothing, honey. It's just that when you women get behind the wheel you turn into lace murderers.'

'Oh, so your mother's a lace murderer, is she? So why are you calling her every five minutes to hear her darling little voice?'

The girl was so furious that the ring in her nostril was shaking. She opened the car door, got out and slammed it behind her.

'Come back here, Maggie! Where are you going? All right, I'm a fuckhead!'

It was as if she hadn't heard him. She dodged between the cars and stepped onto the opposite pavement.

'It's your fault, you surgeon-butcher!' the fellow yelled to Fanis.

'I'm no surgeon,' Fanis replied, laughing. 'I'm a cardiologist, and if you go on like that you'll be needing my services.'

The fellow didn't hear him, however. The lights had changed to green and he edged forward, honking his horn like a madman to get the girl to come back, while the cars behind him were honking their horns to get him to move on so they could pass.

Fanis was splitting himself laughing. I watched the whole scene impassively and Fanis noticed.

'You see, in the past you'd have blown your top with the fellow and with me for laughing. Now you just let it pass you by indifferently. That's a feather in the cap for Mrs Haritos. I didn't think her capable of wrapping you round her finger.'

He pulled up in front of the sports facilities at Aghios Kosmas. By the time he'd found somewhere to park, he had become serious. He turned and looked at me. It was almost dark and we could barely make each other out in the car.

'Katerina is thinking of giving up on her doctorate and coming back to Athens,' he said.

'Why?'

'To do some restoration work on you. She's afraid that before long we'll be spooning you up off the floor.' He paused a moment, while still facing me. 'I told her it's not necessary. You're a person with a lot of inner strength, all you have to do is get the system up and running.'

'Is that why you wanted us to go for a drive? To tell me about Katerina?'

'Because of that, and also because there's no point in swapping one babysitter for another, for your daughter to take your wife's place. The point is that you have to do something for yourself.' He fell silent for a moment, as if weighing up what it was he wanted to say. 'If you go on like this, there's no question of your returning to the service. You'll need more convalescence.'

'Keep your tongue in your mouth!' It was the first time my voice hadn't come out lifeless.

'Katerina is at the most crucial point in her thesis.' Again, he halted. He was worried in case he went too far and I took it the wrong way. 'It's not the right time to put it on hold. And I can't stop her. Only you ...'

He saw that I wasn't going to reply and was about to turn the key in the ignition.

'You're all of you very kind,' I said, and he left his hand on the key. 'My wife, who caters to my every whim, and you, who are always trying to cheer me up, and my daughter, who's willing to give up her doctorate to come and pamper me. So why do I feel so lousy?'

'Because you don't send us all packing and do what you feel like. That's what I'm trying to explain to you.'

This time he turned the key and the engine started up. He waved goodbye to me in front of the apartment block. I didn't ask him up because I knew it was time for his evening call to Katerina.

The kitchen table was laid and waiting for me.

'How was the drive?' Adriani asked me.

'Fine. We went along the coast as far as Aghios Kosmas.'

'In summer, the coastal road is full of life. As soon as you're well, I'll take you for a drive down there in the mornings.' The message was crystal clear. She would be the one to decide when I was well and she would be the one to take me for a drive. 'Sit down and I'll bring you your soup.'

'I don't want soup. It's sizzling outside, people are in the sea and I'm eating noodle soup.'

'Because you have to get better, Costas dear. It'll help you to get better.'

'Which damn quack says that?' I knew that there was no medical truth behind it – the treatment was her own.

Instead of replying, Adriani took the bowl, filled it with soup and tossed a chicken leg into it. She brought it over and put it in front of me.

'If you want, eat it, if not, don't. I'm simply doing my duty,' she said, going out and leaving me alone in the kitchen.

I clutched at the two corners of the table to pull myself up and let out a few choice words, when suddenly my legs went from under me. My anger deflated like a manometer; all the strength went out of my body and I felt paralysed. I sat down again, took a piece of bread, broke it into pieces and tossed it into the soup. I started to eat the soaked bread like an old man. At the third mouthful, I left the spoon in the bowl and went out of the kitchen.

3

I was sitting on the couch beside Adriani and watching the *Aquarium*. The *Aquarium* in question is not inhabited by tropical fish, but by the well-known TV hostess, Aspasia Komi, who every week invites various politicians, businessmen, sometimes a footballer or weightlifter, makes accusations, uncovers scandals and, in the end, sends her guests away smiling. In the past, I would turn my nose up at such programmes and leave the room. Now I turn my nose up and watch them, just like nine out of ten other Greeks today.

Komi was sitting in a comfortable armchair facing Jason Favieros, a well-kept fifty-year-old, who was sitting in the other comfortable armchair. If it wasn't widely known that he had made bags of money in the last twenty years, you would have taken him for a rocker from the seventies who had forgotten to shave and change his jeans. He was the owner of a huge construction company with projects throughout the Balkans, was building a large part of the works for the Olympics, but was wearing faded jeans and a crumpled jacket.

Komi had him with his back to the wall and was questioning him about the accusations that the Olympic works would not be ready in time, but Favieros did not appear to be the slightest bit worried.

'Put it all down to unfounded rumours, Mrs Komi,' he said. 'In undertakings of this kind, a great deal of money is involved, there's a lot of interest generated and Greece is a small country in business terms. Even if we disagree, it's only natural that competitors often resort to trying to discredit their opponents or even eliminating them.'

'So are you telling me that the building projects will be ready on time for the Olympics?'

'No,' he replied with a self-confident smile, 'I'm telling you that they'll be ready much earlier.'

'You realise that you have just made a commitment to our viewers, Mr Favieros.' Komi turned to the camera and was beaming with satisfaction.

'Of course,' replied Favieros completely at ease.

'Yes, I'd just like to see you when we've made fools of ourselves before the entire world,' commented Adriani, who thinks all assurances are fraudulent.

Perhaps she is right, but Favieros had brought the discussion to an end with his commitment and Komi was looking for some other ground to do battle.

'Nevertheless, there's still an unanswered question in business circles, Mr Favieros,' she said. 'How did you manage to create that – albeit by Greek standards – colossal business empire of yours from absolutely nothing in the space of fifteen years?'

'Because very early on I understood two simple things,' answered Favieros immediately. 'First, if I confined myself to Greece, my businesses would be condemned to stagnation. And that's why I opened up in the Balkans. Today, either directly or through my subsidiaries, I'm engaged in projects throughout the Balkans, even in Kosovo. And apart from that, I exploited the traditionally friendly relations that Greece has with a number of Arab countries.'

'And what was the second thing?'

'That a businessman shouldn't have any complexes. A large part of our work is carried out in partnership with other European companies, much bigger than mine. I can assure you, Mrs Komi, that I have never been afraid that they would swallow us up.'

'It seems that you discovered the secrets of globalisation very early, Mr Favieros.'

Favieros broke into laughter. 'I knew the secrets of globalisation long before globalisation.'

'How about that, a pioneer then! And how did you come to discover them?'

Komi came out with a cute little smile as a kind of down-payment for the amusing reply she was about to hear.

'From leftist internationalism, Mrs Komi. Globalisation is the last stage of internationalism. Read the *Communist Manifesto*.'

Whereas, until now, he had been completely open and informal, I suddenly discerned in his voice something like pride and provocation at the same time. The smile on Komi's lips had turned into a smile of perplexity. She had no idea what either internationalism or the *Communist Manifesto* was, much less what they had to say. But she was experienced and quickly recovered her composure. She leaned forward to fix him better with her gaze.

'You might call it internationalism and the *Communist Manifesto*, but others would call it connections with the governing party, Mr Favieros,' she said in a bland tone. 'And they also talk of your dealings with ministers.'

'Not only with the governing party but with all the parties. Do you know any businessman who doesn't have contacts with the parties, Mrs Komi?'

'But we're not talking just about contacts here. We're talking about close personal relations. Only the other day, you were seen eating with a government minister at a well-known and very fashionable restaurant.'

'What are you implying? That the Minister and I were plotting in public and in a restaurant of all places?' said Favieros laughing. Then he suddenly grew serious. 'Don't forget that I am acquainted with many of the ministers in the government since the time of the military Junta, when we were students together.'

'Nevertheless, there are more than a few who claim that the rapid growth of your businesses is due to the fact that you have the favour of the government,' said Komi. 'Perhaps because you were once comrades-in-arms,' she added caustically.

'My business success is due to proper planning, the right investments and sheer hard work, Mrs Komi,' said Favieros gravely. 'And that will be proven beyond a shadow of doubt, and very soon too.' He stressed the last phrase, as if it were about to happen.

Komi opened a folder lying in her lap, took out a sheet of paper and handed it to Favieros.

'Do you recognise this letter?' she asked him. 'It is a letter of protest from five construction consortiums to the Minister of Town Planning and Public Works. They are protesting because the contract for the construction of three junctions was not awarded and will be re-advertised simply to allow your company, which wasn't ready, to take part.'

Favieros glanced at the letter and slowly lifted his head

'Yes, I had heard something, but it hadn't been brought to my attention.'

'As you can see, here we're dealing with very specific accusations. Is there any basis to them?'

'Let me answer you,' said Favieros calmly.

Slowly, his hand went to the inside pocket of his jacket. Komi clutched hold of the armchair, fixed her gaze on Favieros and waited. Through her body language, she was trying to transmit the electrified atmosphere to the viewers, but the staging stank from here to Mesoghia, where the channel was located.

Favieros withdrew his hand from his pocket, but he wasn't holding a paper or even a handkerchief to wipe the sweat from his brow. In his hand was a small Beretta pistol, which he turned towards Komi.

'Heavens above, he's going to shoot her!' shouted Adriani, jumping to her feet.

Komi stared at the pistol as if mesmerised. I don't know if it was her terror that had paralysed her or the fascination that the murder weapon has for the victim, something I've noticed on numerous occasions. At any rate, when she came out of her momentary torpor, she started to get to her feet terrified, except that her legs didn't obey her and she collapsed back into the armchair. She opened her mouth to say something, but her tongue had entered into an alliance with her legs and refused to obey.

'Mr Favieros,' said a voice off set, trying to pacify him, yet trembling with fear. 'Mr Favieros, put the gun away … Please … We're on the air, Mr Favieros.'

Favieros paid no attention. He went on holding the pistol and staring at Komi.

'Switch to the adverts, switch to the adverts,' the same voice cried.

'No adverts!' The voice heard now was categorical, allowing no room for objection. 'Stay with it. I'm the boss here!'

'Mr Valsamakis!' shouted the first voice. 'We'll end up in prison!'

'How often do you think you'll get an opportunity like this, you dimwit. Do you want to spend all your life on news bulletins and game shows or do you want CNN to fall at your feet and beg you? Well, do you or don't you!'

'Patroklos, give me a close-up of Favieros! I want a close-up of Favieros!' shouted the director.

'Aspasia, say something to him! You're on the air, talk to him!' Again the voice of the boss was heard.

Komi made no effort to hide her panic.

'Mr Favieros,' she mumbled. 'Don't … please …'

As Patroklos was zooming in, Favieros made three lightning-quick moves: he turned the gun on himself, pushed the barrel into his mouth and squeezed the trigger. The shot was heard together with Komi's scream. A red fountain gushed from Favieros's head, while his brains splattered onto the scenery, which depicted a huge aquarium with variously coloured tropical fish. Favieros's body slumped forward as if he had suddenly fallen asleep in the armchair.

Komi had leapt to her feet and was retreating almost mechanically towards the exit on set, but the voice of the boss stopped her in her tracks.

'Stay where you are, Aspasia!' he shouted to her. 'Just think that at this very moment we're writing history! The first live suicide on TV!' Komi hesitated for a moment, then turned to the camera, so as to allow a close-up of her face and also to avoid seeing Favieros.

Beside me, Adriani had put her hands over her eyes and, swaying to and fro as if keening, whispered:

'No, dear God, no … No, dear God, no …'

'Aspasia, talk to the camera!' Again the voice of the boss was heard. And on cue the voice of the director: 'Miltos, zoom in on Aspasia!'

'Dear viewers.' This time is was Aspasia's voice that was heard, but instead of her, what appeared was a blurred image with blood and splatters.

'Miltos, wipe your lens! I don't have an image!' shouted the director.

'What can I wipe it with?'

'Your sleeve for all I care. I want an image.'

'Which imbecile left the intercom on? Switch to insert.'

The voices and sound cut out and on the bottom right of the screen appeared the words 'unedited footage'.

'Turn it off!' Adriani screamed angrily. 'Their only problem is that it's unedited. Have they no conscience!'

'I'll turn it off,' I said, 'but you can bet you'll see the suicide on all the news bulletins for the next week at least, like a trailer for a new film.'

'And as for him, what on earth was he thinking of to commit suicide in front of the camera?'

'Who knows what goes on in people's minds.'

I had recourse to this vague reply because if we started to discuss it, we would only end up talking nonsense.

'Everything these days is done for show, even committing suicide.'

There are times when Adriani hits the nail on the head without being aware of it. What reason had a successful businessman like Jason Favieros to stage a public suicide? Unless he was after something else and changed his mind along the way and preferred suicide. But what else? Killing Komi? She needed killing, but Favieros certainly didn't watch so much TV as to have his killer instincts aroused by that blonde Barbie, all covered in glitter like a Christmas tree.

The other alternative was that he had wanted to threaten his rivals. So what was he doing with the pistol? Would he threaten his rivals with a pistol pointing at the camera? I had been a long time out of training when it came to crime investigations and I was coming up with nonsense.

4

I spent another sleepless night. The insomnia was my worst torment. I dreaded the moment when I turned off the light. Fanis told me that this often happens during convalescence and recommended that I take half a sleeping pill before going to bed. I refused to take as much as a quarter, because if you get used to sleeping pills, you can never do without them. I spent half my nights with my eyes wide open, tossing and turning in bed.

The previous night's insomnia, however, had none of the usual symptoms: neither exasperation nor counting backwards from a thousand nor the midnight itinerary of kitchen–sitting room–verandah. On the contrary, each time I felt sleep coming on, I threw some water over my face to stay awake. I couldn't for the life of me work out what it was that had driven Jason Favieros to commit public suicide. I could have accepted his suicide in the office or at home. His business wasn't going well, he had psychological problems, his wife was cheating on him, he was involved in some major scandal and he preferred suicide to the shame of it. It was the public part of it that I couldn't understand. Why in public? Why would Jason Favieros want to make a spectacle of his death? The likes of Favieros hate fuss and move in places far from the public eye, in offices lined with thick carpets to stifle the sound. And suddenly, one of their kind causes the TV ratings to rocket through his death? The possibility that he may have simply flipped could be excluded. He had gone to the studio prepared, with the pistol next to his wallet. Consequently, the public suicide served some purpose; he wanted to reveal something.

Beside me, Adriani was sleeping with that constant, muted, snoring of hers, like a cistern filling all night long. I usually bite the pillow in exasperation, but that night I had hardly heard her. It was the first night of insomnia for months that I didn't want to end and that I revelled in.

For the past month, getting out of bed in the mornings had been a veritable odyssey. I thought of the day before me, the strict programme, without any novelty or deviation, and my feet refused to touch the mat next to the bed. That day, however, I was snug in bed by choice, because I was enjoying it. I had spread my dictionaries around me and was skipping from one to the other. I found the best documented entry in Dimitrakos's Lexicon.

'Suicide: 1. By one's own hand, perpetrator: Aesch. *Suppl.*, 592 *This father; by your own hand, Lord, you planted our stock*; // gen. executioner, perpetrator: Soph. *Antig.*, 306 *If you don't find the same man whose hands dug this tomb, do not appear before my eyes*; 2. partic. one who kills himself intentionally, self-inflicted killing: Soph. *Antig.*, 1175 *Haemon is gone. He drew his blood himself* // mod. Only act or instance of killing oneself, murderer; 3. Soph. *Oed. Rex.*, 231 *If he knows the murder, another, from foreign parts, let him not keep silent*;'

'Are you all right?' She poked her head round the door and fixed her eyes on me in concern.

'I'm fine.'

'Why don't you get up?'

'I thought I'd have a bit of a lie-in.'

'You don't feel out of sorts, do you?'

'No. Nor strain from too much work.'

She stared at me, surprised at my somewhat ironic tone, which of late had faded together with the post-operational symptoms. The truth was that I, too, wondered what was the cause of my unexpected recovery. Was it the brainwashing by Ouzounidis the previous evening? Was it Favieros's suicide? Most likely the latter. Something wasn't right about that suicide, something had been bothering me from the moment that I saw his brains sticking to the huge aquarium on the set, and it was this that had dragged up the policeman, half-drowned and gasping for breath, from the watery depths back to the surface. I told myself it was just bullshit every time my thoughts led nowhere. I was creating crossword puzzles to pass the time. But I knew deep down that there was more to it. Favieros's suicide had something of a show about it that simply didn't add up, and it was this that was bothering me.

I hate idling in bed. In the past I had feelings of guilt about it because I thought I was taking up valuable time from the Force. In the state I was in, it made me feel even more down. I got up and started to get dressed with my mind still on Favieros. When I had finished dressing, I realised that for the first time in months I had put on a suit and tie. I looked at myself in the mirror on the wardrobe door. In appearance, at least, I again saw a police inspector and the sight did me the world of good. The one jarring note was my unshaven face. Shaving is a kind of certification. It certifies that you are healthy and working. On the contrary, an unshaven face means that you're ill, retired or unemployed. For the previous two months I had belonged to the second category and had only been shaving every third day. I took off my jacket and went into the bathroom. Shaving that day was my first brave attempt to move back into the first category. When I had finished, I put my jacket back on and left the dictionaries lying over the bed. It was one of the little privileges allowed me by Adriani following my being shot. Not having to tidy things up, not even my dictionaries, which she loathed and which infuriated her whenever I left them lying around. But now she didn't say even a word, because in her opinion, I mustn't tire myself during my convalescence. Nevertheless, I usually tidied them up myself because Adriani would arrange them higgledy-piggledy as if exacting revenge on them in this way.

She was sitting at the kitchen table and scraping courgettes. She lifted her head mechanically, certain that she would see me in my pyjamas. She remained with her knife in the air and her eyes bulging, staring at the well-groomed version of me, as though seeing a ghost from the past.

'Where are you off to?'

'To get the newspapers.'

'And you've put your suit on to get the newspapers?'

'Actually, I was going to wear my official parade uniform, but I didn't want to overdo it.'

Adriani was nonplussed and tossed the courgette into the rubbish instead of into the bowl of water. I slammed the door behind me so that the noise would wake her up after I had gone.

On coming out of the lift, I bumped into Mrs Prelatis.

'Now you're a sight for sore eyes, Mr Haritos,' she said enthusiastically. 'At last, you're back to being the Inspector that we all know.'

I could have kissed her. With all the foreseeable and unforeseeable consequences. I remembered, however, that Adriani and Mrs Prelatis had a mutual dislike of each other. So she might have been saying that as a dig at Adriani, who hadn't let me out alone for such a long time.

My suspicions dissolved when the newsagent confirmed Prelatis's enthusiasm. 'Hale and hearty, Inspector, hale and hearty,' he shouted. 'First time for a long time that I've seen you looking so well. What can I give you?'

'The papers.'

'Which one will it be today?'

He asked me because each day I would get a different one, either for a change or simply to confirm that I found them all equally boring. I'm still not sure.

'Give me all of them, except the sports papers.'

He stared at me in astonishment, but then his face lit up. 'The suicide, right?' he said, full of satisfaction that he had found the solution to the riddle.

'Yes. Why, do you know anything?'

'No, heavens no!' he replied with the instinctive fear of the ordinary citizen who doesn't want to get involved. 'But from what I saw with a quick glance, the papers don't know anything either.'

He again expressed his delight at seeing me so well and tossed the newspapers into a large plastic bag. I went down Aroni Street and arrived at the little square of Aghiou Lazarou. It had a corner café that had been upgraded into a coffee bar. I chose one of the tables in the shade and took the pack of newspapers from the plastic bag.

The waiter was an unaccommodating fifty-year-old who came over and took my order with a curt 'So what's it to be?' I ordered a sweet Greek coffee, which was met with a scowl tantamount to a stream of abuse, evidently because the Greek coffee downgraded the coffee bar back to a corner café.

All the newspapers had Favieros's suicide as their front-page story. Only the headlines differed. 'Tragic Suicide By Jason Favieros' and 'Mystery Suicide On Camera' were the headlines in the more serious newspapers. From then on, it was all downhill: from 'Favieros's Spectacular Suicide' and 'Suicide Exclusive On Camera' to 'Big Brother Live'. All the papers had a photograph in the middle of the page, showing the same downhill direction. The most serious had a neutral photograph of Favieros shaking the Prime Minister's hand. Two more showed Favieros with the pistol in his mouth. One of the tabloids preferred a photograph of Favieros after his suicide with the blood-splattered aquarium.

I sipped the coffee, which was like water, and read the reports one by one. They were full of questions and conjectures, which meant that no one knew anything and they were all fishing for the answers. One claimed that Favieros had major financial problems and was on the brink of bankruptcy. Another that he had some incurable illness and had chosen to put an end to his life in this spectacular way. One leftist newspaper successively analysed the acute mental problems that Favieros had been left with following his torture at the hands of the Junta's Military Police. It actually presented an interview with a psychiatrist who always features in similar cases with erudite psychological portraits of the victim or perpetrator that leave you wondering why he's not with the FBI. The newspaper with the headline 'Big Brother Live' came up with the idea that, because of some incurable illness, Favieros had struck a deal with the TV channel to publicly commit suicide in exchange for a huge sum that he would leave to his family. Finally, another gutter-press rag, full of colour photos, insinuated that Favieros was gay, was being blackmailed, and preferred public suicide to public scandal.

They knew as much as I did, I thought to myself. In other words, nothing. I glanced at my watch. I had been engrossed in the papers for a full two hours and it was long past lunchtime in my private clinic. I left the two and a half euros they charged for the thimbleful of coffee on the table and headed back home. I was halfway down Aroni Street when it suddenly crossed my mind to call Sotiropoulos, a reporter who for years had been a thorn in my side and with whom I had a love-hate relationship, with the emphasis on hate. I bought a phone card from the kiosk and called directory enquiries to get the number of the channel where Sotiropoulos worked.

'Haritos, what a surprise!' The title 'Inspector' had been dispensed with long ago. 'So, you're fully recovered?'

'More or less. It's all a matter of time.'

'When will you be back with us?'

'I've another two months' sick leave.'

'You'll be the end of me!' he exclaimed disappointedly. 'That Yanoutsos who replaced you is driving us crazy. Getting information from him is like trying to get blood out of a stone.'

I chuckled with glee. 'Serves you right. You used to accuse me of keeping you all in the dark.'

'No, it's not that he doesn't want to reveal his cards; it's that he's unable to put two words together. He writes his statements in a notepad and reads them out as though there were no full stops or commas.'

I almost dropped the phone. 'You mean Ghikas lets Yanoutsos make statements to the press?' I asked flabbergasted. Ghikas, Head of Security, guarded press statements like he did his wallet; he gave them to no one. He had me write them for him and he learned them by heart for the reporters. And now he was handing over his wallet to that blockhead Yanoutsos, who wore his bulletproof vest back to front like a straitjacket?

'Rumour has it that he does it on purpose,' said Sotiropoulos, breaking into laughter. 'He dislikes him so much that he has him garble the statements to compromise him.'

That's something Ghikas is quite capable of.

'I want to ask you a question, Sotiropoulos. Purely out of personal interest. What do you know about Favieros's suicide?'

'Nothing.' His answer was direct and categorical. 'No one knows anything. All as black as pitch. Perhaps his family knows something, but they've shut up shop.'

'And all the talk in the papers?'

'You mean about financial and psychological problems and the like? Hot air, Haritos. When reporters have nothing to go on, they simply dredge the drains to see what they might come up with, and what we usually come up with are old shoes, plastic bags and various refuse. Anyhow, as things stand, that story doesn't have much of a life because there's simply nothing for us to write about.'

I thanked him and he told me he couldn't wait for me to get back on the job.

Adriani didn't hear me entering the house because she was talking to our daughter on the phone.

'Do you realise he's been out wandering the streets for three hours now?' she said to her. It was clear she was talking about me and so I had every right to eavesdrop.

''Three hours, do you hear, Katerina?' Her voice was full of concern. 'Without telling me where he was going, he just opened the door and walked out.' She paused to hear what Katerina said and then went on, even more tensely: 'What harm will he come to? Are you joking? He might have had a dizzy spell and fainted. He might be in hospital right now! I've pleaded with him to get a mobile phone, but he won't hear of it.' This time the pause was cut short with indignation. 'Naturally, it's me who's to blame again!' She felt angry and when Adriani is angry, there's no point in trying to get a word in yourself. 'Fanis, Fanis! Fanis isn't here all day to see how I've rescued him from the hands of death! What I should do is get the police onto it because he's been gone three hours now and I've no idea where he is!'

'I'm here,' I said, appearing in the doorway to the sitting room.

She was taken aback because she hadn't heard me come in, and an expression of relief spread over her face.

'Here's your dad, you wanted to talk to him and here he is,' she said to Katerina with all the cheek in the world. 'Your daughter,' she said, handing me the receiver.

'How are you doing, dear?'

'Me, I'm fine. It's Mum who's not all right. You frightened her out of her wits and she was about to send out a search party for you,' she said laughing.

'I know. She'll have to accept it.'

There was a short pause. 'Can I assume that your chat with Fanis yesterday had some effect?' she asked cheerfully.

'That and the suicide.'

'What suicide?'

'Favieros's. Last night on the TV. Something suddenly clicked inside me.'

She burst out laughing.

'A bit macabre, but a shock like that usually does the trick.' Then she became serious. 'She does it out of love, you know. So don't go now to the other extreme,' she said to me.

'Don't worry! We'll get back on track again.'

We said our goodbyes and hung up. Adriani had gone into the kitchen to get the meal ready. Before going after her, I made a stop in the bedroom and took hold of Apostolides's *Lexicon of All the Words in Hippocrates*. Katerina had bought it for me when I'd gone into hospital after a heart attack.

I opened it at the word 'recover' and went into the kitchen. The table was laid and the food ready: boiled courgettes that she had been preparing in the morning and three meatballs. I went up to her holding the dictionary and read the entry out to her:

'"Recover: regain health after illness; become cured. *Some recovering their health after medical treatment.*" I belong to the "some" of Hippocrates who have recovered their health,' I told her. 'In fact, I feel so healthy that I'm thinking of cutting short my sick leave and going back to the Force.'

'Costas, for heaven's sake, let's not make any hasty decisions!' On the one hand she was beseeching me out of fear and on the other she was reminding me that it wasn't my decision alone but that we would make the decision together. 'And when all's said and done, you pay a fortune for health insurance. Now that you've an opportunity to get back some of what they've been taking from you all these years, are you going to pass up the chance?'

She smiled at me triumphantly because she had found the argument that no Greek can counter. Any Greek who doesn't believe that the state is stealing from him and doesn't feel the need to get his own back is either mad or a communist.

5

I had gathered momentum following my historic sortie and was flirting with the idea of cancelling my afternoon appointment with the cat. But, after careful consideration, I decided that there was more to be gained by my avoiding head-on confrontations and resorting to guerrilla warfare.

A quarter of an hour before the designated time for our little outing, I felt her shadow falling over me.

'Aren't we going to go for a walk today?'

I lifted my eyes from the dictionary and said with a wry smile: 'We'll go, but only if you promise me that tomorrow you'll make me stuffed vegetables.'

'I'd be happy to, but maybe they're too heavy for your stomach just now, Costas.'

'Not again? I've told you a thousand times that I have a bullet wound in my chest not an ulcer in my stomach, but you won't listen.'

She thought about it for a moment and came up with a compromise to save face. 'All right, I'll use less onion so they won't be too heavy.'

I was pleased with myself that my little scheme had worked and now the cat was sitting opposite me and staring at me with that same arrogant expression that my presence usually provoked. I got up slowly, stretched and went up to it. It was alarmed because my action was in breach of our silent agreement. It sat up in readiness and stared at me anxiously. When it saw that I kept on approaching it nonchalantly, it leapt down smartly from the bench so as to withdraw honorably with its tail in the air instead of being forced into a disorderly retreat. From then on, it would at least be on its toes whenever it saw me and I would be free of its arrogance.

Adriani hadn't noticed a thing as she was engrossed in the newspapers that I had bought that morning.

'As if he would commit suicide because of financial problems!' she suddenly exclaimed.

'Do you think it improbable?' I asked, sitting back down beside her.

'Where've you been hiding?' she replied, as though I had just been repatriated along with the communists from the former Soviet democracies. 'Even if he was heading for bankruptcy, his company might have lost out but not him. You can bet your life that he had his personal fortune stashed away in Switzerland.'

'Why Switzerland?'

'Because it's not part of the European Union and they can't check his account.'

I stared at her, dumbfounded. 'Adriani, old girl,' I said to her, 'why don't you go down to Headquarters and I'll stay at home and make the stuffed vegetables?'

'You see what you learn from TV?' she replied with a triumphant smile. 'You're the only one who doesn't learn anything because you can't be bothered.'

'Do they say things like that on TV?'

'Are you joking? Do you realise what you can hear on the box? It's a regular university.'

'One door closes, another opens,' I thought, remembering one of my favourite songs, and in the end it was the box that won out.

'Let's go, it looks like rain,' said Adriani.

I looked up and, through the trees, saw the sky heavy with black clouds. The first big drops caught up with us at the exit to the park. There was no wind at all and the rain fell perpendicularly, like a barber's curtain that doesn't let you see more than ten yards in front of your nose. At the edge of the pavement, we were stopped by a current of water. In less than five minutes, Kononos Street had turned into a tributary of Filolaou Street that had itself become a torrential river.

'How are we going to get across?' I asked Adriani. 'Just look at it.'

She grabbed me by the hand and pulled me into the entrance of an apartment block. 'Wait here, I'll be back,' she said and ran off to the supermarket three doors away.

I was wondering whether she had gone to buy a child's inflatable canoe when I saw her coming out with a handful of empty plastic bags.

'Lift your leg up,' she said, slipping one of them over my shoes and fixing it with a rubber band as though wrapping up a frozen chicken. Any resistance on my part was greeted with a 'Shh, I know what I'm doing!' and she moved on to the second foot.

'You're mad if you think I'm going to dive into that river with plastic bags for flippers,' I told her.

'You're not the only one. Just look around you!'

And she pointed to one woman who was fording the river with plastic bags on her feet and one over her head.

'Be thankful that I had the good sense to bring an umbrella,' Adriani boasted.

The situation overcame all my resistance and in a minute we had crossed over, two pusses-in-boots struggling not to be swept away by the current.

In spite of the umbrella and the plastic bags, we were drenched and once home, we changed our clothes and got out the ointments. Meanwhile the rain had stopped as suddenly as it had begun and the sky in the west was clear and deep red.

This is the most boring part of the daily routine as I don't know what to do to pass the time. I somehow manage to get by till midday by dragging breakfast out till ten and then with the help of the papers and my dictionaries. After lunch, I usually lie down for a while. I never sleep, but I shut my eyes and keep them closed for a couple of hours to fool myself into believing that I'm asleep. This is followed by my appointment with the cat. It's from returning home to the evening news bulletin that there's a black hole that I can't find anything to fill. I thumb through the dictionaries for a bit. Then I pick up the paper, but I've already read it inside out. There's always the crossword, but that only makes me even more irritated as I'm completely useless at it. Not to mention that I feel personally offended at not being able to find the right word after so many years delving into dictionaries. At the third attempt, I end up throwing the paper from the bed towards the door or from the sitting room into the hall, depending on where in the house I am. Then the next day at the same time I start again, a real sucker for punishment.

And that was the case then. I was looking at the squares and I felt more like playing at battleships, like at school, because I couldn't find even one word. After ten minutes, furious with myself, I flung the paper into the hall.

'Why do you bother racking your brains like that, when you know you can't do it?' I heard Adriani's voice coming from the kitchen. She was the ever-vigilant eye in the house that sees all and misses nothing.

I was comforted by the fact that, because of the downpour, the news bulletin would at least be different from the usual and we'd see rivers, flooded basements and buckets, but my delight exhausted itself after four shots, as the afternoon deluge had lasted barely half an hour. By the time the camera crews had arrived, the rivers running down the streets had dried up. I prepared myself to hear for a third time the same news stories that I had read in both the morning and evening papers, but the bulletin was suddenly interrupted by advertisements.

'What, now we've got to have adverts during the news too?' said Adriani puzzled. 'They should be ashamed!'

My first reaction was to get up and walk away. To wait for the adverts to finish just to hear news reports that I already knew was just a bit too much. But then I thought whether I had anything better to do. I didn't so I sat down again. Extraordinarily, my patience was rewarded because the advertisements were interrupted suddenly and the woman newscaster reappeared on the screen. She was holding a sheet of paper and staring perplexedly into the camera.

'Ladies and Gentlemen, just a few minutes ago, our channel received an anonymous phone call. A caller announced that he was phoning on behalf of the Philip of Macedon National Greek Front and stated that they claimed responsibility for the suicide of the businessman, Jason Favieros. The unknown caller said, and I quote, "Favieros did not commit suicide, it was we who forced his hand. The reasons we required his suicide are written on an announcement that we have left in a waste bin in the entrance to the channel's offices."'

The newscaster paused for a moment and stared into the camera. 'In fact, Ladies and Gentlemen, the information given us by the unknown caller proved to be true. The announcement was found in the waste bin outside the entrance to our offices. This is it.' She raised her hand and a sheet of A4 paper appeared on the screen with a logo showing the familiar helmeted head of the father of Alexander the Great with the following large black letters underneath:

PHILIP OF MACEDON
NATIONAL GREEK FRONT

There followed a sparsely written text. Even I could see that the logo and text had been prepared and printed using a computer.

The newscaster began to read the announcement, while at the same time the text appeared, covering half the screen, a method that divides the viewers into two categories: the deaf and the illiterate.

> We wish to announce to the Greek people that yesterday we obliged the businessman, Jason Favieros, to commit suicide. The Philip of Macedon National Greek Front condemned Favieros to death because in his projects in Greece he employed exclusively foreign workers: Albanians, Bulgarians, Serbians, Romanians together with numerous Africans and Asians. Through these activities of his, the Communist, Internationalist, Jason Favieros, systematically hacked away at the very foundations of the Nation. Firstly, because by employing foreign workers from the Balkans, from Asia and from Africa, he contributed to the rising unemployment in Greece and consequently to the weakening of the national fabric to the benefit of foreigners. Secondly, because in this way he promoted the immigration of foreigners to Greece and the gradual undermining

of the Nation by foreign races, who systematically marginalise Greeks and who, in less than a decade, will have succeeded in rendering them a minority in their own homeland. Thirdly, because by employing foreigners at degrading wages, he secured huge profits, without giving even a penny of it to the unemployed Greeks and their families.

We gave Favieros the choice to voluntarily do away with himself, otherwise one by one we would execute all the members of his family.

We call upon all those who employ foreign workers in Greece to dismiss them within a week and replace them with Greeks. Otherwise, they will suffer the same fate as Favieros and either will be obliged to do away with themselves or be executed.

We call upon the authorities to deport all foreigners from Greece within a month. Otherwise, we will kill so many foreigners each day that they will be forced to leave on their own.

Time to put a stop to the pillaging of our homeland by foreign nations!

Time to put a stop to the rising unemployment in Greece so that our enemies can eat and prosper!

Greece belongs to the Greeks and Greeks want it pure and exclusively their own.

Let those who have ears to hear, hear!

PHILIP OF MACEDON NATIONAL GREEK FRONT

The newscaster looked up from the text. 'That was the text of the announcement, Ladies and Gentlemen,' she said. 'The original has already been sent to Police Headquarters.'

I stared at the screen, dumbfounded. Of all the possible explanations for Favieros's suicide, this was the only one I hadn't thought of. It crossed my mind to phone Sotiropoulos to find out whether he'd thought of it, but I immediately dismissed the idea.

That night, it wasn't Philip of Macedon I dreamt about but Bucephalus. He was pure white with a thick mane. He was standing in the middle of a meadow and had raised his head to the sky, like a cock that instead of crowing neighed.

6

It seems that God loves reporters of all kinds. Otherwise there's no explaining how, every time that a story is about to fizzle out, manna falls from heaven and it rises again from its ashes. This time the manna went by the name of the Philip of Macedon National Greek Front and came to completely turn things on their head, without actually changing anything. Because this new line that certain nationalists had supposedly forced Favieros to commit suicide for the simple reason that he was employing workers from the Balkans and Third World countries in his factories and that he committed suicide in public in order to indulge their whims didn't stand up even as the kind of cock-and-bull story told by aunt Lena, who, in any case, only had truck with good nationalists. On the other hand, however, it opened up a whole new ballgame for conjectures, theories and opinions and for all kinds of claptrap so that the news reporters would have plenty to discuss with the usual TV experts for the next ten days or so. This amazing combination where everything seems different, though nothing changes, can only be achieved by God and only with the help of Greeks.

The other thing that stuck in my mind was the name of the organisation. The Philip of Macedon National Greek Front. Where had I heard that name before? I racked my brains but I couldn't for the life of me recall. And yet it kept echoing in my head.

The answer came with a phone call from Katerina, who was dying to discuss the developments in the Favieros case.

'But do you seriously believe that they forced him to commit suicide?' she asked.

'It seems unlikely to me too, and yet the one sure thing is that Favieros committed suicide publicly. What we need to find out is why. There's something we're missing.'

'I agree. Everything they've been saying and writing about his bad financial situation, about incurable illnesses and the like doesn't have any basis in fact from what I can see.'

'That's not what I meant.'

'What then?'

'Why would he commit suicide publicly? There's no logical explanation for public suicide.'

'So what are you saying then? That they told Favieros, who was on first-name terms with everyone in the government and even with the Prime Minister, to go to some TV channel and, in front of the camera, put a pistol in his mouth and blow his brains out?'

'Don't you find it strange that that's exactly what he did?'

'Of course, but I can't believe he was made to do it by some puny little organisation like the Philip of Macedon National Greek Front.'

'Have you heard of it?' I asked surprised.

'Come off it, Pops! They're those cranks who every year celebrate the birth of Alexander the Great by blocking the traffic in the centre of Thessaloniki.'

That's it, I said to myself, that's who they are. I remembered how my colleagues in Thessaloniki raged and cursed each time because a mere handful of people created chaos in the city centre.

'Tell me, Katerina, are we talking here about accessory before the fact?'

'More like incitement to commit suicide, but who could you pin it on?'

'The heads of the organisation.'

'Some organisation!' she said scornfully. 'A dozen or so wackos and as many again who just go along to gawp. Do you know what the biggest gathering they ever managed was?'

'No, what?'

'When they turned up outside the Officer's Club in Ethnikis Amynis Street to protest because at an academic conference someone had given a paper claiming that Philip II of Macedon was a homosexual and that he'd had a thing for Pausanius, his general.'

I laughed and hung up, but despite the laughter, my mind was working overtime. How could an organisation that only made an appearance once a year to cut a birthday cake for Alexander the Great force Favieros to commit suicide? Maybe because they threatened that they'd kill his whole family if he didn't? So why didn't he send his family to the Alps for an extended holiday?

All this led to the only conclusion that Favieros's suicide was for other, still unknown, reasons and that the little group of nationalists had simply seized the opportunity for some free publicity. Perhaps this was the right explanation but it didn't bring me even one step nearer to the reasons that led Favieros to his public suicide. And I would continue to torment myself with the 'public' aspect until some convincing explanation could be found.

I knew that all these thoughts were of no practical value, that it was just a crossword puzzle that I was creating for myself and trying to solve, yet I still preferred this a hundred times more to the crosswords in the newspapers that turned me into a nervous wreck at the first word.

The only way I was going to learn anything more was from the newspapers again. I decided to pop out to the kiosk and as I passed by the kitchen I saw Adriani stuffing tomatoes and peppers.

'I could smell them even before you put them in the oven,' I said to her jokingly.

'All very well, but I'm warning you, they won't be as tasty as usual because I've used very little onion. Don't tell me afterwards that they're not up to standard.'

She has had a complex about stuffed vegetables from the time that she was in competition with my mother and she trembles at the thought of not getting them right.

'For a first step back to normality, it's fine,' I replied and she seemed relieved.

If someone were to ask me why, instead of turning right into Aroni Street, I turned left and from Nikiphoridis Street emerged into Formionos Street, I wouldn't have been able to explain. Nor could I explain what was in my mind when I hailed a taxi and said to the driver: 'Alexandras Avenue. Police Headquarters.'

Nevertheless, as soon as I got out of the taxi and crossed the road at the lights, my reflexes started to kick in. I decided to avoid making a stop on the third floor, where my own department was. I was in no mood to open my office door and see Yanoutsos lolling in my chair and reading the *Trikala News*. After thirty years in Athens, the only newspaper he reads is his village local.

The guard at the entrance was about to ask me for some identification, but my face was familiar to him and he hesitated.

'Inspector Haritos, I'm on my way up to Security,' I told him to help him out of his difficult situation. He was about to get to his feet, but I stopped him. 'I'm on sick leave. There's no need for formalities.'

The lift was playing its old tricks and I waited a full ten minutes before it did me the honour of opening its doors. I prayed I wouldn't bump into my two assistants, Vlassopoulos and Dermitzakis, and even more so into Yanoutsos. Fortunately, the lift raced up to the fifth floor.

I wish I'd had a camera to take Koula's photo when she saw me. The barometer that tells you just how much a person likes you or not is to suddenly appear before them after a long illness or absence. It's then that you can see on their face whether you bring with you high or low pressure. Koula's face shone. She leapt up and shrieked with delight:

'Inspector Haritos!'

She flung herself at me, wrapped her arms around me and kissed me on both cheeks so that neither would feel aggrieved. Koula had always shown a liking for me, though, being a suspicious copper, I had always thought that it was feigned. That day, I had to admit that I had been wrong. The way I saw her looking at me, blonde and beautiful and with a big smile, I reflected that if I had come sooner, most certainly she would have boosted my shattered morale with the help of her kisses.

'You've no idea how pleased I am to see you!' she said joyfully. 'You can't imagine how much I missed you!'

'Maybe, but you never came once to the hospital to see me,' I replied, like a lover complaining to his beloved that she doesn't take enough care of him.

'You're right.' She suddenly felt embarrassed and didn't know what to say. 'But, you know, we ... We don't know each other all that well and I couldn't just turn up suddenly with your wife there ... and your daughter ... It would have gotten around and people here would have started talking ...'

'What do you mean, Koula. Who would have started talking?'

'You know how rumours get started in here ...'

'Rumours about what?'

She nodded her head resignedly. 'Ah, Inspector Haritos. You're so innocent. You live on a different planet.'

I didn't know whether I should be happy or curse myself.

'Anyhow, you're looking fine,' she said to change the subject. 'Healthy, strong, rejuvenated ... When will you be back with us?'

'I have another two months' sick leave.'

'I envy you. Make sure you make the most of it.'

'Is he in? Can I say hello to him?'

'But of course, I don't have to announce you. You won't be interrupting any important discussion.'

It was only on entering Ghikas's office that I realised what Koula had meant. Ghikas was sitting at his desk, which was three yards in length with a curve in it and resembled a race course. Facing him, in the seat I usually sat in, was Yanoutsos. He was around forty-five, quite tall, but thin and sluggish, who was never out of uniform because in plain clothes he looked like a sewing-machine salesman. Serves me right, I should have gone by my assistants' office first to find out where he was lurking.

'Come on in,' said Ghikas on seeing me. 'What brings you here?'

'I just dropped in to say hello.'

'If you've started to miss us, you must be feeling better. Have a seat.'

Yanoutsos didn't take the trouble to greet me, but simply looked at me with an expression that showed him to be both annoyed and worried. Those who show indifference will receive indifference, I said to myself and I fixed my eyes on Ghikas.

'So how are you doing?' he asked.

'I'm getting bored,' was my honest reply. Ghikas smiled.

'You should take up whist,' said Yanoutsos, in an attempt at humour.

'I read the papers, go for walks, watch TV… that's all you can do.' My reply was directed to Ghikas. I had already written Yanoutsos off. 'What about you here, how's it going?'

'Routine, you know how it is.'

'Hasn't Favieros's suicide broken the routine?' I replied, feigning innocence, to see how he would react, but he continued on the same wavelength.

'A new lead-story for the TV channels.'

'And what about this organisation that claims to have forced him to commit suicide?'

'Hardly,' Yanoutsos chipped in again. 'If we'd taken such prattle seriously when I was in the Anti-terrorist Squad, we'd have been running all over the place.'

When you were in the Anti-terrorist Squad, you spent your time playing whist, was what I wanted to say, but I restrained myself so as not to rile Ghikas.

'Another unknown caller phoned a newspaper today to say that the statement did not come from the Philip of Macedon organisation and that it was sheer provocation,' said Ghikas gravely.

'Nevertheless, something doesn't fit.'

'What?'

'The public suicide. Why would Favieros commit suicide in front of the cameras?'

Ghikas shrugged his shoulders. 'Are you looking for logic in someone who's decided to put an end to his life?'

'People like Favieros usually avoid the spotlights,' I insisted. 'They do everything discreetly. That's why I'm surprised.'

'Listen Haritos,' said Yanoutsos, chipping in again. 'We're pleased to see that you're well, but the Chief and I were in the middle of an extremely important departmental matter and you interrupted us.'

I didn't have time to be taken aback by his nerve because Ghikas got to his feet, as if he had been waiting for his cue, and held out his hand. 'I'm very pleased to see you well, Costas,' he said. 'Stop by again and we'll have a chat.'

They want to get rid of me, I thought to myself. They can't wait to see the back of me. I shook Ghikas's hand, turned and walked out without saying a word.

'How do you rate Yanoutsos?' I asked Koula in order to calm down

'He's ill-mannered and always ready to pass the buck,' was the immediate reply. 'It's not enough that he behaves like a boor, he's always trying to hang all his mistakes, which are at least a dozen a day, on me.'

'Be patient, Koula, it's only two months, they'll pass quickly.'

'Amen to that!' she said, laughing.

Despite Koula's comments, my anger still hadn't abated. I stood in Dimitsanas Street, in front of the church of Aghios Savvas, and waited for a taxi, but to find a taxi in the centre of Athens at two in the afternoon you have to have gone through special training. My schooling was only basic so other people grabbed the taxis from under my nose before I even had time to talk to the driver. After much ado I finally managed to grab one myself, I was ready to explode. The moment I sat in the front seat, I realised I'd chanced upon the rule rather than the exception, in other words, on the music-loving taxi driver who has his radio on constantly at full blast. My nerves gave way at the corner of Michalakopoulou and Spryrou Merkouri Streets, when a female voice started singing: *We're getting on so well, I'm starting to hear bells.*

'Shut the damn thing off and honk the horn so we can get through the traffic!' I said to the driver.

He turned and looked at me with that arrogant expression that taxi drivers have. 'Why, are you ill? You don't look ill to me.'

I stuck my police ID in his face. 'I'm a police inspector and I'm on official business. And your radio is interfering with my CB. Turn it off and honk the horn or I'll hand you over to the first patrol car we meet and you'll lose your licence for six months.'

He did exactly what I said without a second thought. He drove like a kamikaze pilot and within two minutes we were at the corner of Aristikleous Street. I asked him how much the fare was.

'Never mind about it, Inspector. I'd rather you let me have your name,' he said as though he were planning to invite me out. 'You never know, it might come in handy some time.'

I flung three euros onto the seat and slammed the car door behind me.

'Where have you been all this time, dear?' Adriani asked, with a worried look.

'Omonoia Square. I missed the illegal immigrants.'

She saw my expression and understood that it was useless to go on. 'Let's go and eat,' she said.

As soon as I took the first bite of my plate of stuffed vegetables, I felt better and my anger evaporated as if by a miracle.

'Tastes delicious, Adriani! That's the best present you could have given me today,' I said, full of enthusiasm.

'Oh come on, you don't have to lie. They're short on onion, like I said.'

I took a second bite and held it in my mouth to allow my taste buds to do their work. There was so much we were short on, I wasn't going to complain about the onion.

7

I was sitting in a deluxe cabin. Not on one of those passenger-car ferries that ply the south Aegean, but in the duty ward of the Cardiology Department in the State General Hospital, that had roughly the same dimensions and facilities as a deluxe cabin. I was waiting for the results of the analyses, for Adriani to finish with the formalities and for the surgeon to examine me. This was my reward for consenting to come for the tests: I would sit in a deluxe cabin while Adriani would do all the legwork. There was nothing wrong with me; I knew it, the doctors knew it, even the nurses knew it. It had been weeks since they had removed my stitches, my wound had completely healed and I only felt it tugging at me slightly with sudden changes in the weather. Adriani, however, insisted that I went for tests, in the hope that the doctors would find some tiny hole that had remained open in order that she might prolong her domination over me on account of continuing ill health.

She stuck her head round the door. 'They're ready, Costas, we can go.'

The duty ward was on the third floor, whereas the Outpatients Department was on the ground floor of the building opposite. Adriani pressed the button to call the lift.

'Never mind, we'll be waiting an hour for it to come,' I said and began walking down the stairs in order to prove to her that I was in fine fettle and not to hold out any vain hopes.

It was unbearably humid and just a few days before I had gone back to wearing a suit and tie so that by the time I reached the Outpatients my clothes were stuck to me. Either it rains and you end up soaking wet or the sun shines and you end up soaking in sweat. Damn weather.

Fanis was waiting for us outside the door of the surgery and we went in for the tests under the astonished gaze of the social security plebs who turn up at six in the morning to get a priority number and are examined at around two in the afternoon.

'What seems to be the problem, Inspector? Do you have any pain?' asked Evkarpidis, the surgeon in charge.

'No, no doctor,' replied my personal government spokeswoman. 'We're fine, thanks be to God, but we thought of having a little check-up just to be sure.'

From the very first day at the hospital, she had been using that 'we', as if we'd been wounded in association. I stripped to the waist and lay down on the couch. Evkarpidis took a quick look, without touching the scar left by the wound. 'You're doing just fine,' he said with satisfaction. 'And your tests are very good. Your white corpuscles are at normal levels and your blood platelets too. That's it, no need for you to come back.'

'Costas dear, why don't we have a cardiograph while we're here?' Adriani said meekly once we were back outside in the corridor.

I knew where she was leading. She couldn't get any blood out of the wound and she was trying to get it out of the cardiograph. I was ready to answer her with a sharp 'no', but I was stopped by Fanis's laughter.

'You had the other tests, you may as well have a cardiograph, you've nothing to lose,' he said.

I accepted in silence as I couldn't say no to my daughter's boyfriend.

We entered the lift to go to the Cardiology Department together with two nurses who seemed agitated and were talking to each other in an intense tone.

'Is it certain?' the one asked the other.

'They just announced it on the radio.'

The first one crossed herself. 'Dear Lord. The world's gone mad.'

We got out on the second floor, so I didn't find out what had been announced on the radio. That the world had gone mad, I already knew.

'Your heart is like clockwork,' Fanis said to me satisfied, after studying the cardiograph. 'How are you doing as regards medicine?'

'He's out of diuretics, Fanis dear. Give him a prescription for another box just in case,' said Adriani, who, like a proper quartermaster, knew off by heart exactly what medicines I had left.

'Get two Frumil and a Pensordil for the Inspector,' Fanis said to the nurse.

A nurse of about fifty, who was waiting for the other cardiologist, raised her head and looked at me oddly. 'You're lucky to be here at the hospital, today,' she said. 'Your colleagues outside have got their hands full.'

'Why?' I asked a little testily. It always irritates me when people start up a conversation with me without knowing me.

'Haven't you heard? That organisation that claimed to have forced Favieros to commit suicide?'

'The Philip of Macedon Front?'

'Exactly. They murdered two Kurds last night. They just announced it on the news.'

I immediately turned to Fanis. 'Is there a TV in here?'

'In the refectory.'

'Why are you in such a rush?' Adriani asked. 'It's going to be on TV for the whole of next week.'

She was right, but I couldn't stop myself. The refectory was situated in a little park full of pine trees. It was packed. Male patients in pyjamas, female patients in nighties, visitors, young doctors and nurses were squashed together at the tables and against the walls and were watching the special bulletin on the TV that was positioned on a bracket on the wall. I happened to get there halfway through the organisation's announcement as it was scrolling down the screen:

> ... Because certain people didn't take our announcement concerning Favieros's suicide seriously, we were obliged last night to execute two foreign workers who were working on Favieros's construction sites, to prove to all concerned that we mean business. We call upon everyone to see sense and take what we say very

seriously. From now on, the responsibility for whatever happens rests with the relevant authorities.

The announcement faded on the screen and the camera descended some narrow steps leading to a basement room, the size of a bedsit, with two divans against the two walls and a Formica table and two plastic chairs in the middle. White sheets were covering each of the bodies on the divans.

'The victims, Ladies and Gentlemen, are two Kurds, who were living here, at 4 Frearion Street in the Rouf district,' explained the newscaster. 'Both were shot through the right eye.'

As I gazed at the screen, the questions were piling up inside me. How had we gone in the space of a few days from the suicide of Jason Favieros to the murder of the Kurds? And why did I continue to insist that the public suicide was a jarring note that no one else wanted to hear? At least not Ghikas or that twerp Yanoutsos. Suddenly, amidst everything, I felt a glowing sense of satisfaction run through me, because the previous day they had looked down their noses at me and now they really had their hands full. They couldn't see what was staring them in the face. Even if we supposed that this nationalist organisation had come out after the event and claimed involvement in Favieros's suicide, they wouldn't have done it if Favieros's suicide had not happened in public and they wouldn't have needed to murder the two Kurds afterwards to convince any doubters.

What does a copper long for at such times? A patrol car. My feeling was so strong that I looked outside the refectory, sure that one was waiting for me. All I saw was some old doctor drooling over one of the nurses.

I turned to Fanis. 'How quickly can I get a taxi?'

Two pairs of astonished eyes fixed themselves on me. Fanis's on the right and Adriani's on the left, because, at least according to Dimitrakos, omens coming from the left are considered not to bode well.

'What do you want a taxi for?' asked Adriani suspiciously.

'I want to have a quick look round the crime scene.'

'You're on sick leave, have you forgotten?'

Her voice rang out like a bell and everyone turned round and stared at us in astonishment. Evidently, I had pushed her to the limit with my gradual extrication from her hands over the previous few days and she was ready to explode. I took the initiative and walked out of the refectory so that we wouldn't create a scene.

'Could you call a taxi,' I said to Fanis.

'Never mind, I'll take you there. In any case, I only stayed for you. Yesterday I had the night shift and I'm off duty today.'

'Well, I'm going home,' said Adriani categorically. She had assumed the look of a crabby governess who doesn't smack her young charge, but nevertheless makes it quite clear that from now on there are no more sweets or chocolates. To be honest, I'd missed that look and I found it amusing.

Fanis put his arm round her shoulders, took her aside and started to talk to her, breathing into her ear. Then he left her and called over to me.

'Wait here and I'll bring the car.'

Adriani came back over to me, but averted her gaze. As for me, by rights I should have explained to her why I wanted to see the two dead Kurds and their hovel, but I had no satisfactory explanation, not even for myself.

Fanis came and stopped in front of us. I let Adriani sit next to him. I tried to guess what they might have been saying and if she was planning to accompany me to the murder scene, which would make me a laughing stock, but I didn't dare ask. I left it in the hands of fate.

Fortunately, I saw Fanis turning from Mesogheion Avenue into Michalakopoulou Street and realised that we were taking her home. When we got to Pangratiou Square, she told Fanis to pull over.

'Leave me here, Fanis dear. I have some shopping to do.' She got out without saying anything to me. It was our first tiff after nearly two months, but I couldn't care less. I was only too happy to be back to old times.

'What did you say to make her change her mind?' I asked out of curiosity.

'That as you would go anyway, it was better at least if your doctor went with you. I'll wait for you in the car. Anyway, this whole business intrigues me too.'

It intrigued everyone except Ghikas and Yanoutsos, I thought with some resentment. This thought obliged me to confess one more reason why I had rushed to the crime scene: I wanted to see Yanoutsos's face when he saw me there after having more or less thrown me out of the office the previous day.

We had turned into Amalias Avenue and were passing by the National Gardens. I began to feel remorse at having taken advantage of Fanis to satisfy my investigative perversions.

'Why don't you leave me here and I'll get a taxi?' I said. 'You're without any sleep and I'm putting you to a lot of trouble for no reason.'

'I told you, the whole business has aroused my curiosity.'

'And Katerina's too. Last night we had a whole discussion on extreme right-wing organisations.'

Fanis laughed. 'I'll confess something to you, but you mustn't tell her. Every night we sit in front of our TV sets, lift up the phone and discuss the various explanations. An amateur and a semi-amateur!'

'And the semi-amateur is Katerina?'

'I'd say so. At least she's studying Law. I'm only a cardiologist. What do I know?'

'And why is she hiding it from me? Why doesn't she say something?' I again felt that lump, just as always when I realise that someone else is closer to Katerina.

'Because she's afraid,' Fanis replied.

'Afraid?'

'Yes, of her policeman father. Afraid of coming out with some drivel and making herself look ridiculous.'

We had now reached Achilleos Street, which at that time of day was chock-a-block with traffic heading in the direction of the city centre, and we turned into Konstantinoupoleos Street. Frearion

Street was on our left as we were going up and so Fanis turned and parked in Megalou Vassileiou Street.

'I'll wait for you here.'

'Won't take long,' I replied, certain that Yanoutsos would spot me straightaway.

The apartment block was one of those overnight constructions that were originally two-storey before their owners greased the palms of the police or someone in the local authorities in order to add another couple of floors on the sly to pay for their daughter's dowry or their son's studies. I saw no ambulances or any TV crews and I concluded that the bodies must already have been taken to the morgue.

As I was going down the steps to the basement, I bumped into Diamantidis from Forensics.

'What are you doing here, Inspector? Are you back on duty?' he asked, as though it were the most obvious thing in the world.

'No, but I'm back in training as you can see,' I said and he broke into laughter. 'What's going on down there?'

He hesitated for a moment as if about to say something, but then changing his mind. 'Go on in and you'll see,' he said.

The door to the flat was open and voices could be heard. The flat was just one room, just as it had appeared on the TV, with a sizeable recess that served as a kitchen. Beside it was a door that must have been the bathroom.

The bodies had been moved as I had thought. Standing in the middle of the room was Yanoutsos together with Markidis the coroner. They were glaring at each other like cocks, ready to begin fighting.

'I'm not saying a word,' shouted Makridis at Yanoutsos. It was the first time in all the years I'd known him that I saw him losing his composure. 'You can wait and read the report.'

Standing behind were my two assistants, Vlassopoulos and Dermitzakis. Their backs were half-turned to the other two and they were pretending to be chatting so as not to appear to be listening in to the conversation.

Suddenly, as though on cue, they all turned and looked at me. Yanoutsos was goggling. Even more odd was my assistants' behaviour. They stared at me at a loss, unable to decide whether they should greet me or not. In they end, they settled for a formal nod of the head accompanied by a smile, before turning their backs again.

The most congenial of all of them was Markidis, who offered me his hand. 'Glad to see you up and around,' he said. His face had become somewhat friendlier as he had exchanged the huge glasses he had worn all his life for an oval-shaped, metallic frame.

'Why are you here?' Yanoutsos asked. 'As far as I know, you're still on sick leave and we've no need of you.'

'I came so you could tell me again what you told me the other day in Ghikas's office,' I replied with spite.

'And what was that?'

'That if you were to take every prattling announcement seriously, you'd be running all over the place. Well now you are.'

'This has no connection with the announcement. This is the work of the Mafia.'

The other three had now turned round and were watching the second cockfight.

'Where were they shot?' I asked Markidis. I knew, but I wanted everyone to hear it.

'In the eye. Both of them.'

I turned back to Yanoutsos: 'Mafiosos wouldn't have wasted their time with details like that. They'd have let fly with five or six bullets and then been on their way.'

'They might have had a reason for staging the scene.'

'What reason when they were only two miserable Kurds? Do you know what work it requires to stage an execution by shooting someone in the eye?'

I turned and cast a look around. Everything was in its place, there were no signs of any struggle. I heard Yanoutsos say to my assistants:

'Dermitzakis, Vlassopoulos, you can go. I've no further need of you.'

I looked up, curious to see whether they would acknowledge me as they left. But they pretended to be engrossed in their conversation and left without even looking at me. I couldn't explain their attitude and I felt infuriated, but I tried to control myself so as not to spoil my mood for riling Yanoutsos.

'From what I see, there are no signs of struggle,' I said to Markidis.

'No.' We looked at each other and Markidis shook his head. 'You're right. I'd noticed that too.'

'What have you noticed?' interrupted Yanoutsos. 'I want to know.'

Markidis thought it superfluous to answer him. 'If they'd shot them in the chest or the stomach or anywhere else, I'd say that they had surprised them and they hadn't managed to resist,' I said. 'But the eye needs planning, preparation. Why didn't they resist, but simply sat and let themselves be executed?'

'Mafiosos. They knew them.'

'Don't keep on so much about Mafiosos, because you'll be in for a nasty surprise,' I told him and headed towards the door.

Markidis caught up with me at the steps. 'So where did that idiot blow in from?' he asked me angrily. 'Vlassopoulos and Dermitzakis would do better on their own.'

I preferred to make no reply, as I didn't want to appear to be biased. 'What do you think it was?' I asked him.

'Spray. The kind used by petty thieves to knock people out in their homes so they can rob them. They found them sleeping, knocked them out with the spray and then shot them through the eye.'

'Can you prove it?'

He reflected for a moment. 'It depends on the composition of the product. If we're lucky, there may be some traces in the urine.'

We were now outside in the street and I suddenly realised that it wasn't just the glasses. Markidis looked as if he'd had an entire facelift.

'You've changed completely,' I said to him surprised. 'You look ten years younger.'

A wide smile spread over his usually unsmiling face. 'I wondered whether you'd notice.'

'How could I not notice? It stands out a mile.'

'I got divorced. I got divorced and I'm getting married again; to my secretary in the department.'

'How long were you married?' I asked him in amazement.

'Twenty-five.'

'And you got divorced?'

'Naturally, she got to keep the three-bedroom flat that cost me a lifetime's savings, but it was worth it.' He suddenly came out with it. 'I've started to live again, Haritos. I've been in a deep sleep all these years,' he said, with the certainty of the person who is the last to find out.

Judging from his dress, he was right. Markidis, who had been going around for the last ten years in the same suit, was now wearing an olive-green jacket with a red stripe, black trousers, an orange shirt and a tie with futuristic designs that gleamed in the sun.

'Does your wife-to-be choose your clothes for you?' I asked, and at that same moment I realised that my mind was done with the running-in stage of convalescence and was ticking over normally again.

'Shows, does it?' he replied, full of pride. 'Post-modern dress. That's what Nitsa calls it. Latest word in fashion.'

Post-macabre would be a better description, just the job for the morgue. But I held my tongue and went to find Fanis.

8

The sweet Greek coffee at the neon cafeteria in Agiou Lazarou Square was like dishwater, the waiter was a sourpuss by conviction, yet, despite everything, I berthed there every morning with my paper. Maybe I'd been won over by the peace of the square, with its two old women and three unemployed Albanians on the benches; then again it might well have been the familiar Greek magnet that always attracts you to places that irritate you, so that afterwards you can happily curse your fate.

My usual table was taken by three lads who were all drinking iced coffee. I sat down two tables further away, in the shade, as the weather had suddenly turned unpleasantly hot, and I opened my Sunday convenience store. From inside the paper I took out: a magazine of general interest, a magazine for arts and culture, a fashion magazine, a TV guide, a crossword book, an advertisement for washing powder, an advertisement with a toothpaste sample, an advertisement for mouthwash and three coupons for interest-free monthly payments. I tossed them all into the plastic bag that my local kiosk owner always gives me with the comment 'Careful, Inspector, don't spill the newspaper,' and kept hold of the main section of the newspaper, which was no more than a dozen pages. I was quickly thumbing through it to find the report on the two Kurds, when I saw the waiter putting the sweet Greek coffee down in front of me and walking away in silence. He had brought it without even asking me.

'Just a moment,' I called out and he turned round. 'How do you know that I don't want an iced coffee today?'

He gave me a bored look and shrugged his shoulders. 'You don't strike me as someone who spends any more on Sundays,' he said and went on his way.

I was ready to give him a mouthful, but my eye fell on a photograph of Frearion Street and a three-column article devoted to the murder. I started to read the article with relish, but after the first few lines I realised it was a rehash. Only the third column had anything new, and that was the names of the two Kurds: Kamak Talali and Masoud Fahar, who indeed had worked on the construction of the Olympic Village that was contracted to Favieros's company. The only new information came from the rejuvenated Markidis, who confirmed what we had both suspected from the beginning: namely that the murderers had used knockout spray on the victims in order to execute them in their own good time.

I scanned quickly through the rest of the paper, but I could find nothing other than the usual screeds with analyses of foreign, domestic and financial policies. I left the exact money for the dishwater on the table and next to it the newspaper with all its accessories.

I leisurely walked up Aroni Street and tried to drive out my sinful thoughts concerning the two Kurds, Favieros and the Philip of Macedon Greek National Front. Besides, it was far more pleasant to think of Sunday lunch with Fanis, which had become established as a regular meeting of the ministerial cabinet, with the exception of those Sundays when he was on duty.

The door of the flat opened, leaving me with the key in my hand. Adriani, a worried look on her face, was standing in the doorway and blocking my way. Evidently she had been listening out for the lift so that she could rush and open the door for me.

'What is it?' I asked her, listening to the trembling sound of my voice, because my mind automatically imagined that something bad had happened. I thought perhaps something was wrong with Katerina and Fanis had come to tell us.

Instead of answering, she stepped out into the corridor, leaned towards me and whispered into my ear in an angry tone: 'That insistence of yours not to want to have a mobile phone. My mother was right: those who wear blinkers become as stubborn as a mule.'

It was true that she had inherited that method of analysing character from her mother. According to my mother-in-law, a blinkered person was stubborn, a slant-eyed person was a dark horse, a large pointed nose signified someone stingy and miserly, while a hooked nose signified someone lecherous and insatiable. These were the character analyses that Adriani had inherited, even though her mother had no connection at all with Lombroso, whose work we studied in the criminology course.

'What is it?' I asked again and received a second shriek in the ear.

'Go inside and you'll see!'

I went into the sitting room and stood there, rooted to the spot. He was sitting in the armchair that formed a corner with the TV, but as soon as he saw me he leapt to his feet. We both stood there motionless staring at each other. He was waiting for me to say something, but I didn't know what to say. It was the first time that Ghikas had ever come to my house. I continued to stare at him in astonishment, while trying to answer two questions together: what was the reason for this Sunday visit and what should I say to him by way of welcome. Should I confine myself to being formally polite, that would sound extremely cold, or should I break into raptures of fake enthusiasm?

In the end, I resorted to a neutral welcome. 'To what do we owe the pleasure after such a long time?' I said, indirectly expressing my grievance that he never came to see me when I was laid up in bed.

'First of all, I came to apologise for my behaviour in my office the other day.'

I reflected that whatever I said would sound false so I decided to remain silent. Besides, that 'first of all' meant that there was more. So I waited.

My silence obliged him to continue. 'It's not that I wanted Yanoutsos; he was forced upon me,' he said. 'There wasn't a thing I could do. He has friends in high places.'

'That explains how he got himself accepted into the Anti-terrorist Squad.'

He burst in laughter. 'The Anti-terrorist Squad were looking for a way to get rid of him and so they sent him to me.'

I had no reason not to believe him because what he said tied in with what Sotiropoulos has told me over the telephone. Adriani came out of the kitchen holding a tray with a cup of coffee. She put it down on the table beside him, returned my thanks with a curt 'You're welcome' and went out of the room.

'I heard that you went by the flat where the two Kurds were murdered.'

He looked at me and waited, this time, for a reply. I shrugged my shoulders.

'If it's in your veins ...' I answered vaguely.

'I want your opinion.'

'I can't tell you very much, but it's for sure not the work of Mafiosos like Yanoutsos says. They were knocked out using spray and then shot through the eye. Mafiosos would have riddled them with bullets and run off. This particular business has all the signs of an execution and it's a case for the Anti-terrorist Squad.'

'Yanoutsos desperately wants the case.' He shook his head slightly and heaved a sigh. 'I don't like this whole business, Costas, I don't like it at all.'

'What business? With the two Kurds?'

'No! Favieros's suicide. Something doesn't add up. Even if he'd already decided to commit suicide, he would have done it discreetly. Not in front of the cameras.'

I saw almost with relief that his tactics hadn't changed. He was still presenting my ideas to me as his own.

'You were of a different opinion the other day in your office,' I said to counter him.

'Because I didn't want to open up in front of Yanoutsos. I have something in mind but I don't quite know how to organise it.'

I kept silent again, but this time in order to hear his organisational problems.

'Officially, I can't order an investigation into the Favieros case. There's no doubt that he committed suicide, consequently the police can't do anything. That's why I didn't open my cards in front of Yanoutsos.'

I smiled without meaning to. 'You don't seem to have much faith in him.'

'I don't have any faith at all,' was the curt reply. 'The other day when I saw you, an idea suddenly passed through my mind. Am I right in thinking you have another two months of sick leave?'

'Yes, you're right.'

He paused for a moment and looked at me. Then he began to speak slowly, as if searching for the words. 'What would you say to making some discreet investigations into the Favieros case? Find out what it was that drove him to suicide?' He paused again and then added: 'After all, it'll pass your time for you.'

I needed quite a bit of time to digest what it was he had just said to me. Who would have believed that Ghikas would turn out to be my saviour, the one who would free me from the boredom of convalescence and put me back into the game? I tried to conceal my delight and at the same time not to seem to be grabbing hold of the lifebelt he was throwing me because if he realised anything of the sort, he would expect me to repay him for at least the next ten years.

'What can I say?' I replied, as if feeling aggrieved that he was asking a chore of me. 'The truth is that this sick leave came just at the right time. As you know, I've never taken many leaves of absence in my time on the Force and this is an opportunity for me to make up for it.' I added this with a smile in order to strengthen my position while waiting for him to go on trying to persuade me so that I might give in little by little.

He stared at me as though wanting to draw up a profile of me, as he'd learned during the six months he'd spent idling his time away with the FBI. I persisted with my smile.

'Yanoutsos is here to stay,' he said suddenly.

His words took me aback and I lost my composure. 'Stay where?' I asked like a twerp.

'They transferred him to Homicide to get rid of him. And on the pretext that you were gravely wounded and you're returning from convalescence, you'll be transferred to a section with less stress and Yanoutsos will get your position.'

I suddenly saw vividly before me the look of my two assistants at the Kurds' flat. That's why they were keeping their distance from me.

It had already got around that Yanoutsos was being primed for my job and they were playing it safe so they wouldn't find themselves in hot water.

'I told you, he has friends in high places and there's nothing I can do,' Ghikas went on. 'But if you get somewhere with the Favieros case, I'll be able to say "Look, Haritos has come up trumps again. We won't get anywhere without him" and they won't dare give him your position.'

What was I thinking of to act like a prima donna? Now he would want to be paid back twice over for the favour he was doing me. 'And if I don't get anywhere with the case?' I said and my voice betrayed my fear and anxiety.

'You will.' The reply was categorical, without any trace of doubt. 'There's something not right about this case and you're the only one who can find out what it is.'

'Why only me?'

'Because you're a stickler and stubborn with it.' His frankness was disarming. He paused for a moment and then went on somewhat uneasily: 'Except that I can't give you any of your assistants or anyone else from the department. If I do, everyone will find out what we're up to and I'll be out on a limb.'

He was right, but how would I manage on my own?

'I can send you Koula. She's the only person I trust blindly. We'll say that her father is on his death bed and I'll give her leave to take care of him.'

'And what about you?' I asked astonished. 'Koula is your right hand.'

He shrugged his shoulders.

'I'll make do with the left one for a while,' he replied vaguely.

'All right,' I said, though my initial delight had been poisoned by the worry of failure, because my job was in jeopardy.

Now that he had secured my consent, relieved and with a big smile on his face, he got to his feet. I looked at him wondering which of us would come out on top in our future confrontation. Would it be him because he would tell me that he'd saved me my job or would it be me for ridding him of Yanoutsos?

We were at the front door when, suddenly, in an outburst of unprecedented cordiality, he gave me a friendly pat on the back instead of his usual formal handshake. 'I've missed you, Costas,' he said, 'I've really missed you.'

I wanted to tell him that I'd missed him too, but it didn't mean very much, because in my case I'd missed everything apart from my own home. So that included him too, but not him personally, he was just a part of the whole.

'It's out of the question!' shouted Adriani, when later we were sitting with Fanis at the table eating our oven-roasted suckling pig with potatoes in a lemon sauce. 'It's out of the question for you to drive that old crock in your weak state.'

The old crock was my faithful Mirafiori that had so far managed to avoid the scrapheap and was about to celebrate, humbly and without any fanfares, its thirtieth year on the road. Adriani had digested the fact that she would have Koula round her feet all day long, but the Mirafiori for dessert was too much for her to stomach.

'I won't be driving it. Koula can drive,' I said to appease her.

'It's out of the question,' she yelled again. 'No one can drive that old banger apart from you.'

'She's right about that,' chipped in Fanis, who was thoroughly enjoying it all. 'Why don't you get a new car? With all the easy instalments that they offer today, you won't have to start paying it off for at least a year.'

'I'm not parting with my Mirafiori. It's still roadworthy.' I said it with assurance though I wasn't at all sure that it would start up again after two months of sitting in front of the house.

'Fine,' said Adriani. 'But if anything happens to you, I'll be straight off to Thessaloniki to stay with my daughter and you can get Koula to take care of you!' In a temper she diced the meat on her plate into tiny pieces as though she were going to feed the grandchild that she didn't have.

9

> 'Continuation: mod. & demotic, Uninterrupted process or succession, sequel, resumption: Arist. *H.A.* 515b, 6 *continuation of the nerves. Sor.* 1/71 *continuation to the embryo's navel.*'

> 'Beginning: med., mod. & demotic, commencement, start. Plato *Rep.* 377[A] *the beginning is the most important part of every task*; 2. place where or from something starts. Thucyd. 1, 128 *of the whole thing this was the start.* Prov. *What starts badly will end badly.*'

The same question had been going round and round in my head all night: was the mission that Ghikas had assigned me to be regarded as a new beginning or as a continuation of my old situation? Officially, I was still the Head of the Homicide Division on sick leave. Ghikas's assignment meant neither change nor conversion. It was simply the continuation towards the embryo's navel as Dimitrakos put it. As though I were a tax official who took care of a few friends' books on the sly each evening in order to make a bit extra for my holidays.

On the other hand, however, it wasn't at all certain that I would remain Head of the Homicide Division. Firstly, because suicide is an act, the success of which is enjoyed in full by the one committing the act and consequently there would be nothing for me to cash in on. Secondly, even if I were to manage to make black appear white and squeeze some mileage out of Favieros's suicide, Yanoutsos in the meantime would have got a firm grip on my position and would pull every string not to have to give up my chair, with its worn leather armrests from which the foam rubber was bursting out. Looking at it this way, the mission assigned to me by Ghikas was a new beginning, which had all the ingredients needed to prove the saying 'a bad beginning betokens a worse end'.

In the morning I still hadn't found any answer to the question and I woke up with my head swimming. In the end, these kinds of dilemmas always come down to the more colloquial 'between the devil and the deep blue sea', so I decided to have a shot at it, despite the limited chances of success, rather than allow Yanoutsos to get the better of me.

Koula phoned me while I was still having my coffee and started talking to me in coded phrases: 'I'll bring the package over tomorrow, Inspector Haritos. Unfortunately, I don't have time today. I need to take care of some details.' She reminded me of my late father, who used to talk in coded language when he wanted to say that there was some order from above and he didn't want anyone else to understand. 'There's a personal order from his nibs.' And he meant the Prime Minister. Anyhow, I understood that she would take up her new duties the next day. In the meantime I could start alone. It was a pity to let the day go wasted.

I drank the last of my coffee and got up to go. At the front door, I bumped into Adriani who was returning from the supermarket.

'Are you going out?'

'Yes. Don't wait for me for lunch. I might be late.'

When I went to work normally, that remark was superfluous. I never came home at midday. Now that I was starting again, after a two-month lay-off, I was obliged to make it clear in order to emphasise that we were returning to the old routine.

'I see. Old habits die hard,' she said, going into the house.

Her vexation was understandable as I had told her nothing of the threat of Yanoutsos. If I were to tell her, she would have jumped for joy. For years she had been trying to persuade me to put in for a transfer to a quieter department with regular hours. 'As they don't promote you anyway, why kill yourself at work on top of everything?' was her foolproof argument, which would have convinced every rational person.

I decided to make my first call of the day at Favieros's residence. I was certain that none of my colleagues would have thought of bothering his family over the suicide, so it was only right I should begin from there. From the TV news reports that have become a kind of contemporary encyclopedia for us all, I found out that Favieros's family lived in Porto Rafti, and so I set to thinking about the best route for getting there. I had no intention of paying for a taxi out of my own pocket and if I were to take the bus I'd get there in the afternoon just in time for tea and cake. In the end, I decided to combine all the forms of public transport that Athens has: I would take the trolley to Syntagma Square, from there take the underground to Ethniki Amyna and then get the intercity bus to Porto Rafti.

Half an hour later, I was going up the escalator in the underground, leaving behind the station's marble mausoleum with its artificial shrubs growing out of granite, its grandiose announcements and its classical music that makes me feel like a European for ten minutes or so. Above, on my right, was the Ministry of Transport and, on my left, the Ministry of National Defence. In between, in the middle of the road, was a line of bus stops and a bustling crowd of people, everyone ready to elbow the other out of the way when the bus appeared so as to get on first and secure a seat. Back in Greece, I thought to myself, and I breathed a sigh of relief.

My own bus was half an hour in coming, but fortunately I didn't have to start pushing and shoving, as it was an intercity bus and there were plenty of empty seats. The fat woman sitting beside me was balancing a plastic bag between her legs and in her arms she was clutching an enormous handbag, half the contents of which were spilling over into her lap. If we exclude some congestion from the Greek Broadcasting Company building as far as the junction at Stavros, the traffic was moving normally. As we approached Porto Rafti, I asked the fat woman whether she knew where Favieros's house was located. Suddenly five or six people, men and women, leaned over to my window to show me what was evidently one of the area's main attractions.

'Get back, I'm the one he asked,' said the fat woman, forcing them back and making them respect her priority. She waited for order to be restored and then turned to me. 'You should get off at Gegos's,' she said.

'Who's Gegos?' I asked, puzzled.

'The supermarket. It's the next stop. Then turn left towards St Spyridon's. When you come to the bend in the road, you'll see it on the slope, to the left. It's a big house with a huge garden.' She turned back and shouted to the driver: 'Prodromos, stop outside Gegos's so the gentleman can get off.'

All the people on the bus had turned round and were staring at me with a strange, inquisitive look on their faces. As I was getting off, the fat woman voiced the collective question:

'Are you a reporter?'

'If I were a reporter, would I be coming here by bus?'

My reply reduced her to silence. 'I'm sorry,' she whispered, blushing, as though she had insulted me by thinking I was a reporter.

I turned left and after about half a kilometre I saw the house before me. It was just as the fat woman had described, except that she had been reserved about the size of the garden, which must have covered more than an acre and led up to a two-storey villa with balconies of various sizes and a patio in front with tables, chairs and awnings all in white, rather like a private cafeteria belonging to the Favieros family. The entire complex was protected by a wall mounted with closed-circuit TV cameras. The interior was visible only through the tall gate.

A gardener was watering the lawn.

'Can I ask you something?'

He heard my voice, turned off the water and came over to me.

'Inspector Haritos. I want to speak with Mrs Favieros or with one of the children.'

'Not here,' he replied abruptly.

'When will they be back?'

He shrugged his shoulders. 'They on boat somewhere.'

His accent showed him to be a foreigner, though he obviously wasn't Albanian.

'Russian-Pontian?' I asked.

'Yes.' When they're not one, they're the other.

'When will your employers be back?'

'Don't know. Ask Mr Ba up in house.'

'Open the gate for me.'

'Can't. Press button, open from house.'

I pressed the button as he told me.

'Yes?'

'Police,' I said sharply

When you're dealing with foreigners, the best thing is to use the magic word 'Police'. They either open up for you straightaway or start shooting at you. As the latter was rather unlikely in Favieros's house, the gate began to slowly open from the middle. I looked around for some sort of golf buggy that would take me up the acre of land to the house, but there wasn't one to be seen anywhere and so I was obliged to climb the steps that were on the left side of the garden. Halfway up, I stopped to catch my breath because I had stiffened up with the sedentary life imposed on me by Adriani and my legs trembled at the slightest effort.

Smart chap that Favieros, I thought to myself as I climbed the steps. He didn't go and build a villa in some expensive suburb like Ekali so he wouldn't be accused of selling out to the system or of turning into a profiteer, but he built it in Porto Rafti so that he would preserve his progressive profile and at the same time get this huge plot of land for peanuts.

Up above, on the patio with the private cafeteria, I was met by a short, swarthy Asian.

'What is it you want?' he asked in a shrill voice.

'Are you Ba?'

'I am Mr Bawan, the butler,' he replied in a formal tone. And again: 'What is it you want?'

How about that? Favieros even had a steward though he went around unkempt, with a beard, crumpled jacket and jeans. Of course, this Thai might have given himself the title of butler just to increase his standing.

'What is it you want?' he asked again, giving a sample of his Asian persistence.

'Are your employers away?'

'Yes. Mrs Favieros, Miss Favieros and Mr Favieros Junior left on the yacht immediately after the funeral.'

'And when will they be back?'

'I have no knowledge.'

He had a foreign accent, but he spoke Greek correctly, as though he were holding a grammar book and searching to find where to put the subject, verb and object. I thought of asking him where I could find Favieros's wife, but I rejected the idea because it might alarm her and lead her to call the police, and my secret mission would go up in smoke. I decided to limit myself to the staff and take it from there.

'I want to ask you a few questions.'

'I am unable to answer. I have no permission.'

I ignored his objection and continued.

'Did it seem to you that Mr Favieros had changed in any way of late? Was he worried or in low spirits?'

'I am unable to answer. I have no permission.'

'I'm not asking you to reveal any secrets. Only whether he seemed different, nervous, let's say.'

'I am unable to answer. I have no permission.'

I reached out, grabbed hold of him suddenly by the arm and started dragging him with me.

'Where are you taking me?' he asked in alarm. 'I have a green card, work permit, health insurance. I am not illegitimate.' He meant illegal. It was his first mistake in Greek. 'I'm taking you to the station for questioning,' I said to him calmly. 'And if you don't want to answer because you don't have permission, you'll stay locked up in the cells till your employers come along and give you permission.'

'Mr Favieros didn't change,' he said with all the willingness in the world, as if nothing had happened previously. 'He was as he always was.'

I kept hold of his arm so as not to lose physical contact with him. 'Did anything else change? His routine, for example? Did he start coming home later?'

'He always returned home between eleven and eleven thirty.

Later? But …' he added, suddenly stopping as though remembering something.

'What?'

'He left later in the morning. At around ten.'

'What time did he usually leave?'

'Half past eight … Nine …'

What might that mean? Who knows? He may simply have been tired and have needed more sleep. 'Who else is in the house now?'

'Two maids. Tania and Nina.'

'Bring them here. I want to talk to them.'

He went to the patio door and shouted out the two names. In less than a minute two blonde girls appeared: the one extremely tall, the other of average height, both wearing light-blue overalls and white aprons. It was blatantly obvious that they were Ukrainians. If, in Favieros's house, the staff represented half the United Nations, I thought to myself, who knows what was the case at his building sites.

I asked the Ukrainian girls the same questions I had asked the Thai and I got the same answers. That meant, at least at first sight, that nothing had changed about Favieros that the domestic staff had noticed.

'What time did Mr Favieros leave home to go to work in recent weeks?' I asked the maids.

'I told you! At around ten,' said the butler, intervening, seemingly annoyed that I might doubt him in front of his subordinates.

'Work'd here,' the one of average height replied.

'And how do you know?' asked the butler as though scolding her.

'I sweep upper floor and see,' answered the Ukranian. 'He work computer.'

'Show me,' I said to her. Not that I was expecting to discover anything, but it was an opportunity for me to take a look around the rest of the house.

The Ukranian girl led me through a living room with expensive marble and with little and modern furniture. We went upstairs by way of an interior staircase and at the top she opened one of the doors facing us. The study was spacious, with a large window that looked on to the garden. Here too there was scant furniture: the desk with his chair and two other chairs in front of it. Two walls were lined with books. Looming on the desk was a huge computer screen that gaped pitch black. The desk's surface was an exact replica of Ghikas's desk: completely empty, without as much as a piece of paper on it. I glanced at the books on the shelves and saw that Favieros had remained somewhere between the Greek Communist Youth and Rhigas Ferraios. There were books on history, philosophy, a large edition of the collected works of Marx and Engels in English, histories of the labour and communist movements and many books on economics. There were no files or folders.

I went back down the interior staircase and found the Thai standing waiting for me at the bottom. The tall Ukranian maid had gone and the other one had remained upstairs. I headed towards the private cafeteria with the Thai at my heels. He saw me descending the garden steps and was at last convinced that I had decided to leave.

The gardener was still watering. 'Didn't Favieros have a driver?' I asked as I got up to him.

'No, he drove himself. A Bimmer convertible.'

'Bimmer?' I asked puzzled.

'BMW,' he answered, casting a contemptuous glance at me for my ignorance.

10

I arrived at the bus station in Porto Rafti at around noon. Since I wasn't going home for lunch, I had time to go on a second little trip that day and visit Favieros's construction site at the Olympic Village. I asked the station superintendent where the buses to Thrakomakedones stopped and he looked at me as though I'd asked him how to get to the Norwegian fjords.

'Try Vathis Square,' he told me. 'All those Third World contraptions start from there.'

As I was walking down towards Vathis Square, I felt my stomach rumbling and I realised that I had gone from my convalescence back to work without celebrating my return. In Aristotelous Street I came across a souvlaki joint and I ordered two souvlakis with all the trimmings. I ate them standing up, leaning forward so they wouldn't drip on me, and I felt myself at last getting back into the work routine. I couldn't care less if I smelled of tzatziki to the builders.

The stop for Thrakomakedones was in the square, but the bus standing there had its doors and windows closed. The driver was chatting with the superintendent and neither paid the slightest attention to those waiting.

'When does it leave?' an elderly woman asked the driver.

'You'll have to wait, there's another one coming,' was the curt answer.

The other appeared after about twenty minutes and after the five passengers waiting had become fifty. I had to use what I still remember from the Police Academy concerning crowd dispersion in order to get on and secure a seat for myself.

The bus set off but stopped every twenty yards either because of traffic lights or because of the congestion. When it was neither of these, it was because someone wanted to get on or off. Somewhere around Kokkinos Mylos, my eyes closed and I dozed off. The voices around me merged into a low droning sound and I dreamt I was still in my sick bed, in the hospital, all wired up and wearing an oxygen mask. I opened my eyes and saw Adriani leaning over me. 'What was I thinking of when I married you,' she said in an angry tone. 'I've known nothing but worry and disappointment since I've been with you! If you were a big shot I could understand it. But you're a copper. Some jackpot!'

I was woken by the jerk of the bus stopping suddenly and I had no idea where I was. 'Are we there?' I asked the man beside me, as if he knew where I was going.

'Next stop is the terminus,' he replied. I breathed a sigh of relief.

I didn't know where the Olympic Village was exactly and I decided to take a taxi so as not to end up searching all over the place.

'Where to?' said the driver as I got in beside him.

'The Olympic Village.'

He braked suddenly before we'd even set off and opened the door for me.

'Not on your life,' he said. 'I've just come from there and I was lucky to get the car out in one piece with all the rubble and potholes. Find another taxi, I've been through that no-man's-land once today.'

Eventually, the third one that passed left me at the border between the Olympic Village and the rest of the world. From close up, the picture was far less inviting than that in the brochure published by the Workers Residence Organisation, that encouraged us to put our names down for one of the flats that would house ten thousand Athenians after the Olympic Games. When Adriani had seen it, she had taken a shine to the idea, but I quashed it there and then. Firstly, because I wouldn't have been able to stand the daily nightmare of commuting between Thrakomakedones and Ambelokipi and, secondly, because the Greek public sector had far more than ten thousand political favours to repay and consequently we would be left looking on. With hindsight, I understood the taxi driver's reluctance. From close up, more than half the places seemed in an embryonic state and the roads were non-existent. Everywhere there were mounds of rubble, excavations and potholes.

I asked a truck driver where the building site of the Domitis Construction Company was. He pointed to some tricolour houses about a hundred yards away. Their corners were ochre, their walls pink and their balconies light blue.

The site's offices were in a caravan behind the houses. I entered without knocking and saw two men: a young man of around thirty, who was sitting at one of the two desks, and another, around forty-five, standing up. They were talking heatedly and paid no attention to me. They evidently took me for a supplier come to sell them prefabricated concrete or bricks and so left me waiting.

'Don't load it on me,' said the elder one heatedly. 'I'm not the one who chooses the workers. That's your job. I work with whoever you give me.'

'Can't you steal a couple of days for zone three?' asked the other in a conciliatory tone.

The elder one shot me a glance that was full of contempt. 'If I steal a couple of days, it will hold up the laying of the sewer system. They bring you straight from university to the site and you think it's like you were taught in the classroom.'

Without another word, he turned round and walked out, leaving the door of the caravan open behind him. The younger man turned his attention to me.

'Yes?' he said in a somewhat bored fashion.

'Inspector Haritos.'

He was taken aback, as he'd thought me a supplier and I'd turned out to be a copper. He got to his feet quickly and closed the door. Then he stood in front of his desk and looked at me.

'About the Kurds?'

Inside I felt thankful that he was taking me where I wanted to go. 'Had you previously received any threats from the nationalistic organisation that claimed responsibility for the murders? I mean, were you ever asked to get rid of the foreign workers you employ here?'

The reply was categorical: 'Never. We heard the name of the organisation for the first time on the TV.'

'Do you know whether your boss had received any threats? Did he seem nervous or frightened to you in recent weeks?'

He reflected. 'Nervous or frightened, no ...' he replied, but it was clear that there was something else he wanted to add.

'But?'

He reflected again. 'Worried ... Preoccupied perhaps ...'

'Did he have any reason to be worried?'

He shrugged. 'What can I say ... If he had any personal concerns I'm not aware of them. As for professional ones, what worries might he have? All his contracts were handed to him on a plate.'

'So you wouldn't have said that he was on the verge of suicide?'

'On the contrary. He was as smiling and as friendly as always.' He paused for a moment, then added: 'Favieros was on very good terms with the staff. Not only with the engineers on the site, but with the ordinary workers too. Whoever had a problem went directly to him to find a solution. He was concerned about everyone and everyone liked him. Okay, he may have put it on a bit, but he did help where he could ... That's the truth of it ...'

'You didn't notice any change in his behaviour?'

'No, other than what I've already told you ... That he was a little worried ... A little preoccupied. Though why, I can't tell you ...'

'Where did the two Kurds work?'

'The sewer system. With Karanikas, the foreman who was here when you came in.' He had a hard time hiding his anger with the elder man.

'Where can I find him?'

'He should be somewhere between the second and third row of houses as you leave the caravan.'

What I had been told by the staff in Porto Rafti had been confirmed. Nothing had changed outwardly in Favieros's behaviour. And yet, for him to resort to suicide, either he must have been receiving threats from the Philip of Macedon National Front or he must have had personal problems.

Between the second and third row of houses I came across a group of workers who were talking to Karanikas.

'Inspector Haritos,' I said as I got nearer to him.

'Do you people come in waves?' he remarked caustically, while his eyes told me that he would have liked to have thrown me out on my ear.

'What do you mean?'

'Two of your colleagues were here the other day and we lost a whole day's work because of them. Now you're here and from what I see we're going to lose another half day. Will there be any more of you coming?'

'What's it to you? I don't have to explain myself to you.' He realised he had gone too far and backed down. 'Those two Kurds, what sort of people were they?'

'How should I know? I learned their names from the TV.'

'Didn't they work here?' I asked surprised.

'Yes, this is where they worked. But they have such strange-sounding names that you forget them as soon as you hear them. That's why it's much easier to call them "Albanian, Bulgarian, Kurd" depending on where they've come from.'

'Do you have a lot of foreigners on the site?'

His ironic tone returned. 'That's a good one … Me, I don't know why we don't build the Olympic facilities in Albania or Bulgaria or Kurdistan. It'd be much simpler as they're the ones benefitting from the Olympic Games. It's provided work for them.'

'Come on now, you're exaggerating. You come out with things like that and you give fuel to all kinds of screwballs!'

'Do you know how many Greeks work on this site? Two engineers and four foremen, six in total. All the others are either from the Balkans or Third World countries.' Then, suddenly getting riled: 'We're a worthless lot, and we're being made proper fools of! Why don't our unemployed do something about it … come here and smash the place up? The only ones to do something about it was that Macedonian lot.'

'Do you mean the Philip of Macedon organisation?'

'Yeah, them. The Macedons.'

'So you agree with what the organisation wrote in its announcement about Favieros's suicide?'

He looked at me cunningly and smiled. 'Don't go putting words into my mouth,' he said, as though reading my thoughts and enjoying it all. 'I don't know what it says in the announcement. All I know is that I have to do with Albanians, Bulgarians, Kurds and Arabs. They're the ones building the Olympic Village and they're building it like their own homes. What do you expect from builders who all their lives have used straw and mud to build their huts?'

I stared at him for some time, but he didn't look away because he believed he was in the right so he didn't feel at all uncomfortable.

'You didn't particularly like Favieros,' I said to him.

He shrugged indifferently. 'Life is like swimming,' he said. 'Some swim in money, others in deep water and others in shit. Favieros was swimming in money. Now, if they made him commit suicide or if he committed suicide out of remorse or because he simply got it into his head, I don't know and I don't care if I don't find out. I mind my own business and I'm happy swimming in deep water, because tomorrow they'll put some foreman from Tirana in my place and then I'll be swimming in shit.'

He considered that our conversation was over and rushed off to oversee the sewer system, which might very well turn out to be his future swimming pool.

11

The doorbell rang at nine o'clock. I was having my morning coffee in the sitting room and searching for the entry under 'washing' in the hope of finding some interpretation of the phrase 'brainwashing'. I couldn't find anything, because in 1955, when the Dimitrakos Dictionary was published, brainwashing was evidently of no concern to anyone, whereas today it's even found its way into our bedroom, where the previous night Adriani had done a veritable laundry job on my brain because I'd been late coming home and was back to my old ways and because I should be ashamed for letting Ghikas make a fool of me by having me cut short my sick leave and because all the good work that she had done for me in those previous two months, I would undo in two days, and … and …

'You're wanted!'

The sound of her voice, sharp and authoritative, came from the front door. As if I were back to my first years in the Force, when I'd hear someone in one of the offices shout 'Haritos!' and I'd jump up and rush to find who it was that wanted me.

'Your new assistant!'

The front door was wide open. Parked outside was a van. Koula appeared at the side door with a computer monitor in her arms. She was followed by a young lad of around twenty-two who was carrying the computer.

'Leave it, Spyros, and go and bring the table,' Koula said to him.

I found myself having to deal with two surprises at the same time and I didn't know to which I should give precedence. First of all, I hadn't been expecting Koula to turn up with a computer, and, secondly, it was quite a different Koula I saw before me. She was wearing a T-shirt and jeans, had tied her hair back into a ponytail and was no longer the model in uniform that greeted me in the entrance to Ghikas's office. She looked like a student or an assistant in a company.

I recovered from the second surprise to return to the first. 'What's this, Koula? The Chief's given you a computer as well?'

She laughed. 'Come on now, Inspector, you know him better than that! It belongs to my cousin Spyros, who's studying computers. He had one spare and he's given it to me.'

The Spyros in question arrived carrying the little table. 'Put it down there, I'll take care of it, Spyros,' she said to him sweetly. 'This is Inspector Haritos.'

The young lad shot me a quick look and mumbled a 'Hello'. Then he went back to the van. It was quite clear that he had no liking for coppers. Koula looked behind her and burst out laughing.

'He's the son of my mother's sister,' she explained. 'I had a hard job getting him to like me because I was on the Force.' Then she pointed to the computer and table. 'Is there somewhere we can put these?'

'What do we need the computer for, Koula?'

'Just think about it! We're working under cover now. You won't have any reports or statements or records. How are you going to remember everything you saw and heard from so many people?'

She was right in what she said, but I didn't know how I was going to persuade Adriani to find us a place for the computer. She'd quite likely put it in the loft without so much as a second thought.

I found her in the kitchen washing the breakfast pots.

'Where can we put a computer that we need for our work?' I asked her.

She dried her hands on the towel and stormed into the sitting room. Without uttering a word, she pushed the carved wooden armchair with the embroidered cushions inherited from her mother to the right; then she pushed the shelves with the vase that I had inherited from my mother to the left, leaving just enough room between them for the computer table. Then she turned to go back into the kitchen. But in the doorway to the sitting room, she bumped into Koula, who was waiting for her with a restrained smile.

'Good morning, Mrs Haritos. I'm Koula,' she said.

'Good morning, my dear.'

You can tell how much Adriani likes or dislikes someone from the shape of her lips. If she likes you, she smiles with her lips at their normal size. The more she dislikes you, the more she purses them. In Koula's case, her lips had virtually disappeared.

Koula went on smiling as though not having noticed her attitude. I, however, was ready to explode. After all, it wasn't the girl's fault if I had decided to clock in for work again. While Koula was connecting up the computer, I informed her about the previous day's visits to Favieros's house and construction site. When I told her that Favieros had been leaving later in the mornings because he had been working on his computer at home, she stopped what she was doing and looked at me.

'How can I get a look at his computer?' she asked me.

'I don't think the butler will let us in before the family returns. But what else might Favieros's computer have on it apart from plans and static studies?'

'You never know, Inspector. Now, with computers, you can discover the entire biography of the user if you know where and what to look for. From his professional business to his personal interests and from the games he liked playing to who he talked and corresponded with. You can come up with the most amazing things.'

I found all this a bit excessive, but we wouldn't lose anything by taking a look. What took priority, however, was a visit to the offices of Domitis Construction so that I might make the acquaintance of Favieros's close circle. I didn't expect to discover anything sensational. What I mainly wanted was to see what kind of atmosphere prevailed following the voluntary exit of its founder and owner.

Koula had switched on her computer and was playing around with it. I left her to go and ask Adriani for the keys to the Mirafiori. I was resolved to keeping my promise and letting Koula drive so as not to overdo it.

Adriani was making dolmades with lemon sauce and was at the stage of rolling the vine leaves with the filling. She heard me come in but didn't turn round.

'Where are the keys for the Mirafiori?' I asked calmly. And I made it clear: 'Koula will drive.'

'You've got them.'

'I don't have them. After the shooting, they gave them to you together with my clothes and all the rest.'

'I gave them to you.'

'You didn't give them to me nor did I ask you for them, because I've had no need of them since then.'

'I gave them to you and you just don't remember.'

I started to get hot under the collar because I knew where she was leading. She wanted to send the keys to the Lost Property Department so that I wouldn't be able to take the Mirafiori. Nevertheless, I succeeded in putting the brakes on my anger and said to her calmly:

'Okay, I'll call the Fiat dealers and get them to send me a locksmith to open up the car and put new locks on. The bill will be around 300 euros because it's an old model and they cost a fortune.'

She tossed the half-wrapped dolma into the pan and went out of the kitchen. In two minutes she was back with the keys to the Mirafiori.

'There!' she said, throwing them onto the table, 'you'd put them in the wardrobe next to your underwear and you'd forgotten!'

I cursed myself for not following her into the bedroom. I'd have caught her red-handed taking the keys out of her hiding place, whereas now she was throwing the blame on me and I had no incriminating evidence to refute her.

Without saying anything, I picked up the keys and walked out of the kitchen. Koula had turned off the computer and was waiting for me.

'Let's be off,' I said to her, explaining that we were going to pay a visit to Favieros's offices.

She stood for a moment in the doorway to the sitting room, then, instead of coming with me, she made a beeline for the kitchen.

'Are you making dolmades?' she asked Adriani with admiration in her voice. 'Will you show me how to wrap them because whenever I do it they always come undone!'

There was a short pause and then Adriani said: 'All right, I'll show you, it's not so difficult, you know!' This last phrase sounded more like: 'Why, are you so incompetent!' But Koula went on undeterred.

'You know, since my mother died, I'm the one who has to do all the cooking for my father. He loves dolmades, but whenever I make them, the poor man ends up eating the filling and the vine leaves separately.'

Adriani had lifted her head and was staring at her. Though her expression hadn't changed, I realised, because I knew her well, that she had been impressed by the fact that Koula took care of her father.

'Come here and watch me one day and I'll show you,' she said with a smile. The smile was still acerbic, but with a bit more lip.

Once outside I handed over the keys to the Mirafiori, which was parked at the corner of Aroni and Protesilaou Streets.

'You drive,' I said to her, 'Adriani has exercised her veto on me.'

She chuckled. 'Don't worry, I passed my driving test with distinction.'

The car doors opened okay, but there the Mirafiori's willingness came to an end. When Koula tried to start it up, it rumbled slightly and then stopped. At the fourth attempt, it lurched so violently that it almost catapulted us through the windscreen, before starting up with a wheezing sound.

The offices of Domitis Construction were in Timoleontos Street, close to the First Cemetary. I was glad it wasn't far from my home so we wouldn't have to overwork the Mirafiori after it had been stationary for two months. Turning into Vassileos Konstantinou Avenue, we hit a wall of traffic. Because of the Olympics, Athens had turned into a ploughed-up field and the drivers who hadn't got themselves a tractor in time were now seeking safety on roads that had still not been dug up, with the result that the traffic had come to a standstill. A policeman at the junction between Vassileos Konstantinou Avenue and Rizari Street gestured at us abusively, not because we would move any quicker like that, but because his eyes had tired of seeing us. Then just as I was breathing a sigh of relief at the fact that the Mirafiori was managing bravely with all the stopping and starting, it gave up the ghost at the red light in Diakou Street. The engine gave out and, when the lights turned to green, it wouldn't start up no matter what. Those behind honked their horns like people possessed, Koula was getting more and more exasperated because with each new attempt, she drowned the engine even more, while those cars that managed to slip out and pass us stuck their fingers up at us just to boost our morale.

'Let me get it started,' I said

While I was trying various tricks to get the thing moving, a convertible pulled up beside us. Sitting behind the wheel was a youngster with a crocodile on his T-shirt and spiked hair. In the past we used to starch our collars, now it seems we starch our hair.

'Eh, you old fogey. What are you doing with the chick in that pile of scrap?' he shouted angrily. 'Get yourself a convertible like us, birdbrain. Look at the face on the old fogey!' And stepping on the accelerator, he smothered us in exhaust fumes to get his own back. In my consternation, I had forgotten that the Mirafiori was stuck at the lights. I cast a sideways glance at Koula, who was trying to remain composed, but failed, and broke into loud peals of laughter.

'At times like these, the bad copper comes out in me and I want to arrest whoever I see in front of me,' I told her.

'Come on, show a little understanding.'

'Understanding?'

'Don't you get it? His girl has dumped him and he's taking it out on you.'

That's one explanation that hadn't occurred to me at all and it filled me with such delight that I turned the key as though caressing it and the Mirafiori started up at the first attempt.

12

I was expecting to find myself before a modern office block of dark concrete and one-way windows, but what I found was a three-storey neoclassical building, recently renovated. The modern office block was behind it. At first, I thought they were two separate buildings, but when I looked from the side, I discovered that there was a small bridge, rather like a glass tube, connecting the two buildings. The same social disguise employed by Favieros could be seen even in his business. At first sight, he didn't want to live in the same neighbourhood with the moneybags in Ekali; his house in Porto Rafti, however, was the house of a moneybag. At first sight, he preferred neoclassical buildings to the modern office blocks; behind the neoclassical building, however, was the modern block. He wore Armani suits, but crumpled and without a tie. Of course, to blame for this might have been the prudishness that leftists feel about their wealth and so they cover it up with a fig leaf, not to stop other people seeing it, but so as not to see it themselves. But perhaps equally to blame is the outlaw syndrome that leftists suffer from and that makes them persist with the disguise, albeit pointlessly, out of an acquired momentum.

Dominating the spacious hallway, facing the entrance, was a portrait of Favieros, draped in black out of mourning. Beneath it was a pile of floral bouquets. The receptionist was a pleasant-looking fifty-year-old woman, simply dressed and without make-up.

'Good morning. How might I help you?' she asked us politely.

'Inspector Haritos. This is Officer Koula ...' I suddenly realised that I didn't know Koula's surname and I got stuck. Fortunately, she understood and cut in.

'... Kalafati. Koula Kalafati.'

'We'd like to see whoever's in charge,' I added politely.

'Is there anything wrong?' she asked worriedly. She had just been through one tragic event and now, fatalistically, she was waiting for the next one.

'Nothing at all. It's purely routine. I'm sure you can imagine that when such a well-known figure commits suicide, and publicly as well, the police are obliged to carry out a routine investigation so as not to be accused of not looking into it.'

Privately, I was hoping that she would go for my little spiel and not suddenly decide to phone the police to verify it.

'Take a seat for just a moment,' she said, picking up the phone.

We sat down in the two metal chairs facing her desk. The hallway had been meticulously renovated. Wooden panelling halfway up the wall, with the rest of the wall painted a light pink colour. The carvings on the ceiling had been restored to their original form and they made you nostalgic for the old light fittings with candles or bulbs. The furnishings were the usual design as in all offices: metal chairs, desks of metal and wood, computers. But it didn't jar; perhaps because it was all so neutral and was absorbed by the neoclassical restoration, rendering it inconspicuous.

The woman put down the receiver. 'Our General Manager, Mr Zamanis, will see you. Please follow Mr Aristopoulos,' she said, motioning to a young man wearing a short-sleeved shirt and tie, who had come and was waiting for us.

We went up to the third floor, over the bridge of sighs and entered the modern block. Here, the decoration was minimalist, not at all recalling the period of the first Bavarian Kings of Greece. Chipboard cubicles, like a line of theatre sets. Sitting inside were men and women either typing away at the keys on their computers or talking on their mobile phones.

Aristopoulos led us to a door at the end, the only door on the whole floor. In olden times, the rich lived in neoclassical houses and the servants in hovels. Now only a door divides them. The actors up front and the impresario behind the door. That was all there was to it.

The second fifty-year-old woman that we encountered had her hair tied back, was wearing white linen slacks and blouse, but like the first woman had no make-up on. I suddenly realised that this was their way of showing they were in mourning for Favieros, and I quite liked it.

'Do go in. Mr Zamanis is waiting for you,' she said, immediately adding: 'Can we get you anything?'

I politely declined and Koula was quick to comply.

Zamanis must have been around the same age as Favieros, but that's where the similarities ended. Favieros was of average height and was ostentatiously unkempt; Zamanis was tall and wearing a smart suit. Favieros had thick hair and was always unshaven; Zamanis was clean-shaven and starting to go bald. He got to his feet to receive us and held out his hand. Then he also shook Koula's hand, but mechanically, without looking at her, because his eyes were fixed on me.

'I have to admit that your visit surprises me somewhat.' He stressed the words one by one as if to underline them. 'Why this sudden interest on the part of the police in the tragedy that's befallen us?'

'It's hardly sudden,' I replied. 'We simply waited for the first few difficult days to pass before bothering you. Besides it's not something urgent. It's purely a formality.'

'Let's get on with the formality, then.' He waited for us to sit down and then shooting his words out at us in a sharp, categorical tone: 'So what do you want to know? Whether I expected Jason to commit suicide? The answer is "no". Whether he had any reason to commit suicide? No, everything was going just fine for him. Whether he was forced into suicide by those fascist idiots? Again no, they simply used it as an opportunity to do their own thing. Whether I expected Jason to make a spectacle of his suicide? Again, the answer is "no" for a fourth time. And now that I've answered all your questions, please allow me to get back to my work. Time is pressing and all the work has fallen on my shoulders.'

Koula wasn't sure whether she should get to her feet or remain seated and looked at me uncomfortably. She saw that I didn't budge and went along with me.

'Thank you for saving us the trouble of asking you the questions,'

I said politely and without the slightest irony. 'But you haven't answered the question as to why Jason Favieros committed suicide.'

He puts his hands in the air in a gesture of ignorance. 'Because I can't,' he said in a sincere tone. 'From the moment I became an eye-witness to that terrible spectacle on TV, I've been racking my brains trying to find an answer but I can't.'

'Is it at all possible that he was being blackmailed by that nationalist organisation?'

He burst into laughter. 'Come now, Inspector. If that was the case, I would have been the first to know and he certainly wouldn't have kept it a secret from the police. And, when all's said and done, if they were going to blackmail us on account of our foreign workers, they would have blackmailed all the Greek construction companies.'

'Did he have any enemies?'

'Of course. All the other public works contractors. We're living in a world where everyone is against everyone else. We all began with dreams of other things but we've all ended up here. I don't see anyone unhappy about it, however.'

'Just before Favieros committed suicide, the reporter had asked about his connections with the government.'

Again he burst into laughter. 'So? Would he commit suicide just because he got preferential treatment? It's the hard-done-by who commit suicide, Inspector.'

I felt like giving up. All his answers were the ones I had thought of and they were sound ones. 'Did he have any psychological problems?'

I asked with the logic that says when you've exhausted everything else, try your luck with psychology. It was the first time that Zamanis's glibness faltered.

'I've been asking myself the same question since that day,' he said pensively. 'The very way that he committed suicide shows an individual who is mentally disturbed.' He paused again and fixed his eyes on the pencil holder on his desk as though trying to focus his thoughts. 'Jason had been through a great deal, Inspector. I don't know whether you are aware of his background …'

'No.'

'You should, really,' he said, looking me in the eye somewhat provocatively.

'Why's that?'

'Because he was one of the leading members of the resistance during the time of the Junta. He was subjected to terrible torture by the Military Police. Once they were afraid that he would die on them and they let him go because they didn't want any trouble from abroad. All that left him with psychological traumas … Sudden changes of mood … affective disorders.'

'Did he have any of these symptoms prior to his suicide?'

He reflected again. 'If I were to interpret the signs with hindsight, yes. At the time, I didn't pay much attention to them.'

'What do you mean?'

'He was – how shall I put it? – somewhat distant, as though his mind was elsewhere. He had turned everything over to me and shut himself up alone in his office. Once or twice when I went in, I found him playing games on his computer …'

'How long was this before his suicide?'

'A week or so … ten days at most …'

'Can we take a look at his computer,' Koula asked rather timidly.

I had told her that morning that Favieros had been doing the same at home. I was impressed that she had linked the two, but Zamanis gave her an ironic look.

'Why? Do you think his playing on the computer is the reason behind his suicide?'

I could have stepped in to take him down a peg or two, but I decided to let Koula deal with it herself, to see how she would react. She blushed bright red, but didn't swallow her tongue.

'You never know what you might find on a computer. The most improbable things sometimes.'

Zamanis shrugged. He didn't appear to be convinced by her argument, but he didn't have any objection.

'Jason's office is on the same floor, but in the old building. It was in there that he had founded the company and he didn't want to leave it. I'll inform my secretary Mrs Lefaki.'

'Between you and me, just what do you expect to find on the computer, Koula?' I said to her once we were outside in the corridor. 'You heard it from Zamanis. The fellow was playing patience.'

She stood in the middle of the corridor and stared at me with a look full of pity. 'Do you know what I do when I have a classified document open on my computer? I open a game of patience as well. Whenever anyone comes into the office unannounced, I maximise the patience and cover the document. Everyone thinks I'm killing time playing patience, but that's how I hide the classified documents from prying eyes.'

She had floored me, though personally I had never seen her playing patience. Perhaps because it didn't matter to her if I appeared unannounced; the most likely explanation, however, was that quite simply I never looked to see what was on her computer screen.

We headed back the way we came, without an escort this time. The decor in the neoclassical building was at the other extreme. Rather like entering a company at the start of the previous century that traded in comestibles and colonial wares. The centre was dominated by a large drawing room, of the kind where *bals masqués* were held in the old mansions, with white doors all around. The doors had no plaques like the one Ghikas had fixed to the door of his office. Evidently so as not to spoil the aesthetics of the place, but that meant that we had to try all of them until we found Favieros's office.

We came across a third fifty-year-old woman. This one was tall, blonde, impeccably dressed, and, naturally, without any make-up.

'Come in, Inspector,' she said as soon as we opened the door. She didn't seem to notice Koula either, and this was starting to annoy me because I had the impression that they all saw us rather like a tow truck with its load.

Lefaki opened a door to her right and ushered us into Favieros's office. Koula stopped in the doorway, turned round and looked at me speechless. My surprise was no less, because suddenly we found ourselves in a lawyer's office from the fifties, with its black leather couch, black leather armchairs, heavy curtains and an enormous walnut desk. The only modern items were a computer screen and keyboard on the desk. Just look at that, I thought to myself, totally different decor from that in his house. And a totally different decor from that in the offices of his associates. In the end, you were totally confused, because you simply couldn't tell who the real Favieros was.

Lefaki noticed our bewilderment and smiled slightly. 'You've guessed right,' she said. 'He had his father's law office moved here just as it was.'

Koula headed straight for the computer. Before switching it on, she glanced at Lefaki, as though asking her permission.

'There's no problem,' she said, 'Mr Zamanis notified me.'

I left Koula tinkering with the machine and went outside with Lefaki. She was the one who saw Favieros more than anyone and perhaps she could verify what I had been told by the Thai butler and Zamanis.

'Had you noticed any change of late in Jason Favieros?' I asked her.

Her answer came spontaneously, as with those people who have no doubt about what they say: 'Yes, he had changed of late.'

'How? Can you explain?'

She reflected a moment before giving her answer.

'He had inexplicable ups and downs. From being hyperactive, he would suddenly sink into complete inactivity. At one moment, he would suddenly explode and shout his head off without cause, the next he would go into his shell and tell me no one was to disturb him.'

'Wasn't he always like that?'

'Jason? Where did you get that idea? He was always amiable, always with a smile and a friendly word. Everyone in here called him by his first name. If you called him "Mr Favieros", he would get upset.'

She suddenly broke into tears, silent tears that were revealed more from the jerking of her shoulders than from the sound of her crying. 'I'm sorry, but whenever I talk about him, I see that frightful scene on the TV before my eyes.' She wiped her tears with the back of her hand. 'I'm sure I'll still see it when I'm in my grave with my eyes closed.'

'What did he do when he shut himself up in his office?' I asked in order to stop her sinking any further.

'He'd sit in front of his computer. One day, to tease him. I said: "What are you doing all day in front of your computer? Writing a novel?" "I've already written it and I'm checking it for corrections", he said in all seriousness.'

Koula came out of the office.

'I'm done, Inspector.'

We said goodbye to Lefaki and left the room. I avoided the lift and took the stairs in order to marvel a little longer at the neoclassical building.

'I need a programme for detecting deleted files,' Koula said on the way down.

'Why?'

'Because I didn't find anything. And because I don't believe that Favieros was playing patience or rummy on his computer, that means that someone has deleted whatever it was he was working on.'

I found her explanation logical. 'And where will you get hold of such a programme?'

'My cousin is a wizard at things like that.'

We were already outside on the street when she stopped suddenly and looked at me. 'Can I ask you something?'

'Go ahead.'

'Why did Favieros only have fifty-year-olds in his company. He could have taken on one or two young girls, who are dying to find work.'

'Because he'd obviously hired all his old acquaintances from his years in the resistance.' She stared at me speechless. 'What are you looking at me for? The kids of police officers get preference in recruitment to the police academy. The kids of army officers get preference in recruitment to the cadet academy. And in Favieros's company, preference was given to his comrades from the resistance. Never mind what the Philip of Macedon lot say, in Greece everyone takes care of his own.'

I didn't seem to have convinced her, but she didn't dare voice any objections.

13

Late that afternoon, I phoned Ghikas at home to find out if there had been any developments in the murder of the two Kurds. Not that I had changed my mind and believed that the murder was connected with Favieros's suicide, but because something might have turned up in the investigation that would be useful to me.

'Don't expect anything,' Ghikas told me.

'Why?'

'Because Yanoutsos is still looking for Mafiosos.'

'It's not the work of Mafiosos,' I said categorically. 'It's what was announced: execution by nationalists belonging to that Philip of Macedon organisation.'

'Try telling him.'

I was almost for telling him that it was his job to make him change his line of investigation, but I knew he was keeping quiet on purpose. He was letting him dig a hole for himself to fall into.

'But I might have something new in a few days.'

'How? Are you going to persuade Yanoutsos to look elsewhere?'

'No, but I think I've found a way to dump the case on the Anti-terrorist Squad. Did you come up with anything new?'

I told him without going into detail about my visits to Favieros's home, to his construction site and his offices.

'So nothing suspicious?' he asked me as though not believing it.

'I told you. He was somewhat distant, lost his temper easily and shut himself in his office.'

'Why? Why would a businessman like Favieros put himself into self-confinement when normally his day should be full of meetings and conferences? Ask me what I have to go through!' he said, emphasising the last phrase and reminding me of the old Ghikas, who had only one point of reference: himself. But then, straightaway, he posed the very same question that had been bothering me: 'Was there something unusual that had happened to Favieros? Why did he suddenly leave everything and withdraw into himself when, so it seems, he had no business or personal worries?'

I had no answer and so I confined myself to simply supplying him with a bit of information. 'Koula had a quick look at the computer in his office, but she told me it needed more thorough investigation.'

'You can trust her when it comes to those things. She's a real wizard!' He paused for a moment and then added: 'And if someone from Favieros's close circle wants to contact the police, give them my name and no one else's.'

We hung up and, if nothing else, at least I had the satisfaction that he had given me a crutch to steady myself when I was stumbling in the dark.

Adriani was sitting in front of the TV, watching a game show. I wasn't in the mood to hear her answer all the questions correctly and then listen to her moaning about all the millions she'd lost. I went into the bedroom to find Dimitrakos. I was stopped, however, by the sound of the doorbell and I went to see who it was. Fanis was standing at the door holding a paper bag in his hand and smiling. I imagined it must have been a little something for Adriani because he'd often bring her little gifts as a way of repaying her for all the cooking she did for him.

I was proved wrong, however, because he held the bag out to me. 'Something from your daughter,' he said.

'From Katerina?'

'Yes, a little gift.'

My surprise increased because Katerina was not in the habit of sending me gifts from Thessaloniki. She even saved money on the heating so as not to be a burden on me. I opened it straightaway and discovered a book with a cheap, garish cover, white, red and black, which reminded me of history books and resolutions by the Greek Communist Party. Its title was: *Jason Favieros. From the Dungeons of the Military Police to the Salons of the Stock Exchange*. The author was someone by the name of Minas Logaras and the name of the publisher was Sarantidis. I flicked through it mechanically and saw that it was 320 pages long.

I was not in the least surprised that some people were trying to exploit Favieros's spectacular suicide. What did puzzle me, however, was how the author managed to write and publish a 320-page biography in the space of only ten days after Favieros's suicide? Unless they had had it ready and were releasing it now. Just a coincidence? Perhaps, perhaps not.

'When did this come out?' I asked Fanis.

'I don't know. They're advertising it though.'

'And where did Katerina come across it?'

'Katerina doesn't only read dictionaries like you do,' he said laughing and winking at me.

'You're wasting your breath, Fanis dear,' Adriani chipped in. 'Costas only concerns himself with small print. Fills his life with it.'

Actually, the small print referred to the dictionary entries I read, but this time she was using it in its wider sense, to include all the little problems, usually to do with work, that filled my time and removed me from her supervision.

I swallowed my anger because I didn't want us to get into a row in front of Fanis. Though I didn't admit it to myself, deep down I didn't want him to think that his girlfriend had parents who went at it like cat and dog.

I preferred to call Katerina to thank her. 'How did you come across it?' I asked her.

'I saw it advertised in the newspapers and I thought it might interest you.'

'Of course it interests me. Thanks a lot.'

'How many pages is it?'

'From what I saw, around 300.'

She started laughing as though she found it funny. 'I feel sorry for you,' she said.

'Why?'

'Because it's not at all your cup of tea and you'll break out in spots trying to finish it.'

'No, I'll fool myself into thinking I'm reading an official file. They're equally boring.'

She came out with the same question I had. 'How did they manage to write and print a 300-page biography in only ten days following Favieros's suicide?'

'They must have had it ready and simply printed it straight after the suicide.'

'In that case, his family must have known about it. Usually the biographer is in contact with the person he's writing about.'

'Brilliant, Katerina!' I shouted enthusiastically. 'Why didn't I think of that!'

'Why do you think I want to become a public prosecutor?' she replied, laughing. 'Kiss Mummy for me,' she said as we were about to hang up.

'Your daughter sends you kisses,' I shouted to Adriani, who was talking to Fanis.

She jumped up from where she was sitting. 'Don't hang up, I'm coming.'

The kisses went on for around half an hour, embellished with all the day's events in Athens and Thessaloniki. Meanwhile I was chatting with Fanis, who found the business with the biography very suspicious and was sure that the name of the biographer would turn out to be a pseudonym.

'Why?' I asked.

'Because if it were a real name, he'd be doing the rounds of the TV channels, giving interviews, at this very moment. What writer would pass up the opportunity of free publicity for his book? But this Logaras hasn't shown up anywhere. Do you find it logical?'

No, I didn't. The biography, together with Katerina's observations and Fanis's comments had roused my interest and I was in a hurry to begin reading. Fanis left at around eleven thirty, Adriani went to bed and I got comfortable in the sitting room with the book in my hands.

Logaras didn't provide much information about Favieros's childhood; he got it out of the way in the first twenty-five pages. Favieros had been born in Koliatsou Square. His father was a lawyer and his mother a school teacher. He had gone to the local primary and secondary schools and had got into the Athens Polytechnic School with exceptional exam grades. From that point onwards, Logaras appeared to know in detail all aspects of Favieros's student life: how good he was as a student, who he mixed with both inside and outside the Polytechnic School, which of his fellow students he was close to. Favieros was one of the leading members of the student movement and he had become involved in the struggle against the Junta from the outset. The Security Forces had arrested him in '69, but they released him six months later. He was taken into custody again in '72, this time by the Military Police. Logaras knew how badly Favieros had been tortured, by whom, even what kinds of torture they used. It made you wonder where he had found and gathered all this information, if not from Favieros himself. Whatever the case, the portrait that emerged from the book was that of an exemplary young man. An exceptional student, liked by everyone, politically active, in the front line of the struggle, who had been subjected to terrible torture but who hadn't broken.

Just as I was coming to the end of Favieros's early years, Adriani, half-asleep and in her nightie, poked her nose round the door. 'Are you right in the head?' she said. 'Do you know what time it is?'

'No.'

'It's three in the morning.'

'I'd no idea. So that's why it's so quiet.'

'Do you intend staying up all night?'

'I don't know. I want to finish the book that Katerina sent me.'

She crossed herself so the evil spirits wouldn't visit her in her sleep and went back to bed.

Favieros's student life came to an end roughly halfway through the book, which is where the account began of his professional life and his rise in the business world. Logaras didn't hide the fact that Favieros received favourable treatment through his contact with ministers and people in high places in the government. He had been in the student struggle with at least four ministers and numerous party cadres. With their help, he had also met the rest of the government cabinet. He had started out with nothing: a small company that constructed pavements and drains for the Water Company, and in less than seven years he found himself the owner of Domitis Construction, plus a ready-mix concrete company, plus a company that manufactured asbestos-cement pipes. According to his biographer, however, over and above any contacts he may have had in the government, he owed all this primarily to his own entrepreneurial instincts, to the profitable operation of his businesses and to his skill in choosing the right people for the job. It was the first construction company to expand its activities in the Balkans following the collapse of the communist regimes and had projects underway in all the neighbouring countries. In short, Logaras was saying what Favieros himself had said just before committing suicide. Instead of giving information which might have helped to explain Favieros's suicide, it merely confirmed what we already knew: namely that he had no reason for committing suicide. In general, it was a biography that flattered him outright.

Only towards the end did Logaras drop one or two hints about suspicious dealings. He devoted just two paragraphs to talk of an offshore company, with numerous international links and with somewhat shady business goals. This was the only slight stain on Favieros's otherwise immaculate suit, even though Logaras barely touched on the offshore company and didn't go very deeply into its activities. This was strange given that he had information on the most intimate aspects of Favieros's life. It was as though he wanted to drop a hint and leave it dangling there.

I shut the book and looked at my watch. It was five o'clock. I wondered whether that offshore company might offer any clue. I decided that, the following day, I would send Koula back to Domitis to see if she could get anything more out of Zamanis. Of course, if we kept on questioning him, he would start to smell a rat, but I didn't care. If the worse came to the worst, I'd direct him to Ghikas.

14

In the end, I spent all night in the armchair. I don't know what time I fell asleep but I opened my eyes at one moment and saw that the book had slipped out of my hands and had fallen to the floor. The hot sun was pouring in through the half-open shutters. I looked at my watch and leapt to my feet. It was already nine and Koula would be there any moment. I threw some water over my face and thought about what my next moves should be. I would begin with Favieros's offshore company. Even theoretically, there was half a chance that the reason for his suicide may lie in the overt or shady activities of the offshore company. It was the only point that Logaras left unclear and it required investigation. I wondered what was better: to search through the books of the Ministry of Trade or to go straight to Zamanis? I'd soon find what I was looking for in the records, but what use would a plain reference be to me? I'd still have to question Favieros's associates. I decided upon the latter solution, but with a slight variation. I wouldn't go in person, I'd send Koula. In that way, it wouldn't be seen to be too important and people wouldn't get suspicious. The next step, or rather the parallel step, would be to find Logaras, Favieros's biographer. That was easily done by a simple visit to the publisher.

The kitchen was empty. My coffee was waiting for me on the table with the saucer covering the cup so that it wouldn't get cold. Before I'd even taken the first sip, Adriani breezed in, wheeling her bag from the supermarket.

'Good morning. Did you sleep well?' she asked in a honeyed voice.

'No. I fell asleep in the armchair without realising.'

'Tomorrow, I'll order you a wooden bed with nails, like those that fakirs use, so you'll be more comfortable.'

I ignored her sarcasm and went on sipping my coffee that was only lukewarm, despite the protection of the saucer. When Koula arrived, I took her straight into the sitting room and told her about Favieros's offshore company.

'I want you to go back to Domitis to talk to Zamanis and Favieros's secretary and to find out everything you can about that offshore company. Where its offices are …'

'Say no more, I've got it,' she said calmly.

'If they give you a difficult time, say that Ghikas sent you. I've informed him.'

'It won't be necessary. Where did you find out about the offshore company?'

I picked up Favieros's biography from the floor and handed it to her. She read the title and whistled: 'That's fast work for you,' she said impressed. 'With him still warm in his grave.'

I found it amusing that she should link the publication of the biography with his remains. 'Do you want to read it?'

She stared at me in alarm. 'Heaven forbid. I'm quite happy driving you around all day, but don't ask me to read big books like that!'

I opened the book and discovered that Sarantidis Press had its offices in Solomou Street, in Exarcheia. We left the house together. Koula went over to her moped which she had parked outside the house. She put her helmet on, started it up and set off, while I headed towards Iphikratous Street to get the trolley to Omonoia Square.

We had been hit by an early heatwave and it was the first really hot day of the summer. There was no breeze at all and even though it was still ten in the morning, the sun was scorching. At every step, the dose of exhaust fumes increased. The trolley was one of the old yellow ones, without air conditioning. Sitting in the seat in front of me was a fat woman furiously fanning herself with a Chinese fan. I don't know whether it was offering any relief to her, but it was certainly filling my nostrils with her sweaty smell. By the time we reached Omonoia Square, I had decided that I was going nowhere in future without the Mirafiori.

Sarantidis Press was located on the third floor of an old apartment block which didn't have a lift. The green iron door was closed. I rang the bell and walked into a large space, more like a storeroom than an office, with an old wooden bench and three chairs. On the walls, there was a variety of shelves and bookcases, all packed with books. A narrow path led from the door to the bench. The rest of the room was filled with packages and copies of Favieros's biography. Sitting on the chair behind the desk was a young man with a beard and hair down to his shoulders; the kind that, were you to run into after the events at the Polytechnic School, you would take straight to Security Headquarters without them having done anything. His eyes were fixed on a computer screen and he was typing away at the keyboard.

'Sarantidis Press?' I asked.

He waited for the printer to start up and then replied with a sharp 'That's me.'

I held up a copy of the biography from one of the piles and said: 'Where can I get hold of this Logaras fellow?'

'Why, do you want his autograph?' he answered ironically.

'No, I want to ask him a few questions. Inspector Haritos.'

The irony changed to sourness when he heard I was a police officer. 'I've no idea where he is,' he replied. 'I couldn't even point him out to you on the street. I've never actually met him face to face.'

'So how did Favieros's biography come into your hands?'

'By post. Together with the manuscript, there was a covering letter saying that if I was interested in the book, he would contact me concerning the details and the date of publication.'

'When did all this take place?'

'Roughly three months ago.'

'Didn't the letter have an address on it?'

'Neither an address nor any phone number, nothing. At first, I paid no attention. You know how it is, even a small publishing company like mine receives a couple of manuscripts each week. I don't have the time to read them all. I put it to one side to read it at the first opportunity. About one and a half months later, I received another letter saying that if I wanted the rights, I had to sign a contract straightaway. I was forced to read it overnight and I decided to go ahead with it.'

'What made you decide to publish it?' I asked out of curiosity.

He reflected for a moment. 'That strange mishmash of political activist and business tycoon. I thought it would sell and I was right. Though he imposed one condition on me.'

'What condition?'

'That he would decide when the book would be published.'

'And you accepted?'

'I modified it slightly. I stipulated that the publication date would be decided jointly.'

'And how did you send the contract to Logaras?'

'By recorded delivery. To an address that was on the second letter. He put the same address on the contract.'

'Can you get it for me?'

On the wall behind him was a shelf full of files and folders. He turned and took down a file.

At that moment, I remembered something that Lefaki had told me the previous day, when Koula was taking a look at the computer. She told me that, when she had once asked Favieros if he was writing a novel, he had replied that he had already written it and was working on the corrections. It suddenly flashed through my mind that perhaps Favieros himself had written the biography before committing suicide.

Sarantidis found the address and wrote it on the back of a piece of paper.

'When did Logaras inform you that you could publish the book?'

He burst into laughter. 'Never. Did he have to inform me? As soon as I saw the suicide, I sent it to the printers.'

'And he never called you?' I persisted with my question.

He reflected and suddenly looked puzzled. 'No, he never contacted me,' he said. 'It's only just occurred to me now that you asked me. With all the madness surrounding the publication and the sales of the book, I completely forgot about it.'

Sarantidis's reply strengthened my suspicions. He didn't call, because in the meantime he had taken up residence in the cemetery.

'Is the book selling well?' I asked.

He looked at me and his eyes lit up: 'If it goes on the way it is, in a month's time I'll be able to move into a bigger office and get myself a secretary.'

Pity, I thought to myself. Favieros's heirs have lost an extra source of income that will be pocketed by the publisher.

When I was back out on the street, I looked at the piece of paper. The address was 12 Nisaias Street, in the area of Attikis Square. I worked out that the quickest way to get there would be to take the electric train from Omonoia Square. As I was walking along Patission Street towards Omonoia Square, I looked straight down Aiolou Street towards the Acropolis, but I could see nothing. The Acropolis had vanished behind a white veil.

The only consolation with the electric train is that it doesn't smell of exhaust fumes, and a slight breeze blew in through the windows along the underground route before reaching Attiki Station. The kiosk owner at the station told me that Nisaias Street was exactly at the other side of the station and joined Sepolion Street and Konstantinoupoleos Street.

I found Nisaias Street easily, but as I started to walk down it, I was gripped by an intense desire to escape. It was a dark and narrow backstreet, that probably only saw the sun at noon when at its highest point. The street didn't only smell of exhaust fumes, you were in danger of suffering apoplexy and needed a portable oxygen apparatus with you.

I walked down the side of the street with the even numbers. I passed by three three-storey houses put up overnight and two cheap apartment blocks whose balconies were decorated with washing lines, mops and cupboards instead of plants. Number 12 was an old house with a wooden door and half-broken closed shutters. Its yellow paint had started to peel. I halted for a moment and gazed at it. I was sure that I wouldn't find Logaras living there, nor even the lowest Tamil dishwasher from Sri Lanka. Nevertheless, with that irrational hope that comes only with desperation, I went up and knocked at the door. I wasn't expecting anyone to open it but I knocked again. The third time, I knocked harder and the door half-opened of its own accord, dragging a piece of paper with it. It was a recorded delivery notice, evidently the contract sent by Sarantidis. No one had been to collect it from the post office.

I went inside and looked around me. Broken furniture, scattered in the two rooms and in the hallway, torn curtains ripped down, the stench of mould. The house hadn't been lived in for at least twenty years. I went back outside and closed the door behind me.

Number ten, next door to the abandoned house, was a two-storey construction. The bells had no names on them. Why would there have been? When you sink to this level, no one looks for you any more, I thought to myself. I rang the first bell and the front door opened. On the top step, a thin, middle-aged woman was waiting for me.

'Do you know if anyone comes to the house next door?' I asked. She put her arms in the air and stared at me. She hadn't understood a word.

I tried the second floor and this time I found myself facing a Muslim woman, her head covered by a scarf, in that oven of a place. She didn't understand either what I was asking her. At the third attempt, I came across a Bulgarian woman, who spoke a couple of words of Greek: 'Don't know.'

It was pointless to go on. Favieros had chosen the house for that reason; so that the postman wouldn't find anyone there to hand over the contract to. He hadn't given any telephone number, the address was that of an abandoned house, consequently, no one could track him down.

I stopped when I reached the corner of Sepolion Street because my investigations had come to an end and all hope of my returning to Homicide had evaporated. Favieros had gone to the trouble of first writing his autobiography in order to immortalise himself before committing suicide. The reason behind his suicide concerned no one; the important thing was that there was nothing suspicious about it. I would remain with empty hands, as I had foreseen all along, and Yanoutsos would permanently step into my position.

15

The thought came to me on the electric train, while returning from Attiki Station to Omonoia Square. It was one of desperation, the kind that you have when logic lays down its arms and looks to madness for salvation. So in the grip of madness, I decided to take a chance on Favieros's offshore company because it was my only hope of keeping the investigation open. Of course, I would have to make a slight breach of faith. I would have to keep quiet about my belief that the biography was in fact an autobiography and, on the contrary, blow up the idea that the secret behind the suicide was to be found in the offshore company. If I got lucky and uncovered any shady dealings, or scandals or scams, I would be able to return to my position via another route. Yes, all this fell under the jurisdiction of the Fraud Squad, but this was a mere detail: when the bombshell burst, it would cover up anything else. Then, again, if the company turned out to be kosher, I would close the investigation and I wouldn't come out any worse for it, given that things couldn't be any worse.

The small extension given to my hopes filled me with a sense of relief, and I went home, if not exactly overjoyed then certainly not down in the dumps. I found Koula in the kitchen getting cookery lessons from Adriani.

'What did you find out about Favieros's offshore company?' I asked her in my strictest professional voice.

'I can tell you now what I came up with.'

'Not now, we have to finish with the food first,' Adriani chipped in, and turning to me she said: 'You go to your dictionaries and I'll call you.'

I was ready to give Koula a mouthful, to tell her that Ghikas had given her leave to help me and not to learn how to make moussaka and dolmades. But on further consideration I had to admit to myself that the smoothing of the relations between Koula and Adriani freed my hands, so I would do well to keep my mouth shut so as not to undermine the newly-established truce. However, I didn't go to the bedroom to get out my dictionaries, but to the sitting room, where I sat doing nothing, to underline the fact that I was in a hurry and they had better get a move on.

Koula came in after about half an hour. 'I'm sorry, but as you weren't here ...' she said apologetically.

'Never mind. Tell me what you found out.'

'Quite a lot about the business done by the offshore company.'

'Did Zamanis give you a difficult time?'

'But I didn't go to Zamanis.'

'Who did you talk to? Lefaki?'

She grinned at me. 'As my daddy always says, better marry over the midden than over the moor.'

'What do you mean?'

'I mean that I'm not in the same league as Zamanis and Lefaki. So I spoke to someone I could deal with.'

'And who was that?'

'Aristopoulos. The lad who took us to Zamanis's office. Do you remember?'

'Vaguely, but what did he know about the company?'

'Inspector Haritos, Aristopoulos is so intent on climbing the ladder that he does exactly what he used to do at school. There he learned all his lessons by heart in order to get good marks and now he's learned by heart the whole history of Favieros and his companies in order to get promoted. He bought me a coffee and told me everything.'

'What did he tell you exactly?'

'Just a moment, I've written it all on the computer so as not to forget anything.'

She went over to the computer, pressed a few keys and began reading. 'Favieros's offshore company deals in property.'

'Another construction company?'

'No real estate. It's called …' She read out the name in English with the same difficulty that I read English. 'Balkan Prospect. Real Estate Agents. They have offices throughout Greece and in the Balkans.'

'And what do they sell?'

'Land, property, apartments …' She stopped and stared at me. 'Don't you find it strange?'

'What?'

'Why would Favieros transform his real-estate agency into an offshore company? Anyhow, Ilias had no idea.'

'Who's Ilias?'

'Aristopoulos.'

'So we're on first name terms now, are we?' I said, teasing her.

She shrugged resignedly. 'There are no free lunches.' I knew that. I might play the untouchable but I'd come unstuck more than once. 'He asked me out on a date,' Koula added with a wily grin.

'And you accepted?'

'I told him I'd call him.' She laughed. 'You know how it works. You say you'll call him, then you forget once you've gone and only remember the next time you want something from him.'

'Never mind Ilias, I'll tell you why he turned it into an offshore company,' I said, ready to return the lesson. 'Because his lawyers and accountants discovered all the benefits he would have from an offshore company. Fewer taxes, certainly fewer inspections and whatever else. Does the company have offices on the mainland?'

'Yes.' She consulted the computer again. 'They're at 54 Aigialeias, in Maroussi. The manager is a Mrs Coralia Yannelis.'

'We'll see what Mrs Yannelis has to say to us.'

I said it though I was certain that she wouldn't have anything to say to me. A woman who manages a real-estate agency might tell you at most in what areas of Athens property values were rising or falling. Or maybe what the building coefficient is for Pangrati. But what could she tell you about Favieros's suicide? If he'd fallen from the penthouse of some apartment block, all well and good. But he had staged his own suicide on TV, what information might you get from a real-estate agency? The signs were not particularly auspicious, but, as I had given myself that flicker of hope, I decided to try my luck.

Adriani caught up with us at the front door. 'Don't forget to take your share of the moussaka with you,' she said to Koula. 'You deserve it. We made it together!'

Koula turned and gave me an embarrassed look. 'You can go home with your food parcel,' I said to her. 'I don't need you any more today. We'll get back down to it tomorrow morning.'

I found the Mirafiori parked in Souliou Square. Once I was out in Vassilissis Sofias Avenue, I realised that I should have waited till sunset to take to the streets. The windows were open and the heat was pouring into the car, while the sun was beating down vertically on the roof and singeing my head. At the Pharos junction, I was held up by the works for the flyover with the traffic bumper to bumper. I curse my fate whenever I stay in Athens in the summer, because I can't bear the scorching heat and I swear to high heaven whenever I go on holiday because I can't stand all the noise and bustle.

I turned right into Frangoklisias Street and again right into Aigialeias Street. Number 54 was close to the Riding Club, one of those ultramodern office blocks, all glass and indoor plants, that look like an aquarium with tropical fish.

The offices of Balkan Prospect were on the third floor. The entrance to the company had nothing impressive about it. A simple white door with a small sign that you had to look at close up in order to be able to read 'Balkan Prospect. Real Estate Agents' in both Greek and English.

The frugality was evident inside too. The outer office was of medium size with simple furniture: a desk with a computer and a small sofa for visitors. Sitting behind the desk was a secretary, who couldn't have been much more than twenty-five and who was dressed simply and wore a modicum of make-up. Evidently, the mourning didn't extend to Favieros's subsidiary companies.

'Inspector Haritos. I'm here to see Mrs Yannelis.'

She had taken me for a client and I'd turned out to be a copper.

That took her aback. She lifted the receiver to make a call, but changed her mind. She preferred to get up and go into Yannelis's office through the door on her right. She re-emerged a moment later and told me I could go in.

Yannelis was the fourth fifty-year-old in a row that I had counted in Favieros's companies. She was wearing a blue and white two-piece, was dark-haired and quite stunning for her age, though the marks of fatigue were plain on her face. She greeted me extremely politely, with a smile and a handshake, then sat back down in her chair and stared at me without speaking.

'This is an unofficial visit, Mrs Yannelis,' I said by way of an introduction. 'We are carrying out a routine investigation into the suicide of Jason Favieros. We're simply trying to discover what it was that drove him to that – how shall I put it? – spectacular suicide.'

'I'm afraid you've come to the wrong place, Inspector,' she said politely and without any hint of irony.

'Why? Doesn't Balkan Prospect belong to the Favieros Group?'

'Yes, but Jason Favieros rarely came here. If he wanted anything, he would summon me to Domitis, where he had his office. So I really don't know what it was that drove him to suicide or what kind of mental state he was in before he committed suicide. I hadn't seen him for months.'

'Do you think it likely that he committed suicide because he had financial problems?'

'If I'm to judge on the basis of our company, no,' she replied with confidence. 'I don't know how his other businesses in the group were doing financially, but I think it highly unlikely that he committed suicide for financial reasons.'

'You are an offshore company, aren't you?' I said, in order to cut to the crux of the matter.

'Yes. And much larger than our head offices show us to be.'

'What do you mean?'

'We don't appear to be a large company, because we have a very flexible infrastructure. All the actual dealings are carried out by the local agencies that are located in Athens and throughout the

Balkans. All we have here is a legal adviser who makes a final check of the contracts, a small accounts department, my secretary and me.'

'Was it Favieros who came up with this flexible infrastructure?'

'All the organisation charts for his businesses were drawn up by Mr Favieros himself. He had no faith at all in management consultancy firms. He thought their systems were no better than manuals for beginners. He said that to organise a business properly, you had to love it and know how its heart beat.'

'Does your company also do construction work?'

'In a few Balkan countries which are lacking in infrastructure, we have set up construction companies to build apartment blocks. In Greece, we deal solely in the buying and selling of property.'

Yannelis was polite and friendly, but in effect was telling me nothing. I made one last attempt.

'Of course, none of this explains why he committed suicide.'

She put her hands in the air and them let them fall back onto the desk. 'No one can explain that to you, Inspector.'

'And what's going to happen to all these businesses now that the mastermind behind them no longer exists?'

The smile on her face reappeared. 'Don't worry. They're in good hands. I won't talk about myself, but Xenophon Zamanis is a very capable individual and knew Jason from their student days together.'

There was nothing else I wanted to ask, so I got to my feet. She said goodbye to me as politely as she had welcomed me.

When I got back to the Mirafiori, I didn't start the engine up straightaway, but sat behind the wheel gathering my thoughts. At first sight, I had learned nothing new, yet that flexible infrastructure was ideal for concealing any illicit dealings if, that is, any existed. The traces all disappeared inside the labyrinth of real-estate agencies. I had to find the right person to show me where I should start looking.

16

Sotiropoulos was sitting opposite me and staring at me. We were at the Green Park in Mavromataion Street. The TV company he worked for was in Melissia, but he was also a partner in a PR company that had its offices in the Pedio tou Areos and so we had arranged to meet nearby. It was ten thirty in the morning and he was sipping his ouzo and waiting for me to open up. In the past, they always served ouzo with a meze: pieces of bread with a slice of tomato and olive, a bit of salami, half an anchovy. As the number of ouzos increased so did the size of the meze, till by the time you were on the tenth, you had a whole platter in front of you. Nowadays, whether it's ouzo you drink or whisky or brandy, it makes no difference. They toss a bowl of peanuts and hazelnuts in front of you so you have something to nibble on.

The idea to talk to Sotiropoulos about Favieros's offshore company came to me while I was having my morning coffee. Of course, Sotiropoulos was not the kind to do something for nothing. But what could he possibly want from me given my current situation? If, by any chance, I managed to get my position back, I would pay him back in forty-eight interest-free instalments in the same way that we pay for everything today, from fridges to favours.

'This is the second time you've asked me about Favieros,' Sotiropoulos said. 'The first time it was by phone, now it's face to face. Why are you so interested in his suicide?'

'No particular reason. Out of personal curiosity,' I replied as vaguely as I could.

'Cut the bullshit, Haritos!' he said vexedly. 'That's why you and I have never been able to get on together. Every time I start to like you and think what a good copper you are, you try to bullshit me and we're back to square one.'

'I don't always tell you the truth because I know very well that in less than an hour, it'll be on the news bulletins.'

'So you sell me a lot of hot air to keep yourself safe.'

He had forgotten his vexation and laughed. 'Listen to me, if what you tell me is not for airing on TV, I won't air it. Because if I did, you'd shut up shop and I'm not so stupid as to want to lose my sources. So, what's bothering you with the Favieros business?'

I continued to look at him hesitantly. He took his identity card from his wallet and placed it on the table.

'Keep my ID as security,' he said. 'Isn't that what we used to do in the old days? If I gave you something and I wanted to be sure you'd return it to me, I'd keep your ID. So keep mine till you're sure that I won't shout whatever you tell me from the rooftops.'

His action persuaded me and I decided to lay my cards on the table, some of them at least. I gave him back his ID and told him that I was investigating Favieros's suicide, but unofficially, because something didn't ring right about it. I kept Ghikas on the sidelines and didn't even mention Yanoutsos. As I had foreseen, he first wanted to make sure I would repay the favour.

'Okay, I'll tell you what I know and keep you informed of whatever I find out, but if you come up trumps, you'll give the story to me first.' He saw that I hesitated and added: 'What are you looking at me like that for? If you're carrying out an unofficial investigation, you're under no obligation to stick to formalities when it comes to impartial dealings with the press.' He laughed, as though suddenly coming up with an idea. 'If I'm pushed, I'll say I got the information from Yanoutsos.'

His argument, though he didn't know it, left me with no choice but to agree.

'Have you read Favieros's biography?' I asked him.

He shrugged. 'No, but what could it tell me? Is there anything about Favieros that I don't know?'

'So tell me about his offshore company, because I have a feeling that there's something fishy about it.'

He burst into raucous laughter. 'You've obviously not found out anything, Haritos. Because if you had, you'd be reeking of fish. Favieros was up to all sorts of tricks. There wasn't one public project that he was involved with that hadn't been cut and tailored to suit him. If, with hindsight, he discovered that some project interested him, the competition for it would be annulled on account of some formality so that it could be repeated and his company could take part. If he wanted to set up some international consortium, the government would go out of its way to exert pressure so that he got what he wanted. There wasn't a bank that he didn't have dealings with and, not only was he not put under any pressure by the banks, but he was able to take out loans without any limit. He got approval for letters of guarantee for any sum simply by making a phone call.'

'Is it true he had close ties with ministers?'

'Close ties? He ate with a different minister every day from Monday to Saturday, and on Sundays he ate with the entire Cabinet.'

'He said that they were friends of his from the time of the Junta.'

'What's the difference between pre-Junta and post-Junta Greece?'

'From being a kingdom, we became a democracy!'

'Wrong. Pre-Junta, when you were asked how you knew some government official, you said "from the army, we did our national service together". Post-Junta, you said "from the Security cells in Bouboulinas Street, we were in the resistance together". An acquaintance in the army got you, at best, a post in the civil service. An acquaintance in Bouboulinas Street made you into a millionaire in five years.'

'If it's as you say, it makes it even more difficult to explain why he founded an offshore company for real-estate dealings.'

'Real-estate dealings?' he repeated as if not having heard properly.

'Yes. A network of real-estate agencies covering Greece and the Balkans.'

'Are you sure it's not just claptrap on the part of his biographer?' he asked me.

'The offshore company is called Balkan Prospect and its offices are in Maroussi. Its manager is a Mrs Coralia Yannelis.'

'That's news to me. I've never heard anything about it.'

'So I found out something after all,' I said ironically.

He stared at me with the look of someone flicking through his mental address book to find a suitable reply. 'Wait a moment, we'll find out,' he said. He took out his mobile phone and dialed a number with the speed of a concert pianist.

'Stathis, Sotiropoulos here. Tell me, does the name Coralia Yannelis mean anything to you?' It appeared that the answer was negative because he went on with a second question: 'Some real-estate agency by the name of Balkan Prospect ...? Exactly, Favieros ... Fine ... Listen, I'm sending a police officer over, Costas Haritos, who wants the lowdown, okay?'

He hung up and turned to me. 'That was Stathis Horafas. He's an estate agent who sold me my apartment and since then we've been friends. Go and see him and he'll tell you all he knows. His office is 25 Karneadou Street in Kolonaki.'

I told Sotiropoulos I'd be in touch and left him in order to go and see the estate agent. I soon got to Karneadou Street, but it took me a good half hour driving around the block between Herodotou and Ploutarchou Streets to find somewhere to park. In the end, I left the Mirafiori right at the top of Herodotou Street, close to Dexameni Square.

Horafas's real-estate office was located in an old, stately apartment block from the fifties, the kind built immediately after the Civil War, in a period when economic growth was identified with building work. Horafas was a smartly-dressed fellow of around forty-five. He ushered me into his office, told his secretary that we didn't want to be disturbed, and closed the door behind us.

I came straight to the point. 'Mr Sotiropoulos has explained to you, I think ...'

'Yes,' he said, interrupting me. He leaned across his desk and brought his face close to mine, at the same time keeping an eye on the door.

'What I'm about to tell you must stay between these four walls, Inspector,' he said in a whisper. 'If you make use of it, you mustn't say where you got the information.'

'Don't worry. Besides ...'

Again he didn't let me finish my sentence. 'Listen, I'm a well-known estate agent with a very select clientele. I don't want to make an enemy of a colossus like Balkan Prospect, owned by the late Jason Favieros.'

'But is Balkan Prospect such a big company.' I still couldn't see what profit a tycoon like Favieros could have got out of a medium-sized business like real-estate dealings. 'Its manager told me of a network of real-estate agencies.'

Horafas smiled. He was more relaxed. 'Correct. It is a network, but you won't find it under the name Balkan Prospect.'

'Why? Is there some other company?'

He reflected whether he should go on and voted in favour. 'Favieros's company is not a very old one. If you remember, it was founded in 1995. Five years ago, it made a dynamic appearance and began buying up real-estate agencies, without, however, changing their business names. Today, there is a whole series of real-estate agencies that still bear the names of their previous owners, while being run by managers belonging to Balkan Prospect.'

Because I'm a complete dunce when it comes to real estate, I wanted to make sure I had understood: 'You mean that the corner estate agents might be called Yorgiou's or Sotiriou's, but in fact belong to Balkan Prospect?'

He burst out laughing. 'Not on this corner anyhow. Balkan Prospect has no interest in Kolonaki.'

'What areas is it interested in?'

'In Sepolia, the area to the left of Acharnon after Aghios Nikolaos, in Liossia and Ano Liossia. And lately, in Oropos and Eleusis.'

I stared at him like a moron, but Horafas wasn't at all surprised. 'Do you find it strange? So do I,' he said with a smile.

'I don't understand why Favieros would buy real-estate agencies in depressed areas like that. With the money he had, he could have easily set up a network in Psychiko or Kifissia or Ekali.'

'What can I say? Perhaps one answer is that there's plenty of work in those areas and no one has to sell his agency.'

'He could have opened his own.'

'But it seems he didn't want to. He preferred to remain inconspicuous.'

'Why?'

He shrugged. 'That's something I don't know.'

Maybe he did know and wasn't telling me because he thought that he'd already said too much. 'Could you give me the names of some of the real-estate agencies that belong to Balkan Prospect?' He grew anxious again and looked at me hesitantly. 'You have my word that I won't use your name.' He looked pensive and continued to hesitate. 'Mr Sotiropoulos will no doubt assure you that I won't compromise you in any way.'

Quite naturally, the client's word was more reliable than the copper's and he was persuaded. He took a thick catalogue out of one of his drawers and began flicking through it. He stopped at a couple of pages and noted down names and addresses on a piece of paper. He closed the catalogue and handed me the paper.

'I'm a hundred per cent certain that these two belong to Favieros's company. The one is in Sepolia, the other in Liossia.'

I thanked him and got up to leave. I didn't have anything else to ask him and, if I had, he wouldn't have answered. He had revealed as much as he was going to.

'Inspector,' he said as I was about to open the door to leave. 'If you want my advice, don't say anything to the estate agents about being interested in buying or renting a flat.'

'Why?'

'Because they won't believe you. Our people neither buy nor rent in those districts. The only way you'll get them interested is if you tell them you have property to sell.'

I thanked him for his advice and left. I walked up Herodotou Street with mixed feelings. On the one hand I was pleased because my nose for things hadn't let me down. When you set up an offshore company to buy up real-estate agencies in depressed areas, without changing their original names, then there's certainly some kind of operation behind it. Favieros wasn't the kind to throw his money away on foundering estate agencies in districts where Greek was a foreign language. On the other hand, my theory that Favieros had himself written his biography had been shaken. If there really was a scam, as I suspected, why would Favieros open our eyes to it and tarnish his name? Unless, of course, he considered it unlikely that anyone would go to the trouble of looking into his offshore company.

The place where I had parked the car was directly exposed to the sun. The seat was like that hot pan on which my mother made me sit to get over the gripes. As soon as I took hold of the wheel, my hands were scorched and I let go of it. The Mirafiori lurched into the Toyota parked in front of me. Blasted summer!

17

The Yorgos Iliakos Real Estate Agency, noted down for me by Horafas, was in Pantazopoulou Square, behind the Peloponnese Bus Station. I drove down Ioulianou Street with Koula in the passenger seat. I had taken her with me because perhaps we would have to carry out investigations in the area after speaking with the estate agent. The heatwave was doing its best to melt the asphalt, the pollution to send us all to hospital and the exhaust fumes to chafe my throat from the coughing.

As we turned into Diliyanni Street, Koula, who up until then had been silent, turned and asked me quite suddenly:

'How shall we present ourselves to this estate agent, Inspector Haritos?'

'As police officers. How do you want us to present ourselves? As fiancés?'

'No, as father and daughter.'

She took me unawares and I braked suddenly. The driver behind started honking his horn furiously, then stepped on the gas and, while overtaking me, stuck up two fingers from behind the closed window, as his car was an immaculate air-conditioned Toyota.

'What made you come out with that – we almost got ourselves killed?' I asked her.

'Can we stop for a moment and I'll explain to you.'

I pulled over and parked between a coach from Novi Sad and another from Pristina.

'Let's hear it then …'

'We're going to this estate agent because you think that there's something fishy going on, right?'

'Right.'

'So why would the estate agent open up to two coppers paying him a visit, and unofficially at that?' She fell silent and waited for a response from me. She saw that I didn't have one and went on. 'But consider if we were father and daughter. You have a two-bedroom flat in the area and want to sell it, to chip in a bit and get me another in a better area. The guy sees the father, sees the daughter, smells a winner and opens up immediately.'

Her idea was simple, correct and most probably effective. 'So we're all right on ideas,' I said laughing, 'but where are we going to get the flat from?'

'My aunt, my father's sister, has a flat a little further down, near the Moni Arkadiou. To tell you the truth, I don't know what's become of it, but maybe the estate agent will know it?'

She had all the answers and all I could do was to agree. We turned from Syrrakou Street into Pantazopoulou Street and drove around the square. We found the estate agency just before we had gone all the way round, on the first floor of a small apartment block.

The office was in a small flat consisting of two adjoining rooms and a sliding door between them. Facing the entrance was a young girl, nondescript in appearance, who was chewing gum and arranging some papers in a file. At the desk beside her a thirty-five-year-old with T-shirt, linen trousers and shaved head was immersed in what was on his computer screen. In the past, they used to shave our heads when we went into the army. Now we shave our own heads after being discharged. The atmosphere was stifling in spite of the fans on the ceilings in both rooms.

'What can I do for you?' said the girl, stopping short her filing but not her chewing.

'We're here to see Mr Iliakos.'

'Mr Iliakos is no longer with us,' said the man with a smile. He got up from his desk and held out his hand. 'My name's Megaritis. How might I help you?'

'It's about a flat …' I began.

'Coffee?' he interrupted me abruptly as if he had forgotten something very important. 'We have Nescafe … Greek coffee. An iced coffee is just the job in this hot weather.'

I politely declined, but Koula accepted the offer. 'I wouldn't mind an iced coffee with a little sugar and milk,' she said.

I shot a look at her. She sat down with her legs close together and an innocent smile on her face, rather like a modest maiden minding her manners in front of her father. The secretary got up with a bored expression and disappeared behind a door, which evidently led to a small kitchen.

'It's about a flat,' I began again. 'I want to sell it and buy something a little better for … Koula, and in another area.'

As soon as he heard the word 'sell', Megaritis resignedly nodded his head and let out a sigh as though it was a question of the fall of Byzantium rather than the demise of Sepolia.

'Where is this flat exactly?'

'Near to Moni Arkadiou,' said Koula intervening, afraid I might have forgotten what she'd told me. 'It's a two-bedroom flat, around eighty-five square metres.'

Megaritis adopted the expression of someone about to say something unpleasant and who doesn't know where to begin.

'It's a tragedy what's happening in that particular area. Ordinary people, family-men, who've managed to build a little place or buy a flat after a lifetime of saving are watching their fortunes evaporate, are selling up and leaving, because the place has been taken over by foreign hordes.'

Just imagine, I thought to myself, on his construction sites, Favieros was the champion of foreigners and immigrants, while the employees in his estate agencies longed for the old neighbourhood with its narrow streets and cursed the immigrants for spoiling the idyll for us.

'Yes, but if they're selling their places, it means they find buyers for them,' Koula observed.

'At the price they're selling them for, anyone can buy them.'

'And what price are we talking about?' asked Koula.

Megaritis heaved a sigh. 'I'm ashamed to say … really I am.'

'Don't be,' I said. 'It's a shame for us not for you.'

'Near Moni Arkadiou, you said? And is it a house or a flat?'

'A flat?'

'How big?'

'Two bedrooms. Eighty-five square metres.'

'Let's see.' He thought for a moment. Then he turned to me. 'You'll be lucky if you get twenty-six thousand euros for it,' he said. 'More likely, around twenty-three …'

'What are you talking about?' Koula jumped up almost spilling her iced coffee. 'That's what you pay just for altering the form factor!'

She was furious, as though she really were selling a flat. I nodded my head approvingly and tried to conceal my surprise at her reaction. Megaritis smiled sadly.

'The good old days are over, miss. Now no one cares about altering the form factor in those neighbourhoods. That's why people are trying to save something of their fortunes any way they can. He took a card from his desk and handed it to me with his fixed expression of sorrow. 'What can I say … Think it over and we'll still be here if you decide to go ahead … Give me a call so we can arrange for me to take a look at the flat and to get the keys …'

He saved the final shot for last, just as we were about to leave.

'You shouldn't lose any time if you want my opinion. Prices are falling day by day. Today it's worth twenty-three to twenty-six thousand, tomorrow it might only fetch twenty.'

Koula didn't even deign to turn round and look at him. I was slightly more conciliatory. 'All right, we'll think about it and if we decide we'll contact you.'

'Did you hear him, the crook!' Koula screamed as soon as we were outside in the street. 'Twenty-six thousand euros! You can't buy a bedsit for that price!'

I was standing on the footpath staring at her. Now that we were outside, I openly expressed my surprise.

'And what do you know about house prices and form factors?'

Suddenly, she looked at me with a feigned expression of sadness. 'You're not concerned at all about my personal life, are you? Have you forgotten that I was engaged to a building contractor?'

Of course, I'd completely forgotten about the contractor who had been building without a licence in Dionysos. As soon as he had become engaged to Koula, he had started using Ghikas's name every time that he had problems with the police. Ghikas got wind of it, threatened to transfer Koula and she had sent the contractor packing.

'So where do you propose we go from here given that you're the expert,' I asked her.

'Why don't you let me ask around a bit on my own and I'll tell you what I find out tomorrow?' she said sheepishly.

'Why, what can you find out alone that we can't find out together?'

'At this time of day, the only people at home are women. And women open up more easily to other women.'

I wasn't at all convinced that she would manage it better on her own, but I saw in her eyes how much she wanted to try, so I gave in. After all, if she didn't manage it on her own, I would come back the next day without her finding out and complete the investigation.'

'All right.'

'Thank you,' she said, glowing from head to toe.

She accompanied me as far as the Mirafiori to get her things. As she was about to go, she leaned over and planted a kiss on my cheek.

'All right, all right, we're done! We're no longer father and daughter,' I said to tease her.

'You're the only male colleague on the Force who doesn't think all I'm good for is filing and making coffee,' she replied in all earnest.

I watched her quickly walking away and started up the Mirafiori.

18

That afternoon, in addition to the heatwave there was a rise in humidity that made your clothes stick to you like postage stamps. Fanis came at nine to pick us up so we could go off in search of a little respite from the heat and we ended up in a taverna in a little back street square, parallel to Pentelis Street. He'd discovered it a few days previously with a group of his friends and he'd found it something of an oasis from the heat. He was right because now and again you felt a few currents of cool air hitting you. And even better, it was an old-style Greek taverna with fresh greens, string beans and split peas.

Adriani found the beans 'a little' undercooked, the split peas 'a little' watery and the main course of meatballs 'a little' dry. She added the 'little' each time to modify her criticism, not wanting to offend Fanis, who had taken us there. However, he knew her by now and was amused by it.

'I brought you here to escape the heat, Mrs Haritos. I know it's no match for your cooking!'

'You know, Fanis dear, compared with the junk we usually get served today, the food here is at least edible,' said Adriani, who always becomes magnanimous once her primacy has been re-established.

'Anyhow, it's paradise here compared to the oven inside the house,' I said, not being one to split hairs.

'The sun hits the house all afternoon and the heat is unbearable,' Adriani explained.

'Why don't you install air conditioning?'

'I can't stand it, Fanis dear. It dries the atmosphere and starts me coughing.'

'You're thinking of the old ones. The new ones don't have those kind of problems.'

'You tell her because she doesn't believe me,' I chipped in.

Adriani made a show of ignoring me and answered Fanis: 'A waste of money, Fanis dear. I manage just fine with the fan. As for Costas, he's back to his old ways, roaming the streets all day. Maybe we should install air conditioning in that old crock he drives.'

My nerves were on edge because of the heat and I was looking for any excuse to let off steam, but I was cut short by the stir that suddenly filled the taverna. People were leaving their meals and rushing inside. We looked around without understanding what was happening.

'What's going on?' Fanis asked one of the waiters passing by at that moment with a tray. He bumped into our table because he, too, had his eyes turned towards the interior of the taverna.

'Stefanakos has committed suicide.'

'What, the politician?' I asked.

'Yes.'

'When?'

'Just now. On TV. While he was giving an interview. Like that contractor! What was his name?'

He had already forgotten Favieros's name, but now, thanks to Stefanakos, he would be dragged up out of oblivion. Because Loukas Stefanakos also belonged to that generation of students who had resisted the Junta and had had his share of prison, the dungeons of the Military Police and torture. Except that he had remained faithful to politics and hadn't gone over to the world of business, with the result that he had become one of the politicians with the highest popularity ratings. In the mornings he was on the radio, in the evenings on TV and in between in the sessions of Parliament, where he was feared by all the parties because he wasn't one to mince his words, not even with his party colleagues. Even I knew that he was the main candidate for succeeding the present leader of the party.

The tables had more or less emptied and everyone was crowding inside the taverna, where there was a TV fixed high up on the wall.

'Do you want to hear what happened?' Fanis asked me.

'I prefer to hear about it in the peace of my own home.'

'I'll go inside to pay because we won't find a waiter to bring us the bill.'

In contrast to the amount of traffic on the way there, there was virtually no traffic on the way back and we only occasionally encountered another car. Fanis was about to switch on the radio, but I stopped him. I wanted to see the scene on TV without having heard the descriptions on the radio.

Outside the electrical shops in Dourou Square, a crowd had gathered to watch the TVs in the shop windows and was taking pleasure in watching the scene in multiple on some twenty different screens.

'Do you think it's connected to Favieros's suicide?' Fanis asked me.

'I'll want to find out how he committed suicide and what his last words were, but at first sight, it would seem so.'

'What reason would such a successful politician as Stefanakos have for committing suicide?'

'What reason did Favieros have?'

'True,' Fanis admitted. I was sitting beside him in the front, while Adriani was in the back. Fanis glanced at me while driving. 'Haven't you found out anything about Favieros?'

'Nothing substantial.'

'Not even from his biography?'

'It hints at some shady aspects of his professional life, but it's too early to know whether that had anything to do with his suicide.'

'If you want my opinion,' said Adriani suddenly butting in from the back seat, 'the TV channel has a finger in all that.'

'What do you mean?' asked Fanis surprised.

'Have you stopped to count how many advertisements are shown each time they play the scene with the suicide? And that's without including all the ones shown during all the talk shows and discussions.'

I turned and stared at her in wonder. 'What are you trying to say? That the TV channel gets them to commit suicide to increase its ratings? Anyhow, how do you know that Stefanakos committed suicide on the same channel?'

'Just wait and see,' she replied with certainty.

'And how does it manage to persuade them?' Fanis asked her. 'By offering them money? Neither of them had any need of money.'

'I don't know, but I can tell you one thing: plenty of people turn their noses up at money, but no one says no to fame,' said Adriani, reducing us to silence.

I didn't go on with the conversation because I knew it was impossible for me to convince her otherwise. She was naturally suspicious. Whenever I got a raise, she was sure they had cheated me and given me less than they should. She read that the new metro would be finished on time and she had no doubt that the contractors had only managed it by cutting corners and in less than three months the whole thing would collapse. You tell her a solution's been found to the Cyprus issue and she smiles knowingly, saying that if it has been solved, it means the Prime Minister must be getting a rake-off from the Turks. The one thing I don't understand with all these rich veins of suspicion that we have in Greece is how the Force takes on men like Yanoutsos.

Because of the heatwave everyone had gone out and it was easy for Fanis to find a parking space outside the apartment block. Once we were inside the house, we all rushed to switch on the TV. We found the right channel at only the second attempt from all the interviews going on. It was the same channel that Favieros had chosen for his suicide.

'What did I tell you? There you are!' said Adriani triumphantly.

I was ready to give her a mouthful, but the phone rang just at that moment. It was Ghikas.

'Did you see it?' he asked.

'No, I was out and I came home as soon as I heard. I'm waiting for them to show it again.'

'All right. Watch it and call me.'

'I hung up and went back to the TV. Sitting at the bottom of the screen was the presenter together with two of Stefanakos's colleagues: one from his own party and one from the opposition party. Various people kept appearing on the rest of the screen, some there permanently, others coming and going, and all of them singing Loukas Stefanakos's praises. What a sharp and spirited parliamentary member he had been, but also what respect he had shown for the parliamentary ethos. How fanatically he had fought against bills that served political self-interest and what a great loss his death was to Parliament. The presenter then moved on to the recent campaign started by Stefanakos for the recognition of immigrants' rights. He had proposed that lessons in their own language be introduced into the schools and that they be allowed to set up cultural associations to maintain their cultural identity. The praise and eulogies dried up and there began the yes-buts, because no one agreed with Stefanakos's position on these issues. The opposition politician claimed that Stefanakos liked to provoke controversy, because he kept himself always in the limelight in that way. The member of his own party claimed that Stefanakos had been extremely disappointed of late with the general movement to the right across the whole political spectrum. The others all flared up at this and wondered whether, in fact, he had chosen that particular programme to make his heroic exit.

'Let's take a short break and then we'll take a look again at the scene with the suicide, perhaps it will give us a clue,' said the presenter, who was only waiting for an excuse to show the scene again.

The discussion is interrupted for a commercial break that lasted a full quarter of an hour.

'You see? There's no end to the advertisements,' said Adriani triumphantly once again.

The director came out with his tricks and, instead of linking up again with the presenter, screened the interview again straight after the advertisements. The interview appeared to have taken place in Stefanakos's office, which was very ordinary with the usual kind of office furniture that you find in any store. Stefanakos was sitting behind his desk. In contrast with Favieros, he was wearing a suit and tie. I don't know if he was in fact as able a politician as his colleagues had made out, but to me he looked more like a bank manager than a politician.

Yannis Kourtis, the reporter, with thick white hair and beard, was sitting facing him. They rarely sent him out on interviews, only in special cases, because, although he looked like Santa Claus, he was their heavy artillery.

'But don't you find all this perhaps too progressive for the situation in Greece?' he asked Stefanakos.

'What exactly, Mr Kourtis?'

'Your wanting to introduce the language of Albanian refugees into the schools in the areas where Albanians live, or saying that they should set up cultural associations, funded by the state, so that they can maintain their cultural identity. You'll not only have the church and the nationalists up in arms, but even ordinary citizens who aren't necessarily hostile to the refugees but believe that there are certain limits to how far one should go.'

'Unless we follow this twin course of incorporating the refugees into Greek society together with allowing them to maintain their national identity, unless the refugees become Greek citizens with Albanian, Bulgarian or Russo-Pontian descent, we will find ourselves facing much more serious problems in a few years' time. We're deluded if we think that we can solve the problem just by issuing them with green cards.'

'May I remind you, Mr Stefanakos, that the same view was held by Jason Favieros, who employed numerous foreign workers on his construction sites. Following his suicide, a nationalistic organisation claimed that it had forced him into suicide. I'm not saying that the claim is true, but, at least officially, it hasn't yet been disproved.'

'Jason Favieros was right,' replied Stefanakos without any hesitation. 'One moment and I'll prove it to you.'

Kourtis remained alone, but the interview was being televised live and the voice of the news presenter was heard in the background.

'Yannis, I want you to put a question to Mr Stefanakos when he returns. I want you to ask him what his opinion is concerning the murder of the two Kurds by the Philip of Macedon organisation and whether he thinks the policies he is proposing may lead to more murders of a similar kind.'

'Okay, I'll ask him, Panos,' Kourtis replied.

But the question was never put. As soon as the conversation between the reporter and the presenter had finished, the door opened and Stefanakos staggered in. Blood was running from three places on his body: from a wound in the area of his heart and two more in the area of his stomach. His suit was dyed red.

Kourtis saw him and leapt to his feet, but instead of going up to him, he took two steps back. Steafanakos continued to stagger towards the centre of the office. He stopped there and opened his mouth in an attempt to say something, but he had no voice. After a great effort, he managed to whisper something.

'I hope Favieros and I are not dying for nothing …'

Without finishing his sentence, he collapsed to the ground. Kourtis found the courage to go over to him but didn't touch him. He leaned over him and said his name: 'Mr Stefanakos … Mr Stefanakos …' as though trying to wake him up.

'Yannis, leave Stefanakos and find out how he did it.' The voice of the presenter was heard giving orders. 'Sadly, the lot has once again fallen to us to have to describe this second suicide on air by a leading figure.'

By the sound of his voice he seemed about to burst into tears. Kourtis moved away from Stefanakos and went towards the door of the office. He opened it wide. The camera zoomed in. Stuck in the back of the door were the blades from three sharp knives, at precisely the points where Stefanakos had been wounded. Two metal handles had been screwed on the two sides of the door.

It was clear what had happened to Stefanakos. He had taken hold of the two handles and pushed his body with force onto the blades.

The scene faded and the discussion was resumed. 'As you know, our TV crew lost no time at all in calling for an ambulance,' said the presenter, as though they had performed some kind of brave feat. 'But the politician Loukas Stefanakos was already dead on arrival at the hospital.'

I had no need either to see or hear any more and I switched off the TV. Fanis turned and looked at me.

'Well, what do you think?'

'Same style as Favieros. There's no doubt about that.'

Adriani thought it unnecessary to remind us for a third time of the fact that she had been right and she confined herself to a smug and triumphant smile. I got up and went to phone Ghikas.

'I saw it,' I said the moment I heard his voice and I repeated what I had said to Fanis: 'Same style as Favieros's suicide. There's no doubt about that.'

'I told you I could smell a rat. I was right!' he said in a voice that rang out like Easter bells with satisfaction.

This time his arrogance had no effect on me. After all, we were both treading on other people; he in order to prove himself right and I in order to save my job.

19

The kiosk owner hadn't seen me since the day of Favieros's suicide. He stuffed all the newspapers, apart from the sports papers, into a plastic bag and winked at me meaningfully.

'That politician's suicide, right?'

He'd also got smart with me after Favieros's suicide and I felt the need to clarify matters:

'Listen, I don't only read the newspapers when someone's committed suicide.'

'Come on now, Inspector! You don't have to justify yourself. I've got customers who only buy the sports papers when their team wins.'

What did he mean? That I, too, only buy the papers when I'm winning? I decided not to give it any more thought and I headed back home. For the first time in who knows how many years, Adriani abandoned her kitchen before three in the afternoon and got stuck into the newspapers along with me.

The climate had completely changed since the first suicide. Then, everyone wondered what reason Jason Favieros had to commit suicide and each newspaper came up with its own version. Now they were all linking Stefanakos's execution with that of Favieros and were openly talking of some government scandal that had sent both of them to their graves. 'Voluntary exit from scandal?' asked one of the opposition newspapers. One politician, also from the opposition party, threatened to make a sensational revelation. 'Olympic Projects' Deadly Secret' was the headline in another newspaper, while a fourth wrote in its leader: 'Though there is no evidence to prove it, at least at present, it is safe to assume that behind the suicides of Favieros and Stefanakos is some scandal that, should it break, will more than likely lead to further victims.'

Actually, the likelihood of a scandal was not at all to be excluded. When Favieros committed suicide, we were all completely in the dark. Now, following Stefanakos's suicide, things were becoming a little clearer. A businessman and a politician committed suicide to avoid public disgrace as a result of a scandal that was about to break. Of course, there was still the matter of two public suicides. Why would people who wanted to avoid disgrace commit suicide publicly? Isn't committing suicide in front of thousands of viewers a kind of public disgrace? Who knows, if we ever found out more, we might be able to explain the public suicide too. Anyhow, even with the facts we had, scandal was a reasonable enough motive, except that it was one I didn't need to investigate. Whether it would come out into the open or not depended on others and I ran the risk of coming a cropper.

An idea suddenly came to me and I called Sarantidis, the publisher of Favieros's biography.

'Do you by any chance have in your hands a biography of Loukas Stefanakos?'

'No, Inspector.'

'Are you telling me the truth?'

'Why would I lie to you? Besides, you couldn't stop me publishing it.'

His disappointment at the other end of the line reached all the way to me. If thanks to Favieros's biography and suicide he had been overjoyed at the thought of having a bigger office and his own secretary, now he was bewailing the villa he wouldn't have in Sifnos.

The lack of a second biography left the field wide open for speculation. The most probable hypothesis was that Favieros had written his autobiography under the pseudonym Minas Logaras, whereas Stefanakos hadn't given any thought whatsoever to his posthumous reputation.

Koula came at nine thirty. She too was carrying a plastic bag with all the day's newspapers. 'I thought you'd want to read them.'

'Thanks, but I already have. You hang onto them.'

'What, read all those pages? No way!' she replied. 'I'll dump them on the way out.'

Adriani, who had heard her come in, put down her newspaper and went into the kitchen. 'Morning, Koula dear,' she said, as she walked past her.

From 'Morning, miss' to 'Morning, Koula dear,' with a warm voice and lips their natural size. The progress was more than impressive. It was only a question of days before the kissing on both cheeks would begin.

'Such a coincidence!' she said when we went into the sitting room. 'First Favieros, then Stefanakos ...' And suddenly, as if wanting to erase the scene, she covered her face with her hands. 'What a horrid spectacle, heavens!'

'Highly unlikely it's a coincidence. Most probably it's what the newspapers are all saying: some scandal about to break drove them to suicide.'

'And what are we going to do?'

'We'll carry on from where we left off.'

She stared at me in surprise. 'And Stefanakos?'

'Do you want a little advice? The worst mistake you can make is to leave an investigation in the middle and go off on another. The only sure thing is that both of them will go up in smoke. We're going to continue with our investigation into the Favieros case, and if it's in any way linked with Stefanakos, no doubt we'll find out as we make progress. Unless we are blinded and fail to see it. So tell me, what did you find out yesterday?'

She looked at me. 'Some rather strange things,' she said.

'For instance?'

'I found three people who had bought houses in the area. Two Albanians, one in Vizyis Street, just up from Pantazopoulou Square, and the other in Aiyeiras Street, a cul-de-sac between Konstantinoupoleos Street and Aghias Sofias Street. And a Russo-Pontian, who had bought a place in Larymnis, which is the second parallel to Monis Arkadiou Street.'

'Prices?'

'The Albanian in Vizyis Street bought it for thirty thousand euros, but it's a one-bedroom flat, around sixty square metres. The second

Albanian didn't want to tell me the exact price; he kept mincing his words, but from what I could understand, he must have paid about the same as the first. Besides, they usually ask one another and then buy. The Russo-Pontian is a bit more interesting because the place he bought is near Moni Arkadiou Street and it's a two-bedroom flat around eighty square metres.'

'How much?'

She looked at me and articulated slowly, so I'd have time to digest it. 'Forty-five thousand euros.'

So that's why Favieros bought real-estate agencies in depressed areas. He paid a pittance to the locals, who sold up at any price in order to get out, and asked forty per cent more from the refugees. The difference went into the coffers of Balkan Prospect, most likely as undeclared earnings.

'And they all paid in cash,' Koula added. 'No cheques, no bills, no nothing.'

How else would they pay? They knew nothing of banks or accounts. They hid whatever money they earned under their mattresses.

'It's downright theft, Inspector.'

'Except that we can't prove it. We have to know how much each one sold the flats for, how much the others paid and then look at the contracts to compare the sums. Perhaps you could get him like that for tax evasion or open the buyers' eyes so the estate agencies would end up in court for fraud. Did you find out the name of the public notary?'

'I tried, but I didn't get anywhere. The people don't speak Greek. They put some documents in front of them and get them to sign. They have no idea who the notary is or what's in the documents, nothing.'

A proper pig in a poke. They were so happy to buy a place of their own that they asked nothing out of fear that the seller might change his mind and not go through with the deal. That's what they were used to in their own countries: if you open your mouth, you lose everything, and they didn't know that in Greece whatever little you gain, it's by shouting and demanding your rights.

'There's something else,' Koula said.

'What?'

'One of the Albanians works at Favieros's construction site at the Olympic Village.'

I hadn't imagined the extent of the scam and I was flabbergasted. So this was the system that Favieros, the champion of the immigrants, had set up. On the one hand, he gave them work, and on the other he took back a sizeable part of the wages he paid them through the houses he sold them. If you consider that he had real-estate agencies throughout the country, he must have been making a lot of money. In Greece, he was selling them property at inflated prices, while in their countries, the real-estate agencies were doing exactly the opposite: they were buying up their houses for a pittance. And all this without Favieros appearing anywhere.

'Well done, Koula,' I said to her genuinely impressed, because I couldn't believe that an inexperienced police officer could come up with all that information in the space of a few hours.

'Did I do well?' she asked and her face lit up.

'Exceptionally. If I'd come with you, we might not have done so well.'

I didn't tell her that I would have liked to have her working with me on the Force, partly because I had no idea whether I would be returning to the department and partly because I had no idea whether Ghikas would let her.

What I had to find out was whether the other foreign workers at Favieros's construction sites also bought flats from his estate agencies. The problem was that I couldn't go to Balkan Prospect, not because they would conceal that information from me, but because they wouldn't know since all the deals were done by the local estate agencies. I would have to go to the offices of Domitis Construction to get a list of the foreign employees and then do the rounds of all the estate agencies and make enquiries. It would take me at least two weeks, even if the estate agents agreed to talk, because without incriminating evidence they couldn't be made to talk. I decided, therefore, to take the shorter route that meant crossing enemy territory, in keeping with the saying that my enemy's enemy is my friend.

The other thing I had to find out was the name of the public notary, because he was the only one who knew the names of both the buyers and the sellers as well as the actual price, since it was he who took the cash from the buyer, paid the seller and kept the difference. A real-estate scam is not possible without a trustworthy notary.

'Koula, do you have the names of the Albanians and the Russo-Pontian who bought the flats from Favieros's agency?'

'Yes, I still have them.'

'Good. I want you to go to the land registry office and find the name of the public notary who prepared the contracts. I'm going to pay a visit to Favieros's construction site at the Olympic Village.'

'All right.'

I left her at home and set off. The Mirafiori was like an oven inside even though I'd parked it in the shade. When I reached the junction at Vasileos Konstantinou Avenue, I wondered whether it would be better to turn left towards Syntagma Square or right towards Vasilissis Sofias Avenue and take Soutsou Street out into Alexandras Avenue. By the time the lights changed to green, I had decided upon the latter route and I was proven right. Apart from the permanent congestion in Soutsou Street, the road was more or less clear.

I got to the end of Patission Street drenched in sweat but without too many problems with the traffic. There, however, I made the major mistake of taking the national road in order to reach Menidi via Metamorphosi. The traffic jammed up because of the works for the new Attica bypass. A policeman directed us down a dirt track that had remained from the time when they still grazed goats in Metamorphosi. It took us the best part of half an hour and three tons of dust to cover a distance of two hundred yards, and with a fair amount of anxiety because the engine was overheating and I was afraid the car would eventually come to a stop in the middle of the goat path. Fortunately, the road soon widened again and the car cruised comfortably as far as the turn for Thrakomakedones.

In less than a quarter of an hour I was at the Olympic Village. I made my way straight to the drainage works that were being constructed by Domitis and looked for the foreman, Karanikas. He was yelling at some workers who were down in a ditch. He saw me but paid no attention and went on with his work. I waited patiently for him to finish because I needed him.

'Why are you chasing after stuff gone stale when there's plenty of fresh around?' were his first words when at last he came over to me.

'Which is the stale stuff and which the fresh?'

'The stale is Favieros, the fresh is Stefanakos.'

His cynicism got on my nerves and I felt like taking him down a piece. 'Do you find it amusing that two people should commit suicide in front of so many people?' I asked him, trying to keep a calm voice.

He shrugged indifferently. 'What do you want me to do? Feel sorry for them because they were playing the TV game?'

'What TV game?'

He repeated, almost verbatim, Adriani's argument. 'Come off it, don't tell me that you don't know that the channel gets them to commit suicide to increase its ratings and cash in on the advertisements. And you're the police!'

'And you're telling me that a businessman and a politician would commit suicide because a TV channel asked them to?'

'Haven't you heard what everyone's saying? Political scandal! And who's to tell me that the channel didn't get wind of it and bribed them into committing suicide in order to get exclusive coverage? Haven't you seen what they put on the top left of the screen? Exclusive scenes! Doesn't that tell you anything?'

It was a good thing that Adriani wasn't there to hear the full theory. She would have had me down for a nincompoop.

'Never mind about the TV. I came here to ask you something else.'

'Ask away, but make it quick, because we've got work to do.'

'Last time you told me that Favieros took good care of the foreign workers.'

He chuckled smugly. 'Yes, but the days of the fatted calves are over. Now we're chasing after cats or the odd stray dog, at most a chicken from Menidi. Each to his own lot.'

'Do you know whether any of them bought houses or flats while they were working here?'

'Any of them? Nearly all of them! You see only misery, do you? It's all playacting. Favieros was the only one to swallow it and he found homes for them.'

'You mean he helped them to buy their own places?'

'He encouraged them to buy! He would even give them advances for the deal or chip in to make up the amount and then stop it out of their wages little by little.'

'Did he do the same for our people?'

'There are none of our people here, didn't I tell you? When I asked him for an advance to buy a new car, he suggested I get the company to intervene with the bank so I could take out a loan. But with all the foreigners he was open-handed. That's why they saw him as their saviour and were all grateful to him.'

Why wouldn't they be grateful? Thanks to him, they acquired their own place, something they didn't have even in their own countries. They had no idea that he was stealing from them and they would never find out. Nor would Karanikas, who took him for a sucker.

20

I got back home at four in the afternoon feeling like a roast chicken. Adriani and Koula were in the sitting room with the fan placed between them. With difficulty, I managed to whisper a 'hello' and went to the bathroom to catch my breath. I took off my shirt, turned on the tap and stuck my head under it. I let the water run for some time until it went from being lukewarm to cold. I dried myself, changed my shirt and trousers and felt somewhat better.

Adriani and Koula had moved into the kitchen. The table had been laid, but the heatwave, the congestion and the Olympic Village had made me feel like a marathon runner who had just entered the stadium after twenty-six miles and didn't even have the strength to open his mouth.

'Sit down and have something to eat,' Adriani said to me.

'Later. I couldn't swallow anything right now.'

'Sit down because you'll miss out on the surprise and you'll regret it.'

She shot a sly look at Koula. So now we're in cahoots, I thought to myself. I decided to play along so as not to spoil the nice atmosphere. Adriani put a plate of baked aubergines in front of me. This was a very pleasant surprise because baked aubergines are my second favourite dish after stuffed tomatoes. To tell the truth, I hate meat. The only meat I eat with pleasure is in kebabs.

'Well, how do you find it?'

I took a mouthful. 'Very tasty. Well done, you've got it just right.'

'Not me. Koula!' she replied beaming with satisfaction.

'With Mrs Haritos's help,' added Koula, who had gone bright red.

'All I told her was how much oil to use. Everything else she did herself.'

I would have to readjust the family budget because now I had to add the cookery lessons for Koula with the use of ingredients thrown in free.

'Well done. Koula, it's very tasty. Congratulations!' Once they had been awarded the citation, they were ready to return to the sitting room. 'Did you manage to get away at all from the aubergines to find time to go to the land registry?' I said, having a dig.

Adriani continued in the direction of the sitting room. Koula stayed behind and didn't seem to have been upset at all by my dig, because she gave me a big smile.

'I didn't need to go to the land registry. I found out the notary's name from Ilias.'

'And who might Ilias be?'

'Ilias Aristopoulos. The young guy at Domitis who helped me concerning the offshore company?' She took a piece of paper out of her pocket. 'His name is Athanassios Karyophyllis and his office is in Solonos Street, number 128.'

'And what did you give him in exchange for the information?' I asked her meanly, because I couldn't stomach the fact that, in spite of the aubergines, she had come up trumps.

She broke into laughter. 'A drink tonight. We're meeting at nine thirty, and at eleven thirty, I'll start to feel sleepy because of the heat and the tiredness and I'll go home to bed.'

'Smart girl,' Adriani commented when Koula had left with her standard Tupperware container filled with food. 'It's in her blood, she's a quick learner.' She paused for a moment and then whispered, as though speaking to herself: 'Not like our daughter.'

'Are you all right in the head? Are you comparing Koula to Katerina?' I protested angrily.

'I'm not comparing, but it saddens me. I'm not saying there's anything wrong with books, education, doctorates and the like, but it wouldn't hurt her to learn how to make a couple of dishes.'

'She must know how to make something. How has she survived for so many years in Thessaloniki?'

'I'll tell you how. With boiled spaghetti bathed in ketchup, eggs and chips. Have you ever eaten chips made by your daughter?'

'No.'

'Good job for you. Usually they turn out like the balls on Christmas trees, because in her haste she throws them in the pan before the oil is sizzling.'

'She still has time. She'll learn once she finishes her doctorate.'

She shook her head as if not believing it. She took it personally that Katerina had no interest whatsoever in cooking.

Fortunately the sound of the telephone interrupted the unpleasant conversation. It was Ghikas.

'Can you come over or are you busy?' he asked me.

'Come over where?'

'To my office.' He realised that I was dumbfounded and he went on: 'Get into the lift and come straight on up. It doesn't matter if Yanoutsos or your assistants or any of the others see you. I'll explain.'

It was the first time since my having been wounded that I made the journey to Aristokleous Street – Security Headquarters – in the Mirafiori and I was filled with a sense of emotion. A huge poster at the junction of Soutsou Street and Alexandras Avenue informed me that if I were to buy the car advertised, I would get the air conditioning free. The car was just right for me and I gave it some thought till the lights turned to green and I turned left into Alexandras Avenue, but I knew that these were just thoughts fuelled by the heatwave. As soon as it had passed, I would abandon my mental adultery and return to my faithful Mirafiori.

When you've been going up to your Chief's office for so many years, always finding Koula at her desk outside, you take objection to seeing a uniformed hulk sitting in her place. Even worse was the state of her desk. The pile of papers had covered the entire desktop, leaving only a small square space, about as big as a cake box, in front of the chair. In this square, the hulk had placed a car magazine and was licking his fingers and flicking through it.

I told him my name as a formality but he was absorbed in Datsun's new model and paid no attention to me.

Ghikas had the air conditioning on full and I felt a shiver run through me as I entered. He lifted his gaze from the *Police News* that he was browsing through and looked at me.

'Good to see you. Have a seat.' He pointed to my usual chair that had been occupied by Yanoutsos during my last visit.

'Do you want to start or shall I?'

'Why, have you found out anything?' he asked hopefully and his eyes shone.

'Yes, though I don't know whether it has any direct connection with Favieros's suicide.'

I began with Favieros's biography, continued with the offshore company and ended with the real-estate agencies and the scam that was going on. He listened carefully to me and when I had finished shook his head resignedly.

'We're going to have our hands full with this business, mark my words.'

'Why do you say that?'

'Because of what the papers are saying and that you've just partially confirmed. Everyone is afraid that there's some scandal behind it all, but no one can come up with it. The government is panicking and is desperately trying to find a solution. This morning the Secretary General phoned me from the Ministry and asked me to recommend a trustworthy police officer to carry out an informal investigation in the hope of coming up with a lead.'

The pleasant sense of anticipation created in me following Ghikas's phone call was slowly turning into a wonderful dream. I saw myself going back to my old office and Yanoutsos packing up his things and leaving for unknown destinations.

Ghikas picked up a piece of paper lying on his desk and handed it to me. 'That's Petroulakis's mobile phone number. Do you know him?'

The name meant nothing to me. Ghikas understood and undertook to give me a profile of him. 'Petroulakis is one of the Prime Minister's advisers. More, he's his right hand. Phone him and arrange to meet with him. The Secretary General is of the opinion that if the investigation is carried out off-duty, the reporters are less likely to find out about it. That's why we came up with this plan. Officially, you're still on sick leave and Petroulakis has no connection with the Ministry of Public Order. So we're more or less safe.'

'Does that mean that I'll still be investigating under cover?' I had been expecting a different turn of events and I felt deflated.

'Yes, but now you are fully covered by me and you can call me and ask for my help at any time. Koula will continue to assist you. If you want another assistant, it won't be so easy for me to find someone equally trustworthy, but I'll do my best.'

'Koula is fine for the time being. How much of what I've found out about Favieros shall I tell Petroulakis?'

'Everything. If a scandal is about to break, as I'm very much afraid, it's better for them to know what they're getting into from the start. If anything else turns up later that you think you shouldn't reveal to him, call me and we'll discuss it.'

'And am I to follow Petroulakis's instructions?'

'Come on now! What instructions can Petroulakis give you? What does he know about police business and investigations? If he gets smart with you, just say "yes" and then get on with it as you think best.'

There was nothing else I wanted to ask him and I got up to leave. As I was going towards the door, I heard him say: 'And give my best to Koula.'

'And I'll tell her how much you miss her. I saw the state of her desk as I was coming in.'

'Don't tell her this, but it's another reason why I want this matter cleared up as soon as possible.'

I imagined that this was the most generous compliment that Ghikas had ever made. Meanwhile, the hulk at the desk had proceeded from the Datsuns to the Hondas.

While in the lift, I suddenly got the urge to go down to the cafeteria for a coffee and croissant just as I did when I used to come to work. I was about to press the button but I thought twice about it and went straight down to the garage. If I was spotted, I would have to lie about why I was there and I preferred to avoid it.

At home, I found Adriani sitting in front of the TV. The scene with Stefanakos's suicide had just faded from the screen.

'You're late and you've missed the special news bulletin,' Adriani said.

'What, not another suicide?' I asked in alarm.

'No, but those nationalists have claimed responsibility for the politician too.'

I didn't have to ask what they had said, because I could imagine it word for word. They had claimed that they had forced Favieros to commit suicide because he was employing foreign workers, even more so Stefanakos, who wanted to introduce their languages into Greek schools. Nevertheless, I impatiently waited for the regular news bulletin. Even if all this was just claptrap and the Philip of Macedon organisation had its finger in someone else's pie, it was quite likely that the announcement would confuse the situation even more and have us turning from scandals to terrorist activities.

In the meantime, I called Petroulakis on his mobile phone. 'It's better if we meet at my place rather than at the office,' he said. 'My address is 21 Dafnomili Street, in Lycabettus. Come along tomorrow at nine, but don't be late because I have a meeting at ten.'

Just as I expected, the announcement was the main news story. Its format and logo were exactly the same as the previous one and, at first sight, the text appeared to have been written by the same person.

It began:

> The Philip of Macedon National Greek Front had issued warnings both in words and in deed …

and went on:

> Unfortunately, those who should have listened to us turned a deaf ear. So, after Jason Favieros, we were also obliged to force the traitor, Loukas Stefanakos, to take his own life. Stefanakos was the biggest rat among all the anti-Greeks. It wasn't enough for him that all the scum from the Balkans has settled in Greece, he also wanted

> to pollute the Greek schools with their languages and spread the infection that would destroy us as a nation. Of all the politicians who, today, are betraying our national interests, he was the one leading the round of underbidding. Loukas Stefanakos received the punishment he deserved. We hope, this time, that all the other zealots and champions of the Balkan rabble will get the message. We will continue with our executions till the stables of Augeias are finally cleansed and the Greek Nation is resurrected.

I thought of Petroulakis's face the following morning after this announcement and I felt like calling in ill and cancelling the appointment.

21

I found a parking spot by the French Institute and said a prayer of thanks. Number 21 Dafnomili Street was a renovated two-storey house from the time when Neapoli was still a petit-bourgeois district in the shadow of the neighbouring high-class Kolonaki. Now, Dafnomili Street and Doxopatri Street, parallel to it, were inhabited by artists, university professors, government officials and all those who couldn't find a place or were unable to afford the Lycabettus ring road, but who wanted to be able to say that they lived in Lycabettus. Rather like the backside of the Hilton, an area ever growing in size.

The wooden door was painted crimson with a golden handle and golden letter box, which testified to the fact that the house dated back to the middle of the previous century. I rang the bell and the door was opened not as in the past by some village girl adopted by the household, but by a Thai girl. She neither greeted me nor asked my name, but turned her back to me and began leading the way. When we reached a door, she stood to one side and allowed me to pass, like a hotel groom showing you into a room in a luxury hotel.

The living room extended through two adjoining rooms separated by an open white door with glass panels. The furniture wasn't from the same period as the house, but nor was it what you would call modern. It was Louis-style furniture, as Adriani would say; the kind that as a child you see in others' houses and hope one day you'll have in yours, even if it's no longer hand-carved but is factory-made. On the table in front of the sofa, I saw the morning newspaper. I picked it up to have a quick look, but I was interrupted by a hasty and commanding voice behind me.

'Sit down, Inspector, and let's get on with it because I have to leave.'

I turned round and saw a man in his forties, tall and thin, with hair starting to grey at the temples. He was impeccably dressed, an exact copy of the type Adriani drools over in *Glamour* and all her other TV soaps. I conformed to his wish and sat down.

'Inspector Haritos, isn't it?' he asked, as if trying to place me.

'That's right. Head of Homicide, on sick leave.'

'Ah, yes. Chief Superintendent Ghikas told me in glowing terms of your act of self-sacrifice.' He paused for a moment, a sign that he was through with the niceties and was about to come straight to the point. 'Mr Ghikas also told me that you are a trustworthy officer and that I can talk quite openly to you.' He fell silent and gave me a searching look. What did he expect? That I would confirm it for him? He saw that I had no intention of doing anything of the sort and so he continued: 'This whole business of the suicides is particularly unpleasant, Inspector. We're talking about people who are extremely well known in the political and business world. However much we were saddened by the suicide of Jason Favieros, we all believed that the reasons were most likely personal. Loukas Stefanakos's suicide, however, has overturned that simple explanation. Stefanakos committed suicide just like Favieros; it's only reasonable to suppose, then, that there's something linking the two events. And so the government has been burdened with a problem that it wasn't expecting and one whose solution is out of its hands.'

'The newspapers are talking of a scandal.'

'There is no scandal, believe me. But that is no consolation to us. If there were, it would come out into the open, we would deal with it and that would be the end of it. But a non-existent scandal is a festering wound that could remain like that for weeks, even for months.'

'I quite understand, Mr Petroulakis,' trying to emphasise my understanding by my tone of voice. 'Tell me how I might help.'

'We want you, very discreetly, to discover the reasons why Favieros and Stefanakos committed suicide.'

'That might take us some time, without even being certain that we'll come up with something.' I reflected as to whether I should continue and I voted in favour. After all, it was better that they should know what they were getting into, as Ghikas had told me the previous day. 'We have no idea what we might uncover in the course of the investigations.'

He looked at me, more out of curiosity than concern. 'What do you think you might uncover exactly?'

I told him about the whole business with Favieros, the real-estate agencies and the foreign workers who bought flats through them. He listened to me impatiently and every so often glanced at his watch to remind me that he had an urgent meeting. When I got to what Karanikas had told me, his patience ran out and he interrupted me.

'I don't believe that the reasons for Favieros's suicide had to do with business, Inspector. You should look elsewhere.'

'Where else, Mr Petroulakis? If he had any personal problems, his family and colleagues would have been aware of it. But they know absolutely nothing. And even if there were any, it would be a huge coincidence if the same personal problems also led Stefanakos to commit suicide.'

'I'm not talking of personal problems, Inspector. I'm talking about those extreme right-wing nationalists who claim to have forced them into suicide.'

I started to wonder whether I really did have an adviser to the Prime Minister in front of me. Even the explanation put forward by Adriani and Karanikas about them being blackmailed by the TV channel was more believable.

'What can I say ...' I replied as cautiously as possible. 'If they had been murdered, I could understand it. Even if they hadn't done it themselves, we would have found some lead. But suicides ... It seems very unlikely to me.'

'But they've admitted it themselves.'

'When we catch them, they'll deny everything, and we won't have any evidence at all to indict them with.'

'And what about the two Kurds who were murdered?'

'We might get them for the murder of the Kurds, but we won't have any evidence linking them to the suicides.'

He leaned over and picked up the newspaper from the table.

He unfolded it and pointed to a particular spot. 'Read it and you'll understand,' he said.

'It was the leading article. I read at the spot he had pointed to.

> All the rumours that the two men were being blackmailed by the TV channel that broadcast the suicides live are ridiculous and completely ungrounded.
>
> Even in the hypothetical case that the channel was in possession of certain information, it is ethically unacceptable for anyone to claim that the channel would endeavour to urge a well-known businessman and a Member of Parliament to commit suicide, regardless of whether it might succeed or not.

'Do you see where all this stuff and nonsense leads, Inspector? As if the supposed scandal weren't enough, before long we'll also have the supposed blackmailing by the channel. They're already starting to put it around.'

'And who will believe it, Mr Petroulakis?'

'Everyone,' he replied, without the slightest hesitation.

I held my tongue, because Adriani and Karanikas had already believed it. The two bodies had turned to mud that they were all throwing at each other: the Opposition at the Government over a scandal and the press at the TV over blackmail.

'You're right, but what connection do the nationalists have with all that?'

He stood over me and looked me in the eye from above.

'The police officers of your generation underestimate the extreme right-wing factions, Inspector. I'm not saying that by way of reproach, I know that's how you were weaned. But, since being a high-school pupil, I've been in conflict with them and I know only too well their methods and what they're capable of doing. If you were to arrest them tomorrow, I can assure you that you would have public opinion on your side and no one would doubt that they had done it.'

So he had finally opened up and I could see now where he was leading. He couldn't care less whether I found the reasons behind the suicides of a tycoon and a politician. All he wanted was for me to pin it on the extreme right so that the case would be closed and he would be able to relax. I was about to tell him straight when I suddenly remembered Ghikas's words: 'Whatever he tells you, just say "yes".' For once in my life, I decided to take his advice.

'I see, Mr Petroulakis. Of course, we'll need to get hold of some evidence to make the accusation stick.'

My reply pleased him and he smiled with satisfaction. 'I'm certain you'll come up with the evidence. I have every confidence in your abilities.' He held out his hand to tell me that the conversation was over. 'And we'll be in touch,' he said, shaking my hand. 'But always call me on my mobile phone, not on the landline.'

It made no difference to me where I called him. My problem was elsewhere. I wondered what I would have to tell him the next time I called him. I was met outside by the Thai girl, who, like a guard of honour, showed me to the door.

As I was going down Octaviou Merlie Street in order to turn into Ippokratous Street and come out into Solonos Street, I reflected that it was the first time that I had felt Ghikas was lending me his support. I couldn't decide whether this was because he had a genuine liking for me or whether it was due to the fact that Yanoutsos got on his nerves more than I did. Most likely the latter. Of course, this support might simply be due to the fact that I was carrying out an unofficial investigation and, not only that, but while on sick leave too. If something were to go wrong, he hadn't given me any official orders and consequently he didn't bear any of the responsibility. Thinking it over again, I decided that this was the more likely explanation. It had nothing to do with his either liking or disliking me, or with his being at cross-swords with Yanoutsos. He was helping me because he was in no danger of compromising himself and, at the same time, he was getting rid of Yanoutsos. I wasn't sure whether this thought angered me because it made me see Ghikas's ulterior motives or whether it relieved me because it put him back in his proper place and didn't upset the existing balance of things.

I found a space for the Mirafiori in the parking lot at the corner of Solonos Street and Mavromichali Street. Number 128 was an old building, something between a large apartment block and a small office block, quite common for buildings from the fifties. Karyofyllis's office was on the fifth floor. I stepped out of the lift into a dim corridor with mosaic floors, the kind that still look filthy no matter how often you clean them.

However, Karyofyllis's office dispelled the previous impression. I crossed a carpeted hallway and entered a spacious and well-lit office with two secretaries sitting in front of computers. Between the two secretaries was a door with plastic casing and gold studs, rather like a square tray of baklava. Judging from its appearance, this must have been the door leading to Karyofyllis's office.

One of the secretaries looked up and stared at me, while the other continued punching the computer keys. I adopted my official tone of voice and said curtly:

'Inspector Haritos. I'm here to see Mr Karyofyllis. It's an urgent matter.'

My tone of voice made the other secretary look up from her computer. 'Please have a seat for a moment,' the first one said as she went through the baklava door. She came back out in less than a minute and told me to go in.

Karyofyllis's office was the same as that of his secretaries, but one notch higher in quality. The carpet was thicker, the desk bigger and the back of his chair higher. The secretaries had a fan; here there was air conditioning. Karyofyllis was about my age, wearing a suit, with black hair and a thin moustache that made him resemble a certain popular singer of bouzouki songs from the sixties. As soon as he saw me, he got to his feet and held out his hand.

'Good day, Inspector. How might I help you?'

Like an uncouth copper, I sat down uninvited in the chair in front of his desk and stared at him pensively.

'The question is how you might help me and how I might help you,' I said.

My introduction took him unawares and he looked worried. 'I don't understand.'

I nodded to him to sit down, as though the roles had been reversed and he were in my office.

'Listen here, Mr Karyofyllis. What I am about to tell you is still unofficial.' I stressed the word 'still'. He had crossed his arms on the desk and was waiting for the rest. 'A Russo-Pontian who bought a flat in Larymnis Street, in the area of Konstantinoupoleos Avenue has lodged a complaint with us. The sale was conducted by a certain estate agent by the name of Yorgos Iliakos.'

I didn't ask him whether he knew the particular estate agency, and he didn't say anything to the effect, but his eyes told me that he did.

'The Russo-Pontian says that he paid forty-five thousand euros. He signed whatever papers were given to him, but he knew no Greek. The other day, however, he was visited by a colleague of his to whom he showed the contract. And it appeared that the price on the contract was not forty-five thousand euros but twenty-five.'

'Let me just say ...'

I didn't allow him to go on. 'I haven't finished yet. It's fortunate that the fellow happened to be Russo-Pontian. They know nothing of lawsuits or lawyers or legal proceedings ... Whether they're hit by a car or have their windows smashed or are deceived about the price of their home, they always come running to the police. This will help us keep the complaint out of the official channels for the time being. So I'm here to talk to you unofficially, Mr Karyofyllis. Is it possible that the contract might state a different price to the one received by the seller?'

I saw his expression change. He looked worried and his gaze wandered round the room with suspicion, almost with a conspiratorial gleam.

'Yes, and it's quite common,' he said. 'But I'm afraid I can't reveal to you how it's done.'

'Why?'

'Because it's a felony.'

'Felony?'

He hesitated and then slowly emitted the words through his teeth: 'Tax evasion.'

'I'm not a tax inspector, Mr Karyofyllis. I'm a police inspector. Your relations with the tax office don't concern me.'

'It's a common practice to declare a lower price in order to reduce the tax.'

'And is that what happened in this case?'

'I would suppose so.'

'And what if the seller did only receive twenty-five thousand euros?'

'What do you mean?'

'If the difference didn't go into the seller's pocket …'

'So who's pocket did it go into? The estate agent's?'

I left the question dangling in the air and changed tack.

'Mr Karyofyllis, I want to be honest with you. I don't have any interest at all in you personally. If I need to, I'll call you into the station and I'll do it without the slightest hesitation. The same is true if I need to arrest you. But the office of Yorgos Iliakos is another matter altogether. It belongs, so we were informed, to Jason Favieros.'

'Who? The businessman who committed suicide?' he asked innocently. 'What connection does he have with the estate agency?'

I shot him a look as though my heart were filled with pity for him. 'Come now. The Yorgos Iliakos Real Estate Agency and a very large number of other real-estate agencies belong to Balkan Prospect, which is a company owned by Jason Favieros. The tragedy that his family has suffered and the confusion that exists at present concerning the future of his businesses obliges us to be very cautious. You stand to benefit from that.'

'Me, how?'

'Because you were the one to draw up the contracts.' I said it so definitively, as though I had verified it from ten different sources, and he didn't dare deny it. 'There are three possibilities, Mr Karyofyllis. First, that the Russo-Pontian is lying. If that's the case, we'll tweak his ear and send him home. Second, an employee in one of the estate agencies is working a scam to cheat the buyers, the sellers and their own bosses. Or third, there exists an organised network of officials and public notaries who are getting rich illegally in this way.'

'The first possibility is the only reasonable one, Inspector.' I had thrown him a lifebelt and he was clutching hold of it.

'So what you're saying is that the Russo-Pontian paid forty-five thousand euros and the same sum was received by the seller minus the estate agent's fee, but that the contract stated twenty-five thousand for tax reasons. And now the Russo-Pontian is being clever and trying through blackmail to get twenty thousand back.'

'Precisely, Inspector. Those people are uneducated and unreliable, just like every other sly animal. They bring the sum in cash, empty it onto your desk, and all they're interested in is getting the key to the house,' Karyofyllis went on. 'Once they've moved in and are settled in the place, their sly minds start working and they try to find ways of getting back some of the money they paid.'

I restrained myself only with difficulty and agreed with him. Given that they allowed estate agents to rob them of so much money right under their noses, what else were they but animals?

'You may very well be right. But what will happen if the Russo-Pontian is only the beginning and from tomorrow the complaints start coming thick and fast? Then the network will come out into the open, Balkan Prospect will be ruined, even if it's not to blame, and so will you along with it.'

'Me, why?'

'Because all the sales and purchases contracts for Balkan Prospect are drawn up by you. We know that from our investigations.'

I had him with his back to the wall and all he could do was jump to his feet and start shouting. 'This is nothing but a damnable plot! Accusations are being made against the executives of a business firm, accusations are being made against a public notary company that has a history going back to 1930, that was founded by my father, just because some lousy Russo-Pontian crook is resorting to blackmail to get back money!'

'No one is being accused of anything yet,' I replied calmly. 'As I told you, this is an unofficial investigation and our aim is to close the case quietly. There's a very simple way for doing that. Give me the particulars of the seller and provided that he confirms that he did, in fact, receive the forty-five thousand euros, the case will be closed immediately.'

He became more and more distraught and hostile. 'That, unfortunately, is something I am unable to do.'

'Why?'

'Because by doing so I would be revealing an illegal transaction and I would be compromising both the seller and the real-estate agency.'

'I told you, I'm not a tax inspector.'

'Agreed. And that may be enough for me, but it won't be enough for the other two parties.'

'I can get the particulars from the land registry.'

He hesitated a moment and then said with resolve: 'That's another matter that doesn't concern me. I'm not interested in where you get the particulars, provided it's not from me.' His refusal confirmed my suspicions, but I kept this to myself. 'In the past, the police would give those good-for-nothings a pasting and threaten them that if they persisted it would be the worse for them,' he said almost complainingly as he gave me his hand.

He knew that only too well, coming as he did from a historic company. I let it go by, so he could make of it what he wanted.

I stopped at the first cardphone I came across and phoned home. I told Adriani to put Koula on the line.

'I want you to go straightaway to the land registry office and find the Russo-Pontian's file,' I told her. 'I want the particulars of the seller. It's urgent and I don't want any delay because of cookery lessons.'

She was silent for a moment and than answered gravely: 'I'm on my way.'

I found her very likeable, but if I left her in Adriani's hands, I ran the risk of her getting the better of me.

22

How quickly can a file disappear from the land registry? It depends on what clout the person who wants it to disappear has. And Balkan Prospect had, so it seemed, plenty of clout. When Koula arrived at the land registry, the file didn't exist. It had been mislaid somewhere and they couldn't find it so she should leave a phone number for them to contact her or pass by again in a few days' time.

In the end, her cookery lessons cost her dearly, because she was forced to spend a whole afternoon in Larymnis Street in order to find the seller's particulars. Just as she had started to get frustrated, she came across an old woman who had paid the bills for the flat before it was sold and she found out that the former owner was an Eirene Leventoyanni, who lived in Polydrosso.

Myself, I spent a whole evening listening to eulogies. Not to the Virgin, but to Stefanakos. And not in church, but on the TV. But apart from the eulogies, it had further interest. The programme was on Sotiropoulos's channel, not the one on which the suicides had taken place. And it was presented by Sotiropoulos himself. His guests began with a round of adulation. The Minister and other politicians spoke of Stefanakos's ethos and character, said what an experienced parliamentarian he had been and how Parliament would be the poorer without him. The two left-wing politicians took a stroll down memory lane, recalling the common struggles during the Junta, the student rising in the Polytechnic School and the torture that Stefanakos had been subjected to in the cells of the Military Police. But perhaps the star attraction was a Balkan minister, who appeared on satellite link-up, and whose mouth dripped honey about Stefanakos: he was the one politician who worked behind the scenes, and on a daily basis, for friendship and cooperation between the Balkan countries; he was a true friend who had helped in the economic revival of his country after the fall of socialism, acting as a bridge between his country, the Greek government and Brussels. He was a politician whose loss the entire Balkans would grieve.

Sotiropoulos allowed them to speak virtually without interruption and then, once they had vented their feelings, he dropped his first innuendo. How close had Stefanakos been with Favieros? I took my hat off to him and thought what a fool I was. It was the very first question I should have asked. The leftists were categorical: certainly they knew each other from their student years as they moved in the same circles. The other politicians minced their words. Yes the two men had known each other from the time of the Junta, but they were not sure whether they still saw each other. Besides, they were both involved in numerous activities and it was doubtful whether they kept in contact.

Just as they were trying to come to some conclusion as to whether they were still in contact, Sotiropoulos dropped his second innuendo: was it just coincidence that the two of them had committed suicide in the same way? And if it wasn't, then what might be behind this double suicide?

It was at such moments that I realised just how effective Sotiropoulos's aggressiveness could be, even though it got on my nerves. The others were completely nonplussed and began to stammer, trying to find some convincing answer, but Sotiropoulos didn't let up. He asked them if they thought that there really was some scandal behind the suicides, as the newspapers were claiming. He had managed to break their unanimity and get them bickering among themselves. The Minister together with the leftists rejected the claim with abhorrence. The former because he would put the government in a difficult position if he were to answer 'yes', and the latter because they would be compromising their two former comrades if they were to accept some such thing. The only ones not to exclude the possibility were the members of the opposition. The Minister put forward the same theory as Petroulakis: that this was the work of the extreme right wing, just as they themselves had admitted. At that point, I started to suspect that this bullshit was slowly becoming the government line. I was expecting everyone to break into laughter, but, as usual, I was mistaken. The leftists fervently supported the same view. Only the opposition politicians were bold enough to say that the theory was a bit far-fetched, but they were attacked by the Minister, who accused them of vote-mongering from the extreme right and the eulogies very nearly turned to curses.

As I was listening to all this, I remembered Zissis. Zissis was an old leftist whom I'd met when he was a long-standing prisoner and I was a rookie copper, who had been sent for on-the-job training to the torture cells in Bouboulinas Street. Afterwards, I lost track of him and forgot about him until I bumped into him one day in the corridors of Security Headquarters. He had gone to get a certificate that would entitle him to the pension given to members of the resistance. They were messing him about and I helped him to get the piece of paper he needed. Since then we had kept in touch on and off and on a strictly personal basis. I hadn't even told Adriani about it, perhaps because I was ashamed to admit that I had dealings with a commie. I was fairly sure that Zissis hadn't admitted it to anyone either, perhaps because he was even more ashamed to say that he had dealings with a copper. So, our mutual shame led to mutual respect, even though it wasn't something we ever admitted to each other.

It was nine in the morning. I had had my coffee and was getting ready to pay him a visit. I wanted to see him early, because he would have just finished watering his plants and would be in a good mood. But I was delayed by the annoying sound of the phone ringing. I picked up the receiver and it was Katerina.

'So then, Pop,' she said, 'when are you going to finish this investigation so that your assistant can go home and we can all get some peace?'

'Do you mean Koula?' I asked surprised.

'Yes, her. Are you aware that she's making my life a misery?'

'Koula? What are you on about, Katerina?'

'Mum phones me every day and praises her to high heaven. How good she is around the house and how wonderful her baked aubergines are and how unbelievably quickly she learned to roll the vine leaves for dolmades; my confidence is shattered.' I suddenly got what it was all about and burst out laughing. 'Yes, you can laugh,' Katerina went on. 'Because so far I've only told you the first act, which is a comedy. But there's a second act, where the drama begins.'

'What drama?'

'That's where she starts handing out advice. That I should take stock, that I'm not only incompetent, but I don't even want to learn the basics and how all her efforts were a waste of time, while with Koula she can see the progress straightaway ... The other day, she even told me that I'd gone and found a man like Fanis, who liked his food, and I didn't even know how to fry chips. I told her that Fanis is someone who likes his food when she cooks it for him. Otherwise he gets by on cheese and spinach pies, just like I do, so we're a good match.'

I understood at last what the drama was. When Adriani decides to go on the attack and start pounding away, you simply collapse, like the Serbians in Kosovo.

'I'll tell Koula to put a stop to all the lovey-dovey with your mother.'

'For heaven's sake, no! I was joking!' she shouted in alarm. 'Let them get on with it. She's found a substitute for me to busy herself with and she's over the moon.' Then she changed the conversation and asked me about Stefanakos's suicide.

'Don't even ask,' I said. 'The bigwigs have started to get worried and I'm afraid it's going to lead to big trouble. Ghikas is of the same opinion.'

'Are you telling me you agree with Ghikas?' she asked surprised.

'Yes.'

'For you to agree with Ghikas means that things must really be serious,' she said and she hung up chuckling.

I stuck to the seat in the Mirafiori because of the humidity. As I turned into Vasilissis Sofias Avenue, I decided to go the top way in the hope of finding a little cool air. Driving up Mouson Street towards the Attiko Alsos, the situation was more bearable. But from the middle of Protopapadaki Street I started to feel the seat beneath me burning and by the time I had reached Galatsiou Avenue, it was just as though I had got into the bathtub with my clothes on.

Zissis lived in Ekavis Street in Nea Philadelphia. It was a narrow little street settled in by Greek refugees from Asia Minor in 1922 and it had remained just as it was then. Three streets below Dekeleias Avenue with all its banks, computer stores and mobile phone companies, you step into Ekavis Street and suddenly expect Eleutherios Venizelos to be there making one of his political speeches. The small houses were on one side of the street with front yards full of geraniums, begonias, carnations and jasmine, all planted in tubs and tin cans, and with an external staircase that led up to the house. It must have been Zissis's family home, because when his circle of activities had closed and he started receiving his resistance pension, he had retired to this house. In Nea Philadelphia, he was a legendary figure, even to the police officers who would go to arrest him. As the years went by, however, he shut himself up more and more in his house. Most of those who knew him had died, and the younger generation knew nothing of this strange old man whom they saw buying a half a pound of feta, a few ounces of olives, two carrots and a packet of beans or lentils, the only food he ate, apart from at Easter, when he cooked roast goat with oven potatoes. His only other needs were coffee and cigarettes.

I found him watering his garden, wearing a vest, shorts and sandals. He had seen me coming towards him but pretended not to notice me. That was his usual tactic in order to show me that my visit was something of an imposition. He washed down the yard, turned off the water, coiled up the hosepipe and then, finally, turned his eyes to me.

'Coffee?'

'Greek, strong and sweet, thanks,' I replied enthusiastically.

He must have been one of the last people in Athens to still make Greek coffee in the embers, with the coffee pot planted deep in the hot ash.

I climbed the external staircase behind him. There are two things that always impress you in Zissis's house. The one evident, the other not. What was immediately evident were the enormous bookcases on every wall. What was not evident was the archive that he had compiled on every public figure in Greece. Now and again, he agrees to give me information from his archive, though he has never shown it to me. In answer to my question as to why he amasses all that material, he said that he did it most likely as a reaction. The state had kept files on him all through his life and he, in his turn, did the same for every public figure so as to bring about some kind of balance.

He came in with an old metal tray of the sort used in cafés and put the coffee on the table together with a saucer containing sweet preserves.

'Since when have you started buying sweet preserves?' I asked him in surprise.

'My neighbour, old ma Andromache, gives them to me. Every time she makes them for herself, she sends me over a jar, the dear old girl.'

We sipped at our coffee in silence. Zissis, because he always waited for me to start the conversation, and I, because I wanted to enjoy my coffee first. Only the door was open. He had the windows shut and the house was like an oven. I took out my handkerchief and wiped the back of my neck with it.

'The heat's a killer.'

'I wish it were hotter.'

I stared at him as if looking at an Eskimo. 'Are you being serious? People are collapsing on the street.'

'I soaked up so much damp in your cells that I can't have my fill of it.'

I should have expected it. Every time he says something seemingly irrational, there follows the standard dig at the police.

As usual, I pretended not to notice so as not to wind him up any further. 'I need to pick your brains.'

'About Favieros or about Stefanakos?'

'Let's take them in turn and start with Favieros.'

'Leading member of the student movement, always in the front line in the demonstrations and occupations, present at the Polytechnic School rising, and all the rest: Bouboulinas Street, Military Police, torture.'

'So how did he end up getting involved in all sorts of shady business?'

'Because he became a businessman. He got involved in whatever was necessary for his businesses.'

'And did his businesses oblige him to pretend to be the champion of the foreign workers while at the same time he was selling them over-priced hovels?'

He would suddenly erupt when you weren't expecting it. Like then. 'For years you broke us trying to get us to recant,' he yelled. 'Prison cells, exile, torture, to make us sign a statement. Now we sign the statement of our own free will with our businesses, the stock market, profits. Such success you could never have imagined not even in your wildest dreams. You've won, what else do you want?'

'Me, nothing. They're the ones shouting their mouths off about struggling on behalf of the underdog.'

'Wake up, why don't you! There are no underdogs when it comes to voting,' he yelled again. 'The real underdogs are those who come from elsewhere, without a voice and so they don't count. The only underdogs when it comes to voting are the smokers! If the Party had had any sense, it would have organised a demonstration on behalf of smokers with the slogan: "Power to the damned" and it would have broken all records!'

When he gets in one of his black moods, it's impossible to have a conversation with him. He explodes all the time at the slightest provocation. I decided not to persist with Favieros, but to pass on to Stefanakos, to see whether he might be a little calmer when it came to him.

'And Stefanakos?'

His eyes lit up. 'Don't even waste your time looking. You won't find anything on him either in the past or present,' he said. 'He wasn't one to give up. He kept on fighting to the end.'

'Okay, okay, Lambros,' I said in a conciliatory tone. 'They were both impeccable. So can you tell me why they committed suicide?'

'Doesn't the way they did it set you thinking?'

'Naturally, but I still can't understand why they decided to do it in public.'

He gazed at me pensively. He wanted to say something but was hesitating. 'If I tell you what I think, don't think I'm crazy,' he said eventually.

'Out with it, I know you're not crazy.'

'Because they couldn't take any more. They were overcome by despair. The one despite all his business success and the other despite all his struggles. That's why they committed suicide publicly, in order to make people sit up.' He saw that I was looking at him in incredulity and he shook his head. 'You don't believe me because you're a copper and you can't understand. Money, fame, power, there comes a moment when you find yourself sinking in all the mud and you want to do something about it.'

I recalled Stefanakos's last words: 'I hope we're not dying pointlessly' or something of the sort. Perhaps what Zissis had said was an explanation, though I was afraid that things were more complicated than that. But I didn't say so. I preferred to leave him under his painless delusion.

'Come round some time when it's not because you need my help,' he said as I was about to descend the staircase.

Anyone else would have felt offended. But, knowing him as well as I did, I understood that it was his way of saying that he liked having a coffee with me.

23

I found Koula alone at home. She was sitting in front of the computer and updating her files. Adriani wasn't there.

'She went out to buy some T-shirts for your daughter,' Koula explained. 'So she'll have something to wear in this hot weather.'

I had never been able to understand her mania for buying Katerina all sorts of small items and sending them to her by parcel post, when she could buy them for herself in Thessaloniki for the same money and probably even cheaper.

'Before she left, she told me to tell you that a Mr Sotiropoulos phoned and he wants you to call him.'

Koula looked at me puzzled. She knew Sotiropoulos, just as she also knew my dislike of reporters, and she was surprised that Sotiropoulos in particular should phone me at home. I considered whether it was better to tell her the truth or to make up some excuse and I settled on the former.

'I'm right in telling the Chief that you're far more flexible than you seem,' she said with a wry smile.

'But he maintains that I'm a stickler,' I retorted, as I knew the storyline only too well.

'Sort of.'

'At any rate, the business with Sotiropoulos is to remain between you and me.'

'Whatever you say, but you're wasting a golden opportunity to go up in the Chief's estimation.'

I should have seen that much earlier. Now I'd missed the boat. I told of the government's wish that we discreetly investigate the two suicides, but I didn't mention Petroulakis's name nor did I say anything about his desire to pin the suicides on the Philip of Macedon

National Greek Front. I ended with my meeting with Karyofyllis, the public notary and I left Zissis out of it completely.

Once I'd updated Koula, I called Sotiropoulos on his mobile phone.

'We have to talk,' he said, as soon as he recognised my voice. 'Where are you now?'

'I have to go to Polydrosso and after that I'm free.'

'Fine, I'll be done in a couple of hours. Let's meet at the Flocafé in Kifissia. Wait for me if you get there first and I'll do the same.'

The weather had changed. The sky had filled with black clouds and it was stiflingly humid. I turned in Vasilissis Sofias Avenue once again and by the time I had got to Kifissias Avenue it was as though night had fallen.

Eirene Leventoyanni lived at 3 Korae Street in Polydrosso. On reaching Varnalis Street, I asked a kiosk owner where Korae Street was. He told me to take the second left off Kanari Street.

'How should we approach this Mrs Leventoyanni who sold her flat in Larymnis Street to the Russo-Pontian?' asked Koula.

'Like we approached the public notary. The notary and the estate agent pocketed the difference and now the Russo-Pontian has made a complaint and we're looking into it.'

'Will it work?'

'Why shouldn't it? Greeks are more afraid of the tax office than they are of the police. Unless Karyofyllis has warned her.'

'There's no question of that if they swindled her and pocketed her money. If they did warn her, that means she was in on the scam.'

Number 3 was a four-storey newly-built apartment block, with lamps and plants in the entrance. We looked at the doorbells and saw that Mrs Leventoyanni was on the third floor.

The door was opened by a round-faced, chubby woman of about forty-five, who was wearing all the colours of the rainbow. She had a cheery smile on her face but, as soon as I told her who we were, the smile faded and was replaced by an expression of alarm.

'Is it Sifis?' she murmured.

'Who's Sifis?' I asked her.

'My son. Has anything happened to him on his bike?'

'No, no, calm yourself,' Koula interrupted smiling. 'Nothing's happened to your son. We're here on another matter.'

Leventoyanni let out a sigh of relief and made the sign of the cross. Then she stood aside to let us enter. If her clothes were all the colours of the rainbow, her house was a veritable greenhouse, with plants that began in the hall and ended on the balcony, more like a jungle. I wondered what possible use the balcony might have when you couldn't sit down for the plants.

'It's the only way we can get some respite from the sun that bakes the house every day from eleven in the morning to five into the afternoon,' Leventoyanni explained on seeing my puzzled expression. 'Coffee?'

Koula declined, I asked for a glass of water. I was surprised that she still hadn't asked us what two coppers were doing on her doorstep. She didn't ask straight out but, after bringing me the water, she sat down and looked at us enquiringly with that permanent smile on her face.

'Mrs Leventoyanni, you sold a flat in Larymnis Street, is that right?'

'Yes,' she replied. 'You see, my husband has played the football pools for years. Once, he came up with a winning line so we sold the flat in Larymnis Street and together with his winnings we were able to buy this house.'

'How much did you sell it for?'

She showed the same alarm that she had when we had introduced ourselves and asked in a voice that was trembling despite her efforts to control it: 'Excuse me, but why are you asking? Is there some problem?'

Koula saw that Leventoyanni was wavering between innocence and alarm and she went to sit next to her to reassure her.

'Mrs Leventoyanni, it has nothing to do with you, nor with the house you sold or the one you bought. It's others we're investigating. You have nothing at all to fear. If you prefer, you don't have to tell us.'

I was about to put the brakes on her, because it's one thing to reassure the citizens we're questioning, but it's another to open their eyes to what we're doing, when I heard Leventoyanni say quite simply: 'Eight and a half million drachmas. Twenty-five thousand euros to the nearest round figure. Twenty-four thousand nine hundred and something to be exact.'

'Are you sure you didn't receive forty-five thousand euros?'

'Why on earth would you say that?' she asked surprised.

'Don't take it the wrong way, Mrs Leventoyanni, but were you the one who collected the amount?' asked Koula very nicely. 'Could your husband, for instance, have collected the amount, kept the twenty-five thousand you needed for the purchase of this house and put the rest in the bank?'

Leventoyanni looked at her very seriously this time and heaved a sigh: 'The transaction was conducted by me and it was I who collected the amount. Both the house in Larymnis Street and this one are in my name. I take care of everything on my own because if I'd left it to my husband, he would have lost it all on the pools or the lottery or at the casino in Loutraki.'

'Now, now,' said Koula smiling. 'Don't forget that it was the football pools that enabled you to buy the flat.'

'Do you think, dear girl, that one winning line makes up for everything my husband has lost all these years in gambling and betting?' Then suddenly she remembered the important question. 'But tell me, why are you asking me all this?'

Because the conversation was going well between them, I let Koula go on. She told her the whole story with the Russo-Pontian, Karyofyllis and the Iliakos Real Estate Agency. Leventoyanni listened to her calmly, but suddenly leapt to her feet.

'Those bastards …' she murmured. 'Those crooks …'

'What's wrong?' Koula asked, taking her hand to stop her going into a panic. 'Sit down and tell us in your own time.'

'I just recalled something that at the time I hadn't attached any importance to. When we were at the notary's office and he was filling out the contracts, he turned and asked the estate agent: "What sum shall we put?" The other one looked at him askance and said: "What are you asking me for? Don't you know?" The conversation ended there and afterwards we signed the contracts. Obviously, the notary was asking whether he should put the actual sum on the contract or the sum I would receive.'

'Was the estate agent around thirty-five with cropped hair?'

'Yes, that's him.'

After what Leventoyanni had told us, there was no longer the slightest doubt that the whole business had been set up with the participation of Karyofyllis. We had learned what we wanted and I was getting ready to get up and leave when Koula stopped me with another question.

'May I ask you something else because otherwise I'll be wondering,' she said to Leventoyanni. 'Didn't the Russo-Pontian understand what was going on?'

'What would the poor fellow understand, dear girl? In one hand he was clutching a folded plastic bag and with the other he was holding his wife's hand and smiling contentedly. They were like two lovebirds buying a little place for themselves so that they could get married.'

'Did you receive the money in cash?'

'No, the notary had the cheque ready and handed it to me. "They always pay in cash and I don't want to inconvenience you," he said. Do you see what he did? He took forty-five thousand in cash from the Russo-Pontian and gave me a cheque for twenty-four thousand nine hundred and something ... And he and the estate agent pocketed the rest.' She leapt to her feet and began shouting: 'I'll sue them, I'll drag them through the courts!'

She was so angry that she even forgot to say goodbye to us. In the distance, you could hear the sound of sporadic thunder. It must have been raining somewhere. As we were going towards the car, I reflected that Koula had a special talent for loosening the other person's tongue. If and when she returned to the office, I'd have her give seminars on how to elicit answers to Vlassopoulos and Dermitzakis, who were still limited to shouting, force and intimidation.

'So tell me, Koula,' I said to her as we left Korae Street and turned into Epidavrou Street. 'Where did you learn how to get people to open up like that? As far as I know, you only deal with paperwork in the office.'

'From my father,' she said laughing. 'My father is unbelievably egoistical and opinionated. But if you're willing to bear with him, he becomes putty in your hands.'

'Yes, and you did exactly the same thing with my wife. In less than a week you became inseparable.'

'Well, that was easy. After all, we have a common interest in cooking.'

I still had a question eating away at me and even though it was a little out of place, I had to ask it or I wouldn't rest. 'What I don't understand, Koula, is why, since you're such a sharp girl, you give an entirely different picture in the office.'

She turned and stared at me with a wry smile. 'What picture exactly?'

'How shall I put it ... that you're a more simple girl.'

She burst into laughter. 'Simple, Inspector Haritos? A simpleton is what you're trying to say!'

'That's going too far, but why are you like that? Is it Ghikas?'

She suddenly became serious. 'It's because I want to get married and have children, Inspector.'

'What's that got to do with it?'

'A lot. In my circles, whether personal and professional ones, when men see a smart woman, they take to their heels. If I want to play the smart type, I'll end up on the shelf. Men prefer the certainty of a simple girl so they can put their minds at rest.' She paused and then continued. 'You shouldn't judge by your own daughter. She went to university, is doing a doctorate and has a doctor for a boyfriend. I have nothing of all that.'

'How do you know about my daughter?' I asked astonished.

'Mrs Haritos told me the other day while we were making the baked aubergines.'

No doubt she also told her of her regret that Katerina didn't know how to cook. 'Don't make it sound so tragic, there's Aristopoulos,' I said to tease her.

'All Aristopoulos wants is to get me into bed,' she said very calmly. 'He's desperate to make it as a company executive; he's not about to get involved with a woman cop. If I say no to him a couple of times, he won't call me a third time. And if I go with him a couple of times, he'll disappear and the only way I'll see him will be to arrest him.' She smiled at me again. 'There's nothing you can say. I've looked at it from every angle.'

'And are you going to spend the rest of your life playing the fool?'

'Of course not!' she said indignantly. 'Once I've got a ring on my finger things will change!'

I turned and looked at her. I suddenly saw Adriani before me. At last I understood why the two of them got on so well together.

24

The heavens opened just as we were passing the old people's home. We were in the underpass and above us we could hear a deafening noise. In less than two minutes from the start of the downpour, the roads in Athens had become jammed and the honking of horns began. We emerged from the underpass after about twenty minutes only to be attacked by a blast of rain that forced the Mirafiori to retreat. The windscreen wipers did their best but to no avail because the rain had created something like a blanket of mist and it was impossible to see further than three yards in front of you.

I decided to take Koula home first and then go to see Sotiropoulos because I couldn't very well leave her to wait for the bus in all that rain. After all, Sotiropoulos would most likely arrive late too. On the way, I congratulated myself for not getting rid of the Mirafiori. It's high off the ground like all the old cars and the water can't touch it. The newer models are closer to the ground and are more like floating barges every time the roads of Athens turn into torrential rivers.

I dropped Koula off in Gyzi and went back up Kifissias Avenue to meet Sotiropoulos at the Flocafé. The rain continued to fall heavily but not with the same intensity. The parking lot behind the Flocafé was full. The attendant looked scornfully at the Mirafiori and obviously thought it an insult to have to find a place for it. He relented half-heartedly when I showed him my badge and told him I was on duty.

Sotiropoulos arrived half an hour later. He went around on a Harley Davidson and was drenched to the bone.

'Time you woke up to the twenty-first century, old boy,' he said indignantly. 'Whoever heard of the Head of the Homicide Division not having a mobile phone?'

'What would I use it for? So that the intended victim could call me to tell me he was about to be murdered?'

'No, but so I could call you and cancel our meeting because of the rain.'

He hung his jacket over the back of the chair to dry and ordered a double whisky to warm himself up a little.

'I watched your programme last night. I liked it.'

He turned to me and gave me an ironic look. 'Really? From what I remember, I usually get on your nerves.'

'Last night, you got on the others' nerves and I thoroughly enjoyed it.'

He burst out laughing and took a gulp at his whisky. 'That's why I called you,' he said, 'because of the programme.'

I saw in his eyes that he was about to deliver a bombshell.

'Do you remember that at one point the conversation turned to how well Favieros and Stefanakos knew each other?'

'Yes, I remember.'

'At exactly eleven, the programme was interrupted for a short news bulletin and adverts. Andreadis, one of the two opposition politicians, turned and said to the Minister: "How could they not have been on close terms given that they were doing business together?"'

As soon as I heard that, I knew my trip had been worth it despite the rain and the traffic. It was the first time I had had some indication that Favieros and Stefanakos were not just acquaintances or friends, but that they were actually involved in some business together. I didn't know whether I should be glad or start to worry because now the situation might begin to get more complicated. I left the apportioning of gladness and worry for later and I asked Sotiropoulos:

'Who was Stefanakos married to?'

'Lilian Stathatos, have you heard of her?' The name meant something to me but I couldn't recall who she was. 'She's the daughter of Argyris Stathatos.'

As soon as I heard the father's name, I remembered her straightaway. Argyris Stathatos had received favourable treatment from the

Junta. He had managed to secure various permits, some legal, some illegal, in order to make himself into the leading hotel owner in Athens and the islands. He raked in money during the years of the Junta, but his hotels were built with interest-free loans and when the Junta fell, the banks began calling in the loans and Stathatos lost everything.

'Is he still alive?' I asked puzzled.

Sotiropoulos laughed. 'God rest his soul! He died about ten years ago. At the height of his power, when he held sway during the Junta, his daughter was studying economics in London and presented herself as a revolutionary, against the Junta. She had cut off all relations with her father and told everyone she was studying with the little money that her grandmother had left her. You can believe it or not, anyhow the truth is that she lived very conservatively. When she returned to Greece, she started work as an executive in an advertising company and she and her father were eventually reconciled. Her father's creditors didn't want to have him put in prison because while he was still on the outside they had hopes of getting some of their money back by blackmailing him. On seeing her father's demise, Lilian Stathatos understood that businesses requiring investment are a double-edged sword and you never know what might crop up. She was quick to foresee the future of TV ads and she set up her own company. It was at that time that she married Stefanakos, who was an up-and-coming young politician. She was very smart and quickly realised that the European Union had plenty of rich pickings for anyone who had their wits about them. And she was one of the first to open a consultancy bureau for European investment.'

What he told me left me speechless. 'Do you keep files on everything?' I asked him, thinking of Zissis.

'No. I knew all about what happened during the period of the Junta. The rest I concluded from reading between the lines of what my guests said last night.' He smiled as if recalling something. 'Do you know what's really funny? During the breaks, while they were all gossiping about Lilian Stathatos, the channel was broadcasting advertisements made by her company.'

'So she still has the advertising company?'

'Are you kidding? Everyone is dependent on Stathatos. She's the one who decides what entertainment programmes the channel puts on the air. If there's some programme or serial she doesn't like, its adverts get cut.'

'And what about the consultancy bureau?'

'No idea. You'll have to ask someone who works with Mediterranean Funding Programmes and the like. But compared to the advertising company, all that's just peanuts.'

'And what did Favieros have to do with all this?'

'Do you expect me to do all your work for you?' he said, taking another gulp at his whisky. 'I've given you enough information to go on.'

'At any rate, I don't think Favieros went to Stathatos to advertise his construction company. I've never come across an advert for construction companies. As for his other business, most probably he wouldn't want it advertised.'

Realising what I'd said I bit my tongue, but it was too late. Sotiropoulos cut straight to the chase.

'You mean the real-estate agencies?' He burst out laughing. 'Horafas called me the moment you'd left his office to ask me if he was right to open up to you. I couldn't understand why he was so worried.'

'Because something doesn't seem right to him, but he doesn't know what it is.'

'And what doesn't seem right to him? Or are we about to start playing games again?' he asked ironically.

We'd come too far for me to keep my cards to myself and I told him all that I'd found out about Favieros's real-estate agencies. When I'd finished, he whistled in exclamation and then shook his head dejectedly.

'You've no idea what you're doing to me!' he said. 'A scoop like that and I have to keep it on ice because I've given you my word. Couldn't I let slip something on the air? Just a few choice titbits?'

I ruled it out without discussion so he wouldn't start trying to bargain with me. 'Out of the question. We've already agreed. I'll give you the whole exclusive story as soon as the case is closed.'

He suddenly turned to me with a worried look. 'Does Ghikas know about all this?'

'More or less.'

'And who's to guarantee that Ghikas won't give the story to one of his own people first?'

'He won't'

He stared at me, holding his glass of whisky. 'You must be walking around blindfolded. Where you are, in Security, every reporter has his own source. From your assistants to Yanoutsos and even higher. Do you think Ghikas, who's got his sights set on making top dog, doesn't have someone?'

'That's precisely why he won't do it,' I answered calmly. 'Because he's not crazy enough to reveal information from an unofficial source.'

My argument seemed to convince him because he emptied his glass. 'Okay, I have to admit there's some logic to that.' Then he suddenly became aggressive again. 'But if anything leaks out, I'm telling you I'll put it all on the air.'

Outside, in the real air, only the wet curb indicated that it had been raining cats and dogs. Apart from that, the sky was crystal clear and the sun was shining. People were shut up in their offices and homes because of the rain and so I was in Aristokleous Street in less than fifteen minutes. But what was an advantage in terms of traffic was a disadvantage when it came to parking, because I couldn't find a place anywhere and I circled the block for a good half an hour. After the umpteenth circle, I saw someone leaving and nipped into his space.

When I walked into the house, I heard the sound of the TV in the sitting room. I went in to say hello to Adriani but she wasn't there. I found her ironing in the kitchen. She often did that: she did her chores listening to the TV in the background as a kind of radio substitute.

'I'm surprised you're not soaking wet,' she said.

'I was indoors and managed to avoid it.'

'You were lucky. Some woman called for you.'

'Who?'

'I don't know, she didn't leave a name.'

'Did you ask her?'

She put down the iron and looked at me with that high and mighty expression of hers that she always adopts when she's about to make some caustic remark. 'I thought that was why you brought Koula round here, to act as your secretary.'

'I took her home so she wouldn't get drenched in the rain.'

'It's a wonder you even thought of it. As for the woman who called, don't worry yourself. If it's serious, she'll call back.'

I let her think she had reduced me to silence and I went into the sitting room to call Ghikas. I gave him a general update concerning my meeting with the Prime Minister's adviser.

'You handled it well,' he said pleased. 'Let him go on believing that you're looking for evidence to incriminate the right-wing nationalists.'

Then I told him about the likelihood that Favieros was doing business with Stefanakos's wife. There was a silence. When he spoke again, his voice sounded troubled.

'If what you say turns out to be true, then I'm afraid we have the worst possible case scenario on our hands.'

'What do you mean?'

'Murder, not by a pistol or knife, but by suicide. And how can you prove that and bring out into the open what's hidden behind it?'

His argument was so solid that I hesitated momentarily. 'Shall I go on investigating?'

'Yes, perhaps we can prevent another suicide from happening.'

I hung up and racked my brains trying to decide where I would go from there. I had to find a discreet way of coming into contact with Lilian Stathatos, Stefanakos's wife. I could simply pay her a visit, but if she didn't have direct access to the Prime Minister, she would most certainly have access to his advisers and so it would get out that I wasn't looking for evidence about the extreme rightists but about the relationship between her and Favieros.

Adriani was right, because the woman called back just as we were about to sit down for dinner. It was Coralia Yannelis.

'Could we meet tomorrow, Inspector?'

'Of course. At your office?' I was trying to prevent her from suggesting that we met in my office at Security Headquarters given that it was temporarily occupied.

'Do you mind coming to the Domitis offices? Mr Zamanis would like to be present.'

We arranged to meet at ten the following day. That phone call was the last thing I wanted. It could be something quite innocuous, on the other hand it could open up new wounds.

25

The sky was crystal clear, and the trees in Athens would have been smelling sweetly if there were any. This time, I myself was driving the Mirafiori and I was on my way to Domitis Construction. I had left Koula at home because I thought that Favieros's heavy artillery executives might not be so ready to open up with her there. I had briefed her on what Sotiropoulos had told me the previous day and had asked her to investigate Stathatos's companies to find me some evidence.

The fifty-year-old woman in reception recognised me immediately. She was still not wearing any make-up but was slightly more cheerful and had a hint of a smile.

'They're expecting you, Inspector. Just a moment while I inform them that you're here.'

Favieros's photo was still hanging in the same place, but without the black ribbon. Also absent were the wreaths on the floor.

It wasn't Aristopoulos, Koula's informant, who came to take me, but a blonde girl of around twenty. We went up to the third floor, crossed the bridge of sighs and arrived at Zamanis's office.

In contrast to the fifty-year-old woman in reception, the fifty-year-old number two, Zamanis's private secretary, was noticeably cool. She greeted me with a faint nod of her head and opened the door to her boss's office to allow me in.

Unsmiling, Zamanis held out his hand to me without getting to his feet. On the contrary, Yannelis smiled at me. Yet, despite the smile, the whole atmosphere, from the secretary outside and all the way to Zamanis, was overcast indicating stormy weather. Zamanis told me to take a seat and my weather forecast was confirmed.

'When you came to see me, Inspector, you told me that you were carrying out a discreet and unofficial investigation into the reasons behind Jason Favieros's suicide.'

He was looking down and reading from a sheet of paper. Evidently, he had had his secretary write down what we had said in order to be able to remember it. The paper, his upright bearing and his suit made me think of an interrogator about to pin me to the wall on the basis of my previous statement.

'Precisely,' I answered calmly.

'You told me the same thing,' Yannelis added.

'That's right. I told you both the truth.'

'And do you believe that the reasons behind Jason's suicide are to be found in the Balkan Prospect estate agencies?'

I shrugged. 'When you're searching in the dark, Mrs Yannelis, you leave no stone unturned. Naturally, sometimes you discover things you weren't expecting, but it's precisely for that reason that you look under every stone.' I had a little dig myself, but neither of them seemed particularly impressed.

'You won't find anything,' Zamanis said, continuing in the same tone of voice. 'All you have succeeded in doing is to upset various people without reason and create a stir which is highly damaging.'

'The stir may be damaging, but the various people have every reason to be worried. What has come to the surface, entirely by chance, is a series of suspicious property deals.'

'Only a sick mind could find those deals suspicious. Neither Jason's background as a leftist, nor his standing as a businessman would allow him to involve himself in suspicious dealings.'

He was making a frontal attack, using his heavy artillery to demolish my arguments. Jason Favieros was a committed leftist and consequently he couldn't possibly be involved in scams at the expense of poor immigrants. Jason Favieros was a businessman of high repute and consequently he wouldn't risk getting involved in suspicious property deals.

'I didn't say that Favieros was personally involved in suspicious property deals. Perhaps certain executives in his estate agencies had been making money on the side. At least in the case of Leventoyanni, there had undoubtedly been some collusion between the manager of the estate agency and the public notary. Who knows what I may find if I dig a little deeper.'

'You won't find anything involving Balkan Prospect,' Yannelis said, interrupting. 'I explained that to you when you came to see me. Our network is an extremely loose one. The local agencies make their own decisions concerning the transactions. Balkan Prospect bears no responsibility.'

'But you told me that you examine the contracts.'

'Only as to the legal side of the transaction, not the money exchanged. And apart from that, I don't see how any of this can possibly be connected with Jason's suicide.'

It wasn't, and because it wasn't, I was fishing in the hope of finding a lead somewhere else so that Yanoutsos wouldn't get his hands on my job.

'Don't waste your time trying to understand, Coralia,' Zamanis said ironically to Yannelis. 'The Inspector is not interested in discovering the reasons behind Jason's suicide. All he wants is to tarnish his name. That's always been the favourite sport of the police.'

In other words, to tarnish the reputation of leftists. That's what Zissis used to say and I respected his opinion. But Favieros was not Zissis.

Yannelis took over: 'I'm curious, Inspector. Why did you decide to investigate the offshore company and its real-estate agencies?' she asked.

'As a result of reading a biography on Favieros published after his death.'

At the word 'biography', Zamanis leapt to his feet. 'That idiot has done nothing but harm,' he cried.

'Come on now, you're exaggerating,' Yannelis said smiling.

'Do you know him?' I asked them.

Zamanis erupted once more. 'No, I don't know him and I don't want to know him! It simply makes me mad that he's exploiting Jason's suicide in order to make money.'

'You're mistaken. The biography was written and submitted to the publisher long before the suicide. We've looked into it.'

They both turned and stared at me in astonishment. 'Then you'll know who the author is,' commented Yannelis.

'No and I doubt whether he even exists. At least with the name Minas Logaras.'

I explained to them the whole story concerning the search for Logaras and how I had come to a dead end. 'Anyhow, the address he had given was close to the Yorgos Iliakos Real Estate Agency,' I added, before concluding.

'What are you trying to say, that the estate agent wrote it?' Yannelis asked with a hint of irony.

'No. But Favieros himself may have written it and submitted it under a pseudonym. Just consider for a moment. He's made up his mind to commit suicide, but before doing so he writes his autobiography and sends it for publication.'

I seemed to have managed to surprise them, because they stared at each other trying to take it in.

'Impossible,' said Zamanis conclusively. 'Jason was continually on the go with the Olympic projects. He was rushing around all day from the construction sites to the ministries and to the Olympic Games offices. He had no time to spare for writing autobiographies.'

'His private secretary told me just the opposite,' I said, countering him.

Now it was Yannelis's turn to be puzzled: 'What exactly did she tell you?'

'When I spoke with her, she told me that Favieros would shut himself up for hours in his office. And when she once asked him, jokingly, if he was writing a novel, he replied that he had already written it and he was simply working on the corrections.'

They glanced at each other. Zamanis was hesitant for a moment, then he pressed the button on his intercom and said to his secretary: 'Tell Theoni I want to see her, will you?'

Lefaki came in with her gaze fixed on Zamanis, ignoring me completely. The rumour that I was working to tarnish Favieros's name was still limited to the third floor and hadn't yet acquired epidemic proportions, I thought to myself, given that the woman in reception greeted me politely and with a smile.

'Theoni, when the Inspector came to see you, you told him that you had once asked Jason if he was writing a novel and he had replied that he had already finished it and was doing the corrections. Do you recall?'

'Of course! It was a Friday. The phone had been ringing all afternoon with people looking for him, but Jason had shut himself in his office and had forbidden me to put his calls through or to bother him.'

'And when exactly did you ask him if he was writing a novel?' Zamanis seemed to be enjoying giving me evidence of his interrogation skills.

'At around eight in the evening when he came out of his office to leave. "What are you doing all the time shut up in your office? Writing a novel?" I said, teasing him. And he answered quite seriously: "I've already finished it and now I'm working on the corrections."'

'Do you remember how long this was before his suicide?' I asked her.

She directed her reply to Zamanis as though he had asked her. 'It must have been around three months.'

I made a mental note to check with Sarantidis, the publisher, when it was that he received the manuscript, but the dates coincided more or less.

'Can I please ask you to stop your investigations into Balkan Prospect?' Zamanis said very formally as soon as Lefaki had left. 'Firstly, because its dealings are completely legitimate and, secondly, because you're not working for the Fraud Squad.' He paused briefly and added meaningfully: 'Unless, that is, you want to go to your superiors for approval.'

Although I've been years on the Force, I still can't understand why it is that every loudmouth who thinks he has some clout considers it proper to end the conversation by bringing up the threat of my superiors.

'Let me tell you what will happen if you were to talk to my

superiors,' I said. 'They will have to talk to me, but they won't be the only ones to hear what I have to say. From then on, it'll only be a matter of time before it reaches the ears of the reporters, who even know when we in Security go to pee.'

Before he had had time to swallow what I'd said to him, I had said goodbye and was outside the neoclassical building. The centre of Pangrati was chock-a-block with traffic and it took me the best part of half an hour crawling bumper to bumper and making liberal use of the horn to get away. Fortunately, the temperature had fallen and I didn't end up drenched in sweat.

At home I was met by an unexpected sight. Sitting before the computer was Koula's cousin, who had come with her on the day she and I had begun working together. Koula was sitting beside him. They heard me come in and turned round. The young lad limited himself to a plain 'hello'. Koula, however, jumped up and, full of enthusiasm, said:

'I don't know where to begin! We found a way into the records of the Ministry of Trade and got the information we wanted about Stathatos's company! Do you know who's a partner with a forty per cent share in the company?'

'Favieros!'

'No. His wife, Sotiria Markakis-Favieros.' I remained silent for a moment to let it sink in, while Koula went on with the same enthusiasm: 'I went to the Ministry just as you told me, but I had to deal with some dolt who didn't listen to a word I was saying. When I told him I was a police officer, he gave me an arrogant look and told me to send my superior and preferably with a warrant from the public prosecutor. That was when I thought of Spyros, my cousin.'

Sotiropoulos hadn't realised that his guests were talking about Favieros's wife and not Favieros himself.

'And there's something else, but I'm afraid that you won't like it,' Koula continued, handing me a magazine from the coffee table. 'Spyros brought it and I came across this while I was thumbing through it.'

It was a full-page advert:

LOUKAS STEFANAKOS

THE MAN – THE ACTIVIST – THE POLITICIAN

By the biographer of Jason Favieros

MINAS LOGARAS

There was a photo of the cover and underneath, the name of the publishers: Europublishers. It was the simplest solution. Logaras had sent the second biography to a different publishing company.

This new development automatically put an end to my theory about Favieros's autobiography that just an hour previously I had served up to Yannelis and Zamanis as my *specialité*. I imagined their smiles when they saw the advert, but this was the least of my worries.

The second biography had appeared in a much shorter time than the first. The first had taken ten days, the second barely a week. That meant that someone had gathered information about the two suicides, then sat down to write the biographies and sent them to the publishers before Favieros and Stefanakos had committed suicide. So there was a mastermind behind all this; someone who had planned the suicides and who had the power to make them happen. Except that I didn't know who, how or why. Just as I didn't know whether there would be another victim. In other words, I knew nothing.

26

'Biography n.: 1. account to a greater or lesser degree detailed of the life and works of a person: Mus. *Rot.* Bibl. 335, 114 *such forms of biography* 2. art of the biographer.'

'Biographer n.: writer of a biography or biographies: *Beethoven's biographer* 2. pl. biographers: the writers, acc. to the ancient Greeks, of short biographies of orators, philosophers, poets, historians, scribes et al.'

Logaras certainly couldn't be classed among the biographers in the plural. Firstly because Favieros and Stefanakos didn't belong to the category of orators, philosophers, poets et al., as stipulated by Dimitrakos. And secondly, because his biographies were by no means short. In fact, the second was much longer than the first, being 350 pages in length. Apart from that, the publication itself was more handsome that the previous one. It had a matt paper cover, with dark blue lettering on a grey background, and in the centre was a recent photograph of Loukas Stefanakos making a speech. It had obviously been lifted from some newspaper or magazine.

This time I went about things differently. I made sure I got hold of the biography in good time so that I would be able to read it comfortably in the afternoon and not have to spend another night in the armchair burning the midnight oil. The visit to the publishers could wait. I was sure that Logaras – whoever he was – had gone down the same road with the second publisher as with the first, one that would no doubt lead me once again to the uninhabited house in Nisaias Street.

We had to start looking urgently for a third biography. I could have kicked myself for not doing it straightaway after Favieros's suicide. I'd been blinded by my certainty that Logaras was Favieros and that the biography was an autobiography. Now that I'd come unstuck, I would have to get my finger out to prevent the worst. I told Koula to get me a list of Greek publishers. After about half an hour, she managed to get hold of one from the Book Publishers Association. She phoned them all, one by one, but didn't come up with a third biography. That was good news, in part, because it meant that there wasn't any third suicide candidate, at least for the time being. Of course, one might be sent to any publisher at any time, so we had asked all of them to inform us immediately if they received anything written by a Minas Logaras. Not that I expected this would lead us anywhere. Whoever was hiding behind the pseudonym Minas Logaras didn't have his eyes shut. He would no doubt have foreseen that we would take measures after the second biography and would be in no hurry to send a third.

It was already turned five o'clock when I sat down in my armchair and opened the book, but I was immediately interrupted by Adriani.

'Do you intend to read Stefanakos's biography?'

'Yes, and as you can see I'm starting early so you won't be griping at me again about my staying up all night.'

'Why don't you read it in the park?' she asked with a sugary smile. The sugar then melted into nostalgia. 'We haven't been for such a long time and it's an opportunity today as it's not so hot.'

Her idea wasn't at all a bad one. On the one hand, I'd be doing what she wanted and, on the other, if I sat for eight hours in the armchair, I'd stiffen up. The walk there and back and the change of air would do me good.

I don't know if anything else had changed in the park, but the cat was no longer in its regular spot. Nevertheless, I kept to our informal arrangement and sat on my usual bench. The park was deserted as always; the sun was piercing through the leafage; everything was just as we had left it, apart from the temperature, which was higher and with an increase in the humidity.

Adriani looked around her and let out a sigh of contentment. 'I've missed it, you know. It was nice when we used to come here every evening.'

I tried to recall whether it really was nice. I was so down in the dumps during that period, so irresolute and lackadaisical, that I couldn't recall anything nice about it. But perhaps it was. Without doubt, they were tranquil days, but tranquillity for me means boredom as I don't know how to fill it.

I kept my silence, which could have meant agreement, and I got stuck into Loukas Stefanakos's biography. After the first few pages, I had the feeling that Minas Logaras had written the same book twice, simply changing the names. The two biographies bore such a close resemblance to each other. Favieros and Stefanakos had sprung from the same social class and had followed the same course. Favieros had attended Primary school, High school and Polytechnic School, Stefanakos Primary school, High school and Law school.

I was halfway through Stefanakos's student activism when the cat appeared. It stopped between the two benches and stared at me in astonishment. Then it opened its mouth slowly. I was expecting it to express its anger at me for having abandoned it, but all that came out of its mouth was a magnificent yawn, as though my presence alone were enough to cause it unbearable tedium.

'Look, it's as though it recognises us. That's instinct for you!' marvelled Adriani, who had looked up from her embroidering.

The cat closed its mouth and, with its tail erect, leapt up and sat in its usual spot, while I went back to Stefanakos's biography.

Logaras was equally generous in his adulation of Stefanakos as he was with Favieros. But now as I read it all for a second time, I had the impression that all the eulogies were somewhat forced – as though the praise was being heaped more out of obligation than conviction. I was sure I'd feel the same way if I were now to reread Favieros's biography.

By the time I'd finished with Stefanakos's student years, which took up half the book, just as Favieros's had done, it was already growing dark. Adriani got to her feet half-heartedly, and I, too, would have preferred to continue my reading there in the park rather than in the stifling atmosphere of the house.

Anyhow, it was around ten when I got back down to reading the biography, after having listened to a boring news bulletin and having eaten a plate of Adriani's beans. Adriani insisted that we avoided red meat in the summer, which meant that we almost always ate vegetables cooked in olive oil or, at most, oven-baked fish.

The similarities between Stefanakos and Favieros continued: years of resistance, struggles against the Junta and his arrest by the Military Police, not long after that of Favieros. As I was reading, it occurred to me that perhaps Favieros and Stefanakos had met in the cells of the Military Police, but I rejected the idea because the Military Police always kept their prisoners in isolated cells so they couldn't have come into contact with each other.

Once I got onto Stefanakos's parliamentary career and his rise as a politician, I was impatient to see just when Logaras would start tarnishing his image, and I didn't have long to wait.

The first innuendo came immediately after the account of his marriage to Lilian Stathatos. Logaras described how hard Stathatos worked during the first years of their marriage in order to consolidate her husband's political profile, while she herself took a back seat; perhaps because she didn't want anyone to connect Stefanakos with her father, Argyris Stathatos. At the same time, however, she had become involved behind the scenes in numerous business activities.

These activities were initially focused on her advertising company Starad, and its rapid growth alongside the growth of TV. Things began to get a little strange where I wouldn't have expected: namely, with the investment consultancy firm Union Consultants that Stathatos founded in partnership with Sotiria Markakis-Favieros. Logaras claimed, perhaps with some irony, that Stefanakos had helped his wife to set up the second firm in the same discreet manner that she had employed to create her husband's profile. For a consultancy firm dealing with European investment programs, this opened up numerous questions.

This, however, was not the main innuendo. Half a page further down, Logaras revealed that Stathatos and Markakis-Favieros had opened offices in Skopje to deal with the Balkan countries seeking accession to the European Union. A large number of the programs intended for these countries were channelled through Greece together with the funds earmarked for the reconstruction of Bosnia and Kosovo.

I finished the biography at around twelve thirty. Adriani had already gone to bed. I got a pencil and some paper and set to work at the kitchen table. I tried to make an outline of the business interests linking Favieros and Stefanakos together with their wives:

FAVIEROS	Domitis Construction Company
	Balkan Prospect: network of real-estate agencies
	Balkan Prospect: network of Balkan real-estate agencies
	Balkan construction companies
STATHATOS	Advertising Company
STATHATOS and FAVIEROS's wife	Union Consultants Investment Consultancy Firm
	Offices of this firm in Skopje covering the entire Balkans and particularly Bosnia, Kosovo
STEFANAKOS	Major politician and with good name throughout Balkans

I gazed at my notes and began making connections. Both Favieros and Stathatos owned companies that were completely above board: Favieros owned Domitis and Stathatos Starad. Behind these honest and reputable companies were others engaged in activities of a more shadowy nature. Both Balkan Prospect and Union Consultants were, on the face of it, entirely legal, but the way in which they earned money was questionable to say the least.

Even more shadowy were things in the Balkans. There, through his estate agencies, Favieros bought land and property for a mere snippet and developed them in various ways. As for the partnership between Stathatos and Favieros's wife, it wasn't at all inconceivable that they were getting a fat slice of the money from the programs intended for the various Balkan countries on the grounds that they were acting as mediators. In the old days, you paid a few drachmas to someone outside the Town Hall to fill out your application form for a birth certificate. Now the Greeks in the European Union were getting millions from Balkan countries for filling out applications for European funding.

And then there was Stefanakos. Activist in the resistance, outstanding politician, feared in Parliament and pro-Balkan. If he had intervened from backstage in order to help Union Consultants secure funds from European programs in Greece and the Balkans, who would have dared to expose him? These things rarely come out into the open because very few are aware of them and those who are keep their mouths shut.

I put the pencil down and tried to put my thoughts in some order. Could this have been the reason behind Stefanakos's suicide? Someone unknown, hiding behind the pseudonym of Logaras, knew the truth and was blackmailing him. And so Stefanakos committed suicide in order to save himself and his wife from the scandal. It seemed that the theory of a scandal wasn't to be thrown out after all.

Nevertheless, there remained the question: why did Favieros and Stefanakos commit suicide publicly? Anyone committing suicide to avoid a scandal doesn't have to do it before the eyes of millions of TV viewers. I still didn't have an answer to that one.

I got up and called Sotiropoulos on his mobile phone. 'That politician who told you about the relationship between Favieros and Stathatos ...'

'You mean Andreadis ... Is there one after all?'

'So it seems. Not with Favieros directly, but with his wife.' He whistled in exclamation. 'Can you arrange a meeting for me with Andreadis, so I can ask him a few things?'

There was a momentary pause. 'Now things are starting to get difficult,' he said and he wasn't joking. He paused again and then added: 'I'll see what I can do.'

27

The heat returned with a vengeance. I had already felt the change in temperature during the night because at one point I woke up drenched in sweat and with the sheets burning hot. It was now ten in the morning and I was on my way to the offices of Europublishers in Omirou Street, between Skoufa Street and Solonos Street. I drove up Skoufa Street behind an old truck full of plastic balcony chairs. As if it wasn't enough that it suffocated me with its exhaust fumes all the way, every time it set off at a green light it emitted a double dose.

'Do something about your exhaust!' I called to the driver as I overtook, trying to save myself. 'You'll suffocate us with your fumes.'

He looked down on me, literally and metaphorically. 'Don't tell me that old crock of yours is fitted with a catalytic converter,' he shouted.

The offices of Europublishers were located at number 22, on the fourth floor. I walked in to find a showcase fixed on the wall, full of the company's publications. Arranged in line was a guide to astrology, a two-volume medical guide, a cookery book, two volumes and a video cassette on major events in the twentieth century and a volume on health care. Between the medical guide and the cookery book was Stefanakos's biography.

Sitting beneath the showcase behind one of those metal desks that you find everywhere and in front of it two chairs that you can also find everywhere was an auburn-haired woman of about thirty-five. She was made up to the nines and was wearing a strapless top revealing two youthful bronzed shoulders. She must have been a model in her youth and had been put there to create a favourable first impression, and probably at little cost given she was well past her prime.

What was a biography about a leftist activist and politician doing in that environment? Sarantidis with his beard and the chaos in his office would have been a thousand times more suitable. Unless he had already moved to the new flat he had been dreaming of and had become like all the rest.

'Yes, what can I do for you?' said the woman in a deep voice.

'Inspector Haritos. I'd like to speak with whoever's in charge.'

She didn't deign to reply but instead picked up the receiver and dialed an internal extension. 'There's a Mr …' Before she could say my name, she had forgotten it and turned back to me. 'What did you say your name was?'

'Haritos … Inspector Haritos …'

'There's a Mr Haritos here, a police inspector, and he wants to talk to Mr Yoldasis.' He must have shouted at her from the other end of the line, because she said in a placatory tone: 'All right … all right … I'll send him in right away.'

She replaced the receiver casting a spiteful glance at it. Then she turned to me: 'Third door on the right,' she said, pointing to the far end of the corridor.

The office behind the third door on the right was exactly the same as the one in reception. The secretary leapt to her feet on seeing me.

'Please go through, Inspector. Mr Yoldasis will see you straightaway.'

She opened the door for me to go in. The man sitting behind the desk was fiftyish, tall and thin, with a pointed nose that almost reached down to his lips. He was wearing an outfit of various shades of blue: a light blue jacket and dark blue trousers.

'Come in, Inspector,' he said very cordially. 'Please. Have a seat.'

The room was air-conditioned, making the sweat on my back freeze. After going through the usual ritual: a routine offer of coffee on his part, a routine decline on mine, he came to the point and asked very politely:

'How might I help you, Inspector?'

'I'd like you to answer a few questions for me concerning Loukas Stefanakos's biography.' His expression suddenly changed and I hastened to reassure him: 'It's nothing for you to worry about.'

'I'm not worried,' he replied quite calmly. 'I simply don't understand what connection there might be between the publication of his biography and his suicide.' Suddenly, he had a moment of divine enlightenment and found the answer for himself. 'Oh, I see. It's because after the suicide of that … building contractor, his biography came out too and was by the same author.'

'Precisely. What I want to know is how and when the biography came into your hands.'

'It came by post, I'm certain of that. I don't recall when, but I can call Iota, who dealt with the publication side of it.'

He lifted up the receiver and asked his secretary to get hold of Iota. Presently, a girl of around twenty-five entered the office. Everything about her was little: she was a little short, a little plump and a little cross-eyed.

'Can you remember, Iota, when it was that the manuscript of Stefanakos's biography came to us?' Yoldasis asked her.

'About three and a half months ago,' the girl replied.

More or less the same time that Sarantidis had received Favieros's biography.

'Mr Yoldasis told me that you received it by post. Can you recall whether there was anything else in the envelope?'

'Yes. There was a letter.'

'What letter?'

'I can bring it for you. I kept hold of it.'

'Smart girl,' Yoldasis said to me as she went out of the door. 'I had completely forgotten about Stefanakos's biography and it was Iota who reminded me of it.'

Iota soon came back with the letter and handed it to me. I took it in my fingertips and examined it. It was printed from a computer, with no address or phone number. Under the signature, simply, was the name 'Minas Logaras'. It said roughly the same as the letter to Sarantidis: that if Europublishers were interested in the manuscript, Logaras would contact them concerning the terms of the contract and the publication date.

'May I keep this?' I asked Yoldasis. Not that we'd be able to get any fingerprints from it after such a length of time and it passing through so many hands, but sometimes miracles do happen.

'Of course. All I would ask is that you return it to me. I don't have any other proof that the text came into my possession legally. And if at some point this Logaras shows up … You understand, I'm sure …'

'What do you mean? That there's no contract?' I asked surprised.

'No. Logaras never got in touch with us again, and, as I told you, I had completely forgotten about the biography. Iota remembered it the day after his suicide. From then on, it was a race against time. I paid a fortune to the printers and bookbinders to get the book ready inside five days.' He paused and smiled. 'But it was worth it,' he said with satisfaction.

'And you published the biography without a contract?'

He shrugged. 'Where was I to find Logaras given that he'd provided neither address nor phone number? If he shows up, I'll pay him his legal rights. But he won't,' he added with certainty.

'How can you be so sure?'

'After all the hullabaloo created by Stefanakos's suicide, he would have already shown up to claim his percentage. As he hasn't come already, he won't. I recouped the high cost of production from the author's rights and still some.' He was overjoyed by his decision and made no effort to hide it.

'And why in your opinion hasn't he shown up? Why throw away so much money?'

I asked in case he had thought of something that hadn't occurred to me. He simply shrugged.

'I've no idea, though I can offer a guess. It's almost certain that Logaras is a pseudonym.'

'That much I've worked out for myself. Go on.'

'Who's to say that the man hasn't died in the meantime, is six feet under, and no one has the slightest idea that he wrote two biographies that are selling like hot cakes?'

His explanation suited him to a tee because, in this way, he would never have to pay any author's rights. If Adriani had set eyes on him, she would have immediately come to the conclusion: large, pointed nose equals skinflint and money-grabber.

I knew what he said was wrong since in Sarantidis's case there was both a contract and a fake address, but I didn't say anything. Why should I give him cause for concern, when in any case Logaras wasn't going to show up? I was beginning to understand the way he thought, though I didn't know how this might be of benefit to me. In the case of Favieros, it was the first biography and he wanted to make sure, albeit theoretically, that it would get published. That's why he signed the contract and gave a false address. On the contrary, in the case of the Stefanakos biography, he did nothing because he was certain that Yoldasis's eyes would light up after Sarantidis's success and that he would publish the biography without delay in order to cash in on the suicide. That's why he sent the second biography to Europublishers, who bring out anything so long as there's profit in it.

Logaras couldn't care a jot about the rights. For some reason, he simply wanted to be sure that the biographies would be published. I wish I knew why but I didn't have the faintest idea.

'Can I ask you one last thing?' I said to Yoldasis. 'No doubt you know that Sarantidis Publications brought out the biography of Jason Favieros following his suicide?'

'Yes. Those highbrow publishers look down on us, but when they find themselves with a winner, they're far more ruthless than we are when it comes to making the most of it. Compare our publication with Sarantidis's and tell me which is the more attractive of the two.'

Whichever, I couldn't have given a monkey's. 'All right, but given the other biography, didn't you think to contact someone when, after Stefanakos's suicide, you found yourself with a second biography in your hands?'

'Contact who?'

'How should I know? His family ... The police.'

He shrugged. 'I'm under no obligation to inform the family that I'm going to publish the biography of a well-known politician, even less so when it's full of eulogies about the deceased. As for the police, the era of censorship has long gone, Inspector.'

I had no counter arguments so I got to my feet to leave. The goodbyes were much more formal than my welcome had been.

After the coolness of the office, the oven outside seemed unbearable. I arrived home, where Koula was waiting for me on tenterhooks.

'Spyros and I have discovered another company,' she said as soon as I walked in.

'What company?'

'An offshore one.'

'Belonging to Favieros, his wife or Stathatos?'

'Stathatos and Favieros. Hotel and tourist enterprises in Bulgaria, Romania and the Dalmatian coast.'

She handed me a piece of paper on which the name of the business was written: 'Balkan Inns – Hotels and Cruises.'

So there it is, I thought to myself. Like father like daughter. Stathatos had only renounced her father inside Greece. Outside Greece, and in the area of the Balkans, she was carrying on in the same line of business. I suddenly found myself faced with a network of businesses both inside and outside Greece run by two families: one belonging to a businessman and the other to a politician. The common denominator in both cases was student activism, resistance to the Junta and the Military Police. How all this resulted in pan-Balkan enterprises and how it was linked to the suicides of the two heads of the families was a puzzle I had little hope of solving.

Nevertheless, because attack is the best form of defence, I decided to pay another call on Coralia Yannelis at Balkan Prospect, since she was an expert on Favieros's offshore companies.

I was about to telephone her when the phone rang and it was Sotiropoulos: 'A bummer. Andreadis won't agree to talk.'

'Why? What did he say?'

'He didn't say anything. He simply started yelling at me: how those who agree to appear on my show regard me as being trustworthy and that it's not right for me to abuse their trust and talk to others, and if I go on like that, before long I won't be able to find people who'll agree to appear on my programme.'

'All that?'

'Yes. I sensed that he was scared, but it may have just been my imagination.'

Whatever the case, that door had closed for good and I would have to look for information elsewhere.'

28

Yannelis welcomed me in her office. Our appointment had been for five and I arrived twenty minutes late, but that didn't seem to bother her. I once again confirmed her weakness for outfits because this time she was wearing a pale orange one with an enormous sunflower on the bust, while her trousers were of a single colour. As soon as I had sat down, her secretary appeared with a tray and put in front of me a glass of fruit juice and a plate of assorted biscuits. I was unprepared as I hadn't been expecting such a welcome and I felt obliged to thank her even though I detest fruit juice and I generally don't eat anything between meals, apart from souvlaki that is. In spite of my thanks, she read the surprise on my face and smiled.

'I know you're here for a friendly chat,' she said, 'so let's start with some refreshments.'

Yannelis was something of a mystery to me. She somehow managed to remain likeable even when she wasn't on your side, as had been the case a few days previously in Zamanis's office. However, you also got the feeling that somewhere she set a limit, that you'd come up against a wall if you went a step further.

'My visit is neither a friendly nor an unfriendly one,' I said to put an end to the joking. 'I simply want you to confirm a piece of information for me.'

'Normally, I shouldn't say anything to you. Because of the conversation we had the other day in the office of Xenophon Zamanis but also because, thanks to you, Leventoyanni threatened to sue us if we didn't give her the extra money we are supposed to have taken from the Russo-Pontian.'

Not exactly 'supposed to', I thought to myself, but I preferred not to open up old wounds. 'I haven't come to ask you about Balkan

Prospect but about Balkan Inns, the other offshore company owned by Jason Favieros dealing with hotel and tourist enterprises.'

'You're very thorough, Inspector,' she said with the same calm smile. 'You leave no stone unturned. You don't miss a thing.'

'It's my job.'

'As you're so good at your job, it can't have escaped you that the company you're referring to now belongs to Jason Favieros's heirs and to Mrs Lilian Stathatos.'

'It didn't escape me.'

'So, why have you come to me? If you want information about Balkan Inns, you should talk to Mrs Lilian Stathatos.'

'I came to you because I considered it still a little early for me to bother Mrs Stathatos.'

I had recourse to my standard argument, but this time it didn't seem to work because she burst out laughing.

'Let's leave mourning out of it, Inspector. The problem is elsewhere. You're afraid that if you go to Mrs Stathatos with some indiscreet questions, it may reach the ears of your superiors, perhaps even those of the Minister of Public Order, and that will no doubt have consequences for you. And you can't go to Xenophon Zamanis either because he doesn't appear to like you particularly. So you've come to me because you find me more manageable. I don't intend, however, to talk about matters or about companies which have nothing to do with Balkan Prospect.'

Once again she had read my mind. I decided to change tack. 'Let's look at it from another angle,' I said. 'Does an offshore company by the name of Balkan Inns have dealings or any connection with Balkan Prospect?'

'What sort of dealings?'

'For instance, has Balkan Inns ever purchased any real estate in the Balkans from Balkan Prospect in order to build hotels?'

She shrugged. 'That's something only our local estate agencies would know.'

'Come now. Surely, you're not telling me that the local offices don't keep Headquarters informed?'

'Even if there were any such dealings, what would that prove?'

I left her question unanswered and continued: 'Do you know whether the local construction companies belonging to Jason Favieros had been contracted to build such hotels?'

'The person able to answer your question is once again Xenophon Zamanis, but personally I wouldn't rule it out.' She paused for a moment and then leaned forward. 'Why do you suspect illegal practices in all this, Inspector? What's more natural than for three companies belonging in whole or in part to the same owner to cooperate?'

'I repeat what I told you at the outset. I'm not looking into illegal practices but into the cause of Jason Favieros's suicide. And now, too, into the cause of Loukas Stefanakos's suicide.'

'And do you think you'll find it in the businesses owned by Jason Favieros or by Favieros and Mrs Stathatos or by Mrs Favieros and Mrs Stathatos? Both Jason Favieros and Loukas Stefanakos committed suicide before the eyes of thousands of TV viewers. So any criminal action is out of the question. Jason left no explanation for his suicide, not even a letter. He took the secret with him to the grave. You have to respect that and stop your investigations.'

She looked at me with some satisfaction thinking she had closed all the doors so that I had nowhere to turn. But she had said it all in a way that suited her and had left out the most important element.

'Do you find it natural that two such well-known personalities, a businessman and a politician, should commit suicide in public and in such a violent way? And do you find it natural that ten days after the death of the one and one week after the death of the other, two biographies of them should appear, both written by the same person?'

She reflected for a moment. 'I have to admit that it's not so natural,' she answered. 'But it may just be a coincidence. This Logaras fellow may simply have wanted to exploit all the fuss in order to sell books.'

'The biographies had been sent to the publishers three months previously and more or less on the same day. Whoever this Logaras is, he knew very well what was going to happen.'

She was thinking about it, either because I had convinced her or because she was searching for some counter-argument, when the secretary came in and whispered something in an agitated fashion in Yannelis's ear. As soon as Yannelis heard it, she jumped up out of her chair.

'What? When?'

'Just two minutes ago,' replied the secretary, leaving the office and closing the door behind her.

Yannelis turned to me. 'There's no need for you to continue with your investigations into the causes of the suicides, Inspector,' she said slowly. 'Just a short while ago the police arrested three members of that nationalist organisation ...'

'Philip of Macedon?'

'Yes. They've been charged with the murder of the two Kurds and as accessories before the fact in the suicides of Jason Favieros and Loukas Stefanakos.'

'When did this happen?'

'It's just been announced in a special news bulletin.'

29

I don't remember how I got to Aristokleous Street. I suppose I must have been led by my reflexes – both in my choice of route and in my observance of the highway code. As for the rest, the only collision I tried to avoid throughout the journey was the one between my thoughts and my feelings. On the one hand, I was trying to think calmly in order to understand what was behind this act, and on the other my thoughts were being confounded by my anger and indignation.

I barged into the sitting room and found Adriani, as every evening, with the remote control in her hand.

'Where on earth have you been? All hell's broken loose!' she shouted, as though I'd been down to the beach at Varkiza for a swim.

I stood facing the screen waiting anxiously for the world-shattering news, but the TV was earning its name as the gogglebox. A presenter was testing the general knowledge of two young contestants. He was apparently overjoyed when they gave a right answer and he had to pay out and grief-stricken when they got it wrong and he saved his money. I grabbed the remote control and began switching channels, but I ended up flicking from one piece of tripe to the next.

'Don't be like that,' Adriani said by way of consolation. 'They've been putting it on every hour. It was on at seven, and it's sure to be on again at eight.'

It was the voice of years of viewing experience so I gave up. I waited for fifteen minutes for the programme to end and another ten minutes for the ads to finish. Finally, after half an hour, the title appeared: ARREST OF RIGHT-WING EXTREMISTS FOR MURDER OF TWO KURDS AND AS ACCESSORIES IN SUICIDES OF FAVIEROS-STEFANAKOS.

The same instant, three close-cropped, brawny types appeared on the screen. They were handcuffed with two of our lot on either side of them and were walking down the familiar corridor outside my office. The first was wearing a T-shirt with some monster from hell depicted on it. The other two were so close together that their trademarks weren't visible. Lined up along the sides of the corridor were reporters trying to thrust their microphones in the faces of the youths. The questions were coming thick and fast: 'What do you have to say about the charges against you? Did you kill the two Kurds? How did you feel when you shot them? What do you think about racism? How did you convince Favieros and Stefanakos to commit suicide?' The youths had their heads bowed and didn't answer, while the police officers were pushing them in an effort to break through the ring of reporters. As soon as they disappeared, the main attraction was gone and the screen split into various windows.

'The arrest of the three suspects took place today at three in the afternoon following a coordinated operation on the part of the police,' said one reporter, who had made his appearance just prior to my being shot. 'The suspects are Stellios Birbiroglou, aged twenty-three, unemployed, Nikos Seitanidis, aged twenty-two, a student at the Physical Education Academy, and Haralambos Nikas, aged twenty-five, an electrician by trade. All three are are being held at Security Headquarters, where their interrogation is ongoing.'

'Have the police made any statement, Vaso?' the newscaster asked.

'Yes. We have a statement from the Head of Homicide, Inspector Polychronis Yanoutsos.'

'And when on earth did he take over your position,' Adriani asked in astonishment.

'As I'm on sick leave, someone had to fill my position.'

'Yes, but shouldn't they say that he's only standing in for you?'

'Now you're asking for too much.'

Nevertheless, I was surprised that it was Yanoutsos who was making the statements and not Ghikas. Ghikas considered statements to the press his own little domain. How come he was letting Yanoutsos trespass on his patch and in such an important case too? Yanoutsos read out the the previously prepared statement from a piece of paper, but the microphones pressed up close to his mouth made him feel uneasy and he coughed at every second word.

'Already, following the suicide of the businessman Jason Favieros, and the ensuing statement by the Philip of Macedon National Greek Front, there was evidence that the aforementioned nationalist organisation was planning to proceed to blackmailing well-known figures and even to political murders. Following the murder of the two Kurds, both of whom were employed on the construction site of Domitis Construction, owned by Jason Favieros, the police began a coordinated operation in order to apprehend the guilty parties. We are now in a position to state that the culprits had been blackmailing Jason Favieros and Loukas Stefanakos for many months, applying more and more pressure and eventually causing both to commit suicide.'

I was spinning in a huge vacuum. First of all, I had never heard anything about the police having had their eye on the Philip of Macedon National Front. And even if they had, it was work for the Anti-terrorist Squad and not for my department, even less for Yanoutsos, who until just previously had been looking for Mafiosos in order to pin the murder of the two Kurds on them. And why was it Yanoutsos and not Ghikas making the statement, or, for that matter, the head of the Anti-terrorist Squad, who was the one most competent to do so?

As I was racking my brains to work out what was going on, the lawyer for one of the three accused appeared.

'My client is innocent and is being prosecuted for nothing more than his ideas,' he said angrily. 'These are actions that do damage to the validity and functioning of democracy. What person in their right mind can believe that three youths were the instigators in the suicides of two leading figures in the financial and political world such as Jason Favieros and Loukas Stefanakos?'

'And what about the two Kurds?' one reporter asked.

'My client had no involvement whatsoever in the murder of the two Kurds and we will prove it in court.'

'So you believe that the charges are trumped up?' another reporter asked.

'What I believe is that some people are looking for scapegoats so that all the fuss surrounding the scandals, which is harming the government, will blow over.'

'You see, now, that you didn't believe me?' Adriani said triumphantly.

I nodded my head as though acknowledging her, because I was in no mood at that moment for an argument. The lawyer's words had opened my eyes and I realised the game that was being played. Petroulakis, the Prime Minister's adviser, had seen that I had not been in contact with him and had assigned someone else to hush up the business. And so it had fallen to Yanoutsos, without the Anti-terrorist Squad having any part in it.

This was the *coup de grâce* as far as the loss of my position was concerned. From the moment that Yanoutsos willingly carried out orders and rounded up the three extremists, there was no way that they wouldn't reward him. And his reward would be to permanently take over my job. My sick leave would be up in less than a month and so I had to start looking for some refuge straightaway.

The sound of the phone roused me from my thoughts. Adriani never answered it when I was in the house because she thought it ninety per cent certain that it would be someone from the department for me. I lifted the receiver and heard Katerina's voice. 'Dad, have you heard?'

'Yes.'

'Are they right in the head? Are they trying to say that three village idiots forced a business tycoon and a leading politician to commit suicide? What a load of nonsense!'

'Don't ask me, dear. I know as much as you do about it.'

'Anyway, I'll tell you one thing. With all that nonsense they've no chance in court of making the charges stick.'

'Perhaps there's more that they're not saying.'

'Possibly. But more likely, they're looking for a way to close mouths just like that lawyer said.'

'We'll see. Let me put your mother on.'

I was in no mood to go on with the conversation. What Katerina told me I already knew, but that didn't do anything to change my own fate. They would decorate me for my bravery and put me out to pasture.

As I was reflecting on all this, I had one of my sudden flashes and understood what Ghikas was up to. The anti-terrorist people may not have known anything, but Ghikas was certainly in on it. Not even a leaf fell to the ground in Security Headquarters without Ghikas knowing about it. With some bitterness I realised that the conclusion I had come to on the day I visited the public notary was correct. Ghikas had supported me as long as the investigation was unofficial and he was in no danger of being compromised himself. However, as soon as he had received orders from his superiors to close the case, he had left me playing blind man's buff and supported Yanoutsos because it suited him.

I felt anger rising inside me and rushed to the phone. I called Ghikas at home. I let the phone ring at least a dozen times, but no one answered. Of course, I thought to myself, he suspected I might call and he's not answering so as not to get into an unpleasant conversation with me and lose his peace of mind.

Adriani shouted from the kitchen that the meal was ready. I sat down to eat a little ratatouille but it just wouldn't go down.

'Anyway, what are you brooding for?' said Adriani, seeing me eating without any appetite. 'Let them gouge each other's eyes out. You're not going to save the honour of the Police Force on your own.'

She thought I was brooding because the Force would be compromised, as I had told her nothing of what was eating away at me. I didn't care a jot about the Force; what bothered me was losing my position. Of all the transfers I had had, this was the one that suited me to a tee and I liked the job, even though I was always walking a tightrope. Now they would stick me in some operations or planning department and I'd be pushing papers all day long.

'I know what,' said Adriani rather coyly, and I knew immediately that she was about to come out with something. 'What would you say to us going to stay with Eleni for a while on the island? She's always inviting us. If you want my opinion, after the hospital and all we've been through, it will do us good. You still have another twenty-seven days' sick leave.'

She had counted them down to the very last one, but her idea provided me with a way out. If I got out of Athens for a while, at least I'd get a little peace. I'd get my strength back and I'd come back able to fight for a new position that wouldn't damage my pride. But despite the positive side to it, I tried not to show too much enthusiasm so she wouldn't get her hopes up and start nagging at me all the time.

'We'll give it some thought. It's not such a bad idea.'

'Wonderful. I'll call up tomorrow to find out the times of the boats. Eleni told me that there are some new ones that do the trip in six hours. They're a bit pricey, but it's worth it.'

When she really wants something, there's no need for you to say 'yes'. All she needs is a 'we'll see'.

'All right, find out. But don't take it as definite.'

I left half the food on my plate and went to take up position in front of the TV. I knew that apart from losing my appetite, I was also going to lose my sleep. I again watched the three youths dashing down the corridor outside my old office, again listened to Yanoutsos's statement and again became riled. However, then they showed interviews with the parents and neighbours of the three youths, something that was of interest to me. The parents of all three stated categorically that their sons were innocent. They swore at the government and cursed the police for plunging them into grief and stigmatising their offspring. The truest thing was said by a young lad from the same neighbourhood. 'Okay, I'm not saying he was a saint, but a murderer? You've got to be joking.'

Just after eleven, I chanced upon a discussion concerning the danger of the extreme right in Greece, once again chaired by Sotiropoulos. The participants were a minister, a prominent member of the opposition, a reporter and a lawyer. The game was being played in the usual way, with little variation: the minister claimed that the danger from the right was always lurking in Greece and the state had to be ever vigilant; the opposition politician rejected all this and accused the government of political exploitation, the minister responded by accusing the opposition of deliberately underestimating the danger in order to benefit from the votes of the extreme rightists. In between, like a wild card, there was, on the one hand, the lawyer, who was trying to explain whether and to what extent there were grounds for a case against the three youths, and, on the other, the reporter, who was trying to engage in a political analysis of the situation. Both were wasting their time as no one was paying any attention to them. Sotiropoulos was playing his usual game of hot and cold: first he would come out with some innuendo to get the participants to flare up and then he would try to maintain a balance.

That was it, I thought to myself. They've managed to do what they set out to do. The next day, all the newspapers, the radio stations and the channels would be talking about the danger of the extreme right and the three youths would come to a bad end.

It was one of the few nights that before going to sleep I longed to hear the waves breaking on the shore of an island. As soon as I closed my eyes, however, I saw Yanoutsos before me, sitting in my chair, and I opened them again.

30

It usually means one of two things when you can't get to sleep: either you're full of fear and worry or of vexation and anger. In both cases, you need some kind of sedative. My sedative was my decision to square accounts with Ghikas. Instead of this bringing with it agitation and anxiety, it brought me relief and I managed to sleep a couple of hours.

So, at ten in the morning, I left the Mirafiori in the garage at Security Headquarters and took the lift up to the fifth floor. Koula's replacement was there again with a magazine in front of him.

'Inspector Haritos,' I said, certain that he would have forgotten me as I wasn't either a Toyota or a Hyundai.

He cast a glance at me and went back to reading his magazine. As I walked past, I saw his eyes bulging as he had his ugly mug stuck in a two-page advertisement for mobile phones.

I knocked on Ghikas's door and went straight in without waiting for an invitation. I found him standing with his back to the desk gazing out of the window into Alexandras Avenue. This was a sign that something was eating him, otherwise he never budges from his chair. As soon as he turned round, I stood on the brake and stayed where I was. I saw a man who was tired, his eyes red from lack of sleep, looking at me as if some great misfortune had befallen him.

'I know what you're going to say to me,' he said, 'but I had no idea.' He sat down and fixed his eyes on the matching set with the scissors and paperknife on his desk. 'I had no idea, Costas. Everything happened behind my back.'

In all the years we had worked together, I had seen him enraged, indifferent, fawning, cunning, secretive … This was the first time I had seen him an emotional wreck and all my anger dissolved. I put everything I had prepared to say to him in the pending tray and sat down in my usual chair without waiting for an invitation. He slowly lifted his eyes and looked at me.

'All these years I've been on the Force, I knew the political leadership at the Ministry had faith in me. If anyone had told me anything to the contrary, I wouldn't have believed him. And they didn't only have faith in me because of my ability, but because I always played by the rules, I carried out my orders without question or any disagreement or pretending not to have heard them. Yesterday, for the first time, I felt I was being passed over. I realised that it's not enough just to follow orders, I have to carry them out to the letter. Not in my own way, which because of my experience is the correct way, but exactly as they are dictated to me, even if what they ask of me is irrational and compromises me.'

His voice sounded tired and weary, yet sincere. Perhaps because he wasn't one of those people who easily open themselves to you.

'I have another six years to go before I'm up for retirement,' he went on. 'And in those six years, I'm going to have to live with the doubt as to whether they're telling me the truth or not every time. I'll be constantly niggled by the thought that behind my back they're issuing other orders that I won't know about and that I'll eventually have to deal with. I ask you, is that a way to live?'

It wasn't easy for me to find any comforting words. Not just with Ghikas at that moment, but with Adriani and Katerina too. There are times when I pray that my sympathy shows on my face because the words stick in my throat and won't come out. That's how it was then. All I could say was something quite innocuous.

'Didn't you ask Yanoutsos for an explanation?'

'Yes. Do you know what he replied? Orders from up above. Talk to the Secretary General.'

'And did you?'

'Yes, and he told me that it wasn't his job to keep me informed and that those beneath me should have informed me earlier.'

'What does that mean?'

'Don't you understand?' he cried. 'You! They think it was you who didn't tell me that there were orders from above to go and nab those troublemakers!'

'Let them put themselves on the line. They won't find a court anywhere to convict them.'

He stared at me and shook his head sorrowfully. 'Ah, Costas. You're right in what you say, but you don't see clearly. They'll put them away and they'll start saying: "Let justice take its course." And by the time it has taken its course and acquitted them, two years will have passed. In the meantime, the case will have been forgotten and no one will give a damn.'

He was right. At the rate that the media today come out with scandals, world-shattering revelations and exclusive reports, three times a day, like cough syrup, in two years' time no one would remember anything about Favieros and Stefanakos.

'You realise that I can no longer make any promises to you concerning your position,' he said. 'Whatever I say or do, it'll be difficult to get Yanoutsos out of it.'

'I realise that.'

He heaved a sigh. 'Finish your sick leave and then come back and I'll see where I can put you so that at least you'll be content.'

I wouldn't be content, but at least I appreciated his efforts. 'And what shall I tell Koula?'

He shrugged. 'As she's on leave, let her finish it and then come back.'

Outside the office on my way to the lift I bumped into Yanoutsos.

'Something reached my ears about you investigating the two suicides on the q.t.,' he said ironically. 'There's no need for you to go on looking. The case is closed and you can take yourself off fishing.'

As I was opening the lift door, I heard his laughter behind me. I reflected on just how much we would miss Ghikas if he retired and Yanoutsos were to take his place.

Throughout the journey back home, my own problems gave way to Ghikas's. The way I'd seen him, vulnerable and betrayed, I felt an unprecedented sense of solidarity with him. It was the second time

I had felt that, and on each occasion for the same reason. The first time was when I had left Petroulakis's house in Dafnomili Street. Once again, I was tormented by the question of whether I'd been wrong about him all those years. Perhaps yes, perhaps no. Yes, because I always regarded him with suspicion and doubted his good intentions. No, because when someone admits to you of his own accord that throughout his life he did whatever his superiors told him without ever questioning their orders, it meant that he couldn't care less about you, his associate, and merely used you in keeping with the needs of the moment. Consequently, I was right to be cautious with him and to play my own game, just as he played his. Solidarity was all well and good, but those who made it their banner in the coalition government of '89 came a cropper.

I walked into the house and found Fanis talking to Adriani. Next to them was someone unknown to me, who looked like a technician and who was looking around at the walls.

'But, Fanis, dear, why do we need an air conditioner? I told you, I don't like them because they dry the atmosphere in the room. We're fine with the fan.'

'Do I have to say it again? You have a husband with a heart problem. For heart sufferers, the heat increases the risk of death. Do you know how many cases we get in Emergency when there's a heatwave?'

'Maybe, but we're leaving for a few days. We're going to stay with my sister on the island.'

'And what are you going to do when you get back and Athens is boiling hot?'

The technician interrupted the conversation, which was taking place in my absence, as did every conversation that had to do with me.

'Can I just ask? Do you want it to cool the whole place?'

'No, just the sitting room,' Fanis replied.

'Then 12,000 BTU will be ample.'

Fanis took the decision on his own. 'Okay. It's settled.'

The technician turned to leave, saw me in the doorway and halted. It was only then that Fanis and Adriani noticed me.

'Do you have any objections to us putting in an air conditioner?'

asked Fanis. 'It's a special offer. You can pay in instalments and the first one is in two years' time.'

'Go ahead,' I replied. With all that had been happening, I would need to take care of my heart.

Adriani walked out of the sitting room, leaving us alone. She always did that when she didn't get her own way.

Once she had gone, Fanis leaned over to me and said confidentially: 'It was Katerina's idea, but I didn't say anything because her mother would have gone into a huff.'

Before I had time to reply, the phone rang. It was Sotiropoulos. 'Are your lot out of their minds?' he said as soon as he heard my voice. 'They think they can pin it all on those three yobs, do they?'

'Don't be ungrateful,' I said ironically. 'Those three yobs gave you the topic for your programme last night.'

He understood that the dig was aimed at his programme on the danger of right-wing extremism, and he didn't reply straightaway. When he did at last open his mouth, it was one of the rare occasions that he sounded uptight.

'I've got people over my head too, Haritos. And I can't say "no" to them when they want to profit from some event, even if I disagree.' He paused for a moment and went on: 'So what do we do now?'

'Nothing. We might have succeeded in doing something if I'd been able to talk to Andreadis.'

'I tried, but he was adamant. I told you.'

'Andreadis was adamant because he had got wind of what was cooking and he didn't want to compromise himself.'

'It's possible. At any rate, keep hold of the material you've come up with. It won't go wasted.'

Yes, I thought to myself. I could sell it to you to pay for the air conditioner.

'Which Andreadis were you talking about? The politician?' asked Fanis, who had been an unwilling listener to the conversation.

'Yes, I wanted to ask him a few things about Stefanakos, but he refused to talk to me. Anyhow, now they've pinned it on those three yobs.'

As he was opening the front door to leave, Fanis bumped into Koula. I made the introductions.

'So you're the famous Koula who's so impressed Mrs Haritos,' Fanis said, laughing.

Koula blushed to her toes, mumbled a 'she's very kind', and went into the house. When I had closed the front door, she stood there looking at me gravely.

'No need for you to say anything,' she said. 'I saw it all on TV and I know.'

'I saw Ghikas today.'

'And?'

'He said for you to finish your leave and then go back.'

'That's something, I suppose. At least I'll get a bit of swimming in,' she said with some sarcasm in her voice.

'Are you upset about it?' I asked.

She shrugged. 'I have a father who paid dearly for his stubbornness and his tongue. And we paid for it along with him. It was all that upset that finished my mother off. And so I went to the other extreme. Get on with your job and whistle indifferently.' She looked at me as if waiting for me to say something. But I had nothing to say and so she continued: 'I came to tell you how happy I am to have met you and how much I'll miss you. Both you and Mrs Haritos.'

Saying that, she went into the kitchen, where Adriani was preparing oven-baked perch. She waited patiently while she was regulating the temperature. 'My work with the Inspector is finished and I came to say goodbye,' she said. 'And to tell you how happy I am to have met you.'

'I'm happy to have met you, too, dear,' said Adriani warmly, kissing her on both cheeks. 'What will you do now? Go back to the office?'

'No, I'm going to go swimming,' said Koula, unable to hide her bitterness.

'And we were thinking of going to see my sister on the island.'

'You should. The Inspector needs it after all he's been through.'

'Keep telling him that,' said Adriani, happy to have found an ally.

'If I need your help now and again when I'm cooking, may I call you?'

'Of course, whenever you want!' Adriani replied enthusiastically. 'And you can come round so I can show you.'

They kissed each other again and Koula rushed out, as if afraid she may change her mind and stay.

'Wonderful girl,' said Adriani as she watched her go. 'And we never invited her to come and eat even once. Shame on us.'

'Let's have her round on Sunday.'

'Good idea.' But then she thought better of it. 'No, perhaps not on Sunday.'

'Why?'

'Sunday is when Fanis comes.'

'So?'

She didn't reply, but the expression on her face made clear what she was thinking.

'Are you in your right mind? Fanis is with women doctors and nurses all day. You don't think Koula is going to turn his head, do you?'

She thought it over again and came out with her philosophical aphorism: 'She's a pretty girl and you never know.'

When I thought of it, as things had turned out for me, I was ready to believe it.

31

The high-speed are every Tuesday and Thursday,' said Adriani. It was nine in the morning and she was dressed, decked out and ready to go for the tickets.

'High-speed?'

'The fast boats that do the trip in six hours, stopping only at Paros and Naxos. The regular boats leave every day, apart from Saturdays.'

'Buy tickets for the fast one.'

She left at high speed lest I changed my mind and told her to leave it for later. I was about to revert to my old ways in order to pass my time till Thursday. I would go by the kiosk and pick up all the papers, then plant myself in the little square of St Lazarus, at the cafeteria with the sourpuss waiter, who brought you watery Greek coffee after you'd asked for strong and sweet.

I was wondering how I would pass my time on the island and whether I should buy myself a fishing rod and folding chair before going or buy it there when the phone rang.

'Inspector Costas Haritos?' The voice was that of a young woman.

'Speaking.'

'Inspector, a few days ago you had asked for an appointment with the politician, Kyriakos Andreadis.'

I couldn't believe my ears. If I'd been told that the three yobs had been released and that Yanoutsos had been looked up in their place, I wouldn't have been more surprised. I only just managed to whisper a 'yes'.

'Mr Andreadis will expect you at two o'clock today in his office. Please don't be late because at three he has a parliamentary session.

'I won't be late. Where is his office?'

'34 Heyden Street, on the third floor.'

I hung up and tried to take in what I had just heard. What had happened to change Andreadis's mind? Most probably the arrest of the three yobs and the attempt by the government to pin the whole business on the extreme right. If that were the case, Andreadis must have information to dispel that scenario and he probably wanted to release it anonymously so as not to compromise either himself or his party. I phoned Sotiropoulos to find out if he knew anything more about it, but his mobile phone was switched off. The people at the channel told me that he still hadn't arrived.

I had another three hours to kill so I decided to stick to my previous plan. This time, the kiosk owner was surprised to see me buying all the newspapers given that the arrests had been made two days before and nothing sensational had happened the previous day. He racked his brains thinking he must have missed something, but I left him wondering.

My turn to be left wondering came at the would-be cafeteria. Instead of the sourpuss waiter, an eighteen-year-old girl with miniskirt and platforms came over to me.

'Where's my usual friendly waiter?' I asked surprised.

'You mean Christos? He's left. Every year around this time he goes to Anafi. He has some rooms there that he rents out.'

The strange thing was that I wasn't glad to be served by a young girl; on the contrary, I felt peeved because Christos had spoiled my plans. At least the Greek coffee was still watery and that was something of a consolation.

Though forty-eight hours had already passed, the arrest of the three nationalists was still front-page news in most of the papers. This was the first thing in common. The second was the consensus of opinion. All the newspapers expressed objections to the arrests. The scale of the objections gradually rose from the mild reservations of the pro-government papers to the plain sarcasm of the opposition papers. Anyhow, the consensus of opinion, even with the political bent, testified to the fact that the ploy thought up by the masterminds was not working. It crossed my mind for a moment that perhaps this was why Andreadis wanted to see me. No doubt he had seen the morning papers, had decided that the time was ripe and had called me in order to speak to me. I couldn't rule out the possibility that he wanted to open up a second front in order to put the government in an even more difficult position.

But what was I to do with Ghikas if things were as I imagined them to be? Should I tell him what I had found out from Andreadis? By rights, I ought to keep him informed. After all, he too had been left with his tail between his legs and I felt a moral obligation towards him. Then again, if some information should emerge from my meeting with Andreadis that I felt I should keep to myself, I would decide when the time came.

I took a last sip at the watery coffee and got to my feet. The Mirafiori was parked in Protesilaou Street. It was noon and the heat was at its most oppressive. By the time I had walked down Aroni Street, I was drenched in sweat and I stopped off at home in order to change my shirt. Fortunately, Adriani still wasn't back so I didn't have to do any explaining.

There was one long line of traffic all the way from Vassileos Konstantinou Avenue to Omonia Square. I turned into 3 September Street and, taking Ioulianou Street, I came out into Acharnon Street in order to find the beginning of Heyden Street. Number 34 was between Aristotelous Street and 3 September Street. I double-parked outside the apartment block, certain that the traffic wardens never passed by there.

The office of Kyriakos Andreadis was a spacious three-roomed flat of the kind they built in the sixties, in other words a good twenty square metres bigger than they built them today. I was received by a woman of around thirty, tall, slender, dressed impeccably and looking as though she had just come from the hairdresser's. She had manners to match.

'Please be kind enough to wait a moment, Inspector,' she said on hearing who I was. 'He's on the phone. Can I get you something because he may be some time. Those phone calls are often like personal visits.'

I asked for a glass of cold water to go with the air conditioning that was working overtime and I waited, passing the time by looking at the photos on the walls, all of which showed a man of about sixty, always smiling and overjoyed, either giving a speech or standing beside a spitted goat with wine glass in hand. The other thing that made an impression on me was the amazing resemblance between Andreadis and his secretary. It didn't take much for me to realise that he had hired his daughter. My suspicion was confirmed when she showed me into his office.

'Inspector Haritos, Daddy.'

The man got up from his desk and came over to greet me with the same smile that he had in the photos.

'Welcome, welcome!' he repeated and, after shaking my hand, he led me by the arm not to the metal chair reserved for his voters, but to the sofa reserved for more friendly visitors and sat down beside me.

'What is Doctor Ouzounidis to you?'

The question came right out of the blue and I was tongue-tied. How was I to explain my relationship with Fanis? If I said he was my in-law, it would be premature and a lie. To say my future in-law wouldn't sound right. If I called him a friend, which was perhaps nearer to the truth, it would do him an injustice. Fortunately, Andreadis himself got me out of my difficult situation.

'Fanis told me that you are to be his future father-in-law.'

'The evidence seems to be pointing in that direction,' I replied and we both broke into laughter.

'You know, I owe him my mother's life.' He became serious. 'I took her to the hospital one night with a severe heart attack and not only did he manage to save her, he also stabilised her condition. Since then, my mother swears by Fanis and won't hear of any other hospital either in Greece or abroad. So when he phoned and told me that you wanted to talk to me, I couldn't refuse him.'

If I had been told that the meeting had been set up by Ghikas, or the Minister or even the Prime Minister, I would have believed it more easily. Fanis was not in the plan. I could never imagine him picking up the phone and succeeding where Sotiropoulos had failed.

Andreadis looked at his watch. 'So, ask me what it is you want because, unfortunately, I have to be in Parliament soon.'

'I happened to see you on a TV programme following the suicide of Loukas Stefanakos.'

'Ah yes. It was that fellow's programme ... what's the man's name?'

'The reporter, you mean? It escapes me.'

If Sotiropoulos had heard us, he would have been hopping mad that he wasn't a household name. But if Sotiropoulos's name were to crop up, Andreadis may very well clam up out of fear that what he said would leak out.

'First of all, I have to confess to you that personally I don't believe that theory about right-wing extremists obliging a businessman and a politician to commit suicide.' I said. 'I can come right out and say it because I am officially on sick leave and so off-duty.'

A smile of pleasure appeared on his face.

'At last, a member of the Police Force who thinks in the right way,' he said with some satisfaction. 'Because, in its panic, the government has come up with such a crude solution that it must take us all for fools.'

'Certain information has come to my ears, nevertheless, and I'd like to verify it – let's say out of personal curiosity.'

'What information?'

'Concerning the business relations between the families of Favieros and Stefanakos. I was informed that, apart from Jason Favieros's construction company and Lilian Stathatos's advertising company, there are two other consultancy companies for European investments that the wives of Favieros and Stefanakos are partners in. One of these operates in Greece and the other in Skopje, covering the Balkans. Favieros also had an offshore company Balkan Prospect, which operates a network of real-estate agencies throughout Greece and the Balkans, together with various construction companies. Finally, there is another offshore company owned by Favieros and Stathatos that deals in hotel and tourist enterprises.'

'Thank God you're a police officer and not a tax official. You'd have us all at your mercy,' he said, without losing his smile. 'So where are you leading?'

I began to explain to him the whole network of business relations linking Favieros and his wife with Stefanakos and his wife. I outlined my theory about the two bona fide companies, the construction and advertising ones, and how behind these operated the more shady ones, Balkan Prospect belonging to Favieros, and the consultancy companies and hotel enterprises.

He didn't interrupt me even once, but nor did he show any great interest. 'What is it that you want of me exactly?' he asked impatiently when I had finished.

'I'd like you to tell me if, in your opinion, there is anything unusual behind all this and how it might operate.' I tried to formulate my question as innocently as possible so as not to bring him down to earth with a bang.

'I see nothing unusual about it,' he said, astounding me.

'Not even in the way that Balkan Prospect runs its real-estate agencies?'

'Why would I find it unusual? Every business operates by buying cheaply and selling dearly. If it doesn't succeed in this in the first year, it will close.'

'Yes, but the difference is not declared to the tax office. It goes straight into the pocket of the real-estate agency as undeclared earnings.'

He laughed. 'Do you own the flat you live in, Inspector?'

'No.'

'Well, if you buy a flat for your daughter in view of her upcoming marriage, I suggest you don't declare the whole amount to the tax office. No one does it. Consequently, the tax office doesn't lose anything. It gets the tax it would anyway.'

'Except that various Romanians, Bulgarians and Albanians end up paying more.'

'Why do you just see the negative side? Personally, I'm only too happy when I see foreigners who came to Greece wretched and miserable succeeding in the space of a few years to become householders and property owners. It proves something about the dynamism of our little country.'

I saw that I wouldn't get anything out of that conversation because I was coming up against the dream of every Greek to acquire his own flat. So I decided to change tack.

'And the consultancy firms?'

'Is it bad that there should be companies that advise Greeks how to take advantage of the funds made available by the European Union? On the one hand, we're always complaining that we don't absorb the funds given by the EU and on the other we accuse those who actually do something with them.'

'I'm not accusing them. I simply wonder whether Loukas Stefanakos was using the political means he had at his disposal to secure the requisite participation of the Greek public sector in order that the company owned by his wife and Favieros's wife could absorb the European funds.'

'The important thing is that the funds are absorbed, not by which company they are absorbed.'

'I imagine this was why that Balkan minister on the programme with you praised him so highly.'

Despite all my efforts, it seems I was unable to conceal my irony, because he registered it immediately and tightened up a little.

'I don't understand your irony. You have no idea of the difficulties these countries face in order to secure funding, credit and loans. Stefanakos helped them through the mediation of his wife's consultancy firm.'

'And a large slice of the funds went into the pockets of Mrs Stathatos and Mrs Favieros as a fee for their mediation.'

'Isn't it only natural that Greece should get something in return for the help it offers to a third country? Otherwise, what would be the incentive for such mediation? What does it matter if Stefanakos channelled the fee through the firm run by his wife and Mrs Favieros? After all, both Greece and the Balkan country benefited from it. The poor wretches in the Balkans recognised that and were grateful to him.'

I had no words to counter his. After all, I was a copper who dealt in dead bodies; I was neither a politician nor a financier. Andreadis, however, took my silence as acquiescence.

'Everything you've described to me so far, Inspector, is in keeping with the rules of a self-regulating, free market. Our great success is that we managed to convince even fanatic leftists like the families of Favieros and Stefanakos to accept these rules and apply them. And now that we've convinced them after so many decades, you want us to accuse them of illegalities. For heaven's sake!'

All his rhetoric had made him forget the time and he suddenly looked at his watch. 'And now I'm afraid I have to go as I'm already late.'

He accompanied me to the door. He halted there and slapped me on the back. 'We've won, Inspector. As a member of the Security Force, that traditionally has always been closer to our party, you yourself should be happy. Give my best regards to Fanis.'

He gave me another friendly slap on the back and handed me over to his daughter, who accompanied me to the front door.

32

> 'Capture: 1. med. & mod. seize, conquer, destroy. Eurip. *Trojan Women*, 95 *A fool he who destroys cities and temples* / mod. seize, see citadel or fortification / mod and metaph. *He captured her heart* 2. take as plunder, as spoils. Thucyd. 4, 57 *They burnt the city and plundered all that was in it* 3. pass. metaph. be undone. Soph. *Trach.* 1104 *and here I lie dismembered and undone.*'

I was looking to see which meaning best suited the taking over of my post by Yanoutsos. It was very close to two of the first meanings: those of 'seize' and 'destroy'. He had seized my post while I was in hospital and, given the way he was handling the cases in the Homicide Department, he was undoubtedly destroying it. The other meaning was redundant because 'he hadn't captured my heart'. On the contrary, the second meaning 'take as plunder, as spoils' suited him to a tee. Yanoutsos had done what the adviser had asked, bypassed Ghikas, rounded up the three blockheads and had taken my post as his plunder and spoils. As for me, that was perfectly expressed by the third meaning: I was completely undone.

It was one of the rare occasions when I had taken Dimitrakos with me into the sitting room. The bedroom resembled a street market with Russo-Pontian wares. The wardrobe had been emptied out and all the clothes were scattered over the bed, the armchair and the dressing table, where Adriani was sitting and putting on her make-up. Decorating the centre of the double bed were two open suitcases, which operated on the lines of communicating vessels: the one emptied and the other filled. All this was part of Adriani's preparations in view of our departure the following afternoon on the high-speed. Actually, she had time the following morning to pack the cases, but it took her so long to overcome her indecisiveness that she felt safer when she had a whole night in front of her.

> 'Flight n.: med., mod. & colloq. hasty or secret departure, fleeing. *Odyssey* X, 117 *but the two others running away in flight came back to my ship*. 2. escape, avoidance, release from something. Aesch. *Suppliants* 395 *escape from this cruel rape* 3. eviction, expulsion, exile from the homeland. Herod. 7.3 *and having gone into voluntary exile from Sparta*. 4. coll. noun: exiles, fugitives. 5. refuge, sanctuary. Diod. XVIII, 17 *refuge in the mountain*.'

'Come and choose what trousers and shirts you want to take with you.'

'Pack as many shirts as I need to have a clean change every second day, and throw in three pairs of trousers and a jacket for the evenings when it's windy.'

So then, a hasty departure. Even if it wasn't secret, it was certainly fleeing, as Dimitrakos had it. Put more simply, I was taking to my heels in search of the meaning in 5: refuge, sanctuary, except that the refuge was on an island and not in a mountain.

While I was investigating the lexicographic formulation of my situation, the idea became lodged in my mind that my self-sacrifice in saving Elena Koustas from the bullet of her adopted son had, in the end, brought me nothing but bad luck.

Fortunately, Fanis appeared at just the right moment to dispel my pessimism. That was the good thing about Fanis. He always breezed in with a smile on his lips and in two minutes he had raised your spirits.

'I just popped round to say bye and wish you happy holidays,' he said as I opened the door for him.

'Except that I don't have any treat for you this evening,' said Adriani, who had emerged from the bedroom. 'I decided not to cook given that we're leaving tomorrow.' She always apologised to him when there was no home-cooked food in the house, as she considered it her duty to make up for her daughter's culinary incompetence.

'What do you think tavernas are for?' Fanis replied.

She liked the idea, because she immediately showed willingness. 'Let me finish packing and I'll get ready.'

She jumps for joy when it comes to going out to eat but as soon as she sits down in a taverna, the one dish smells funny to her and the other she thinks is off. You just can't win with her.

'It seems Andreadis thinks the world of you,' I said to him when we were in the sitting room.

He laughed. 'Because of his mother. The patient and all his family think that you're a good doctor, but you yourself know that you just got lucky. When they brought her in, she had a blockage the size of the Anatolian fault. I was certain she wouldn't make it through the night, but the old woman's organism reacted and she got away with it. I gained Andreadis's gratitude.' He looked at me gravely. 'Did you find out what you wanted?'

He had no idea what game was being played at the office at my expense, but he realised that it must be something serious for me to want to talk to a Member of Parliament.

'He was helpful and polite with me, but I didn't expect to learn what it was I wanted.'

'Why?'

'Because I was looking for a needle in a haystack.'

'It's a good thing your wife's not listening. According to her, that's what you've been doing all your life,' he said, laughing.

'A drowning man clutches at straws.'

He saw my expression and became serious, but at that moment we were interrupted by the sound of the doorbell and I went to open the front door. Standing in the doorway was a young lad of the kind that delivers letters sent by courier.

'Costas Haritos?'

'Yes, that's me.'

'Sign here, please.'

I signed and he handed me a thick and heavy A4-size envelope. The young lad turned and left, leaving me wondering who might possibly have sent me an envelope by courier and at seven thirty in the evening. I looked at the name of the sender and froze. The sender was Minas Logaras, 12 Nisaias Street, Athens 10445. The addresses of both the sender and the recipient were typed on labels.

I went back into the sitting room, tearing open the envelope in the same way that in the village my mother would skin a rabbit to make rabbit stew. Inside was a thick pack of printing paper. My eyes fell immediately on the title:

MINAS LOGARAS
APOSTOLOS VAKIRTZIS
THE JOURNALIST – THE ACTIVIST – THE MAN

I was unable to shift my gaze from the name Vakirtzis. Apostolos Vakirtzis was one of the most well-known newspaper and radio journalists. His articles were something of a barometer for the political scene and his morning radio programme was heard by the whole of Greece, from bus drivers and barbers to car mechanics.

I tried to understand why Minas Logaras was sending me the typed manuscript of his new biography. Fanis came over to me and looked over my shoulder. He murmured to himself bewildered:

'Apostolos Vakirtzis? The journalist? Why would Vakirtzis commit suicide? He's got the government and the opposition in fear of him. He can make and break ministers. He's made more money than he knows what to do with. Houses, villas, yachts, whatever you can imagine.'

Then he came out with the same question that had passed through my mind: 'And why has Logaras sent the biography to you?'

'He's warning me,' I said. 'He's warning me that Apostolos Vakirtzis is going to commit suicide.'

'I don't understand,' he said with a troubled expression. 'Why would Logaras warn you? So that you'll prevent him from doing it?'

His bewilderment suddenly opened my eyes for me. Correct, why would he warn me? He knew that I would immediately move heaven and earth to prevent Vakirtzis committing suicide. I tried to imagine what Logaras had in mind, but I was flustered and my mind was working at half speed.

Adriani walked into the sitting room all dressed and spruced up. 'I'm ready,' she said with a smile of satisfaction.

I grabbed Fanis by the arm and began shaking him. 'He's playing with me!' I shouted angrily. 'He's playing with me! He's not warning me that Vakirtzis is going to commit suicide. He's telling me that he's doing it at this very moment and there's nothing I can do about it!'

Adriani stared in amazement, first at me, then at Fanis. 'What's wrong with you both?' she asked.

'We're not going. It's off!' I shouted.

'But didn't we say we'd eat out?'

'Not that! The holiday is off! There's been a third suicide!'

She remained speechless for a moment, then she raised her eyes to the chandelier and began crossing herself. 'Holy Mother of God, enough of all these ups and downs. Let my husband have a normal job, let him go to work at nine and come back at five, and I'll light a candle to you that's as big as I am.'

She had no idea just how close she was to having God fulfil her wish. I rushed to the phone to call Ghikas at his home. No one answered. I searched for his mobile number. He only allowed us to use it in extreme circumstances, but this was as extreme as they came. I heard some old mother hen saying that my call would be forwarded. I called the exchange at Security Headquarters in the hope that he might still be in his office or that they might be able to tell me where he was.

'Turn on the TV and find the channel where Favieros and Stefanakos committed suicide!' I called to Adriani, while I waited for them to answer. If Vakirtzis had already committed suicide, they would lose no time in announcing it. If not, perhaps there would still be some hope, but every moment that passed counted in favour of Logaras.

'Inspector Haritos! I want to speak to the Head of Security, Superintendent Ghikas! It is extremely important!'

'Just a moment, Inspector!' I waited, at the same time trying to bridle my impatience and my nerves. 'The Superintendent will be away for a few days, Inspector. Would you like to speak to someone else?'

The 'someone else' would be Yanoutsos. 'No,' I said and hung up.

Ghikas had obviously moved in the same direction as I had, but more quickly. He had turned his back on it all and gone on holiday. I cast a quick glance at the TV, but there was nothing that looked like a special news bulletin. I grabbed hold of the remote control and began switching channels at random. All the channels were much of a muchness. That relieved me somewhat though it didn't bring me any nearer to preventing Vakirtzis's suicide.

'What if it's just a farce?' asked Adriani, not believing it herself, but simply saying it to calm me down.

'And what if it's not?' Fanis asked her.

'It's not,' I answered categorically. 'No one sits down and writes a three-hundred page biography as a farce.'

As I was replying to Adriani, I had a sudden flash of inspiration and I remembered Sotiropoulos. I called him on his mobile, praying that he would answer it. God left Adriani's wish in abeyance and fulfilled mine. At the second ring, I heard his voice.

'Sotiropoulos, listen to me and don't interrupt.' I told him the whole story with the biography. 'Do you know where Vakirtzis might be now and how we might notify his family?'

'Give me a minute to think.' Silence followed. Then I heard his voice again, this time with a much more anxious tone. 'It's his name day today and he's throwing a party at his place in the country. He invited me, but I have a TV programme and I couldn't go.'

That's it, I thought to myself on hearing this. He's going to commit suicide at the party in front of his guests. There'd no doubt be at least one TV crew there that would record the scene and broadcast it as an exclusive on the news bulletin. For nothing to have been broadcast yet meant that he was still alive.

'Can you inform anyone in his family?' I asked Sotiropoulos.

'I've got Vakirtzis's mobile number, but I doubt if he's going to answer.'

'Don't call him! If he's made his mind up that he's going to go through with it, he'll only speed it up and we won't be able to prevent him.'

'I've no idea who else will be there.'

'Where is his place?'

'Somewhere near Vranas.'

'Exact address?'

'I don't know, but I can find out.' Suddenly, he changed his tone and shouted angrily. 'And how the hell am I going to communicate with you when you don't have a mobile phone?'

'I'll give you another number.' I gave him Fanis's mobile number.

'You get going and I'll be right behind you.'

That meant he would set off after first securing a TV crew. 'You drive, please,' I said to Fanis. 'I don't want to take the wheel. I feel too shaken.'

'Okay.' He turned and glanced at Adriani. She had remained in the middle of the sitting room, at a complete loss.

'I'm sorry we've ruined your evening, but it's not our fault,' he said to her tenderly.

'Never mind, Fanis, dear. It's not the first time.' She didn't say it with spite, but rather with a sigh of resignation that made me go over to her.

'Listen,' I said, 'we're not cancelling the trip to the island, just postponing it for a while. We still have the whole summer ahead of us. We'll go for sure. I give you my word.'

'All right, all right. Now go quickly so we won't have another suicide on the screen.'

It was one of her good points. As soon as you acknowledged the sacrifice she was making, she stopped feeling sorry for herself and paid you back tenfold.

33

Fanis drove a Fiat Brava, a sort of great grandchild of the Mirafiori. I sat beside him in the front seat, holding his mobile phone in my open hand. I was waiting for Sotiropoulos to call and give us the exact address of Vakirtzis's place in the country. But Sotiropoulos was delaying and I kept casting an impatient glance at the screen of the phone, which showed the time and simply increased my anxiety.

Fanis was of the opinion that we shouldn't go via Stavros, but via Penteli, then drive down past the former pine forest and present-day charred forest of Dionysos to Nea Makri, from where we could continue on to Vranas. It had only been forty-five minutes since we had left the house and we were already driving up towards the forest at Dionysos. Fanis turned out to be right, because if we had followed the route Mesogheion Avenue-Aghia Paraskevi-Stavros, we would still have been stuck outside the ERT-TV building in Aghia Paraskevi because of the Olympic works underway at Stavros. Nevertheless, another idea began gnawing away inside me. Did Fanis know the way from Dionysos or would we get lost in the mountains and vales and Vakirtzis would commit suicide while we were still looking for someone to ask for directions? I saw him driving with great assuredness and that relieved me somewhat.

The phone rang just as we were starting our descent from the top of Dionysos.

'No one has Vakirtzis's exact address,' Sotiropoulos said. 'You'll have to ask when you get to Vranas. Everyone knows his place.'

'Okay.'

'I'm leaving in fifteen minutes.' There was a short pause and then he asked, somewhat tensely: 'Have you talked to anyone else?'

'Like who, for instance?'

'To some other reporter. Have you?'

'Do you think I've time to engage in chit-chat with your lot, Sotiropoulos?' I said furiously and I pressed the button that Fanis had shown me in order to hang up.

By the time we reached the straight road leading to Nea Makri, night had well and truly fallen. There was virtually no traffic as far as the coast road, but at Zouberi we came up against an endless line of cars crawling bumper to bumper.

'That's it,' I said to Fanis. 'We'll be lucky if we get there tomorrow.'

'We've done well to get this far. Imagine if we'd come via Rafina.'

He was right, but it was no consolation. While we were trying to escape from a line of at least a hundred cars, Vakirtzis might have already committed suicide and have been laid out. My one last hope was that among so many guests someone might have stopped him. However, I knew from experience that in such cases people become paralysed when faced with the unexpected and, instead of doing something to prevent it, simply watch like pillars of salt.

Beside me, Fanis suddenly exploded and began pounding the steering wheel with his hands. 'In summer they all go for fish, in winter for souvlaki and in between just for the excursion,' he shouted angrily. 'How are you ever going to find an open road?'

For a moment I forgot about the prospective candidate for suicide and tried to calm the prospective candidate for dangerous driving, but to no avail. He suddenly twisted the wheel to the left, pulled out into the opposite lane, which was empty given that no one goes in the direction of Athens for fish, put his foot down and started speeding like a man possessed.

'Stop, you'll get us killed!' I shouted, but he wouldn't listen.

In the distance I saw an intercity bus coming straight for us at full speed. Fanis quickly turned the wheel to the right and began honking at the line of cars to open up and let him back in. He managed it just as the bus whisked past us.

'Are you crazy, you numbskull?' shouted a man of about sixty from one of the cars. 'And a doctor too. You should know better!'

'He must be looking for custom,' shouted a forty-year-old redhead at the wheel of a Honda.

'That's why we have more victims every weekend than the Palestinians!' replied the sixty-year-old.

'He's right,' I said to Fanis. 'Do you think if we get killed, we'll stop the suicide more easily?'

'I'm a doctor!' he yelled. 'Do you know what it means when someone's dying and you don't get there in time?'

'No. I'm a policeman and I always arrive there after the death.'

He was so absorbed in his thoughts that he didn't even hear what I said. He was equally deaf to the comments and protests from the other drivers. It was the first time I had seen Fanis, who was always composed and conciliatory, beside himself. He went on with these guerrilla tactics for several more miles: swerving out into the opposite lane, overtaking three or four cars and then dodging back into the proper lane whenever something was coming in the opposite direction.

Despite the abuse we got, we at least managed to get away from Nea Makri and continue on the coast road towards Marathon, where the traffic was back to normal. When we eventually turned left towards Vranas, it was already almost ten o'clock. After the turn, the road was clear and Fanis stepped on the accelerator so the Fiat raced along.

'It was my mistake,' he said as he drove. 'We should have come by Stamata.'

'And how long would it have taken us to get to Stamata from Drosia?'

'You're right.'

At ten o'clock at night, Vranas is lit up with garlands of fairy lights. The taverns are all packed and instead of pine, the air smells of barbequed meat and burnt oil. We stopped at the first kiosk and asked directions to Vakirtzis's house.

'What, you too? What's going on tonight that everyone's headed for Vakirtzis's house?' the kiosk owner asked as he showed us where to turn.

'We're too late,' said Fanis disappointed, as we set off again.

'Don't be too hasty. He's celebrating tonight. All those asking the way may just have been guests.'

'You're right. I'd forgotten he had his name day.'

Fortunately, we didn't have to search for very long. We found Vakirtzis's house on our right, just off the road, as we left Vranas heading for Stamata. It was a huge farming estate that rose up and culminated in a white, three-storey house. Both the fields and the house were ablaze with light. Fanis turned right into a parallel track where the entrance to the estate was. The enormous iron gate was wide open. Inside and outside the estate were parked all the latest models of the world car industry: from jeeps to BMWs and from Toyotas to Mercedes convertibles. Fanis couldn't find anywhere to park and had to leave the car at a distance.

It was only when we got closer to the estate that we saw the turmoil. As we had passed by to park the car, we had been impressed by all the cars and lights. Now we saw that the entrance was deserted and unguarded. I looked around and high up, close to the villa, I saw a crowd of people pushing and jostling, as though watching a parade. Except that instead of cheering and applause, there was the sound of screaming and yelling. Panic prevailed on the terrace running round the whole of the three-storey building. Some were gesticulating frantically, others running in and out of the house and others going up and down the steps leading from the terrace to the surrounding estate.

Fanis and I halted for a moment and stared. 'You were right,' I said. 'We're too late.'

As though someone suddenly pushed us, we began running up to the place where the people were crowding. Halfway up, Fanis suddenly stopped and looked at me.

'Perhaps I shouldn't come with you?'

'Come on, no one's going to ask who you are.'

We were still going up when, behind us, we heard the siren of an ambulance and its headlights lit our path. Behind the ambulance was a patrol car. I motioned to the driver of the ambulance to stop.

'Why are you here?' I asked him when he came up beside me.

He stared at me in surprise. 'We were notified to come and take someone to the hospital.'

'Who?'

He consulted his book. 'Vakirtzis, the journalist.'

A sergeant got out of the patrol car and came up to me.

'Who are you?' he asked.

I showed him my badge. 'Inspector Haritos. Stay here, both of you, till I call for you.'

They both looked at me in surprise, but didn't dare object. Fanis and I set off up the slope again.

'If they sent for an ambulance, he may be still alive,' he said.

I had the same thought and prayed he would be. I struggled to push through the crowd, constantly saying my name and rank. As I passed through the crowd, I heard frightened whispering, crying and sobbing. Many of the people were wearing wet clothes.

I eventually reached an open space with grass and a swimming pool in the middle. My gaze automatically fell to the swimming pool. Perhaps it was the result of noticing the wet clothes, but the swimming pool was empty and everything was calm. Sitting in a chair next to the pool was a woman. She was bent over the grass as if looking for something and her body was shaking from her sobbing. Her clothes were also wet.

I continued to cast my gaze this way and that, till at a distance of fifteen metres from the pool, beneath a trellised vine, I saw a white mound. The spot was poorly lit and I couldn't quite make it out, but when I went nearer, I saw straightaway that it was a human body covered with a sheet.

I approached the mound and looked at it from above. Any hopes that had sprung up when we saw the ambulance dissolved at the sight of the covered body. I leaned over and lifted up the sheet. The sight of the charred face took me so much by surprise that I let the sheet fall from my hands and had to steady myself against the trunk of the vine. I was prepared to see a head blown apart by a bullet, or a throat cut by a knife, but not a charred body. I looked about me.

The grass all around was yellowed in places and completely blackened in others.

I left the body and went back to the woman sitting in the chair. Her sobbing had abated. She was standing erect, motionless, and with her hands covering her face.

'What happened?' I asked her. She didn't answer but simply continued standing there in the same position. 'Inspector Haritos. Tell me what happened.'

She slowly took her hands from her face and looked at me. She took a deep breath and tried to find where to start. 'We were playing, pushing each other into the pool,' she said after a while. 'You know the game at parties.'

I had seen it in some Hollywood films, but it was no time for games. 'And then what?'

'Apostolos suddenly appeared. He was wet and we thought that in all the hullabaloo he had dived in too. But he was wet with … paraffin …' She began sobbing again and could barely whisper. 'He went over there where he is now and waved to us as if saying goodbye. Then …' She was unable to continue as she broke into sobs. 'Then he took a lighter from his pocket and set fire to his clothes.'

I let her calm down a little from the sobbing. 'Did no one think of dowsing him with water?'

'No. We all froze. The flames engulfed him in less than a few seconds. We watched him leaping and screaming, but we didn't dare approach him. When he finally collapsed on the grass, we came round and began looking for buckets and hosepipes. There was no hosepipe anywhere. Some people who ran into the house found a bucket. They filled it with water from the pool and threw it over him, but it was too late.'

'Where's his wife?'

'He doesn't have a wife, he's divorced. Rena, the girl he lives … lived with, is in shock and they took her upstairs.'

People reacted as they always do in such cases. As soon as they see someone taking charge, they feel reassured and leave. I let her go to Fanis, who was standing beside the pool watching me.

'He burnt like candle.'

At my words he was struck by awe. 'All right, it's one thing to commit suicide. But in such a horrible way? Why?'

'I don't know. Tell the ambulance to come and get him. And go into the house to find his girl. Her name's Rena. See what state she's in and do something to bring her round, because I need to talk to her.'

He turned and quickly walked away, while I looked around me. As I had lost the race with the inevitable, all I could do was investigate whether there were any similarities with the other two suicides. At first sight, Vakirtzis's suicide differed on two counts. Firstly, the biography accompanying the suicide hadn't been sent to a publisher but had come directly to me. That meant that whoever was hiding behind the pseudonym Logaras knew that I was investigating the suicides. Consequently, it was someone belonging to the circle of the three men and quite probably someone who knew me or knew who I had interrogated. Secondly, this was the only suicide that had taken place before an audience, but not on TV. Suddenly, Andreadis emerged from a group of people.

'Terrible tragedy,' he said on seeing me. 'Terrible tragedy.'

'Did you see it?'

'Everyone saw it. It happened right before our eyes.'

'Did you talk to him at all tonight?'

'We exchanged a few words, that's all. I greeted him when I arrived and wished him all the best for his name day, but then we didn't bump into each other again.'

'How did he seem to you?'

He thought about it for a moment. 'As always, cordial and jocular. "You know how I feel about you, Kyriakos," he said to me, "but I'm never going to see you in power."'

Did he mean that he wouldn't see him in power because his party would never win the elections or because he would commit suicide? Most probably the latter.

'I didn't expect to see you again under such unpleasant circumstances,' Andreadis said to me.

'It was these unpleasant circumstances that I was trying to prevent when I visited you.'

He looked at me astounded. 'Do you think Vakirtzis's suicide is in some way connected with the suicides of Favieros and Stefanakos?'

'Of that I'm certain. What I don't know is when the circle will close or whether there will be any more suicides.'

He looked at me worried, almost panic-stricken, but I had neither the means nor the time to reassure him.

At the other side of the pool I saw a TV crew and a redhead getting interviews from the guests with the cameraman behind her, rather like a pageboy holding the bride's dress. So there's TV coverage, I thought to myself. The crew belonged to the same channel that had broadcast live the two previous suicides. I found it strange that only its crew should be there. I took hold of her arm and pulled her to one side. She was surprised to see me before her.

'Inspector, you're better. Are you back on duty?' she asked me.

I left her question unanswered for obvious reasons. 'How did you come to be here? Is it usual for you to cover parties thrown by your colleagues?'

'No, but we received a phone call to send a crew to Vakirtzis's party because there would be surprises. At first, the director thought it was probably just the grapevine, but then he changed his mind and told me to get a crew together and come just in case.'

'I want a cassette with the interviews you've taken.'

'Of course, I'll drop it in at your office tomorrow.'

'No, not at my office. I don't want it going astray. Send it to the Superintendent's office and I'll pick it up from there.'

I left her to go and see Rena. I was hoping that Fanis had managed to bring her round so that I could question her. So, in the first two suicides, Logaras had arranged a TV spectacle. In the third, as he wanted to provide a spectacle in the countryside, he had ensured there would be TV coverage. But how did he know when Vakirtzis would commit suicide? How was he so sure about the day and time? I was thinking all this over as I climbed the steps to the terrace and I came to the conclusion that it was only in the present case that he had taken a risk. In the first two cases, he had taken care in advance to send the biographies to two different publishers and had relied on their astuteness to publish them immediately after the suicides, as had indeed happened. With the third case, however, he had taken a risk. Not with the TV channel. If Vakirtzis hadn't committed suicide, they would simply have taken it to be a farce. But what would have happened if the biography had come into my hands and Vakirtzis hadn't already committed suicide? Wouldn't I have tried to prevent it? For him to have sent me the biography meant that he knew I was investigating the suicides, consequently I wouldn't have sat with folded arms waiting for the inevitable to happen. So why, then, had he sent me the biography approximately an hour before the suicide with the certainty that I would fail to prevent it? How could he have been so sure? Unless he had agreed with Vakirtzis himself on the day and time. How did he have such a tight hold over them? What did he have on them? The question would remain pending until I could find out how and with what he was blackmailing them.

I asked one of the girls wandering around like a sleepwalker on the ground floor of the house where Rena's room was. She pointed to a staircase leading from the vast ground-floor sitting room to the first floor. As I was going up, I bumped into Petroulakis, the Prime Minister's adviser. We came face-to-face halfway up the stairs. The way he looked at me suggested he was expecting me to pay him my respects. However, I thought that following Vakirtzis's suicide, he would most likely fall into disfavour and I decided not even to return the slight nod of the head he directed towards me. I turned my head away in time and continued climbing the stairs.

On the first floor, I found myself facing three closed doors. The first one opened onto a cold, impersonal room with a double bed, an armchair with a low back and a shelf with books. It was evidently the guest room. The next door revealed a gymnasium complete with bars, bicycle and running machine. I tried my luck at the third door and found Fanis holding a girl's wrist and taking her pulse. The girl heard the door opening and turned towards me. She was dark-haired with dark mauve lipstick and dark mauve nails. She was wearing a red top with shoulder straps, which left her shoulders and navel bare, and beige slacks. From what I knew, Vakirtzis was fifty-five, so there must have been a good twenty-five years between them as she couldn't have been over thirty.

Fanis came up to me and whispered in my ear. 'She's come round a bit, but don't overdo it.' And he left the two of us alone.

I sat down on the edge of the bed. The girl followed me with her gaze as though hypnotised. 'I'm Inspector Haritos,' I said. 'I don't want to tire you, but I need to ask you a few questions.'

She made no reply, but continued to follow me with that same gaze. I assumed she understood what I was saying and went on:

'Had you noticed anything unusual in Vakirtzis's behaviour lately?'

'Such as?'

'I don't know … was he irritable … did he suddenly lose his temper … was he prone to shouting?'

'Yes, but it wasn't unusual … he was always abrupt and prone to shouting … then he would quickly forget everything and be all lovey-dovey.'

'Was anything worrying him … some trouble perhaps?'

A faint smile came to her lips. 'Apostolos never had any worries. Other people had worries because of him.'

I wasn't certain whether she meant the people he savaged on his shows or herself. Probably she meant both.

'So he didn't give you the impression that he was about to commit suicide.'

'Apostolos?' The faint smile turned into a bitter laugh. 'What can I say?'

I concluded that things weren't too good between them, but that was of little interest to me. 'So you hadn't noticed anything unusual in his behaviour lately?'

'None whatsoever.' She paused momentarily as though reflecting. 'Unless …'

'What?'

'During recent weeks, he would spend hours on end shut up in his study in front of his computer.'

Just like Favieros. The same scenario was repeating itself and I was a real twerp for not investigating the case of Stefanakos to find out whether perhaps he had done the same. That was one of the difficult aspects of carrying out unofficial investigations while on sick leave: you don't dare turn up to see whomever you want, whenever you want.

'Didn't he spend much time in his study normally?'

'He didn't spend even one hour. Apostolos had everything. A study that covered the entire top floor with computers, printers, scanners, internet connection, everything. But he didn't use any of it. He only had it because his friends and colleagues had it. He couldn't bear for others to have something that he didn't. He was envious. Until lately, when he really did shut himself up there in front of his computer.'

'Didn't you ask him what he was doing?'

'Whenever I asked him, he always replied that he was working, regardless of whether at that moment he was watering the garden or watching a match on TV and swearing at the referee.'

I realised that I wasn't going to learn anything more so I left her to recover. I went out of the room and made my way up to the third floor. There were no doors at all there. It was an open space with a desk, a TV with a huge screen and various other machines. Scattered all around were loudspeakers of different sizes and a couch with a coffee table facing the TV.

On top of his desk was all of the equipment that the girl had listed for me just previously. What surprised me was that there was not a single book to be seen anywhere in the study, just a few magazines piled on the coffee table in front of the couch. Even I had four bookshelves on the wall, albeit in the bedroom. Vakirtzis didn't have one.

There were three drawers on the left-hand side of the desk. I opened them one by one. The first was full of empty notepads and a variety of ballpoint pens. The second was of more interest because it was crammed with cassettes. I made a note to have someone come to collect them and take them to the lab. I tried to open the third drawer but it was locked. I bent down and saw that it had a security lock. We would have to get hold of the key, though I wasn't sure, even in a case of suicide, whether we had the right to investigate. If not, we would have to find a way to get permission from the legal heirs and I had no idea who they were. It certainly wasn't Rena. She was one of those victims who live with much older men, spend a few great years with them and then end up left in the lurch and penniless.

As I was walking back down the terrace steps, I bumped into Sotiropoulos. 'Nothing here for me,' he said to me resentfully, as if I were to blame. 'They'd already taken the body away and most of the guests were gone. Fotaki got here first and she got all the interviews. How did she find out?' he looked at me suspiciously.

'From an anonymous phone call. Someone said that there would be surprises at Vakirtzis's party.'

He thought about it and whistled in amazement 'So you mean that …'

'Exactly. He sent the biography to me and informed the channel that had screened the previous suicides.'

I started to walk away towards Fanis, who was sitting in a chair waiting for me, but Sotiropoulos grabbed me by the arm.

'There's no way you're going,' he said. 'I have to get something out of this story too.'

'And you expect me to give you something?' I was ready to explode but that didn't daunt him at all.

'Yes. I want you to tell me about the biography. How did you get hold of it and how did you get here so quickly? I'm not saying you'll turn up trumps because I know what a crank you are and you might say no.'

I would turn up trumps, but not for the reason he imagined. If I talked, I would compromise Yanoutsos and those supporting him irrevocably. After all, I wasn't there on duty. I was on sick leave and had been replaced by someone else. If I had to, I could say that I had phoned Security Headquarters, been unable to find Ghikas and so had rushed there myself to try to prevent the suicide.

'All right. I'll tell you,' I said to Sotiropoulos. 'But you won't ask me if I was carrying out investigations here or what I came up with, because I'm obliged to report all that back at Headquarters.'

He stared at me, evidently thinking I was joking. He held the microphone to my mouth waiting for me to spill the beans. But I began to relate the whole story, from the moment that the envelope was delivered to my house to the time I arrived at Vakirtzis's estate. With every word I added, his smile got bigger as though he were experiencing the crazy rise of the stock market minute by minute.

When I had finished, he shook my hand for the first time in his life. 'Thanks. You're a good sort,' he said.

I made no comment and went over to Fanis, who had got to his feet.

'Did you come up with anything?' he asked me.

'Same symptoms as Favieros. Lately, he'd taken to shutting himself in his study in front of his computer. I found a drawer in his desk with a security lock, but I couldn't find the key.'

This time, we took the route that went through Stamata. It was after midnight and the traffic in Kifissias Avenue had thinned out.

'So, that's an end to your sick leave,' Fanis said suddenly.

I stared at him in surprise. 'Why? What makes you say that?'

'Because all the silly nonsense about thugs and right-wing extremists has gone out of the window and things will start to get serious.'

I didn't know whether things were starting to get serious. But, one thing was for sure, Petroulakos's expression showed just how difficult it would be for them to pin this suicide too on the Philip of Macedon organisation.

34

'The situation only improves as it worsens.' That's what one of our instructors at the Police Academy used to say. It was during the period following the fall of George Papandreou's government with all the ensuing demonstrations, marches and daily clashes between the students and the police. The instructor would come into the lesson, rub his hands and say: 'The situation only improves as it worsens.' To his mind, this meant that although things were daily going from bad to worse, this was in fact an improvement because it brought the dictatorship all the closer. He would say it, expound on it and, in the end, it happened. Of course, with the Junta, things did anything but improve, but everyone has a different idea of what improvement means.

These were the thoughts running through my mind as I looked diagonally across at the Minister. With Vakirtzis's suicide, the situation had most definitely worsened. Ghikas, who had returned by Flying Dolphin from Spetses, had phoned me because the Minister had called us to an urgent meeting. When I entered the Minister's office and saw that Yanoutsos wasn't there, I realised that 'the situation improves as it worsens'. There were four of us in the office: the Minister, who was sitting in his ministerial chair, Ghikas and I at either side of him, and the Secretary General was in the chair facing him. In the case in question, the Secretary General's chair was more like the dock, as the Minister was giving him a rollicking.

'I honestly don't understand you, Stathis,' he said. 'You give an order to the Head of Homicide to go and arrest those louts without bothering to inform the Superintendent? And when he's not even the Head of the Division but merely a temporary replacement?'

'When I asked the Secretary General to brief me, he replied that it was the job of those under my command to keep me informed,' said Ghikas, adding one more nail to the Secretary's coffin.

The Secretary avoided Ghikas's gaze, preferring to retain eye contact with the Minister. 'But I've explained to you. The order came from high up,' he said.

'If it was from so high up, shouldn't I have been informed too? Are you trying to tell me that there are orders from high up that don't go through me?'

He waited for an answer in vain. The Secretary General limited himself to giving the Minister a meaningful look.

'And what are we to do now?' The Minister continued with his questions, perhaps because like that he was constantly putting the Secretary in a difficult position. 'If we release those three louts, we'll look like idiots. And if we keep them in custody, we'll have everyone on our backs.'

'We can stall for a while,' suggested the Secretary.

'And what will we gain by that? In the meantime we'll have become a laughing stock.'

The Secretary hesitated for a moment, but eventually spat it out. 'Is it out of the question that this latest suicide has nothing to do with those right-wing extremists? After all, the three that we arrested are not the entire organisation.'

Ghikas was ready to explode and almost leapt up from his chair. The Minister saw his reaction, but kept his composure.

'Completely out of the question, Stathis,' he said to the Secretary with an ironic smile. 'Vakirtzis was in favour of the enforced repatriation of the illegal immigrants. He had even done a series of programmes on the topic. Would the extremists kill someone who wanted to get rid of the illegal immigrants? You'd better pray that none of his colleagues remember the programmes, because then we really will look ridiculous.' Suddenly, no longer in any mood for humour, he said to the Secretary coldly: 'Thank you, Stathis. That will be all.'

The tone in which he said it sounded more like he was firing him. The Secretary left the office in silence without saying anything to anyone. As soon as the door had closed behind him, the Minister turned to us.

'Will someone please tell me what's going on?' he asked, looking at Ghikas.

'Inspector Haritos will explain. He gave up his sick leave to carry out investigations at my request,' he replied.

The Minister's gaze fell on me. In such circumstances, the difficult thing is not to paint too pretty a picture and at the same time avoid sowing the seeds of panic. 'I honestly still don't know what's going on, Minister, and why Favieros, Stefanakos and Vakirtzis committed suicide. I am certain, however, that someone made them do it.'

I told him about the biographies, about Logaras's fake address, about the different publishers, and how Vakirtzis's biography had been delivered to me at home by courier. He listened carefully and his expression grew increasingly worried.

'What was it that aroused your curiosity?' he asked me when I'd finished.

'Two things. The fact that the suicides took place publicly. Figures like Favieros, Stefanakos and Vakirtzis would never make a spectacle of their suicides by choice.'

'And the second thing?'

'That although the biographies were, on the whole, eulogies to the deceased, nevertheless there were allusions to shady activities.'

He looked at me gravely and said very calmly: 'In other words, we're not going to avoid a scandal?'

'What can I say? It's certain that Logaras, whoever he is, knows what he's writing, at least in the cases of Favieros and Stefanakos. I haven't had time yet to read Vakirtzis's biography.'

'Who else knew about all this?'

I had been wondering when this question would come up. Ghikas and I were the only ones who knew about it all. To arrive at the arrests of the three toughs meant that one of us had spoken to someone else. I turned and stared at Ghikas. He avoided my gaze and spoke directly to the Minister.

'Mr Petroulakis, the Prime Minister's adviser, asked me personally for certain information. The Inspector visited him and told him what we knew.'

What he couldn't tell him was that we both had something to gain from talking to Petroulakis: Ghikas because he was looking to his promotion and I because I was fighting for my job.

'And why didn't you tell me all this?'

'Because we didn't have any tangible evidence whatsoever,' Ghikas replied immediately, obviously having anticipated the question. 'First of all, these were not murders but suicides, therefore, officially speaking, we couldn't carry out any investigation. And what emerged from the Inspector's investigations naturally gave rise to certain questions, but without any evidence. It was only after Vakirtzis's suicide and after Logaras had sent the biography to the Inspector that we had grounds for suspecting that this was instigation to commit suicide.'

'And because you had no tangible evidence, you preferred to talk to an ignoramus, who immediately tried to hush the matter up in the most puerile of ways.'

The comment was warranted and we kept our mouths shut. He took it as a silent admission of our guilt and sugared the pill for us.

'I wouldn't want you to think I'm trying to ascribe blame for the handling of the case, I'm aware that everything happened behind your back,' he said to Ghikas. 'The truth is that we're stuck with a very unpleasant business, whereas we could have done what every good politician in Greece does: we could simply have ignored it. Now we don't know how to get ourselves out of it.' He again looked at Ghikas. 'Do you have any ideas?'

'Yes. We won't release the three extremists just yet. We'll announce that we're still questioning them concerning the murder of the two Kurds. In the meantime, we'll let it leak that the successive suicides have given grounds for suspicion and that we are investigating the reasons behind them. As for the latter, we won't escape some ironic comments from the press, but at least no one will be able to accuse us of holding the three youths as scapegoats.'

The Minister reflected for a moment. 'All right. That's how we'll proceed. We don't have any options.' He reflected a little more and then turned to me. 'Do you think we'll have more suicides, Inspector?'

'I wish I knew, Minister. Perhaps Vakirtzis's was the last, perhaps not. Unfortunately, we don't know why they're committing suicide and we don't know who Logaras is, because evidently he's the one who's pulling the strings.'

'The idea that there may be more terrifies me.'

'Me too. But there is one ray of light after yesterday.'

Ghikas and the Minister both turned and stared at me in surprise. 'And what's that?' asked the Minister.

'The biography that Logaras sent me. He sent it because he wanted to open a channel of communication with me. And I believe he'll continue.'

'Why did he do that?' asked Ghikas.

I shrugged. 'Perhaps because he thinks he's smart and he wants to play with me. Then again, perhaps he's getting ready to reveal why he forced them into suicide. The one sure thing is that he knows that I'm the one dealing with the suicides. And for him to know that means that he must be one of the circle of people I've questioned.'

Just as I said it, the thought flashed through my mind that Logaras may have found out from Sotiropoulos. I had told Sotiropoulos almost all the details of my investigations. It wasn't unthinkable that he had discussed it with a colleague and that it had leaked out that way. I didn't dare reveal to the Minister and to Ghikas that I had had dealings with Sotiropoulos and let him in on my investigations. The former would have given me a dressing down and the latter would have thought I'd lost my wits during my sick leave because he knew how I detested reporters of all kinds.

It wasn't often that Ghikas did me the honour of giving me a lift in his limousine, but that day he made an exception. Perhaps because that case was an exception to the rule. When you're dealing with the murders of locals and foreigners, underground bosses and Russian Mafiosi, the patrol car is more than enough. But when you're moving in the big league where business tycoons, politicians and hotshot journalists commit suicide, you acquire a different air and find yourself now and again stepping into a limousine.

As we entered Ghikas's outer office, I saw the policeman quickly hiding a magazine in one of Koula's drawers. It seemed that Ghikas had taught him well in the meantime, because he made sure he turned his head in good time to the wall.

'Are you thinking of cutting short your sick leave and coming back?' he said, once we were sitting in our usual seats.

I had already thought of it, and this time it wasn't Adriani who was holding me back. 'I'd prefer to carry on with the investigation in a discreet way and with Koula's help. If I start investigating officially, the reporters will be all over us and the suicides will turn into murders. I'm afraid we might run up against the families of the three men. They're big names and they could put a spoke in our wheels whenever they wanted.'

'So at long last you're starting to take those with clout into consideration. In future, I'll be able to sleep more peacefully,' he commented, breaking into an ironic smile.

'It's a case that needs careful handling.'

He reflected for a moment and then sighed. 'You're right, though it would suit me to have you return to the office.'

'Why? Because of Yanoutsos?'

'No. Because of Koula. I need her back to put some order in here.'

'Why, isn't the officer outside any good to you?' I asked innocently, though I knew what his reply would be.

'Me, no. But I might send him to my wife so they can exchange magazines. When she goes to the hairdresser's, she takes a pile of them with her.'

We both burst out laughing at the same time, as though we had been waiting for an opportunity to find a moment's relief from the stress.

'What are you going to do about Yanoutsos?'

'I'll send him back to where he came from and I'll personally take charge of Homicide till you're ready to return.'

I left after promising to give him regular updates. I was about to press the button to go down to the basement when I had a sudden change of mind and pressed the button for the third floor. I walked down the corridor and burst into the office where Vlassopoulos and Dermitzakis, my two assistants – former assistants till just previously – were sitting. Obviously, they had written me off for good because they stared at me as if seeing a ghost. After a moment of embarrassing silence, they leapt to their feet.

'Inspector!' they blurted out in unison.

Because I still owed them for their conduct at the home of the two Kurds, I dispensed with the greetings and formalities.

'I'm here to tell you that my leave is over in two weeks' time. If you need me in the meantime, you can call me at home. I'll be in Athens.'

'You mean … you're coming back?' asked Dermitzakis timidly.

'Why wouldn't I be coming back, Dermitzakis? Have you heard mention of a disability pension?'

'No, no, Inspector. It's just that …'

'Just what?'

'Just that we'd lost all hope of you coming back, Inspector,' said Vlassopoulos, who was always more forward because he'd been with me longer. 'We're the ones who've been contemplating retirement with that idiot over our heads.' And he pointed to the door of my office. 'Anyway. I don't want to get started. Even the walls in this place have ears, as my old mum always says.'

They wanted to buy me a coffee for changing the terms of their retirement plan, but I used the excuse that I had jobs to do and that I was in a hurry. I had no wish to bump into Yanoutsos. I wasn't out for revenge and seeing him with his tail between his legs would have ruined my good mood.

'If I need your help before I'm back officially, I'll let you know, but you'll do what I want without asking for details,' I told them.

They stared at me without having understood a word, but such was their delight that I was returning that they didn't even try to fathom it out.

'Anything you want, Inspector.'

I told them to arrange for a patrol car to take me home. I had no intention of roasting in the midday heat. In less than three minutes, the car was at the entrance waiting for me.

As we said, the situation only improves as it worsens.

35

The offices of Starad were in Vikela Street, opposite the Hygeia Clinic. Mrs Stathatos must have spent a small fortune on decorating her advertising company. As soon as you walked in, your feet sank into a thick carpet that deadened the sound of your footsteps. You sat down and the armchairs wrapped themselves around you lest you had any thoughts of getting up and leaving them. The paintings on the walls in their white frames depicted straight lines, cubes and circles in a variety of colours, but always with a dash of red as a trimming.

Stathatos's office was different from the others because she had two expensive rugs on top of the carpet and on the wall behind her, where in our offices we usually put a picture of Christ wearing a crown of thorns, she had a painting of a tiny harbour, with fishing boats and a woman with a door opening in her back.

Stathatos was a well-preserved woman in her fifties, who, with make-up, would have looked much younger. That day, she was without make-up, wearing a dark blue outfit with some discreet white additions round the collar and she looked at me with a somewhat haughty expression that she had no doubt inherited from her father. Sitting at the side of Stathatos's desk was Sotiria Markakis-Favieros. She, too, was without make-up, and wrinkled as she was and with short-cropped hair, it made her sex and age difficult to tell. When I had visited their home in Porto Rafti after Favieros's suicide, I had been told that his family had gone away on their yacht. She must have shut herself up in the cabin all day because she was as white as white. She was sitting with her ankles glued together and was looking at us with a suspicious and frightened expression. When you saw them side by side, you understood from the first which of the two ran the business and which was there as a stand-in for her husband.

They had banished Koula and myself to the couch with its glass coffee table in front, at a distance of some ten yards from Stathatos's desk. Koula was the one who had her work cut out for her as she tried to take notes with her notepad balanced on her knees. She had returned that morning from holidays in Aigina, suntanned and wearing linen slacks and sandals. And because she was smart and knew which way the wind blew in our house, she didn't come to me to express her delight that we were starting the investigation again but went straight to Adriani to express her sorrow. 'I'm so sorry you had to postpone your holidays, Mrs Haritos!' Then she looked up to heaven and added: 'Heaven forbid that I should marry a police officer.' And instead of telling her that police officers are honest and sincere and, on the whole, good family men, Adriani stoically shook her head and replied: 'Unfortunately, Koula dear, heaven has its own way of working!'

We were sitting facing the two women and trying to discover whether there was anything strange in the behaviour or actions of their husbands prior to their suicides, particularly with regard to Stefanakos, as we already had plenty of information on Favieros. The portents, however, were not good because the two widows were tight-lipped and made no attempt to hide their displeasure.

'Why are you digging, Inspector?' asked Stathatos. 'Our husbands chose to kill themselves. Will your investigations bring them back?'

'No, but we may be able to prevent others. That's why we're asking for your help. Up until now, we've had three suicides that all conform to the same model. Doesn't that seem suspicious to you?'

'The police may find it suspicious,' she replied almost with contempt. 'But as there's no murder, I don't understand what you're looking for.'

'Did your husband have any reason to commit suicide, Mrs Stathatos?'

'As far as I know … no.'

'Then why did he?'

She shrugged in a manner indicating resignation. 'Why do people kill themselves, Inspector? Because their lives didn't turn out the way they expected … Because they don't like the world around them … Because they're tired of life and can't take any more …'

'Do any of those reasons fit your husband's case?'

'No. Loukas had everything he wanted and he was a person full of life.'

'So?'

'He went mad,' she replied abruptly. 'It happens sometimes that people suddenly go mad for no good reason. That's what happened to Loukas. He went mad. It's the only explanation.'

'Do you think it was madness that drove him to commit suicide in public?'

'If you'd met him, you'd know that Loukas liked grandiose gestures. He wanted to be in the limelight, he wanted his every word and action to create an impression. That in combination with madness can lead to extreme situations.'

If Stefanakos's had been the only suicide, I might have believed it. But three people don't go mad in quick succession, nor does anyone foresee that they'll go mad and write their biographies. On the other hand, Greece is a country in which everything is explained away as madness. I turned to Mrs Favieros in the hope that she might have a different answer.

'What about you, Mrs Favieros? Do you have any explanation?'

Panic-stricken, she looked first at Stathatos, then at me, at the same time crossing and uncrossing her legs.

'What can I say? I don't know. All I know is that I was living with a man who was in his office from morning to night, even at weekends; who arranged to go to the cinema with you and then called you at the last minute to say that something had come up and he couldn't make it, or who, while you were ready and dressed up to go out for dinner, told you that someone had phoned and he had to go to meet him.' And suddenly, without any warning, she erupted: 'Leave me alone, I don't even want to think about it!' she cried hysterically. 'Jason's dead! Why he killed himself, what got into him, I don't know! All I know is that he's left me with his businesses, the inheritance, the houses and yachts to sort out and with two children that are in a world of their own and are going on as though their father were still alive!'

She covered her face with her hands and started sobbing. Stathatos rushed over to her and took hold of her by the shoulders. 'It's all right, dear,' she said reassuringly. 'It's all right. I know what you're going through, but be brave. It's a bad time, it'll pass, you'll see.' She lifted her head and looked at Koula. 'Tell the secretary outside to give you a glass of water,' she said to her commandingly as though talking to an office girl.

Koula put down her notepad and went out of the office. Stathatos then turned her gaze to me.

'You see where all this pointless questioning leads, Inspector? You're upsetting us unnecessarily and only making things harder, while we're trying to put it all behind us and get on with our lives.'

I tried to keep my temper because it was not in my best interests to get into an argument. 'I'm sorry for causing you any upset, Mrs Stathatos. However, we find it difficult to believe that three people suddenly went mad and committed suicide. And even if we were to accept that, there's the question of the biographies that followed, all written by the same author and all written before the suicides.'

'What are you saying exactly? I'm trying to understand.'

'That there's something behind the suicides, something that as yet we are unaware of. If our hypothesis is correct, then there may very well be more suicides. I'm sure you understand what that means, particularly when it concerns well-known figures.'

The glass of water brought by Koula saved Stathatos from having to reply because she took it from Koula and turned all her attention to Mrs Favieros. I waited for Favieros to empty the glass and for Stathatos to give her a pat of encouragement and sit down before I went on.

'I won't keep you much longer. I'll try to be brief. Had you noticed any change in your husband's behaviour in the period just prior to his suicide?'

A faint smile appeared on Stathatos's lips. 'Loukas and I both had very busy schedules and we rarely saw each other, Inspector. He spent all day rushing between his office and Parliament, while I was tied up with my businesses. In the evening, each of us had our own obligations: his were political, mine business. The only time that we saw each other was in the morning over coffee and even then we barely had time to discuss the essentials. Stella can tell you better than I can if there was any change in his behaviour.'

'Who's Stella?'

'His secretary.'

If anyone had asked Adriani about me, she would have been able to tell them even when the rhythm of my blinking changed. I turned back to Mrs Favieros. I didn't ask her anything so as not to oblige her to answer if she didn't feel well. But she understood my questioning look.

'Yes, I did notice a change in Jason,' she said. 'But there was a reason for it.'

'Can you tell me what it was?'

She reflected as to whether she should tell me or not. Eventually, she took the decision and said very tensely: 'He was very concerned about a serious problem that our son has.'

The way that she said it left me in no doubt as to the nature of the problem their son had, but it was still unclear to me whether it was his son or something else that so overcame Favieros as to lead him to suicide. Most probably it was one thing on top of the other.

'Do you know whether your husband was acquainted with Apostolos Vakirtzis, Mrs Stathatos?'

She laughed. 'What a naive question, Inspector. Is there any politician or would-be politician, or even town counsellor for that matter, who doesn't know Apostolos Vakirtzis?'

'Do you know whether he was on friendly terms with him?'

'Another naive question. You couldn't be on anything but friendly terms with Apostolos Vakirtzis. You had to appear on his show, give him interviews whenever he wanted, always supply him with the information he asked for. Otherwise, he would declare war on you and, sooner or later, he would succeed in eliminating you.'

'And what about your husband, Mrs Favieros?'

She shrugged to stress that she had no idea. 'Jason knew so many people, from politicians to businessmen, that it was impossible among all that crowd to distinguish Vakirtzis or anyone else.'

There was no point in my going on. Even if he had known Vakirtzis, Favieros certainly wouldn't have told his wife. My next question was a difficult one because I didn't know whether I should ask it and also because I didn't know what answer I might get.

'Could your husbands' suicides be connected at all with your own business activities?'

'I don't see what possible connection there could be …' Favieros began, but Stathatos cut her short.

'None whatsoever,' she said abruptly. 'The partnership was between Sotiria and myself. Jason and Loukas had no involvement at all and, what's more, I have no intention of discussing my business activities with you, Inspector.'

'And I have no intention of asking you about your business activities, Mrs Stathatos. They're of no concern to me. Though what you just said, that Loukas Stathatos and Jason Favieros had no involvement in your businesses, is not exactly true. If I recall correctly, you had, together with Jason Favieros, an offshore company that dealt in hotel enterprises in the Balkans.'

She wasn't expecting me to know that detail and so I caught her off guard, but she quickly recovered.

'Ah yes, Balkan Inns,' she said complacently, as though she had forgotten about it. 'But I was never personally involved in that. It was run by Jason and Coralia Yannelis.'

I began to think of Coralia Yannelis as a sort of Minister for Balkan Affairs in the group of companies. I would have to try my luck with her once more. I found her far more likeable than Stathatos, even though she hadn't really told me anything despite all her smiles and friendliness.

Koula opened her mouth for the first time as we got up to leave. 'May we have your permission to search the computers used by Mr Favieros and Mr Stefanakos in their offices and in their homes?'

Mrs Favieros turned and looked at her in astonishment. Mrs Stathatos once again adopted her haughty expression as though the very sound of Koula's voice was an annoyance to her.

'And just what do you expend to find on the computers, young miss? If Jason and Loukas had left suicide notes, we would know about it.'

'I'm not looking for suicide notes, Mrs Stathatos,' Koula answered in a firm voice. 'Mr Favieros's private secretary informed us that Mr Favieros had been spending hours shut up in his office in front of the computer prior to his suicide. So much so that it had caused her to wonder. Mr Vakirtzis's partner had also said the same thing about him to the Inspector – namely that he, too, had been spending a great deal of time in front of his computer. So we would like to search them in case they contain some evidence.'

Mrs Stathatos shrugged.

'Loukas didn't have a computer at home, only in the office. I'll tell Stella, his secretary, who is still working there, to allow you access.'

The way she said it revealed her certainty that we wouldn't find anything. Koula thanked her and I nodded to her that we should be going. The secretary sitting outside didn't even raise her eyes to look at us as we left. Perhaps she didn't hear our footsteps on the thick carpet.

36

'I really don't understand, Inspector.'

Coralia Yannelis looked at us with an expression that was both ironic and inquisitive at the same time. We had gone straight there from the offices of Starad, because it was only five minutes' drive from Vikela Street to Aigialeias Street.

'If I'm not mistaken, this is the fourth time you've come here and I can't understand your interest in these suicides. I'm starting to suspect that there's something else behind all this that you're not telling us.'

'There's nothing else behind it, Mrs Yannelis.'

'So are you telling me that your interest is purely on a human level? That you're desperate to learn why Favieros and Stefanakos committed suicide in such a tragic way?'

'And Vakirtzis. The day before last, Vakirtzis also committed suicide in an even more tragic way.'

'All right, Vakirtzis too.'

'Did you know him?'

'Of course, along with ten million other Greeks. You couldn't open a newspaper without coming across Vakirtzis, or turn on the radio without hearing his voice.'

'But you didn't have any connection or dealings with him?'

She laughed. 'You still think that the reasons behind the suicides of Jason and Stefanakos are to be found hidden somewhere in Favieros's group of companies or in their joint companies or in their wives' companies. But where does Vakirtzis, a journalist, fit into all that?'

She waited for an answer from me, but she didn't receive one because I didn't have one. I didn't have any answers, and the ones I did have were not all that convincing. Those who shared my suspicions did so simply because they had the same gut feeling that I had, like Ghikas for example, or because they were scared of some scandal, like the Minister.

Yannelis saw from my silence that I was at a loss and continued: 'I can assure you that Jason and Stefanakos, at least, did not commit suicide because of the prospect of bankruptcy. If you don't believe me, all you have to do is ask to see their companies' balance sheets and give them to a specialist to examine. He'll tell you that the companies are doing just fine.' She paused for a moment and her tone suddenly became cold. 'Three people have died by their own hand, Inspector, and before thousands of eyes. That's tragic for their families and also for those who knew and loved them. But they weren't murdered, so why do you care?'

Her irony had turned into controlled indignation. They were dead anyway, I thought to myself. If they had been murdered instead of committing suicide, I would have come up with a lead far more easily. How was I to explain to Yannelis, without any evidence, that to my mind the three suicides were indirectly murders? And how was I to convince her that if we didn't come up with the reasons behind them soon, it was very probable that the suicides would continue and we'd be faced with a suicide epidemic that we wouldn't know how to stop? If I had been dealing with a murder, I would have been able to involve another three or four divisions. I would collect evidence, have bank accounts opened and, sooner or later, I'd get to the bottom of it. But now I had neither evidence nor arguments and I was going round in circles like a mouse on a wheel.

'Do you think it a mere coincidence that three leading figures from the world of business, politics and journalism should commit suicide in succession?'

She shrugged. 'Some coincidences are inexplicable.'

'And the biographies? The two were published within ten days of each suicide and the third was delivered to my door at the very moment that Vakirtzis was committing suicide.'

This time, she didn't answer straightaway. 'Agreed. The biographies lend some weight to your argument. But who's to say they weren't already written and the author is simply cashing in on the events? All three of them were well-known personalities and lived action-packed lives. That's a temptation for any biographer. After all, there's the example of that nationalist organisation that wanted to take advantage of the suicides to draw attention to itself. Perhaps the biographer was doing the same thing.'

'He had three biographies of three hundred pages each ready and waiting, Mrs Yannelis. Two of them were already in the hands of the publishers. He can't have written three biographies expecting his three protagonists to eventually commit suicide. Not to mention that this Logaras didn't give any address to his publishers, or even a bank account so they could pay him his royalties.'

'He's not going to lose them. He can turn up at any time and ask for them.'

'Perhaps, but his actions suggest that he won't.'

She looked at me gravely this time and her question sounded sincere: 'What are you looking for, Inspector?'

'I told you. I want to find out why Favieros, Stefanakos and Vakirtzis committed suicide.'

'And you think you'll find out by investigating our companies?' she said, again in an ironic tone of voice.

I was about to reply, but Koula beat me to it: 'Excuse me, Mrs Yannelis, but are you sure there won't be any more suicides?' she asked politely. 'We've already had three that follow exactly the same pattern.'

Yannelis turned and stared at her with a surprised look on her face, as though she had just noticed her for the first time. 'How should I know, my dear girl?' she said in the same disparaging tone used by taxi drivers when they talk to young women. 'Let's face it, not even you know.'

'Precisely. And because neither you nor we know, you can try answering our questions so that we might get somewhere before we have more suicides on our conscience.'

Yannelis stared at her even more surprised. 'All right, I'll tell you whatever I can,' she said in a conciliatory tone. 'And if you ever get fed up with the Police Force, come to me and I'll hire you.'

Koula blushed, which was an encouraging sign that she hadn't lost her modesty. I took advantage of the window she had opened for me and I began my questioning.

'Do you know whether Jason Favieros had any connections with Apostolos Vakirtzis?'

'If you mean professional ones, no. Vakirtzis is neither a partner nor an associate in any of the companies in the group. I can tell you that with certainty.'

'Do you know whether they had any personal connections?'

She thought for a moment. 'I think they knew each other from the time of the Junta. From what I remember, Vakirtzis was also involved in the resistance. Jason mentioned his name now and again, but I can't tell you whether they were still in contact.'

'Would Mr Zamanis know?'

She looked at me and smiled. 'My advice to you would be not to ask him. You're not one of Mr Zamanis's favourite people at the moment.'

I was about to tell her that I wouldn't lose any sleep over it, but I held back. The important thing was that there was another link between the three suicides apart from the public spectacle and the biographies: namely, the fact that the three of them knew each other from the time of the Junta and had all been involved in the resistance to the dictatorship. And what might that mean? Was something buried in their anti-Junta past and someone who knew about it was blackmailing them? Perhaps my conjecture was correct, but I'd have to find out first if there was any such secret and what it might be.

I returned to the present to go on questioning Yannelis, but I saw her picking up the phone and I waited.

'Hello, Xenophon. Tell me something because I'm curious. Did that Vakirtzis who committed suicide the other day know Jason?' I didn't expect her to call Zamanis on my behalf and I was astounded. Koula glanced at me with a hint of a smile on her lips. 'No, no particular reason for asking,' Yannelis went on. 'It's just something that's stuck in my mind since yesterday and I thought you'd be able to satisfy my curiosity.' She listened, nodding her head. 'And were they still in contact?' she asked cautiously, while turning her eyes to me. 'They'd talk every so often over the phone, I see. So I was right when I thought I remembered Jason once talking about Vakirtzis.'

She thanked him and hung up the receiver. Then she turned to me. 'You heard. They'd talk every so often over the phone. The rest is as I told you. They were together during the Junta and did time together in the cells of the Military Police.'

'Thank you very much, Mrs Yannelis.'

She smiled. 'You constantly make me change my feelings towards you, Inspector. One moment I find you a little irritating and the next I'm full of admiration for the way you continue to search in the dark.'

'That offshore company that Favieros had with Mrs Stathatos ...' I said, getting back to my line of questioning because I didn't want to be thrown off track by her civilities.

'Balkan Inns?'

'Precisely.'

She looked at me once again with that same ironic smile on her face. 'We've already had that conversation if I remember correctly.'

'You don't remember correctly. You had told me then that the person best able to tell me about it was Mrs Stathatos and that you only concerned yourself with Balkan Prospect. But Mrs Stathatos told me today that she knew very little about it and that it was you who managed Balkan Inns.'

She realised that I had her with her back against the wall, but she didn't lose her composure. 'Anyhow, let's not turn it into a sticking point.'

'Does Balkan Inns have any connection with your other offshore company?'

Without saying a word, she got up and walked out of the office. Koula turned and stared at me perplexed.

'What's suddenly got into her?'

'Wait and we'll find out.'

We didn't have to wait long. Yannelis returned more or less straightaway with two pamphlets in her hand. 'This is the background to each company together with the most recent balance sheets. If you examine them, you'll find all the answers you want.' She remained on her feet and handed me the two pamphlets. 'Unfortunately, the Balkan Inns pamphlet is in English, we're out of the Greek ones,' she added with a slight hint of irony.

It was all the same to me. I'm equally a dunce when it comes to balance sheets whatever language they're in. Koula had already got to her feet. I got up too and took the pamphlets. It was time for us to leave. We'd been handed our cards, as my dear departed mother used to say.

37

I had come to learn who the experienced reader was. Not the one who reads quickly or even the one who reads carefully, but the one who knows what to read and what to pass over. I was now in the third category thanks to the three biographies by Logaras. I'd read the first, about Favieros, word by word. I'd read the second, about Stefanakos, just by looking at the beginning of the sentence in many instances because I understood what Logaras wanted to say due to my experience from the previous biography and so I concentrated only on the main points. With Vakirtzis's biography, which I'd started the previous night, I had arrived at the essence of what it meant to be a good reader: I skipped the first part, which was about his childhood and youth, as in the first two biographies, I also skipped the part with all the eulogies about what an important journalist he was, and I went straight to the third part of the book where, as usual, Logaras started with his innuendos.

To my great satisfaction, I wasn't wrong. With the last of the adulation and flattery came the first innnuendo:

> They say that in order to be a good journalist, you have to be ruthless. And Apostolos Vakirtzis was ruthless. He would terrify first one then blackmail the other till he got the information he wanted. Ministers, politicians, mayors, officials were all afraid of him and did whatever he asked of them so as not to have to come up against him. Apostolos Vakirtzis made use of all this to come out with accusations and revelations.

So far there was nothing reprehensible. After all, a great many journalists used similar means even if they weren't as aggressive as Vakirtzis. Logaras's main dig came immediately afterwards.

> Rumour has it that Vakirtzis exploited these 'special relations' he cultivated on behalf of the companies in which he was either a visible or invisible shareholder. Apart from providing him with his journalistic revelations, these 'special relations' had secured preferential treatment for the companies. But all this is only rumour. There's no proof or evidence of it.

My first reaction was that Logaras was exaggerating. But then I reflected that everything he had said up until then had proved to be correct. Did Logaras have evidence of it, and if he had, why didn't he come out with it? That was another question. Why didn't he state outright the names of the shady companies that Vakirtzis was involved in, and Favieros and Stefanakos for that matter, instead of allowing all his innuendoes to poison the atmosphere? One possibility was that he had heard things here and there, but didn't have any concrete evidence. Another possibility was that he had evidence but couldn't reveal it because by doing so he would also reveal his identity. The third possibility was that he was keeping it secret so that he could go on blackmailing. Who? The families of the three men, of course. Favieros's wife and children, Mrs Stathatos, and Vakirtzis's relatives, who must have existed.

The third possibility seemed the most probable but also the most alarming, because as long as the blackmailing continued, so would the suicides. We already had three and it was like the morning traffic report on the radio: jams everywhere and no sign of them clearing.

The good thing about the experience I had acquired as a reader was that I didn't have to stay up all night to finish Logaras's biography. In fact, I finished reading it so quickly that I even managed to catch the late-night news bulletin, which was full of reports, interviews and clips concerning Apostolos Vakirtzis. I listened to it all, only to conclude that this mysterious Logaras knew far more.

It was already ten in the morning and I sat down with Koula to make a plan for the day. I told her to rope in her cousin again and go to the records department at the Ministry of Trade and search through Vakirtzis's companies.

'I don't know what you'll find,' I said. 'Logaras spoke about companies in which Vakirtzis was either a visible or invisible shareholder. If we're lucky, we might come across the companies where he appears as a shareholder.'

'And what about the victims' computers?'

'Afterwards. First let's find out what companies Vakirtzis was involved in. I can smell at rat, though it might be my nose that's to blame what with all the pollution I'm breathing in constantly.'

I left her to call her cousin so they could get down to work.

Loukas Stefanakos was a Member of Parliament for a constituency in the suburbs of Athens and had his office at 22 Dardanelion Street, close to the park in Aigaleio. With the traffic, it was like going from Athens to Patras, a good three hours' drive.

The sky was full of rain clouds and the sun nowhere to be seen. That meant that we were in for a bout of unbearable humidity till we got our fifteen-minute downpour and the sky cleared. In Athens, the weather finds relief in the same way as the people: a sudden outburst that sweeps your legs from under you and then it's as if nothing had happened.

The traffic flowed normally, albeit slowly, as far as Peiraios Street. There was even less traffic in Peiraios Street and I got my hopes up, but the miracle was short-lived. At the lights at the junction with Iera Odos, I ran into an endless line of traffic dotted with patrol cars and ambulances. After ten minutes, I began cursing Stefanakos to high heaven for having opened his office in Aigaleio. What was wrong with Glyfada or Nea Smyrni? But Stefanakos, being a leftist, wanted to be in a traditional working-class district like Aigaleio, even though today the working-class district is hidden behind boutiques and fashion stores, rather like Stefanakos was hidden behind his wife's businesses.

After twenty minutes or so, I finally reached the lights and came upon a pile-up involving a coach and three cars. The coach had been left abandoned in the middle of the junction, facing in the direction of Kifissou Avenue, while a car coming from Iera Odos had evidently crashed into it and two other cars had crashed into the back of the first car. The road was almost completely blocked with only one car getting through every five minutes, and that thanks to a policeman who kept emptying his lungs into his whistle.

Once past the point of the accident, Iera Odos opened up before me like the National Road on Easter Sunday and I sped along. It's a fact that you always make up the time you lose. What you don't get back is your health and peace of mind.

Dardanelion Street was parallel to Thivon Street. Number 22 was a new block of the type put up overnight. This, too, was part of the game of hide and seek played in the district: pulling down the old workers' houses and putting up new blocks of flats overnight. Stefanakos's office was on the second floor; a two-room flat with adjoining rooms – the one for the secretary, the other for the politician. Stella, Stefanakos's secretary, had already been informed by Mrs Stathatos because she recognised my name. Before sitting down, I glanced around me. There was nothing that particularly attracted my attention, other than the flowers. The entire outer office was filled with flowers. There were vases everywhere: on the desk, on the coffee table, on the floor.

'The constituents keep bringing them,' she explained when she saw my surprise. 'I've already thrown half of them away, but more keep coming. His door was always open to them, he did everything he could to deal with their problems and they worshipped him.' She sat down at her desk and waited. 'So what can I do for you.'

'In the cases of Favieros and Vakirtzis, there were noticeable changes in their behaviour prior to their suicides. I wanted to ask you whether you'd noticed any changes in Stefanakos's behaviour.'

She thought for a moment. 'I thought that he was ill and that he was trying to hide it,' she replied eventually.

Her reply surprised me. 'What do you mean?'

She thought again. She was one of those people who think before they answer. Usually, you get good statements out of them.

'He looked run-down and was in very low spirits, as though he had some serious illness. Whenever he was here at lunchtime, we would go to a taverna just down the street to eat. It had become a regular habit. But of late he never had any appetite. Either we didn't go at all or, when we did go, he hardly touched his food.'

'Didn't you ask him what was wrong with him?'

'Yes, when I found the tranquillizers on his desk.'

'Tranquillizers?'

'Yes. Loukas was a cheerful person, outgoing and with amazing self-confidence. He didn't have any need of tranquillizers or anti-depressants. When one day I opened his desk drawer, I found a box of tranquillizers. It surprised me and I asked him abut it.'

'And what did he say?'

'That everyone has their ups and downs.'

'How long before his suicide did all this take place?'

'About two weeks before.'

Suddenly, I thought of a question that I should have asked Faviеros's secretary, too.

'Do you recall whether during that two-week period he received any phone calls that may have upset him?'

'A Member of Parliament gets phone calls in his office from people he knows very well or people he doesn't know at all, Inspector. So I can't tell you with certainty whether some unknown caller had upset him. But I don't remember anything of the sort.'

'Did you happen to notice any other change in his behaviour?'

I deliberately left my question vague, not wanting to mention the computer and perhaps influence her, but she replied categorically.

'No.'

'Did Mr Stefanakos have a computer?'

'Yes.'

'Did he spend a long time at his computer?'

She laughed involuntarily. 'Loukas spent countless hours at his computer, Inspector. That's why he had a laptop so he could take it around with him. He wrote everything on his computer, from his speeches and the results of his research into various topics to the notes he kept concerning the various requests of his voters. Consequently, I can't tell you whether he had been spending more time at his computer given that he always had it on in front of him.'

That was encouraging. If Stefanakos recorded everything on his computer, we might possibly find some evidence that would give us a lead.

'Where is his computer now?'

'In the office.' She gestured towards Stefanakos's office.

'May I take it with me?' She looked at me hesitantly. 'I've spoken to Mrs Stathatos.'

'I know.'

'As soon as we're done with it, I'll have it returned to you.'

She thought for a moment and then shrugged. 'Why not? It can't do any harm.'

She went into Stefanakos's office to fetch the computer and left the door open. I glanced inside the office and suddenly, flashing before my eyes, I saw the scene from the TV: the nails on the door on which Stefanakos had impaled himself. The TV presenter had said that the interview had taken place in Stefanakos's office, but this door bore no resemblance to the other.

'Excuse me, but did the interview Stefanakos gave on the night of his suicide take place in this office?'

'Do you think I'd still be here if it had taken place here?' She regained her composure immediately and added more calmly and politely: 'No, Loukas had another office on the floor below the offices of Starad in Vikela Street.'

I put the computer on the back seat of the Mirafiori and then sat for a moment behind the wheel to collect my thoughts. Favieros and Stefanakos had both exhibited the same two-sided behaviour. The foreign workers swore by Favieros, who helped them, but, as well as helping them, he made a pile of money on the side through the houses and flats that he sold them at bloated prices. As for Stefanakos, his voters sent flowers to his office to honour his memory, but he offered them only crumbs while using all the means at his disposal to make sure his wife's businesses got preferential treatment.

Suddenly an idea came into my mind, but instead of filling me with delight, it sent a shiver through me. What if the suicides had no connection with scandals? What if someone knew what Favieros,

Stefanakos and Vakirtzis were up to behind the scenes and decided to punish them in order to render justice?

38

> 'Computer: n. *mod.*: 1. clerk subordinate to an accountant, assistant accountant. 2. esp. naval, title of finance officer corresponding to chief petty officer or warrant officer. 3. *rec.* intellectual, thinking person who computes or calculates.'

Of course, I didn't expect to find in Dimitrakos's Lexicon, published in 1954, the contemporary sense of the word 'computer'. Besides, the first 'computers' that circulated in Greece were actually calculators. When the real computers arrived, we didn't call them computers but rather 'calculators'. In other words, there was neither rhyme nor reason to it. Anyhow, it seemed to me that the first sense of the word given by Dimitrakos, 'clerk subordinate to an accountant', was closer to the modern computer. Nine times out of ten, I encountered it as an assistant accountant at the chemist, at the garage, at the service station and so on. 'The computer is the cleverest moron you'll ever meet,' I'd once heard from one of the forensics experts. 'It all depends how you use it.' Because I knew how I'd use it, I kept it at a distance so as not to have a moron getting under my feet.

In any case, Dimitrakos had provided me with a sense of the word that suited Vakirtzis, 'intellectual, thinking person who computes or calculates'. At least so it seemed at first sight.

Koula, with the help of her cousin, Spyros, had been trying to find the businesses owned or jointly owned by Vakirtzis in the Ministry of Trade records, but they still hadn't come up with anything. I got them to stop because in the meantime I had brought home Stefanakos's computer and I wanted them to search through that first.

I was sitting in the kitchen on hot coals, trying to contain my impatience by thumbing through Dimitrakos while they were doing a first search of Stefanakos's computer. The kitchen stank of vinegar because Adriani was cooking okra and she was of the opinion that if you first soaked them in vinegar, they didn't turn 'gooey'.

I looked up from the dictionary at the sound of Koula's footsteps as she came looking for me to inform me of the results of the search. Her cousin had pushed the screen belonging to Koula's computer to one side and was bent over Stefanakos's laptop.

'You explain, Spyros. You're better at it than I am.'

Spyros didn't even bother to look up from the screen. 'Well, he had a cleaning program.'

'What program?'

'Cleaning.'

All his answers were abrupt and he kept his eyes glued to the screen. I found it irritating, but I restrained myself because I didn't want to upset Koula and also because he was helping on a voluntary basis.

'Listen, when I hear the words cleaning program, my mind goes straight to the housecleaning,' I said calmly. 'Can you spell it out for me?'

He lifted his head for the first time and stared at me with an expression somewhere between surprise and contempt. But he saw Koula standing beside me and bit his lip so as not to come out with anything rude.

'When you delete something from the computer, it's not permanently deleted,' he explained to me slowly and patiently. 'It remains on the hard disk and there are various ways that you can retrieve it. There are some programs, however, that clean the disk and permanently delete what's written on it. You can run them when you want or you can programme them to start up on their own. When one of these programs is installed, you can retrieve what hasn't been deleted on the disk before it starts up again.'

'And Stefanakos had one of these programs on his computer?'

'Yes, and it was set to clean the disk every three days.'

'So you're telling me that with the frequency that it ran, we won't find anything?'

'Looks like it.'

Disappointed, I turned to Koula. 'Zilch!'

She didn't appear to share my disappointment because she grinned. 'Not exactly. We did come up with a few things that may be of interest.'

'Such as?'

'The good thing about Stefanakos is that he kept notes on everything. Read for yourself.'

She pressed a few keys and a series of squares with notes opened up before me. It reminded me in reverse of the boxes of Ethnos cigarettes, on which my father would note down what he had to do. Every so often, he'd bang his head and say, 'Oh no, I'd written it on my cigarette box and I've thrown it away!' Since then Ethnos had gone bust, cigarettes were now in packets and computers had become cigarette boxes. I was slowly starting to understand a little. I leaned over and read the notes one by one.

> What A is asking is absurd. L doesn't even want to discuss it. He says he's already paid M in gold. He's right.

The good thing was that they were all dated. This one was dated May 10th, when I was still in hospital. In another one, dated May 12th, he wrote:

> I spoke to M. He says one thing and A another. I have to speak to K.

Another two or three followed that at first sight seemed irrelevant, then on May 20th:

> K won't even discuss it. He says his position is at stake.

And on May 22nd:

> I heard A's programme last night. He's blackmailing me openly. I'll

have to talk to his station and persuade some journalist to interview me so I can reply.

Again, there were a few irrelevant notes followed by two successive ones on June 2nd and 3rd:

> Where did he sprout from? And what does he want? He says he has irrefutable evidence. It's probably just hot air.

And on June 3rd:

> He'll send me the evidence and what he's asking for is outrageous. The world's gone mad. J told me that he can't refuse to call M. A knows too much and he's scared of him.

I reread all the notes and tried to see what I could make of them. There was no doubt in my mind that 'A' was Vakirtzis. 'L' was most likely Lilian Stathatos, Stefanakos's wife, and 'J' had to be Jason Favieros. I had no idea who 'M' and 'K' were. That said, there were more or less three main conclusions: first, Vakirtzis was putting pressure on Stefanakos to facilitate him with his businesses, and Stefanakos, in his turn, was putting pressure on his wife and on 'K', who was quite probably someone high up in the government, perhaps even a minister. Secondly, Jason Favieros was scared of Vakirtzis because he knew too much. Third, and more important, Vakirtzis was blackmailing Stefanakos on his radio programmes to force him to succumb. The only blank was the note of June 3rd. It was evidently referring to someone unknown who had irrefutable evidence. What evidence and about whom? About Vakirtzis? It wasn't at all unlikely. Anyhow, from the way the note was written, it didn't give the impression that Stefanakos was collecting information about Vakirtzis. Probably this unknown person was offering his services. And evidently at a price given that Stefanakos had noted that what he was asking for was outrageous.

After so long, it was the first time that we had some clues and connections. At least, I was now certain that Favieros, Stefanakos and Vakirtzis not only knew each other, but also had dealings, and seemingly shady ones at that.

'Print out two copies,' I said to Koula. I intended to rush with it to Ghikas. Why shouldn't he have a bone to lick, like me, to slake his hunger a little.

'Well done, both of you. You've done a good job.'

A smile spread over Koula's face, but Spyros didn't appear to be too impressed by the honourable mention.

'Can we take a look at Vakirtzis's computer soon?' he said, still with his eyes fixed on the screen. Apparently, it was the only view that interested him.

'You'll get your chance, but why is it so urgent?'

Once again he gave me the look that was somewhere between surprise and contempt. 'Because you told Koula that he had a computer, but that he didn't use it much. There's a fifty-fifty chance that it had a cleaning program. Maybe sixty-forty. But even if it did, his suicide was just the other day and we might still find some data on the hard disk.'

'All right. I'll arrange it for tomorrow. In the meantime, go on searching through the records at the Ministry of Trade in case we turn up something on Vakirtzis.'

While they were printing out the notes from the computer, I phoned Ghikas to tell him to expect me.

It appeared that the police officer with the magazines had either been sent packing or had gone to find Ghikas's wife at the hairdresser's. Sitting in his place was a young man, who, if nothing else at least, had his computer switched on and asked me my name and what I wanted.

Ghikas was so anxious that he didn't even bother to greet me. 'Give me something that I can pass on, because the Minister is phoning me every few hours.'

Without a word, I spread out the notes from Stefanakos's computer on the desk before him, as though I were laying out the cards for patience. He read them carefully, one by one, then lifted his eyes and looked at me. 'Conclusions?' he asked.

'First of all, the most obvious. Vakirtzis wasn't just a journalist, he was a businessman too. We're trying to find out what businesses he had his hand in. It's just a question of time. The second conclusion is that Vakirtzis was blackmailing Stefanakos, either because he wanted a share in his wife's business or because he wanted to work with her. It seems, too, that Favieros was caught up in all this business.' I paused for a moment and looked at him. 'I don't know how pleased the Minister will be about all this stuff on Vakirtzis.'

He shrugged. 'I don't think he'll lose any sleep over it. He'd become a pain in their necks of late. He never let up with his attacks and he'd really got on their nerves. If I'm to judge from what you've told me, his attacks were aimed elsewhere.'

'I still don't know who "M" and "K" are.'

He shook his head and sighed. 'I can't imagine who "M" is either. But if "K" is who I think it is, then the Minister will have trouble swallowing it.'

'Who do you think it is?' I asked curiously.

'Karanikas, the one who's overseeing the Olympic building projects at the Ministry of Public Works.'

Ghikas was thinking of the Minister, but I was imagining Petroulakis's face when he learned where we'd got to.

'Can you arrange for me to talk to Karanikas?'

He stared at me with an expression of both anger and amazement. 'Are you out of your mind? What evidence do you have to talk to Karanikas? Are you going to open up your hand to him? The next day, it'll be all over the newspapers, the radio and the TV channels.' He paused for a moment, then added slowly: 'Old habits die hard, it seems. You're back to your old ways.'

I didn't persist, because at bottom he was right. I really didn't have enough evidence to get Karanikas to talk and, if the investigations leaked out, it wouldn't only be Ghikas who hung me up by my fingernails, but also Sotiropoulos, who was banking on an exclusive scoop.

'I want one more favour from you.'

'Like the one with Karanikas?'

'No. I want you to get me the cassette of Vakirtzis's programme from May 21st, the one where Stefanakos says he was being blackmailed.'

'If there is one, I'll get it for you.'

'Tomorrow, I'll send Koula to take a look at Vakirtzis's computer. If I have any problems, I'll call you.'

'Do that and I'll sort it out.'

The good climate was back again, but as I got up to go, he fired a warning shot at me: 'Take care, Costas. We're walking on a tightrope and if we put one foot wrong, there'll be no one to save us. Did you see what happened with Petroulakis?'

I preferred not to answer so as not to commit myself, though I knew he was right when he said that we were walking a tightrope.

39

The way things were going, the Green Park looked like becoming a regular haunt for my clandestine meetings with Sotiropoulos. If it had been winter, we would have gone to sit aside in some quiet booth. But it was summer and the previous day's lousy weather was continuing with the humidity stultifying. So we chose a table at the back, among the trees, to avoid any indiscreet eyes.

I'd asked to see him because the search done by Koula and her cousin, Spyros, had not revealed even one company owned or joint-owned by Vakirtzis. Spyros had even managed to get into the tax returns, but had found nothing. I began to have doubts about Logaras's reliability, but then I reflected that he no doubt knew what he was saying; we were the ones who didn't know where to look. And so I had decided once again to have recourse to Sotiropoulos, who was after all a colleague of his and, as was usually the case, would know far more than the Ministry of Trade.

This time, however, I was facing an uneasy Sotiropoulos. He took a sip of his iced coffee and stared at me with the look of someone in a tight corner.

'You're asking me to reveal the secrets of a colleague who died in a tragic manner. It's not exactly easy for me.'

'Secrets or skeletons? Because Logaras, who knows everything, seems to be talking more of skeletons.'

He remained silent and took another sip of his iced coffee.

'And there's another thing,' he said, even more tense. 'Vakirtzis and I both came from the same ideological background.'

'So what?'

All that stuff concerning ideological background meant nothing to me and I was at pains to understand where he was leading.

Apparently, however, he took my reaction as an expression of disparagement because it rankled him.

'You're quite right. It was my mistake to bring up ideology,' he said sarcastically. 'You coppers don't have a clue about the meaning of comradeship and solidarity.'

After several weeks, Sotiropoulos was back to his normal self. Except that, in the meantime, we had grown familiar and the relations between us had changed.

'You know, Sotiropoulos, how I used to refer to you before we got to know each other better?'

'How?'

'Robespierre in Armani. And with those little round glasses that you and your intellectual friends wear, like the ones that Nazi butcher Himmler used to wear.'

He stared at me for a moment in astonishment and then burst out laughing. 'You know, you're not far wrong.'

'But I'll give you one thing.'

'What?' he asked, genuinely curious.

'You're above board. You might use pressure to come up with a story or exaggerate your reports or make us out to be incompetent, but you never do it for your own ends. You don't try to scare or blackmail to make money for your businesses.'

He eyed me with satisfaction. 'I'm glad you give me that at least,' he said, his face beaming.

'So what's your relation with Vakirtzis that makes you want to cover for him? Didn't you see his place?'

'Yes.'

'And you're still in any doubt?' I didn't want to say anything about the notes we'd found on Stefanakos's laptop because it would only start his mouth watering. 'I still haven't found out how and from where he was filling his pockets, but he certainly had his finger in several pies, and I think you know about it. So why give me all that stuff about solidarity? What kind of solidarity is that? The "heat of the moment" kind?'

'Or the "anything for a comfortable life" kind,' he replied with a bitter smile. 'Why bother yourself about it?' He was silent for a moment and then added without looking at me: 'Vakirtzis had a brother, Menelaos Vakirtzis.'

The 'M' in Stefanakos's notes, I thought to myself. An entire cooperative was starting to appear. Favieros and his wife, Stefanakos and Lilian Stathatos, and the two brothers, Apostolos and Menelaos Vakirtzis. Of course, the last two were probably on the fringes of the group as they had to secure their participation through pressure and blackmail.

'You may have heard of Menelaos Vakirtzis as a mayor,' Sotiropoulos went on. 'But he's also a businessman. One of those who, unofficially, are surrounded by misappropriation, scandals, unfair trading and so on. Officially, however, nothing ever comes out into the open. On the contrary, he's continually nominated for mayor and he's been elected on the last three occasions. It's rumoured that all the hushing up and the nominations are due to his brother.' He turned and looked at me with that ironic expression of his. 'If you want, wait another three years. If he doesn't stand at the next local elections or if there's suddenly a shower of allegations, it means that the rumours were right.'

'Too long to wait.'

'So start investigating Menelaos Vakirtzis right away.'

'Don't you know what businesses he was involved in?' I asked, in the hope he might know something and save me some time.

'No, and I'm not interested any more. Since Vakirtzis died, his brother has ceased to concern me. He'll either make it as a businessman or he'll come to a bad end as mayor.'

The idea flashed through my mind to assign this too to Ghikas. But I immediately rejected it. I didn't know whether Menelaos Vakirtzis still had clout even after his brother's death. And it would have been a mistake to ask Ghikas to investigate people with clout. If he didn't refuse straight out, he'd no doubt feel so uncomfortable that he would go too easy on them.

I was about to settle on Koula and her cousin again when Zamanis suddenly came to mind. He'd be sure to know whether Favieros had any delings with Menelaos Vakirtzis. I also remembered something else that Stefanakos had noted: that his wife had paid 'M' in gold. It might have meant that she had contributed financially to his election campaign just as Favieros might have done. Again, Zamanis would be the one to know.

Of course, I knew from Yannelis that I wasn't his favourite person, but I wasn't going to lose any sleep over that. I wanted answers. Whether he gave them to me with a smile or with a frown made absolutely no difference to me.

On the other hand, it would be a good idea to get Koula to investigate Menelaos Vakirtzis so that I could go to see Zamanis prepared.

'Excuse me a moment,' I said to Sotiropoulos and I got up to phone Koula.

When I returned, Sotiropoulos had finished his iced coffee and was about to get up, but I stopped him.

'There's something else I want you to tell me. Do you know whether Favieros and Stefanakos's wife contributed to Menelaos Vakirtzis's election campaign?'

Sotiropoulos shrugged. 'It's very likely. But what do you have to gain by finding out? Parliamentary candidates, candidates for mayor, even candidates for the town council all find various ways of getting money out of businessmen. The businessmen give something to everyone, not because they expect to get it back, but because they believe in being safe rather than sorry. In my opinion, you'll get far more mileage out of investigating Menelaos Vakirtzis's businesses.'

'I intend to do that anyway. But if I manage to unravel the thread linking Vakirtzis's campaign contributors, I may come up with a lead to something else.'

Sotiropoulos gazed at me and smiled. 'You're a smart customer,' he said. 'It's not that common in the Greek Police Force, but you're a smart customer.' He paused for a moment and added: 'I'll make a few discreet enquiries. If I find out anything, I'll call you.'

We both got up to go: he to his TV channel and I to see Zamanis. I reached into my pocket to pay, but he stopped me.

'My turn,' he said. 'You paid last time.'

I hadn't paid, in fact, but I appreciated his kindness.

40

The fifty-year-old receptionist put down the receiver and looked at me with a sad expression on her face.

'Unfortunately, Mr Zamanis is extremely busy and can't see you.'

I was grateful to Yannelis for tipping me off and I had come prepared. I got up out of the armchair, beneath Favieros's watchful eye on the wall, and approached her.

'It's a pity he's not available now,' I said calmly. 'Please tell Mr Zamanis that tomorrow we'll ask him down to Security Headquarters to make an official statement.' The woman looked at me, trying to work out whether I meant it or whether I was bluffing. 'Following Apostolos Vakirtzis's suicide, things have taken a more serious turn,' I went on. 'We're now putting all our efforts into investigating the causes behind each suicide, because we want to prevent any more happening. If Mr Zamanis thinks I'm bluffing, he has only to call the Head of Security, Superintendent Ghikas, and have him confirm what I say.'

I finished my little speech and headed towards the exit, but, as I expected, the woman's voice stopped me.

'Please wait a moment, Inspector.'

I remained standing to show her that I wasn't going to wait for long. She again lifted up the receiver, used her other hand to screen her mouth, and began whispering something. Before very long, she put the receiver down and said to me with a smile: 'Mr Zamanis has agreed to see you.'

I walked towards the lift, expressing neither gratitude nor satisfaction in order to show her that it was all the same to me.

'Wait, someone will come to accompany you.'

'There's no need. I know the way,' I replied coldly.

I went up to the third floor, passed by the tiny stage-sets with the actors and actresses, and walked into the office of Zamanis's private secretary. She greeted me with the same slight nod of the head as before and, without saying a word, opened the door to Zamanis's office for me.

Zamanis had all the topographical surveys and plans he could find in his office open on his desk and was poring over them to underline just how busy he was.

'You seem to make it a habit of coming unannounced,' he said to me without looking up.

'Murders come unannounced too. Of course, the police take them on as contractors, are assigned to them, but neither the culprits nor their victims make any announcement.'

My reply made him lift his head and look at me. 'Murders?' he asked surprised. 'Up until now, we've been talking about suicides.'

'Following Vakirtzis's suicide, we're now talking openly about instigation to commit suicide, which is tantamount to murder. I'm no longer satisfying my personal curiosity. I'm trying to find out who drove your boss and two others to kill themselves and how I might avert any further suicides.'

He stared at me pensively. What I had told him had caught him off guard and had lessened his composure. 'Even if there's some logic behind all this, what I don't understand is why you believe that the cause is to be found somewhere in our companies. There are no deadly secrets hidden here, believe me.'

He said this with a degree of irony, perhaps in an attempt to regain his aplomb. I decided to be honest with him because, in that way, he would be more likely to open up to me.

'There are two elements common to Favieros, Stefanakos and Vakirtzis. One is their past. All three had met during their student years, had been involved in anti-Junta activities and had spent time in the cells of the Military Police. In other words, they knew each other very well.'

'And what's the other common element?'

'Their businesses. Apart from the businesses belonging to Jason

Favieros and Stefanakos's wife, Lilian Stathatos, there were also businesses owned jointly by Lilian Stathatos and Sotiria Favieros and by Lilian Stathatos and Jason Favieros.'

'There's no secret about all those. But where does Vakirtzis fit in to the businesses?'

'He doesn't, but his brother, Menelaos Vakirtzis, does.' I remained silent to see his reaction. He looked at me, waiting for me to continue. 'Apostolos Vakirtzis was a journalist and didn't want to expose himself as a businessman for two reasons: first, because he would lose his credibility, and, second, because by remaining inconspicuous he could help his brother much more effectively. Menelaos Vakirtzis had a mechanical and electrical installations company and a security systems company.' Again I waited to see whether he would say anything, but he remained quiet. 'What was the nature of your cooperation with the companies owned by Menelaos Vakirtzis?'

He shrugged and answered indifferently: 'We worked together on the same construction sites at the Olympic Village. We were responsible for the construction, and Menelaos Vakirtzis's company, Electrosys, took care of the electrical installations.'

'Is that all?'

'Yes, that's all.'

Without a word, I reached into my pocket and took out a photocopy of Stefanakos's notes and put it down before him. He read it, then slowly lifted his head and looked at me.

'What is it?'

'They're some notes that we found on Stefanakos's laptop. It says that Jason Favieros couldn't refuse Menelaos Vakirtzis because his brother knew too much and Favieros was scared of him. So there are two questions. What couldn't Favieros refuse Menelaos Vakirtzis and why was he scared of Apostolos Vakirtzis?'

He sighed. 'Menelaos Vakirtzis had become a pain in the neck,' he said slowly. 'To start with, he forced us, through his brother, to enter into a consortium with him. We would take care of the construction works and his company, Electrosys, the electrical work. Jason didn't want to even hear about it.'

'Why?'

'Because they're incompetent and do slapdash work. They're always behind schedule and we end up rushing around to pull the chestnuts out of the fire. Or the work they do is so shoddy that half the things don't work and we have to put them right.'

'Yes, but these notes are much more recent, they can't be referring to the consortium.'

'No. They're referring to the security systems at the Olympic complex.'

His reply took me by surprise. 'Do you also do security systems?'

He laughed involuntarily. 'No, but in order to get a letter of guarantee from the bank to tender for such a big contract, you need to have a high credit limit. And Menelaos Vakirtzis owes a great deal. So he was putting pressure on us to intercede in some way so he could secure the letter of guarantee.'

'Does that "in some way" mean that he wanted you to cover him?'

'More or less.'

'And you accepted, because his brother was putting pressure on you.'

'Exactly.'

'And why was Apostolos Vakirtzis putting pressure on you and not anyone else in order to help his brother? The banks, for instance?'

'Because he couldn't touch them. He could put pressure on various government circles, but they had grown tired of him and even more so of his brother.'

'That brings me to my second question. What did Jason Favieros have to fear from Apostolos Vakirtzis?'

He didn't answer immediately and I wasn't sure whether he was trying to order his words or restrain his accumulated anger.

'The real owner of the businesses was not Menelaos but his brother. Apostolos Vakirtzis collected information on everyone and everything. When the genuine information he had was not sufficient, he fabricated information himself and used this to exert pressure and to blackmail people till he got what he wanted. I'm sure that he had nothing on Jason. But how would we have been able to stop him if he began to defame us or sully our reputation on his programme or in his newspaper? We're businessmen, Inspector. And any defamation of our good name is detrimental to us.'

'At any rate, Jason Favieros, Loukas Stefanakos and Apostolos Vakirtzis knew each other from the time of the Junta.'

Zamanis shrugged. 'Perhaps, but of what significance is that? If you're looking to their common past and common struggles, forget it. After a certain point, each of them went their own way and, if it ever happened that they had a conflict of interest, you can be sure that solidarity and common struggles would have counted for nothing. Each of them would have looked to his own interests.'

Two irrational scenarios unfolded before me: three friends and comrades with a common past. The two of them – Favieros and Stefanakos – remained associates, while the third was blackmailing them in various ways in order to exploit them. The public life of the first two could explain their suicides. The third had gone a step further than just blackmail and had coerced them into committing suicide. That might have held up if the third hadn't committed suicide too. If it was murder, it might be the case that the first two had come to the end of their tether and had killed or had had someone else kill the third. But it wasn't murder, it was suicide. And the first two had committed suicide before the third. I couldn't work it out, and there was no point in my thinking about all that in Zamanis's office, so I got up to leave. This time he held out his hand.

'I don't know what to say,' he said. 'If it's as you say, then I hope with all my heart that you find the person who forced Jason into suicide. However, without wanting to disappoint you, I doubt very much that you'll succeed.'

I shook his hand, without saying anything. I didn't need his doubt too. My own was more than enough. As I was crossing the bridge of sighs, my pager, that I had started carrying around again, beeped. It was Ghikas's number. I called him from the phone in reception.

'Koula phoned me. Go straightaway to Vakirtzis's house in Vranas. She's found something that she thinks may be important.'

Koula and Spyros had gone that morning to take a look at

Vakirtzis's computer, after Ghikas had arranged it. I glanced at my watch. It was almost noon. I reflected that with the heat and the traffic I'd be well and truly sizzled by the time I got to Vranas, but I didn't have the luxury to wait till the sun went down.

41

To go from the First Cemetery to Vranas at midday is not the easiest thing in the world. I racked my brains trying to decide which was the shortest way, but there was only one: from Kifissias Avenue to the new Athens ring road. It's easy to say, but not at all easy to do, because the journey from Vassileos Konstantinou Avenue to Kifissias Avenue is an ordeal in the sweltering heat. At the section in Psychiko where the new flyover was being built, I ran into an endless traffic jam. While crawling along I passed the time reading the billboards: *Maroussi-Metamorphossi in three minutes via the Athens ring road*; *Yerakas-Koropi in four minutes via the Athens ring road.* Athens was, due to circumstances, truly the most Christian city in the world: you had to pass through fire and brimstone before entering paradise. You have to spit blood on the roads of Athens, which are either being dug up, are blocked off or are full of potholes, before attaining the paradise of the Athens ring road. I stepped on the accelerator and let rip, which as far as the Mirafiori was concerned meant fifty miles per hour maximum. The wind hit my face, but the freshness it brought was more psychological than anything, because the air was scorching.

The journey to the junction at Spata was, relatively speaking, a delight, but from the moment I turned into Marathonos Avenue, I left paradise behind and entered hell once more. In total, I had been driving for over two hours and by the time I reached Vakirtzis's three-story villa at Vranas, all I wanted to do was jump fully-clothed into the swimming pool. I resisted the temptation and climbed the steps leading to the terrace. It was baking quietly and tidily, with its swing seats and tables beneath umbrellas. There were no signs of the turmoil from the night on which Vakirtzis had committed suicide. It was as if it had never happened.

I walked into the sitting room and came upon a chubby woman of about forty, wearing a T-shirt and white shorts. Her hair was dyed auburn and her shorts revealed legs that would have been the envy of any footballer or even wrestlers.

'What do you want?' she asked as though talking to a house-to-house salesman.

'Inspector Haritos.'

My name must have rung a bell with her, because she came out with a ready smile. 'Ah, yes, Inspector. I'm Charoula Vakirtzis, Apostolos's er … widow.'

She took me by surprise, because I knew that Vakirtzis was separated. As her appearance had nothing of the look of the distraught widow, I dispensed with the condolences.

'From what I understood, Apostolos Vakirtzis was separated,' I said, more to needle her and see how she would react.

'Yes, we were living separately, but we weren't divorced.' She stressed this last phrase in order to justify the legality of her presence there. 'As I'm sure you can understand, as soon as I heard the tragic news, I rushed straight over. Besides, Apostolos has no family and someone had to tidy the place up.'

In other words, not only am I here legally, but I am also his legal heir, given that he didn't get a divorce. The more time went on, the more she was starting to get on my nerves.

'On the day of the incident, I spoke to a young woman …'

'Ah, his little floozy!' She cut in. 'The slut got her things together and took off when she heard I was returning. She'd had plenty out of him. Eventually the freebies come to an end.'

'Where are my assistants?'

'On the third floor, in Apostolos's study.'

I took to my heels, not out of fear but so as not to lose my temper with her. I climbed the stairs and in one breath reached the third floor, where Apostolos Vakirtzis had his study. Koula was kneeling down in front of the desk. She had opened the second drawer and was searching through the cassettes that I had seen on the night of the suicide. Spyros's eyes were still glued to the screen.

'Why did you call me urgently?' I asked Koula, who jumped to her feet as soon as she saw me.

She didn't reply, but went over to the desk, took a pile of papers and handed them to me without a word. I took one look at them and almost dropped them. In my hands, I was holding Vakirtzis's biography, the same copy that Logaras had sent to me.

It took me a moment to recover from the shock and think more clearly. So before sending the biography to me, Logaras had already sent it to Vakirtzis. Evidently, this had been part of the plan, but why? I had been taken aback and couldn't think straight. I decided to leave it for later and asked them whether they'd found anything on the computer.

'The guy simply had it for show,' Spyros cut in. 'At most, he played the odd game of patience or surfed the internet once in a blue moon.'

'Why do you say that?' I asked him. 'Because he didn't have a cleaning program?'

He turned round and gave me an ironic look. 'Not just because of that. When you turn on a computer, you can tell straightaway whether it's still set up as it was in the shop or whether it's been changed because it's been used. This one is like it was delivered this morning!'

'Did you come up with any other information?'

'No, but that doesn't mean that there wasn't any.'

He'd got me confused again and the way my head was spinning at that moment, I was ready to give him a clout round the ear. 'Spell it out for me slowly, will you, because I'm not with you.'

'Sometimes messages are sent to a computer together with a little program that automatically deletes them after a short while. Then there are others that come with a program that automatically returns them to their sender. So if there were any messages with programs like that attached, we won't find them.'

'And the biography? Why wasn't that deleted or returned?'

He shrugged. 'How should I know? Maybe they left it longer because the guy would need time to read it.'

I gradually started to understand what it was he was trying to explain to me. Logaras had sent other stuff to Vakirtzis too, but only for him to read. Once he had read them, they would be deleted or returned. He'd left the biography longer because it would take time to read it but also because it would be published in any case so there was no point in deleting it.

As there was no hope of our finding anything else on the computer, I turned my attention to more prosaic and humble hiding places, such as the drawers.

Did you find anything?' I asked Koula.

'From what I've seen, they're tapes of Vakirtzis's programmes.'

I leaned over and took hold of one of the cassettes. Written on it, like on all the others, was the date of the programme. I began looking for the programme of May 21st, the one on which Vakirtzis had blackmailed Stefanakos, according to what Stefanakos had written in his notes, but it wasn't there. My eyes fell on the bottom drawer with the security lock. It was still locked

'I searched, but I couldn't find the key,' Koula said.

'Go and bring Vakirtzis's wife here.'

'That's it. There's nothing else here,' said Spyros.

He switched off the computer and went over to the TV. He picked up the remote control, switched on the TV and planted himself in the armchair facing it. Forget the trees, forget the swimming pools. The only view that interested him was the view of a screen.

Koula came back with Mrs Vakirtzis. It seemed propriety had got the better of her because she had put on a pair of slacks.

'I'm looking for the key to this drawer, do you happen to have it?'

'No. Apostolos always carried it with him.'

Consequently, it had melted when Vakirtzis had set fire to himself and we would never find it.

'I have to open it.'

She shrugged indifferently. 'Open it if you want.'

'Call Ghikas and get him to send over a locksmith from Forensics,' I said to Koula.

I went down to the terrace to wait till the locksmith came. I sat down in the shade of an umbrella and tried to focus my thoughts. The fact that Logaras had sent a copy of his biography to Vakirtzis meant that he had most probably sent their biographies to the other two as well. They may have been deleted, but that didn't change anything. The question is why he sent them. If we excluded a few insinuating remarks here and there, the biographies were exceptionally flattering about the two men. Consequently, the only logical explanation was that Logaras wanted to convince the men that their reputation was safe. But what need had Favieros, Stefanakos and Vakirtzis of any posthumous reputation when they were top names in Greek society anyway? Would they have committed suicide in order to enter the pantheon on the basis of a biography by a certain Minas Logaras, a complete unknown? Unless their reputation was linked to something else. And that something else may have been hidden in what Spyros had told me upstairs. Together with the biography, Logaras had sent them various other documents that either deleted themselves or were returned to the sender. And what documents were they? We would never know, but they certainly must have had some connection with the biography. That's why when I'd read Stefanakos's biography, I'd had the impression that it was concocted, manufactured.

Another idea, of the kind that comes out of the blue, suddenly struck me. What if the public suicides had to do with the biography? What if the condition that their reputation would be saved was that they had to commit suicide before an audience? The explanation was plausible, but that still didn't answer the question why they agreed to this. What had motivated them?

No matter from what angle I looked at it, I could find no answer to the question. I got up and went down into the garden. In less than two minutes my head was like a hot brick. I walked past the pool and went to the place where Vakirtzis had set fire to himself. The traces had completely disappeared. The ground where his body had been and the burnt grass around had been dug over and freshly planted. Whether it had been planted with flowers or cucumbers I didn't know, because nothing had sprouted yet.

I heard the sound of a motorbike approaching in the distance. It was the locksmith from Forensics. He came to a stop a little way off, opened the box on the back of the bike and took out a smaller box with his tools. I waited for him beside the terrace steps.

'Good day, Inspector. What is it you want me to open?' he asked, coming up to me.

'A desk drawer with a security lock.'

We went up together to the third floor. Spyros was still sitting in front of the screen. Koula had put all of Vakirtzis's cassettes on top of his desk and she was arranging them.

'This drawer here,' I said to locksmith, pointing to it.

He glanced at it. 'Child's play.'

True enough, the second key he tried opened it. Koula and I looked inside it with anticipation. It contained just five cassettes. One was the one from May 21st that we had been looking for. The others were dated October, December, January and February, but without the year. It didn't take a great deal of imagination for me to realise that this was where Vakirtzis had hidden the tapes of those he had been blackmailing for favours.

'Take them and have them transcribed,' I said to Koula.

'I'll take all the others with me too.'

'Take them, but have these five transcribed first. They're the ones with the goods.'

Beneath the cassettes I found two envelopes. I opened the one and found a copy of the letter of protest to the Minister that Komi had shown to Favieros just before he committed suicide. Beneath it was a photocopy of a cheque for the sum of forty million drachma, around one hundred and seventeen thousand euros in today's currency. The cheque had been made out to cash and had no stamp, so it must have been one of Favieros's personal cheques. It wouldn't be too difficult to discover who had cashed it, but it would be more difficult to discover who was behind whoever had cashed it. That blackmailer Vakirtzis wouldn't have kept a photocopy if it wasn't a cheque for greasing someone's palm or buying someone off. Beneath this were photocopies of three property contracts. In all three, the public notary was Karyofyllis. So Vakirtzis knew about the network of real-estate agencies owned by Favieros and how they operated. That's why Favieros was scared of him.

The second envelope was on Stefanakos. But the only thing that related to Stefanakos was the draft law on the cultural identity of Albanians in Greece. Everything else concerned his wife. A quick glance revealed three photocopies of approvals for large amounts of funding from the EU. For Vakirtzis to have hold of them, they must have been granted to Stathatos as a result of her husband's political intervention. I also found another one, in English, that I would have to have translated, as my English wasn't up to it. Underneath all this, I unearthed another cheque for three hundred thousand euros. However, this one wasn't drawn on a Greek bank but on a bank in Bucharest.

If Vakirtzis had been murdered, we would have had Favieros and Stefanakos at least as accessories before the fact. He was blackmailing them and they had him killed. But the blackmailer had committed suicide too. This was where it all got complicated and you started to tear your hair out.

The locksmith was the first to leave. He was most likely swearing at us under his breath for having made him come all this way in the scorching heat for something that was child's play, but that was one of the joys of the profession.

It was the first time that we actually had our hands on some tangible evidence, even if we didn't know where it would lead.

'Well done, you two. You did a good job,' I said to Koula and Spyros, as we walked past the pool.

'I told you,' said Koula full of enthusiasm, 'Spyros is a whiz kid when it comes to computers. They're in his blood.'

'Yeah, okay, don't overdo it,' Spyros commented indifferently, because with today's generation modesty is usually expressed as indifference.

'You know, Spyros is thinking of going into forensics,' Koula went on, unabashed.

'Cut it out, Koula. Enough, for fuck's sake! All that was just between us, because I'm still toying with the idea. You're acting like a cop and it gets up my nose, damn it!'

'Hold on a bit, it's just a friendly chat. It's not an official interview!' I said, cutting in. 'All I want to ask you, and you don't have to answer, is why you want to enter the Police Force.'

'Okay then. If it means studying computers like I want to and having a job waiting for me on top of it, it'll be a real gas.'

My generation spoke about a 'golden opportunity', today's speaks about a 'real gas', but they're just as concerned to get themselves set up as we were.

'Think it over in your own good time. And if you decide, let Koula know. We'll take care of the rest.'

After all, Ghikas owed Koula a favour. And it wasn't a very big favour to put in a good word for her cousin. We reached the front gate. I saw Spyros getting on Koula's bike and Koula climbing on behind him. Before they set off, Koula turned and winked at me. I realised she was doing it to let Spyros show off.

I had parked the Mirafiori in the shade of a tree, so it wasn't like an oven inside, as usual. Whether it would get me to Athens without the radiator boiling over, I had no idea.

42

The idea came to me during the night. I suddenly felt myself jump and sit up in bed. I didn't know whether it had happened in a dream or not, though I don't recall dreaming about Logaras or about the three suicides at that moment. Whenever I jump like that in the night and my mind is fuzzy, I do what everyone does: I go to the kitchen for a glass of water. Then I went into the sitting room and sat down in the doorway to the balcony, half inside and half outside.

What Logaras had sent to Favieros, Stefanakos and Vakirtzis and then deleted or had returned to him was incriminating evidence. Logaras had the proof in his hands and was threatening them with public vilification. The biography was the alternative solution, the lesser of two evils, so to speak: either you agree to commit suicide publicly and I publish a flattering biography and so safeguard your reputation, or you remain alive and I vilify you so you vanish from the scene. He'd sent them the incriminating evidence electronically so that they could see that he wasn't bluffing. After they had seen it, it was automatically deleted or returned to the sender by means of the program that Spyros had explained to me. As for the biography, he let them keep it so they could read it and see that he wasn't selling them a pig in a poke.

The question still remained, however: what were the trump cards that Logaras was holding and where had he found them? And the question that followed on: if they really were trump cards, why weren't they known to others? How come nothing had leaked out? We were talking here of three public figures. Was it possible that all three had such skeletons in their cupboards that they preferred death to exposure and that no one else had heard anything about it other than Logaras? And given that no one else had come up with this information so far, how was Logaras able to dig it up?

When I eventually went back to bed at around six, the questions were still unanswered and I couldn't get back to sleep. With some effort, I managed to doze a bit till around eight, when I jumped up for a second time at the sound of the phone ringing. Ghikas had called me to tell me that the Minister was expecting us at ten. Before I left, I phoned Koula and told her to get her cousin and go to Domitis and make a thorough search of Favieros's computer. I didn't expect them to find anything, but it's always a good idea to tie up any loose ends.

I found myself sitting, together with Ghikas, facing the Minister and I was watching him comparing the two copies of Vakirtzis's biography: the one that had been sent to me and the one we'd found on his computer. I had brought both of them along with me so that he could see that they were identical.

He looked up and slowly asked me: 'Do you think he sent their biographies to all three of them first?'

I explained my theory to him. Ghikas had already heard it outside in the corridor and agreed with me. I told him how, in my opinion, the public suicide was Logaras's condition for publishing the biography. Then I went on to outline the conclusions I'd come to early that morning: that Logaras had been in possession of information detrimental to them and that the biography was a respectable way out for them. They could choose public suicide and safeguard their reputation or go on living and have it tarnished.

'What information could this Logaras have had?' asked the Minister.

'I'll only be able to tell you that when I discover who he is. I think it's someone from their immediate environment and, probably, someone from their past.'

He looked at me curiously. 'How did you reach that conclusion?'

'Because such secrets can only be secrets from the past. If they had to do with present-day scandals, eventually every reporter would have got hold of them and we'd have read about them in the papers. I'd go so far as to say that whatever the secret is, it's probably common to all three. It's no coincidence that all three had a common past and were working together in the present, even though this involved blackmail in Vakirtzis's case.'

He looked at us and we could tell from his expression that he could find nothing to counter what I'd said. 'What are our chances of discovering who this Logaras is?'

'Our one and only chance is if he reveals himself,' Ghikas replied. 'Otherwise, the chances are zero. He's hiding behind a pseudonym and so far he's managed to avoid leaving any traces.'

The Minister leaned back in his seat and looked at us in disappointment. 'In other words, he has us where he wants us.'

'Not exactly. We can go down a different route,' I countered. 'We can investigate the past of all three and try to discover their common secret for ourselves. If we succeed, it's quite probable that we'll also discover the identity of Logaras.'

'And what do you need to do that?'

'Apart from mobilising the department,' Ghikas said, cutting in again, 'we'll also need to involve the Fraud Squad.'

'Can we exclude the possibility that it has some connection with the Junta? Perhaps they succumbed to the torture and spoke, for example, and Logaras knows about it?'

'All that's been written off, Minister. No one cares anymore.'

'Besides, it's highly improbable that all three were informers,' I added. 'I'm certain that whatever their secret may be, it's one they have in common and at least involves the three who committed suicide. Let's hope it doesn't involve others, too, because the deaths will continue.'

'All right. I'll undertake to inform the Fraud Squad. But the investigations must be discreet and there must be no leaks.'

'Given that we've kept them under wraps so far, I think it's safe to say that we'll be able to continue to do so,' Ghikas replied. 'Having the Inspector conduct his own private enquiries has paid off.'

I didn't know whether I would be able to continue working from home or whether I'd need to return to the office. I decided to leave that question for later, depending on how things panned out.

We returned to Security Headquarters in Ghikas's limousine.

Since Vakirtzis's suicide, he'd been giving me the kid-glove treatment.

'This case has turned my life upside down,' he said to me as we were driving down Mesogheion Avenue. 'I even had to cut my holidays short and come back to the office.'

'And I had to postpone mine, even though I'm on sick leave,' I replied, so he wouldn't think he was the only one making sacrifices.

'I wouldn't care so much about the holidays if it wasn't for my wife. I left her on her own in Spetses and every day she phones me to ask me when I'm going back. It's getting on my nerves.'

'I know what you mean,' I said. He looked at me, I nodded my head, and we were in complete accord.

When we reached Security Headquarters, I went straight up to the third floor and into my assistants' office. Dermitzakis was arranging some files, while Vlassopoulos was immersed in a hi-fi magazine. As soon as he saw me enter, he leapt to his feet mouthing 'Inspector!' while trying, blindly, to stash the magazine in one of the drawers.

'Never mind. I'm on sick leave, have you forgotten?'

Dermitzakis turned and greeted me: 'Good to see you, Inspector.'

'Listen to me very carefully,' I said to them, closing the door of the office. 'You know about the suicides of Favieros, Stefanakos and Vakirtzis?'

'How couldn't we? They've created such a buzz,' said Dermitzakis.

'I want you both to look into their pasts. Systematically and in detail. And, most important of all, with the utmost discretion. Nothing must leak out, no one must hear about it.'

'Why?' asked Vlassopoulos.

'What did I tell you the last time I was here, Vlassopoulos? If I tell you to do something, you'll do it without asking for any explanations.'

'Right you are, Inspector.'

'What are we looking for, exactly?' said Dermitzakis, cutting in.

'I don't know. Most likely all three of them committed suicide for the same reason, so it must be to do with something they all have in common. But I can't give you any more details than that, nor can I tell you where to start looking. If you need any help, contact me or go direct to the Chief. I've spoken to him.'

'How urgent is it?' Demitzakis, who had a weakness for superfluous questions, went on.

'Why aren't you already on your way?' was my answer.

I was about to leave when Vlassopoulos stopped me. 'Just a moment, Inspector. Would you come with us?'

I saw them shooting a meaningful look at each other and I was curious. Vlassopoulos opened the door and went out first. I followed him and Dermitzakis brought up the rear. They took me as far as the door of my office. Vlassopoulos opened the door and stood aside to allow me to pass.

I halted in the doorway. My office was empty.

'Where's Yanoutsos?' I asked.

'He got his marching orders the day after you came by,' Vlassopoulos said smiling. 'The Chief called him upstairs and since then he's never been seen again. It seems he collected his stuff while we were out.'

My desk was clean and tidy, just as I always left it when leaving work.

'Seems he tidied up, too,' I muttered.

'Are you joking? We did that. So that you'd find it just as you'd left it.'

So that was what was behind the look they'd given each other. 'Thank you. You've made my day.'

I walked in and sat down at my desk. The two of them left me alone, closing the door quietly behind them.

43

Sotiropoulos found me the following morning in the same place. Not that I had spent all night in the office; it was simply that it was no longer possible for me to work from the house and I had decided to return. I had said a prayer and then announced it to Adriani. She'd given me one of those icy looks of hers that she had been keeping in the freezer because of the summer.

'Now you're cancelling your sick leave, it'll be our holidays next,' was her only comment.

I almost told her to go and keep Mrs Ghikas company in Spetses, but I held my tongue, because it would have been at least a week before we were back on speaking terms. Then we'd have to go through the whole rigmarole of my having to wait for her to cook me my favourite stuffed tomatoes as a sign that she was ready to make up. Besides, I intended to keep my promise to her about the holidays.

'It's a good thing we didn't leave. Ghikas had to cut his holidays short and come back. The Minister himself has taken a personal interest in the case so what can you do? When it's all over, we'll take off the day after, I promise.'

She didn't reply, indicating that she had noted what I'd said though she wasn't fully convinced. Anyhow, it softened her attitude.

My other problem was how to persuade Ghikas to let me have Koula till the end of the investigations. His face turned sour.

'I don't want her to get a taste for it because I won't be able to keep her under control afterwards.'

'Koula has been on the case from the beginning. She's been keeping notes and she knows all the details. It'll be even worse for you if I have to keep coming and disturbing her from her work every so often or if I'm obliged to keep asking her to come down.'

He saw that there was no other way and half uttered, 'Okay'. My two assistants gawped when they heard that Koula was moving into their office for a time and that she would be assisting in the investigation. Dermitzakis was about to ask something, but I reminded him that I didn't accept questions.

I don't know how the press reporters found out that I was back, but they suddenly all burst into my office with Sotiropoulos at their head, as he was justifiably their leader. I had agreed with Ghikas to tell them that my sick leave was over and that I had returned to work. First we got the 'welcome backs' and the 'thank yous' over with.

'You've become something of a legend,' said one short brunette, who wore red tights in winter and a red skirt in summer.

I made a joke of it. 'Don't overdo it because it'll go to my head and I'll start seeing you by appointment one by one.'

'Anyhow, you didn't miss very much while you were away,' said one conventional-looking young man with shiny hair and a crocodile printed on his T-shirt.

'Apart from the Philip of Macedon business,' added a well-coiffured blonde.

'What happened in the end with those three?' asked another woman. 'I've been away on leave and I've missed a few episodes.'

'From what I know, the file on them is being prepared and they are to be indicted for the murder of the two Kurds,' I replied. I had no idea if that was the case, but I'd agreed with the Minister that this was what we would say.

'And the suicides?' asked the young man with the shiny hair.

'Suicides are suicides and there's nothing we can do about it.'

'Inspector Yanoutsos thought differently.'

'I don't know what Inspector Yanoutsos thought. All I know is that when someone commits suicide, we can neither interrogate him nor arrest him. Consequently, the case closes automatically,' I replied with some effrontery.

Fortunately, Sotiropoulos hastened to my rescue. 'Come on now, let's not bother the Inspector with nonsense on his first day back in the office,' he said with the authority of a leader. 'Whoever wants to know what Yanoutsos thinks can go and ask him.'

It appeared that the hint was taken, because all of them had heard in the meantime that Yanoutsos had been given his marching orders and there was the sound of ironic tittering. Then we once again went through the formalities of the 'welcome backs' and the 'thank yous' and they all left, apart from Sotiropoulos, who closed the door and came and stood in front of me.

'Any news?' he asked.

I didn't want to tell him about the biography we'd found on Vakirtzis's computer. After all, he was a journalist and I couldn't keep subjecting him to temptation. Eventually, he'd succumb and I'd be left regretting it.

'All we know with certainty is their common background.'

'What do you mean?'

'All three of them mixed in the same circles, were involved in the struggle against the Junta and spent time in the cells of the Military Police. This Logaras must know something from their past that he was using to blackmail them.'

He thought about it. 'That makes sense. It also explains the biographies.'

'How? Enlighten me,' I said, curious.

'He brought out the biographies afterwards in order to muddy the waters.'

I might have had the same thought, if I hadn't known that Logaras had sent the biographies to his victims first. On the other hand, it would suit me if he were to come out with his version, because he, too, would be muddying the waters and that would be to my advantage.

'We can't exclude the possibility.' He gave me a wily look, pleased with himself. 'Could you see what you can find out?' I said to him.

'Find out about what?'

'Something from their past.'

'If it's a long way in the past, it'll be difficult. Maybe the files kept during the Junta would be of more help.'

'They were burned in Keratsini, have you forgotten?'

He laughed. 'Come on now, Haritos. The only things that got burned in Keratsini were storeroom inventories and newspapers!'

'No matter how unbelievable it may seem to you, they were burned,' I insisted.

He went on laughing. 'Okay, then search among the ashes. I'm sure that not everything was burned,' he added meaningfully. 'Anyhow, I'll do what I can.'

He left and I called Koula in. She was wearing jeans, a T-shirt, no make-up and her hair in a ponytail, just as on the first day she had come to my house. Ghikas's model in uniform was still not back on duty.

'What happened with the computer in Favieros's office?'

'Just as you expected. Zilch.'

'Not even a copy of the biography?'

'No.'

'And the papers with the cassettes that we found at Vakirtzis's home?' She placed an envelope she had been holding under her arm in front of me. 'Did you send the cassettes to be transcribed?'

'This morning, all apart from one. The one from May 12th that we needed urgently. I had Spyros transcribe it last night. If he wants to join the Force, he can afford to show a little eagerness. You'll find it in the envelope,' she said with a coy smile.

'Well done. What else is there?'

'Spyros and I thought of going and taking a look at the computer in Favieros's home in Porto Rafti.'

'I don't think you'll find anything, but take a look so we don't leave any stones unturned.'

Koula left and I sat comfortably to read the transcription of Vakirtzis's programme. My first reaction after reading the first few pages was that if Vakirtzis had wanted to incite the toughs belonging to the Philip of Macedon organisation to kill Stefanakos, he couldn't have done it in a better way. The entire programme consisted of Vakirtzis ranting and raving about Stefanakos's proposals for the recognition of immigrant culture and for the introduction of their languages into the state schools.

Vakirtzis wasn't advocating nationalism, on the contrary, he attacked Stefanakos from the left. He set himself up as the voice of the unemployed. The reason, according to Vakirtzis, why unemployment was not falling even though the number of job opportunities was rising was because the new positions were going to the immigrants. The result was that Greek workers were being done out of their rights. The immigrants were preferred because they worked longer hours for below the minimum wage. If Stefanakos's proposals prevailed, immigrants would become a permanent feature in Greece which would increase the prospect of unemployment for the Greeks. The parting shot crowned it all:

> All right, Mr Stefanakos. I can accept that the issue of human rights has become a personal crusade for you. I can even ignore rumours that you do this purely for personal gain. Can't you see, however, what cost your proposals entail? Are you proposing, then, that we keep all the Albanians, Bulgarians, Romanians and Serbs here and send our own people to Albania, Bulgaria and Romania to find work?

That question alone would have been more than enough to incite the Philip of Macedon nationalists to kill Stefanakos and all the members of the Greek Parliament along with him. The remainder of the programme confirmed this. The phone calls came one after the other from idlers of both sexes with streams of abuse about the foreigners who were stealing their jobs and ruining their wonderful country.

I was starting to lose interest from constantly reading the questions and answers between the listeners and Vakirtzis when, towards the end of the programme, Vakirtzis came out with another comment that I found intriguing:

> Who doesn't want to see our neighbours in the Balkans progressing? But a much greater service is done both to them and to us by those who create jobs and make investments in their own countries. If

> Stefanakos wants to help our Balkan neighbours, he should support those Greeks who are creating jobs there and not the foreigners who are taking our jobs in Greece.

That was the two-sided game that Vakirtzis was playing. On the one hand, he was making a scathing attack on Stefanakos that could only harm him politically, yet, at the same time, he was showing support for his wife, who secured EU funds and consequently jobs in the Balkan countries. So that was the message. He was making it clear to Stefanakos that he too was interested, using his brother as a front, in opening up in the Balkans.

Why didn't Stefanakos take Vakirtzis to court? Given what he had said against him and, more particularly, the way he had said it, Stefanakos could have easily sued him for defamation of character. So why didn't he? Out of a sense of hackneyed comradeship and belated solidarity, perhaps? I thought about it for a moment but rejected it. The answer was to be found in the envelope that Koula had left in front of me: in the photocopy of a cheque for three thousand euros drawn on a bank in Bucharest that Vakirtzis had had in his possession.

44

Stathatos had her eyes glued to the photocopy of the cheque drawn on the bank in Bucharest. Her problem wasn't with the Romanian, but with how she might gain time while deciding how to confront its bearer, in other words, me.

'Where did you find it?' she asked me eventually.

'In a drawer in Apostolos Vakirtzis's desk. Together with other information he was safeguarding. Among which was a recording of a programme about your husband.'

'Ah, the infamous programme,' she commented.

An embarrassing silence followed. Stathatos didn't know how to continue, nor I how to begin. I wondered whether I should come straight to the point or whether I should use a roundabout way. I decided upon the first approach.

'Was Apostolos Vakirtzis blackmailing you?'

Almost mechanically, she adopted her self-confident and condescending expression. 'Now, now, Inspector. You see conspiracies everywhere ...'

'I listened to the programme and the attack made by Vakirtzis on your husband. Were there any other motives behind it in your opinion?'

She shrugged. 'No, that's what he believed. Following the fall of the communist regimes, leftist nationalism became very fashionable.'

'Perhaps, but towards the end of the programme, Vakirtzis came out with something rather interesting.' I reached into my pocket and took out the sheet of paper where I had written Vakirtzis's words and I read aloud: '"Who doesn't want to see our neighbours in the Balkans progressing? But a much greater service is done both to them and to us by those who create jobs and make investments in their own countries." That comment should make you sit up, Mrs Stathatos. He's sending you a message that he regards what you are doing as something positive and he would like to be involved in it. If you take it in conjunction with the cheque we found among his papers, it says a lot.'

She was no longer in any mood to help me shed some light on the matter. She simply looked at me in silence.

'I've said it several times, to you, to Mr Zamanis and to Mrs Yannelis, that we are not investigating your businesses or your dealings. All we are interested in is finding out the reasons behind the three suicides and for one reason alone: in order to prevent any others. This is our only concern.'

She continued to look at me pensively and let out a sigh. 'You're right. He was blackmailing us. Both Loukas and myself. And, naturally, we weren't the only ones. Vakirtzis was blackmailing politicians, businessmen, publishers, not to get money out of them, but for favours and information that he then used against them.'

'And you … what favours were you doing him?'

'Business people want their peace of mind, Inspector. Vakirtzis was well aware of that.'

'And?'

'I secured two large projects in the Balkans for his company Electrosys. Also …' She stopped abruptly.

'It would help me if you were to tell me more,' I urged her gently.

She shrugged. 'Anyhow, it's no longer of any importance. I secured him a fee for promoting a Balkan country on his programme. I'm not going to tell you which country, but the fee didn't come out of the country's funds. I paid it out of my own pocket.' She smiled quite unexpectedly. 'At least I'll save on that now. But I'm continuing to support the projects undertaken by Elecrosys because, if anything goes wrong, I'm the one who'll be compromised.'

She had been extremely honest with me and I didn't want to be any less with her. 'I can't see in what you've told me any motive for your husband's suicide or that of Jason Favieros for that matter and certainly not of Vakirtzis.'

She smiled with satisfaction. 'I knew that from the start, but you wouldn't believe me.'

'Do you think they might have had some common secret from the past that could have led them to suicide? I'm asking because they knew each other, took part in the same struggles and had been locked up together in the cells of the Military Police.'

'What can I tell you? I couldn't say no with certainty. But I was studying in London then and I had no idea what was going on here. I met Loukas much later, after the fall of the Junta, when I returned to Greece.'

'Would Mrs Favieros know?'

She let out a spontaneous laugh. 'Good Lord, no. Ioanna kept out of all that and she got upset whenever Jason talked about the resistance.' She reflected a moment. 'The only person who might know something is Xenophon Zamanis, but even if he did, he wouldn't tell you. He's one of the old school and he still believes in the underground's code of silence.'

I may have felt some satisfaction at finally having persuaded Stathatos to open up to me, but that was of little practical value, because she had told me nothing that would give me a lead.

I got up to take my leave of her, but her farewell was far from cordial. 'I trust this will be the last time that we meet, Inspector,' she said. 'I find your presence distressful, as I don't like talking either about my husband or about my businesses.'

'I quite understand,' I said in all sincerity.

As I turned into Vikelas Street, I toyed with the idea of paying a call on Zamanis. But I thought better of it, coming to agree with Stathatos's opinion. Apart from his dedication to the ideals of conspiracy, Zamanis was even more fed up of seeing me than Stathatos and he would send me packing as soon as he heard my name. I would wait first to see what Vlassopoulos and Dermitzakis came up with. I very much doubted they would discover the common secret linking the three men, but they might discover something that would help me to break Zamanis's silence.

It was six in the evening and I decided to go home. Before I'd left the office, Koula had phoned me to say that I would have to rule out getting anything from Favieros's computer in Porto Rafti. So I wasn't expecting any more earth-shattering news unless, of course, another new biography by Logaras was delivered to me. The thought made me shudder, but I tried to convince myself that no such thing would happen.

Everything was quiet when I got home and I heaved a sigh of relief. Adriani was sitting in her usual place of honour in front of the TV. The air conditioning was on and the room was cool. She had had it on regularly during the previous few days.

'I see you've got used to the air conditioning,' I said to tease her.

'I put it on so the money we paid for it won't go to waste,' was her glib reply.

I sat down beside her to watch whatever was on till it was time for the news bulletin, but the only choice was between indifferent chat shows and game shows. After five minutes, I'd had enough. I was about to withdraw to my dictionaries, when I felt two hands covering my eyes.

'Katerina!' I shouted, because we had played that game when she was a little girl.

'So you haven't forgotten our game, eh?' I heard her say, as she pulled her hands away from my eyes and wrapped them round my neck.

'What time did you arrive?'

'On the 12.10 from Thessaloniki. We were at Larissa Station just after six.'

'And why didn't you tell us you were coming?'

'So I could see you as you are now,' she said laughing.

'How long are you staying?' I asking, hugging her. From the moment she came home, I was always immediately gripped by the fear of her leaving.

'I'm staying a week. Then Fanis and I are going on holiday and in August, when Athens is empty, I'll be back here again.'

'We'd better make plans for going in July, because I can't see us leaving in August,' said Adriani, cutting in.

'We'll go, don't worry. Besides, I can't see this case going on for much longer.'

'Do you really believe that?' asked Katerina.

'It's like this, dear. Either the investigation will stop or the suicides will.'

'And what if the suicides don't stop?' asked Adriani. She had made a hobby of bringing bad luck.

'Then we'll go away so I won't see them.'

I almost believed it when I said it. I would have found it unbearable to stay in a scorching Athens waiting for my daughter to get back from her holidays. Whereas being on a cool island counting the days till I would return to Athens and find my daughter waiting for me seemed a much better prospect, whichever way you looked at it.

45

It had been months since I had experienced the delight of the family breakfast in the kitchen. I certainly hadn't felt it since returning from the hospital. It was nine in the morning and the three of us were sitting round the table: Adriani with her cup of tea, Katerina with her iced coffee and me with my sweet Greek coffee. We were all sipping at our beverages, with Adriani casting a sideways glance at Katerina every so often. I attributed it to the fact that she had missed her and couldn't get enough of looking at her, but, as usual, I was wrong.

'So, Pop, do you have any objections to meeting Fanis's folks?' Katerina suddenly asked me.

I immediately understood Adriani's sideways glances. She had been waiting impatiently for her daughter to broach the topic. I must have been expecting it too, because it didn't surprise me.

'Is there an engagement in the air, or am I mistaken?' I asked calmly.

'Call it what you like, but Fanis knows you both and I know Fanis's parents, and only our parents haven't met each other. So we decided to get you together before we go off on holiday.' She paused momentarily and then added somewhat restrainedly: 'Fanis's parents are quite keen on the idea.'

'The question is whether it's something you and Fanis want.'

'It is,' she answered without hesitation.

'So arrange it for whenever you want.' She got up and planted a kiss on my cheek.

'Anyhow, my opinion is that if we're going to meet, we should exchange the rings too,' Adriani cut in.

'Mum, don't start rushing things. Everything in its own good time.'

'Katerina dear, your father is a police officer, and when the bonds aren't tied officially, the rumours start to fly.'

'And when did the police start arresting couples not wearing engagement rings?' I asked her.

She was about to have a go at me when the doorbell rang and Katerina got up to see who it was. Adriani took a time-out and waited for her daughter to return before continuing.

'Dad, it's for you!' Katerina shouted from outside.

I suddenly feared the worst. I left my coffee and rushed to the front door. I encountered a young lad wearing a helmet and carrying a shoulder bag, the classic attire of a courier.

'Sign here!' he said and thrust the envelope together with the receipt into my face.

It was exactly the same kind of envelope as the one containing Vakirtzis's biography. Instead of taking hold of the envelope, I grabbed hold of the lad and pulled him into the house.

'Tell me who gave you this envelope and where! I want the exact address and a full description!'

'What's got into you, Dad?' I heard Katerina's voice but it was no time for explanations.

The young lad looked terrified and didn't know whether he was dealing with a policeman or a madman. '12 Nisaias Street,' he murmured. 'It's written there.'

It was the deserted ramshackle house that Logaras always gave as his address.

'An old house?'

'Yes.'

'And where were they waiting for you? Inside or out?'

'Outside, on the pavement.'

'And who gave you the envelope? I want you to describe him to me in every detail.'

He reflected for a moment. 'An Asian girl. Thai, Filipino, I couldn't say. Small, a little chubby, wearing jeans and a brown T-shirt.'

The simplest thing in the world. You send your Filipino maid to hand over the envelope in front of a deserted house so the police would have no chance of ever finding her.

'Where did the order to pick up the envelope come from?'

'I don't know. The orders are taken by the people at the central office. They notify the courier for that area to go and pick it up.'

I scribbled my initials on the receipt and took the envelope. The lad ran through the door and jumped into the lift before I changed my mind.

'What's got into you?' Katerina asked again, staring at me strangely.

'Vakirtzis's biography was sent to me by courier and in exactly the same kind of envelope!'

She realised what that meant and stood over me to see what was in the envelope. The biography wasn't as thick as the previous ones because, as I held the envelope, I could tell that whatever was in it was thin and light. I ripped it open, but, instead of finding paper, I found a piece of red material folded into four. I opened it up and it turned out to be a T-shirt imprinted with the face of Che Guevara.

Something fell out of the T-shirt. Katerina bent down and picked it up. It was a CD in its case.

I stared at the T-shirt with the Che Guevara face and at the CD and I didn't know what to make of them.

'What does it mean? Is he sending you the Che Guevara T-shirt as a gift?' asked Katerina, who was equally puzzled.

'He wants to tell me something. It's a message, but I don't understand it.'

Before going any further, I decided to finish with the formalities. I looked at the shipping document attached to the envelope to find the number of the agency and I phoned straightaway.

'Inspector Haritos, Homicide Division. I've just received an envelope from you and I want to find out some details.'

'Could you give me the number of the shipping document, please?' came the sound of a woman's voice.

I gave it to her, waited just a few seconds and heard her voice again.

'Yes, Inspector. What is it you want to know exactly?'

'I want to know how you were contacted to pick up the envelope.'

'By phone, from what I can see.'

'Did you by any chance keep a phone number?'

'No, Inspector. Just the address. 12 Nisaias Street, behind the Attiki Station.'

'All right, thank you.'

Katerina was standing in front of me and staring at me with that inquisitive look of hers.

'Nothing. They didn't leave a phone number, just an address. The derelict house.'

'What are you going to do now?'

'I don't know. I need to think a little.'

'So you've managed to infect your daughter now,' said Adriani, always coming out with her opinion at the most inappropriate times. 'Come on, Katerina dear, come and tell me what you want me to cook for Fanis's parents.'

Katerina winked at me and went off with her mother without brooking any objections. Evidently, in order to leave me in peace to think, though in the meantime I had decided that it would be better if I got my things together and went to the office. Perhaps Vlassopoulos and Dermitzakis would have come up with something. I stared again at the T-shirt and the CD I was holding in my hands, but they still meant nothing to me. So what? A Che Guevara T-shirt that you can find in any wastebin or hanging in any number of shops that sell boots and imitation army uniforms. As for the CD, I was unable to listen to it because I didn't have a CD player. Our audiovisual needs were met by the TV and occasionally by a radio-cassette player, of which only the radio had ever been used.

I put the T-shirt and the CD in a plastic bag and went out of the house. Halfway to the corner of the street, where the Mirafiori was parked, I suddenly stopped in my tracks. Why the office? If there was a message behind these two objects, the most suitable person to decode it for me was Zissis. I'd go to see him instead.

46

When it's hot in Halandri, it's sweltering in Ambelokipi. And when it's sweltering in Ambelokipi, it's boiling in Acharnon. And when it's boiling in Acharnon, it's sizzling in Dekeleias Street. I left the boiling pot of Acharnon and turned into the frying pan of Dekeleias Street. As I drove up it, I had the impression that the asphalt, the concrete and the glass were all emitting red-hot lava that was burning my face. A few ladies and several pensioners were sitting under the umbrellas at Kanakis's and were gazing languorously at the orange juice or ice cream before them, barely able to reach out and pick it up.

I stopped at the first kiosk and bought a bottle of water that I downed in one go to clear my parched throat. I prayed that Zissis wouldn't have finished watering his plants that morning so that I'd be able to cool down under the hose.

I must have arrived about a minute too late as the cement in the yard was still wet and steaming. Zissis was sitting upstairs, in the doorway, half inside the house and half outside on the balcony, drinking his coffee. He saw me coming but continued drinking his coffee as though he hadn't seen me, either because he didn't want to notice me or because I wasn't particularly noteworthy. I would discover that as soon as I saw the expression on his face when I had him before me. I slowly climbed the steps leading up to his place, holding the plastic bag in my hands.

'I need to pick your brains.'

We had dispensed with the usual 'good mornings' and 'welcomes'. Sometimes months passed when we didn't see each other, yet it was as if we were going in and out of each other's house all day long. He got up without saying a word and went inside. I watched him going into the kitchen and I sat on one of the two old wooden chairs that, together with the café-style table, constituted his furniture. In less than five minutes, he was back with my coffee, which he put, still not saying a word, in front of me on the table.

I suddenly had a vision of how things would be if I didn't have Adriani and Katerina. Every day, we'd sit together, two miserable old men, and make coffee for each other that we'd drink in silence. It would be the first copper-commie cooperative in the history of the world. I went along with his game and, without saying a word, I took the red Che Guevara T-shirt out of the plastic bag and handed it to him. He took it, looked at it carefully on both sides, and said slowly:

'What is it, a gift for me for the summer?'

'It's a gift for me. It was sent to me by Minas Logaras, the one who wrote the biographies on Favieros and Stefanakos.'

I began telling him about all the similarities in the circumstances of the three suicides, and also in the biographies of the three men. I explained how Logaras had sent the third biography to my home, just before Vakartzis's suicide.

'Do you see what I'm telling you? First the biography and now this. He's playing games with me and now he's sending me messages. That's why I've come to you. Maybe you can help me discover what it is he's trying to tell me.'

He again examined the T-shirt, turned it inside out, but didn't seem to come up with anything. 'One of those T-shirts that you can find anywhere and that make a mockery of Che,' he said, shrugging his shoulders. 'So what's he trying to tell you?'

'There was another gift too.' I took out the CD and handed it to him. 'Perhaps together they might make more sense.'

He took hold of the CD and went over to the stereo system on the edge of his huge bookcase. Despite the stifling heat, I felt overcome with excitement. What was I expecting to hear? Perhaps a recorded message from Logaras explaining why he was doing all this or why he had obliged the three men to commit suicide, or some challenge, perhaps, in the form of a game, or even some ironic remarks. Instead, I heard a Latin American song with guitar accompaniment.

It was pleasant enough, but it didn't solve the mystery for me; on the contrary, it only deepened it. A Che Guevara T-shirt and a Latin American song, with the usual guitar accompaniment. What could they mean? And what connection could Favieros, Stefanakos and Vakirtzis possibly have with Latin America? So far, I hadn't found the slightest shred of evidence that might connect them in any way. Consequently, it must have been something else that Logaras was trying to tell me, or perhaps he wanted to turn my attention elsewhere. But where?

I was awakened from my thoughts by the sound of Zissis's voice. There he was, an old man, bald and stubbly, with half his teeth missing, holding a cigarette between his yellowed fingers, singing a Latin American song in a loud voice, while the tears ran down his cheeks. I got the impression that he was singing with a slight Vlach accent, but I wouldn't swear on it because I didn't understand a word. I couldn't understand the song or why Zissis was crying, or anything for that matter. All I managed to catch were the words 'Commandante Che Guevara' every so often. It was the only phrase connecting the song with the T-shirt.

I waited for the song to end in the hope that some explanation or message would be forthcoming, but all that followed was silence. There was nothing else on the CD. Zissis had fallen silent, too. His eyes were still filled with tears. I've said it before, I'm not very good at expressing my feelings. That's why I preferred to fast-forward and come straight to the point.

'Make anything of it?' I asked him.

He got up without saying anything and went out of the room. I suspected that something had flashed through his mind, but I knew I would have to be patient and go along at his pace. Before long he came back holding a small card covered in scribbles. Because I had seen cards like that before at his house, I knew that it was from his secret archive and I waited.

'Favieros, Stefanakos and Vakirtzis claimed that, politically, they belonged to the left but that they were not members of any particular leftist party.' He stopped and twisted the card in his fingers. 'But they were only telling half the truth. It's true they didn't belong to any party, but they were members of a group.'

'Which group?'

'A group that called itself the Che Independent Resistance Organisation. When you gave me the T-shirt I didn't think of that straightaway, but the song brought it back to me.' He heaved a sigh and said, as though to himself: 'Songs always take you back. They did then and they do now.'

I understood what he meant, but I preferred not to make any comment. I let him go at his own pace, even though I was sitting on hot coals.

'Don't imagine it as being any big or important group. At most it had about ten members. But they believed in armed resistance. Not that they ruled out other kinds of struggle: gatherings, occupations, demonstrations. But they believed that in order for all these to be more effective, they had to be backed by armed resistance. I don't know whether they ever actually planted bombs or whether they remained at the planning stage, like lots of groups did then. At some stage, the Military Police announced that they had broken up the "Che" ring of terrorist bombers. Of course, that doesn't mean that they had actually planted any bombs. In those days they arrested you on suspicion, and then they tortured you until you confessed what they wanted to hear.' He paused and added meaningfully: 'You of all people should know that.'

Whenever he came out with a dig about my police careeer, I automatically defended myself.

'I didn't have anything to do with the Military Police,' I said coldly.

'You don't have to tell me that! Neither did I. It was your lot on the Force that I had to do with! Do you want me to show you how they left my body? It's all your lot's work!'

I fell silent and waited for the storm to pass. I knew that if I aggravated him, the conversation would take a different course and I still hadn't got what I wanted out of him. And, true enough, after a few moments, his tone changed and calmly he said to me: 'I'm talking about your predecessors. I don't put you in that category.'

He said that because when he had been locked up in the cells in Bouboulinas Street, and I was just beginning my career then as a guard, I used to let him out of his cell late at night to stretch his legs or have a smoke and warm his clothes on the radiator after he'd been left fully clothed in cold water for hours.

'Do you know who else was in the group?' I asked to bring the conversation back to the topic that interested me.

'I know of three, but there may have been more.' He gazed at his card. 'Stellios Dimou, Anestis Tellopoulos and Vassos Zikas. But I can't tell you where they are, or whether they're alive or dead.'

I took out my little ringed notebook and noted down the names.

'The only one of them who's dead for sure is the organisation's mastermind,' Zissis went on. 'He must have started it on his own initiative and then recruited the others. It seems the Military Police thought the same way too, as he was tortured more than the others. The younger ones called him "uncle" because when the Junta came to power in '67, he must have already been about forty-five. In other words, around twenty-five years older than they were. After the fall of the Junta, he disappeared and nothing was ever heard of him again. About a year ago, I learned quite by chance that he'd died.'

'Give me his name so I can note it down with the others.'

'Thanos Yannelis'

I clutched at my notebook to stop it falling from my hands. What connection might there have been between Thanos Yannelis and Coralia Yannelis? Was it simply a coincidence? If Yannelis had still been alive, he would have been over seventy-five. So Coralia couldn't be his sister. Perhaps she was his daughter?

'Do you know whether Yannelis had a daughter?'

'You never stop, do you!' he shouted, indignantly. 'You're not satisfied with the information I give you, now you want his family tree. No, I've no idea whether he had any kids, or any pets for that matter!'

I suddenly remembered all the women in their fifties who worked at Favieros's companies and something that I'd said to Koula: that Favieros had known them all from his years in the resistance and that's why he had hired them. If Coralia Yannelis belonged to that category, then it was certain that she was related in some way to Thanos Yannelis.

As I was getting up to leave, he threw the T-shirt to me. 'Take it, I don't want it,' he said. 'But is it all right if I keep the song?'

'Keep it, if you want.' Besides, it wasn't as if it were evidence in a murder enquiry.

'Thanks, Lambros,' I said, while putting the T-shirt back into the plastic bag. 'I know you can't stomach coppers, but you're always a big help to me and I'm grateful.'

He avoided having to answer by lighting up a cigarette. When I was out on the balcony, however, I heard him say behind me: 'Ah, you coppers. We used to despise all your people when they had money to burn. Now our people have turned the revolution into T-shirts. And everybody's profited.'

47

My first thought was to go straight to the offices of Balkan Prospect and speak with Coralia Yannelis. That thought, coupled with my impatience, filled me with momentum till I turned into Alexandras Avenue. From there, however, I began to have my doubts, which increased in direct proportion to the uphill slope. What would I gain by going to Yannelis unprepared? First of all, I wasn't sure whether she was at all related to Thanos. It could simply be a coincidence. Secondly, even if they were related, I didn't know how closely. They may have been cousins three times removed who hadn't seen each other for twenty-five years.

And, apart from Thanos Yannelis, what would happen with the other three? There may even have been other members of the group that Zissis didn't know about. The correct thing would be for me to investigate, to collect information on Thanos Yannelis and the others and then to confront Coralia. If the other three were alive and living in Greece, they might very well be in danger from Logaras's suicide mania. And if he'd already been in contact with some of them, we might manage to avert the worst and get some new information on Logaras.

I had got as far as the High Court building when another thought suddenly came to me. Zissis had told me that Thanos Yannelis was dead, but that he didn't know exactly when he had died. What if Logaras's first victim wasn't Favieros but Yannelis? If he, too, had committed suicide, for his own worse luck and ours, then we would have to start looking for a biography. Whatever the case, all this convinced me that I should leave Coralia Yannelis for the time being and collect information on Thanos Yannelis, the other three and any others in the group, if they existed.

These thoughts were still running through my head as I reached the third floor of Security Headquarters and made a beeline for the office of my assistants. I found all three of them working feverishly. I didn't know whether they really had work to do or whether they were pretending to be occupied because of Koula, afraid that she might snitch on them because she was Ghikas's private secretary.

'Come into my office,' I shouted to them.

When I walked in, I got a surprise, because waiting for me on my desk was a coffee and croissant, my breakfast every day at the office. A croissant wrapped in cellophane and a so-called Greek coffee made with an espresso machine. I usually got them myself from the cafeteria. I attributed their willingness to bring them for me to my recent return from sick leave and I felt moved.

'Who brought my coffee and croissant?' I asked when they came into my office.

'I did,' replied Koula, overjoyed. 'My colleagues here told me that's what you have for breakfast.'

I immediately understood what was going on. Vlassopoulos and Dermitzakis had decided to demote her to filing and bringing coffee in order to keep her out of their way.

'I didn't assign you to bring me my breakfast,' I said to her sternly. 'I assigned you other work and that's what I expect you to be doing. I can get the coffee and croissant myself.'

It was the first time I had asserted my authority. She turned pale and I saw that she was ready to burst into tears. I felt sorry for her, but I didn't want the other two having her run errands.

'We still haven't managed to discover any secret from their past,' said Vlassopoulos in an attempt to change the subject.

'Forget the past for the time being. There's something more pressing.' I tossed the red Che T-shirt to Vlassopoulos, who caught it in the air. 'I want you to find out who manufactures those T-shirts.'

He looked at the T-shirt and shook his head. 'It won't be easy! It's shoddy work and there must be at least ten different factories that could have made it.'

'Find out which ones. It's urgent.' I reached into my pocket and took out my notebook with the names that Zissis had given me. I looked at Dermitzakis. 'Stellios Dimou, Anestis Telopoulos and Vassos Zikas. I want you to find out everything you can about them. And if they're dead, how they died and when. If they're alive, where they live and what they do for a living. And I want the information quickly, today if possible.'

I turned to Koula. 'Does the name Yannelis mean anything to you?'

She hadn't recovered from the scolding and still had tears in her eyes. 'Coralia Yannelis at Balkan Prospect,' she mumbled with some difficulty.

'Exactly. Now I want you to search for a certain Athanassios or Thanos Yannelis. He's probably dead, but, if he were alive, he'd be over seventy-five now. I want you to find out his particulars and check them against those of Coralia Yannelis. I want to know if they're related and how closely. You've met Coralia Yannelis, you've talked to her and you know exactly what to look for.'

I stressed this last sentence to make it clear to the other two that Koula was more in the know concerning the case than they were and that they should stop treating her as though she were the errand girl. It seemed that Koula understood because I saw a smile appearing on her face.

'And one more thing. Go up to the fifth floor and tell the Chief that I'd like to see him and Stellas from Anti-terrorism concerning the suicides as soon as possible. Tell him it's urgent.'

They left, with Koula leading the way, while I removed the cellophane and began eating my croissant. I may have had to scold Koula for preventative reasons, but the coffee and croissant testified beyond any doubt to my longed-for return to routine. I took a sip from the coffee that, meanwhile, had gone cold. I got up to go down to the cafeteria and get another one, but then I immediately sat down again. Never mind, I thought, Adriani has spoiled me. At work, I almost always end up drinking my coffee cold.

As I was taking the last sip, Koula phoned to say that Ghikas was ready to see me. The lift kept me waiting a good ten minutes, evidently to take the wind out of my sails so I wouldn't have any illusions about its workings.

I arrived at Ghikas's office and saw Koula sitting at her desk outside, tidying up a mass of papers.

'What are you doing here?' I asked her.

'He told me to spend an hour or so putting his papers in order because he was getting buried under them and didn't know where to find anything.' She took a deep breath and added: 'It's difficult to know where to begin.'

'Don't get yourself worked up about it. Till we're through with this case, he's not going to get you back. I made that clear to him.'

'No, you don't understand. I'm talking about afterwards. From what I see, it'll take me at least two months to put everything back in order.'

'Go and find out what you can about Yannelis and leave the rest to me. I'll sort it out with him.'

The old Ghikas. Never missing an opportunity. But now we were in a hurry and there was no time for luxuries of that sort.

I found him poring over the brochure of the Worker's Housing Organisation concerning the houses in the Olympic Village that would be allotted to the lucky few after the Olympic Games. I didn't know whether he met the requirements, but if he were to enter the draw, no doubt he'd come out with one of the first-choice houses.

'What's happened all of a sudden?' he asked, as he folded up the brochure and stuffed it in one of his drawers. 'Have there been some developments? And why Stellas?'

I gave him a full and detailed report: about the T-shirt and the song and about all I'd learned from Zissis, without, of course, referring to his name or to the names he'd given me.'

'In other words, we're making progress,' he said with satisfaction when I had finished my report.

'It depends. Maybe yes, maybe no.'

We'd known each other for years and he could read my reactions. 'What's bothering you?' he asked.

'It's not so much that we are making progress as that Logaras is leading us by the hand. That's what troubles me. I'm not sure whether he's leading me or setting traps for me that I keep falling into.'

'When we were with the Minister, you said you wanted him to play cat and mouse with you.'

'Yes. In the hope that while following his trail I'll come up with something unexpected, something he hasn't foreseen, and that I'll get a lead from there. That's what I'm counting on.'

Our conversation was interrupted as Stellas, deputy head of the Anti-terrorist Squad walked in. He took a seat opposite me and then looked at us in hierarchical order: first Ghikas then me.

'So, what is it?' he asked.

Ghikas glanced at me and left it to me to take the initiative.

'Tell me, Nikos, have you heard of any resistance organisation from the time of the Junta called the Che Independent Resistance Organisation?'

He reflected for a moment. 'You mean Yannelis?' he asked.

'Yes. Do you know him?'

'Not personally. But I know what my older colleagues used to say about him.

'What did they say?'

'They did everything but get to their feet when they mentioned his name. Seems Yannelis was one of those few that you fight against and respect at the same time.'

'Do you know who else was in the organisation?'

'No, that's all I know. It was the Military Police who dealt with them and their records were all burned in Keratsini. I'd know them only if they'd continued their activities after the fall of the Junta.'

'And didn't they?'

'Not under that name, at least. We'd have known.'

'And what if they used another name?'

He shrugged. 'I can't tell you anything more for certain. The business of anti-terrorism is still an impenetrable tangle, you know that. All I can tell you is that Yannelis vanished from the scene after the fall of the Junta and cut all ties with his former comrades. We don't know why, but it seems he decided to retire. I can't tell you if the others in the group continued their activities, because we don't know who was in the group during the Junta.'

So Zissis's records were more up-to-date than those of the Anti-terrorist Squad, I thought to myself. Pity that we couldn't incorporate the illegal workings of the Greek Communist Party into the Security Forces. We'd be sitting pretty now.

There was nothing more to be said and I got to my feet. Stellas said his goodbyes and left first. I halted in the doorway and turned to Ghikas.

'I almost forgot. Let the tidying up of your office wait till we've finished with this case. Then you can have Koula back.'

He gazed at me with the expression of a wounded deer. 'You've come back from your sick leave a changed man,' he said. 'Without any compassion.'

I don't know why, but I liked what I heard.

48

It's something of a delight to see a journalist pounding his head with his hands. Sotiropoulos was doing it to punish himself for his stupidity.

'Why didn't I think of it?' he cried. 'Why didn't I think of it? With all that drivel I come out with every night on the box I've gone gaga!'

'Did you know about the group?'

'Come off it! We knew all the groups, big and small. We could recite them off by heart, like the National Anthem.'

'And did you know that Favieros, Stefanakos and Vakirtzis were all members of "Che"?'

'Okay. No one knew anything about anyone for sure. But there were plenty of rumours going around. You know how it is: so-and-so belongs there, so-and-so belongs somewhere else, so-and-so fell out with the one group and went over to the other. They themselves said nothing and you didn't ask them. You always found out from the circle. Some of it was true, some of it was made up.'

I told him the other three names and he reflected for a moment. 'The name Dimou sounds familiar,' he said. 'The other two names mean nothing to me. Of course, it all depended on who you knocked around with. Secretiveness was the rule so you might know some from one group close to your own circle and not know others who weren't.'

'Do you know when Yannelis died?'

'I can't tell you the exact year, but it must have been a decade ago.'

'How did he die?'

He stared at me before answering. 'Wait for it,' he said. 'He committed suicide.'

So, then, my fears of the previous day when I had learned that Yannelis was dead turned out to be justified. I had guessed right that there was some common secret from the past linking everything together. The question was whether the secret had anything to do with Yannelis's suicide.

It seemed that Sotiropoulos read my thoughts, because he elucidated: 'Anyway, Yannelis didn't commit suicide in public. He hanged himself from the light fitting in his house. He was hanging there for three days till the building started to stink and the neighbours called the police, who broke down the door and found him.'

All right, but that didn't overturn my hypothesis in any radical way. Everything may have started with Yannelis's private suicide before the rules of the game were changed and the others continued with public suicides. There was something to this explanation if you consider that the other three were well-known public figures, whereas Yannelis was known to only a handful of those in the resistance.

'Do you know whether Yannelis had any children?'

'No idea.' He paused and looked at me. 'How much of all this can I use?'

I didn't take the wind out of his sails. On the contrary, I thought about what he'd said. What gain would there be for us if he were to come out with anything I'd discovered so far? For example, the connection with Thanos Yannelis and with his suicide? It might alert Logaras to the fact that I saw Yannelis's suicide as the starting point for the case, forcing his hand, making him reveal something more or go on playing cat and mouse with me until he tripped up.

'If you want, you can talk about the "Che" organisation and question the connection between Yannelis's suicide and the recent suicides.'

His face lit up. 'At last, a start! I'm on my way!' he called enthusiastically as he rushed out of my office.

I didn't share his enthusiasm, but I couldn't rule out the possibility that something may come of the ruse. I called my three assistants in to find out whether there'd been any new developments in the investigation. The indirect scolding of the previous day had worked because Vlassopoulos and Dermitzakis had begun to acquire chivalrous habits. They opened the door for Koula and let her come in first. All three sat down in front of me and waited in expectation.

'Do we have anything new?'

'Nothing on the Che T-shirts yet.' Vlassopoulos was the first to speak. 'It's crude work, but nevertheless. In a couple of days at most, we'll know who's manufacturing them.'

I decided to leave Koula till last, because I'm something of a masochist and I wanted to prolong my agony, so I turned next to Dermitzakis.

'Did you find out anything about the three names I gave you?'

'Nothing about Stellios Dimou yet. Anestis Tellopoulos went abroad to study after the Junta and settled in Canada, where he's a university lecturer. I got the information from his mother, who lives in Sparta. Vassos Zikas died two years ago.'

'How?'

They saw my alarm and stared at me in surprise. Koula was the only one not perplexed because she knew the reason behind it.

'Of a heart attack, while at the wheel,' Dermitzakis said.

'Right. Make sure you find out about Dimou.' I turned to look at Koula.

She was holding a large desk diary, which she opened. 'The name of Coralia Yannelis's father is Athanassios. Her mother's name is Vassiliki.'

Could that, too, have been a coincidence? It was highly unlikely. 'Anything else?'

'She was born in 1955 in Bogotá, Columbia. Athanassios Yannelis lived in Columbia from 1953 to 1965 and then moved to La Paz in Bolivia. He returned home in 1967.'

So that's it, I thought to myself. There was no doubt that Coralia Yannelis was the daughter of Thanos Yannelis.

'There's a son, too,' Koula added. 'Kimon Yannelis was born in 1958, in Bogotá. He left Greece in 1978 and never came back. His whereabouts are unknown.'

'And the mother?'

'Vassiliki Yannelis, née Papayannidis, from Nigrita, Serres. Born in 1935 and died in 1970.'

'Find out if there's any biography of Thanos Yannelis or any other book about him.' I turned to Vlassopoulos. 'I want you to find me the manufacturer of the T-shirt, at all costs. And I want to know what happened to Stellios Dimou,' I added, looking at Dermitzakis.

When they had left, I phoned Ghikas to inform him that we had established beyond a shadow of a doubt that Coralia Yannelis was the daughter of Thanos Yannelis and that there was also a brother whose whereabouts were unknown.

He asked me the classic question: 'What do you propose to do?' From the tone of his voice, however, I could tell that he was pleased.

'First, I'll talk to Coralia Yannelis, and take it from there.'

He agreed. In less than ten minutes I was down in the Security Headquarters garage. I didn't take Alexandras Avenue, but went along Alpheiou Street into Panormou Street and turned into Kifissias Avenue at the lights by the Red Cross building in order to avoid all the traffic. Fortunately, it was almost the start of July. The school exam period was over and the traffic was moving at an acceptable pace. It took me just fifteen minutes to reach Aigialeias Street and I parked outside number 54.

49

Coralia Yannelis made me wait. Her excuse was that I had come without an appointment and that she had to deal with a serious professional matter. I was over half an hour in reception, like a patient waiting to see his GP or a voter waiting to see the MP for his constituency. I felt uneasy and I shared this feeling with Yannelis's secretary, who didn't much like having a copper hanging around her office. I could have left and called her down to Headquarters, but my kid-glove tactics had proved effective so far and I didn't want to change them now that there was some light at the end of the tunnel.

She received me after about an hour, but she didn't ask me to sit down. 'This business has got to come to and end, Inspector,' she said in a cold and annoyed tone. 'You've visited me on numerous occasions, you've asked me the most irrelevant questions about the companies in our group and without any authority whatsoever. I answered your questions because we've nothing to hide and because I'm a law-abiding citizen. Whichever you prefer. But I've no intention of going on with this game. Next time you want to question me, send an official request and I'll come with my lawyer.'

She finished protesting and waited for me to leave, but I didn't move from the spot.

'I haven't come to talk about your companies,' I said very calmly.

'But?'

'About your father, Thanos Yannelis.'

I was banking from the beginning on the element of surprise and I wasn't wrong. 'Is this some new business?' she asked, taken aback.

'No. It's old business, going back to the Junta and the resistance organisations of the time.'

She considered whether it was worth abandoning her hardline approach, decided that it was and told me to take a seat.

'During the period of the Junta, your father was a member of a resistance group known as the Che Independent Resistance Organisation.'

I waited to see how she would react before proceeding. She looked at me and smiled calmly.

'In 1967, I was twelve years old, Inspector. Do you imagine that my father would discuss resistance organisations with me?'

'No, but he might have discussed them with you later, after the fall of the Junta.'

'My father never talked about his activities. He did it to protect us. He used to say that no one knew how things would turn out and the family had to be protected.' She had regained her composure and smiled calmly.

'Favieros, Stefanakos and Vakirtzis belonged to the same organisation as your father.'

'It's the first time I've heard that.' She appeared to be surprised, but she may have been playacting. You never knew with Coralia Yannelis.

'So your father never spoke about the resistance. Didn't you hear anything from Favieros either?'

'Only once, when he was about to hire me. He told me that he had met my father during the period of the Junta.'

'And didn't you ask him where and how?'

She shrugged. 'No. So many people knew my father that there was no point in my asking every time. Perhaps his acquaintance with my father played some role in Jason's decision to hire me. All of those in Jason's close circle go back to the Junta and the student struggles. Not only Xenophon Zamanis, but also his private secretary, Theoni, and Zamanis's secretary, and a whole group of others, mainly engineers and lawyers.' She paused for a moment and then added: 'All I remember from that time is the day the Military Police came to arrest my father.'

'There's another common element from the past: your father's suicide.' She said nothing. She nodded her head resignedly. 'When did your father commit suicide?'

'In the early nineties.'

'And now the other members of the organisation are all committing suicide in turn.'

She stared at me as though not believing what she had just heard. 'What are you saying?' she asked astonished. 'That the suicides of Jason, Stefanakos and Vakirtzis have some connection with that of my father?'

'I can't prove it yet, but nor can I rule it out.'

'More than ten years have passed between my father's suicide and those of the other three.'

'Yes, but there were at least ten members of the organisation. Apart from those who committed suicide, we've tracked down another two. The one died of natural causes and the other is living abroad. But we don't know who the rest were. There may have been other suicides that we don't know about.'

She propped her head up on her hands and closed her eyes, as though she were trying to revive the images in her memory.

'My father was a very unhappy man, Inspector.'

She said it without emphasis, but categorically, as an indisputable fact. Then she opened her eyes and looked at me.

'He lived his life in the movements and the illegal political organisations. That's what he knew. He had close ties with Castro's regime and he worshipped Che Guevara. We moved from Bogotá to La Paz just before Che started his guerrilla war in Bolivia. When my father was deported from Bolivia, we returned to Greece. Then came the Junta and he was back in his element, till the day they caught him.' She paused again, trying to order her thoughts. 'The period after the fall of the Junta was a disaster for him. From one day to the next, he found himself on the scrap heap. No one wanted him and he didn't have any way to make a living. He made a trip to Cuba, but conditions had changed there, too. He returned, and from then on he began to waste away. When the communist regimes fell, he realised that it was the end and life no longer had any meaning for him.'

She stopped to get her breath, as though the effort had exhausted her. What she had told me was totally logical. There was nothing irrational or outrageous about it. All that was required was to compare her father with Zissis. Despite his bitterness, and the anger that he vented every so often, Zissis had endured. Yannelis hadn't and that was the only difference.

'My father committed suicide quietly in his room and we found him three days later. He didn't die in front of the cameras or in his villa or in Syntagma Square.'

It was the first time that she had voiced anything resembling a reproach concerning Jason Favieros and the others. It was also the first time that she had lost both her smile and her composure. She had put it all in place and it all appeared totally convincing, but was it? What if there was something behind all this linking the recent suicides with Yannelis's? And there were others in the group we didn't yet know about and who might, therefore, be in danger? They might include ministers, government officials, scribes and Pharisees, whatever you could thing of. What could we do? Announce in the press and on TV that anyone who was once a member of the 'Che' organisation should contact the police?

'What did your father live on?'

'He had a small pension as a former member of the resistance. He didn't have any other income.'

'Didn't you help him?'

She was silent for a moment and then added, without hiding her sorrow: 'My father was a proud man. He wouldn't accept help from anyone.'

'You have a brother, isn't that so? Kimon Yannelis.'

'Yes.'

'Does he live in Greece?'

'No. From what I know, he has a fishing business in South Africa.' She saw that I was perplexed by her answer and added: 'My brother and I never got on, Inspector. We've not had any contact for years now.' Her smile reappeared, even though it was a little affected. 'And because I'm sure you want to know about my mother, I can tell you that she died in 1970, shortly after our return to Greece, of acute meningitis.'

At the end of my previous visit, she had given me her companies' balance sheets. Now she was giving me the details of her mother's death without my having asked. It was her way of saying: we're done, on your way.

'All in all, I think I prefer it when you ask me about our companies,' she said as I reached the door. 'What you asked me today was far more difficult for me.'

It was difficult for me too, because I couldn't get it out of my mind that her father's suicide was the starting point for the other three.

50

I wasn't superstitious, but there was definitely something strange about it. Whenever we formally invited Fanis round for a meal, I was always in a state. The last time, I had been suspended and the meal very nearly turned into a wake. Now, when his parents were coming to meet us, my mind was fixed on the suicides. So I was worried in case I got lost in my thoughts in the middle of their visit and they took it to mean that I was fed up and couldn't wait for them to leave. That was what had happened during Fanis's first visit and we were on the verge of a life-long misunderstanding till I confessed that I had been suspended and the situation was resolved. And, when you come to think about it, suspension was a life-long matter. But how was I going to convince anyone that the suicides of three sharks were as serious a matter. I couldn't expect any support from anyone other than my daughter and Fanis. Adriani would be the first to crucify me.

The said Adriani had spent her day between the supermarket, the butcher's, the greengrocer's and the stationer's. She had been shut up in the kitchen all afternoon. At that particular moment, she had laid out in front of her about a dozen scooped-out tomatoes, rather like empty piggy banks, and half a dozen headless peppers that she was getting ready to fill. That was the first dish: stuffed vegetables in the traditional way. In other words, not *à l'orphelin* or without onions, as she had made for me during my convalescence so that I wouldn't suffer from indigestion. The main course was a dish she made rarely, which is why she was anxious: veal *à la jardinière*. Veal loaf with vegetables, wrapped in greaseproof paper and baked in the oven. She had been running all over the previous afternoon trying to find greaseproof paper, which is hardly used any more as it brings back memories of a poor old Greece, and everyone had advised her to use tinfoil, which is just as good. In the end, she tried the stationer's and found exactly what she wanted.

Katerina was against all this. She thought that there was no reason for going to all this trouble and that we could just as well have invited Fanis's parents round in the afternoon for tea and cakes. The conversation was over in less than five minutes with Adriani exercising her veto.

'I was brought up differently, Katerina,' she said. 'In our house, the parents of the bride had to invite the parents of the groom for a meal.'

'Mum, I'm not the bride and Fanis isn't the groom. Can you get that into your head!'

'Ask your father,' Adriani went on, unperturbed. 'Would his parents have been pleased if they'd gone round and the bride hadn't cooked for them?'

Katerina didn't ask me. She preferred to swallow her anger and to go for a walk, but Adriani wouldn't hear of it.

'I think you could help me, Katerina, so I don't have to do everything myself.'

So, there were two hotplates next to each other in a kitchen no bigger than five by eight. Adriani was worried that everything wouldn't be ready in time and was impatient with Katerina, who, it had to be said, wasn't exactly a star in the kitchen. On the other hand, Katerina was ready to storm off and take Fanis's parents out for ice cream, but she gritted her teeth and held back so as not to seem ungrateful to her mother.

I decided to heed the popular proverb about too many cooks spoiling the broth and I went for a walk in Katerina's place, out of fear of getting caught in the crossfire and of having to assume the role of mediator. Whereas, if the hostilities erupted in my absence, the two of them would hide it from me when I got back so as not to upset me.

My first thought was to go to the little square of Aghiou Lazarou. I rejected this idea immediately, however, because on Saturday afternoon, the café would be full of people and the square full of kids. So I changed direction and headed towards the park and my familiar bench. At that time on Saturday in the summer, people would still be at the beach or sleeping or lazing somewhere with an iced coffee or an ice cream.

It was as I expected, because only the cat was there waiting for me. It had come down from its usual place and was sprawled on the sunny side of the bench. It heard me approaching and half-opened its eyes. It saw who I was and closed them again, indifferent to me.

The park was quiet, not a soul around, apart from me and the cat, so it was an ideal place for thinking, provided that you had some ideas. I didn't. I was at the recycling stage, but the recycled product hadn't appeared yet. I had managed with Logaras's help – the word 'lead' was an affront to my ego – to arrive at the original suicide by Yannelis. I could understand his daughter's objections and I could accept that there were real differences, which were not confined to the 'public' and 'private' nature of the suicides, but to something else: Yannelis wasn't wealthy, nor was he involved in businesses in Greece and the Balkans. He lived on his meagre resistance pension. Perhaps his children had helped him financially, but given the image of the proud revolutionary that I had gleaned from Coralia Yannelis's description of him, that was something I ruled out.

I was aware of all these counter-arguments but my gut feeling told me that, nevertheless, there was some thread linking Yannelis's suicide with that of the other three. What this was I didn't know and there were only two ways I would find out: either Logaras would lead me to it step by step, as he had done so far, or I would have to uncover another member of the group who would tell me what it was. I didn't imagine that they would cover my travelling expenses to visit Tellopoulos in Canada, nor was I crazy about the idea if the truth be told.

The sun had moved and the cat woke up. It stretched, sat back on its hind legs and yawned magnificently. Then it turned its gaze to me and gave me a curt miaow. It was the first time after an acquaintance of several months that it had spoken to me directly and I wondered how I should react, but it wasn't necessary. It noticed the sun, which was now on the edge of the bench, curled up in its rays and shut its eyes again.

I got up and headed home in the hope that the preparations for the meal would have been completed and that the temperature would have returned to its normal level for the time of year. It was, indeed, quiet in the house, with Katerina setting the table.

'All prepared for the meal?' I asked her.

'As you can see. I'm setting the table.' She finished arranging the glasses and took the empty tray to bring the knives and forks. 'Do you know where Fanis and I went wrong?' she asked me, as she went to the door.

'Where?'

'We should have taken you all and sat you down together round a table at a taverna.'

'It's a bit late for that now.'

'I know, but it's my being away in Thessaloniki that's to blame. I'd forgotten what Mum's like.'

The prospective in-laws together with the prospective groom, as Andreadis would have collectively called them, arrived promptly at eight thirty. A couple, Prodromos and Sevasti Ouzounidis, both of average height and both of a portly build, were standing between an embarrassed doctor and an embarrassed prospective magistrate, waiting to hear our 'welcome' so that they could respond with their 'nice of you to invite us', before we all moved on to the quadraphonic 'so we meet at last'.

Once in the sitting room, we proceeded from our introductions to our professions. Prodromos Ouzounidis already knew that I was a police officer. I learned there and then that he was a classic Greek jack-of-all-trades: part farmer, part self-employed businessman. He had some land on which he grew tobacco and a neighbourhood corner shop in Veria. When he was working on the land, Sevasti Ouzounidis kept the shop, and when Prodromos was keeping the shop, Sevasti kept home.

Most of the information was supplied by Sevasti Ouzounidis.

Prodromos stayed quiet most of the time and kept wiping the sweat on his face with his handkerchief, because he had thought it only proper to wear his best suit, which was a thick, woollen one. I was about to switch on the air conditioning to help him out, but his wife beat me to it.

'Prodromos, why don't you take your jacket off? Look, the inspector isn't wearing his.'

I didn't know whether that was a simple observation or a chiding remark aimed at me for not being appropriately dressed, wearing as I was a short-sleeved shirt. Whatever the case, the offer was a godsend for Prodromos, who took off his jacket and his tie, heaving a sigh of relief. On the contrary, I came out the worse for it as I received a reproachful look from Adriani. The only one to find it amusing was Fanis. He had caught sight of his father and Adriani and looked at me, ready to burst out laughing.

I followed Katerina with my gaze. I didn't know how she was when she was sitting exams at the university, but it was the first time I had ever seen her so ill-at-ease and quiet. She was sitting uncomfortably on the edge of the chair and smiling at everyone in turn. She was simply dressed, but her clothes seemed too tight for her; she was wearing sandals, but they were pinching her feet. I suddenly thought how much more relaxed Koula would be if she were in Katerina's place. She would have taken part in conversation, she would have had something to say to everyone and it wouldn't have taken ten minutes before she was liked by all. My daughter was educated, knew what she wanted, no doubt she would have a brilliant career, but I was obliged to admit that in circumstances like those, Koula could leave her standing.

Adriani got up to start getting the meal ready. Katerina jumped up, too, probably because Adriani had forewarned her that when she got up, that would be the signal for Katerina to go with her into the kitchen.

'You sit with the men, Katerina dear,' said Sevasti. 'I'll go and help Mrs Haritos.'

Adriani was about to protest, but Sevasti wouldn't hear of it. 'But

I insist, Mrs Haritos!' she said. 'If you were in my house, wouldn't you want to help? Don't even mention it!'

Katerina was stuck in the middle and didn't know whether she should obey her mother and go into the kitchen or her future mother-in-law and stay in the sitting room. Fortunately, Fanis got her out of her dilemma.

'Stay here,' he said, smiling. 'Didn't you know that the kitchen is where housewives get to know each other better?'

Adriani and Sevasti went off, Katerina remained, and the atmosphere became more relaxed. Ouzounidis *père* began talking about tobacco: how they only grow Virginia tobacco now and how this had increased the competition and drastically reduced the income. I listened to him patiently, without feeling at all irritated. My own father may have been a police sergeant, but both his brothers had land that they struggled with all through the year and so I understood his plight.

However, perhaps I would have been somewhat less understanding had I known that once he'd finished his report, I would have to begin mine. He reminded me with a 'And what do you do in your line of work?'

The easiest thing would have been for me to tell him that all my life I'd been dealing with corpses, murders and, of late, suicides, but I was afraid that it might be too much for him. So I endeavoured to be as vague as possible, but it seemed that Mr Ouzounidis had seen what the cameras show on the news bulletins countless times and he was keen to learn in every detail what they didn't show. He demanded that I recount everything from the moment the Flying Squad took the call to the moment they opened the plastic bag with its contents.

I did it to please him, answering all his questions one by one. Fanis was about to intervene and restrain his father, but he saw how I was dealing with the questions willingly and in detail, in a way that Ghikas would no doubt have envied, so he suspected that perhaps I was enjoying myself and remained silent.

I wasn't enjoying it at all, however, and I was relieved when I saw

Adriani coming in with the dish of stuffed vegetables and Sevasti behind her with the veal *à la jardinière*. We sat down at the table and the praise for the food began. Adriani was flattered and the Police Force was forgotten. The rest of the evening passed with idle chatter till around eleven. Fanis's parents got up to go, but, before leaving, they insisted on making us promise that we would visit them in Veria.

'You're certain to like it,' Sevasti said warmly. 'It's a quiet place with clean air. And besides, when you go to see Katerina in Thessaloniki, Veria is on your way.'

Adriani agreed without a second thought, while I reflected that they would only have to cater for half the family, Adriani that is, because in all the years that Katerina had been in Thessaloniki, I couldn't have gone there more than a couple of times.

As soon as she had closed the front door, Katerina flung her arms round my neck and kissed me on both cheeks.

'Thanks, you're the best,' she said, full of enthusiasm.

'Come on. You must have had a dim view of me. Your grandfather was from a farming family too.'

'That's not why I kissed you, but because of your patience in answering all the questions about the police. I know how much you hate it.'

'I did it for Fanis,' I said completely spontaneously.

'I know. And he knows it too. That's why you're so fond of each other.'

When Katerina had taken up with Fanis, I had been afraid she would give up her PhD studies to marry him. Now that I was convinced she would finish it, it seemed I was starting to hear the sound of wedding bells.

51

The telephone rang early on Monday morning while I was in the bathroom shaving. Sunday had passed quietly with that pleasant languor that follows on from the previous night's festivities. Adriani was pleased because everyone had commented on her cooking and she had every reason to be happy, Katerina because a weight had been taken off her shoulders and she felt relieved and, finally, I was pleased because I had managed not to let the suicides affect me and had been smiling and affable to the point that Fanis's parents must have been wondering whether they had had a mistaken view of coppers, who weren't all sour and sullen, as perhaps they had thought.

I heard Adriani's voice from the hallway: 'Vlassopoulos!'

I wiped my face and rushed to the phone. I must have had a look of terror in my eyes because I was filled with panic that perhaps there had been another suicide. Thankfully, I heard Vlassopoulos full of enthusiasm and that reassured me.

'I've found him!' he shouted.

'Who?'

'The one who makes the T-shirts. Do you know who it is?' I half expected to hear the name Minas Logaras. 'Christos Kalafatis.'

The name meant absolutely nothing to me and I tried to place it. Vlassopoulos realised from my silence.

'Doesn't the name remind you of anything?' he asked surprised.

'No.'

'Christos Kalafatis … That big strapping military policeman, who was tried for torture and got ten years. The prosecution witnesses at his trial were Favieros, Stefanakos and Vakirtzis. It's all documented. I looked into it.'

'And now he's making Che T-shirts?'

'Exactly!'

A military policeman, a former torturer for the Junta, who was manufacturing Che Guevara T-shirts. Could it be that the suicides had been an act of revenge because the three men had testified as prosecution witnesses and Kalafatis had been put away for ten years? If that was the case, then he most certainly would have been blackmailing them with something from their past. And the secret must have been from the period of their incarceration in the cells of the Military Police. Otherwise, how would Kalafatis have known about it?

'Do you have an address?'

'Yes. His factory is at 8 Liakou Street, near the Aghiou Nikolaou Station, between Ionias Avenue and Acharnon Street.'

'If Ghikas asks for me, tell him I'll be there in a couple of hours. Well done, you did a good job.'

'Eh, we can't be having the Chief's secretary running rings round us!' he said ironically and hung up.

The shortest route in the Mirafiori was by way of Patission Street, then down Agathoupoleos Street and into Ionias Avenue. On second thoughts, it occurred to me that the next suicide victim would be me. So I decided to leave the Mirafiori in the Security Headquarters garage and take the metro. Changing twice, at Syntagma and Omonia, I would be at the Aghiou Nikolaou Station in no more than twenty minutes. Liakou Street was more or less opposite.

Number 8 was an old warehouse, built of stone and concrete, with small windows and a double iron door that was half-open. I pushed it open. The area inside wasn't particularly spacious. It was just big enough for the three machines that made the T-shirts, a machine for stamping the design on them, an ironing board and a packaging machine. The T-shirts were piled all around the walls. Six women, all foreign, were operating the machines. The floor was covered with boxes, cardboard and rags, as though the place hadn't been cleaned up for months. At the back, sitting behind a desk, was a tall, brawny man of around forty-five, with a beard and thinning hair. His build told me that he might very well have been a military policeman in his youth and I approached him. He looked up and saw me.

'Yes?'

'Inspector Costas Haritos.'

Nothing changed in his expression. He continued to gaze at me with the same questioning look.

'May I sit down?'

'Why? Is it necessary?' he asked ironically.

I made no reply, but simply drew up a chair and sat on it. 'You were in the Military Police at the time of the Junta, were you not?'

'And now you've found out?' It seemed that he was becoming annoyed, but I tried not to lose my temper. 'Listen, all that business is over with. I was tried, I became famous. I went away for ten years and everybody forgot about me. I was released after six and a half years for good behaviour and I put all that behind me.'

'It has nothing to do with you. It's something else I'm interested in. Have you heard about the suicides of the businessman, Jason Favieros, the politician, Loukas Stefanakos and the journalist, Apostolos Vakirtzis?'

'Yes, but I didn't lose any sleep over it.'

'All three were political prisoners in the cells of the Military Police when you were there.'

'Perhaps. I don't remember. People came, people went, how am I supposed to remember them all?'

'You're sure to remember them because they testified as prosecution witnesses at your trial.'

He was taken aback by the fact that I knew and, to hide his shock, he became aggressive. 'So what? Do you know how many testified to get me put away for ten years of my life? Why do you think I've grown a beard? So I won't be recognised on the street. I can't stand being stared at.'

'Is that why? I thought you'd grown it to look like Che Guevara,' I said ironically.

'What do you mean by that?' he asked, surprised.

'What do I mean? During the Junta, you fought against the commies and all their kind. And because of them you were put away for ten years. And now you're selling Che Guevara T-shirts?'

I persisted in the hope that I would provoke him into opening up, but he just stared at me as though I were from another planet.

'Open your eyes. Today's not for commies, today's for T-shirts,' was his reply. 'We no longer fight, we feather our nests. Do you remember what Pattakos used to say?'

'The dictator? What's Pattakos got to do with anything?'

'Do you remember what he used to say?' he repeated.

'He said a lot of things. How should I remember everything?'

'Let me remind you of one thing he said that turned out to be prophetic: Greece is an enormous construction site.'

'And why was it prophetic? Because of the Olympic Games?'

'No. Because, today, it's an enormous stock exchange. From an enormous construction site to an enormous stock exchange. Prophetic words. Pattakos was right and, together with him, we were too. In this enormous stock exchange, Che is just another face that sells. Tomorrow, it might be the other dictator, Papadopoulos, or the day after, that other commie Mao with his little cap. It's not important. Everything today is just a stamp. So says Christos Kalafatis, the right-hand man of Major Skouloudis.'

'Skouloudis? The torturer?'

For the first time, he got angry and his eyes bulged in their sockets. 'The Military Police interrogator,' he said angrily, correcting me. 'But, naturally, all you coppers looked down their noses at us MPs.'

'Was he the one who interrogated the three who committed suicide?'

'Yes, and they were all milksops,' he said with contempt. 'And I'm not saying that because they testified against me. They were miserable wimps who squealed like little pigs as soon as you laid a hand on them. Only one of them had any backbone and he was a good twenty years older than the rest.'

'Who?' I asked, though I already knew the answer.

'Yannelis. He was the only one with any balls. Whatever you did to him, you always had to take your hat off to him in the end.'

'He committed suicide, too, only much earlier. At the beginning of the nineties.'

'It's a wonder that he survived that long.'

What did he mean? Something told me that concealed in this simple sentence was the secret I'd been looking for, but I tried to keep my composure and not show any excitement in case I scared him and he shut up shop.

'What makes you say that?' I asked, as calmly as I could.

'Because he paid more dearly than all the others. Maybe the stronger end up paying more, it's one way of looking at it. At any rate, it was a huge blow to him and it's a miracle he survived till the nineties.'

'What huge blow?'

'His daughter married Major Skouloudis.'

He looked at me, pleased with himself that he'd succeeded in shocking me. And he had succeeded in shocking me, but for other reasons. Coralia Yannelis was the wife of Major Skouloudis, her father's torturer? Was this the secret? Was this the start of the thread that would unravel the whole case?

'A real rosebud!' said Kalafatis with old-fashioned admiration. 'She was no more than eighteen and would come to the Major for news of her father, to plead with him to tell her when he would be released. And Skouloudis could be very charming. When he talked to you, you'd never imagine that this same man could torture anybody. That's how it was with the girl. In less than a month, she was totally smitten with him.'

'Did Skouloudis say anything to Yannelis about his relationship with his daughter?'

'Are you kidding? It would have been like killing him. And as I told you, the major respected Yannelis.'

'I thought he might have let him go,' I said provocatively. 'After all, he was the father of his girlfriend.'

'He couldn't. He would have found himself in deep trouble. Yannelis and his group had been accused of bombings. He did stop interrogating him, however. He closed the file on him and sent him before a military tribunal. Yannelis was still in prison when they got married. He found out about it from his son.'

I could now, with hindsight, understand why Coralia Yannelis had been so tense and uneasy when talking about her father and her brother. She'd meant it when she said it was less painful for her to answer questions about Favieros's companies. Evidently, she had fallen out with her brother over her marriage. But if she had fallen out with her brother, she must also have fallen out with her father. Yet, again, I had uncovered a secret that might lead to murder, but not to the suicides of three people. If someone had murdered Skouloudis, his marriage to Coralia Yannelis would have provided the perfect motive. But what connection could this marriage possibly have with the suicides of Favieros, Stefanakos and Vakirtzis? The only ones who could answer this question were Coralia Yannelis and Minas Logaras, whoever he might be.

'Are you still in contact with Skouloudis?'

'No, when I got out of prison, I didn't want any more bother. I started this little business, married a girl from my village and kept myself to myself.'

I got up to leave, but just then I thought of one last question that I asked more by way of fishing than for any other reason.

'Do you know anyone by the name of Minas Logaras?'

He thought about it, but came up with nothing. 'No. Never heard the name before.'

'That's all, then,' I said and walked towards the iron door that was still half-open.

'Don't bother coming back,' I heard him say behind me and I turned round. 'I've had my fill of military police, coppers, cells and prisons. I've paid through the nose and I have a right not to want to set eyes on any of you.'

I opened the door and went out without replying. He was the third person to tell me not to come back. First there was Zamanis, then Coralia Yannelis, albeit indirectly, and now it was the former military policeman, Christos Kalafatis. And everyone was happy, just like Zissis said, those who ended up making enough money to burn and those who ended up turning the revolution into T-shirts. And no one wanted to remember. It reminded me of that song I'd heard in the taxi on the day I'd returned from my meeting with Ghikas and Yanoutsos: 'We're getting on so well, I'm living in fear of hell.'

52

I called her as soon as I got back to the office.

'You again, Inspector?' she asked as soon as she came to the phone. 'I thought we were done.'

'So did I, but I was wrong, Mrs Skouloudis.'

The line went quiet for a moment. When she spoke again, her voice was calm and grave. 'So you've discovered who I am?'

'Yes. Just this morning.'

'May I ask how?'

'From Christos Kalafatis, who manufactures the Che T-shirts.'

Her cheeriness returned. 'I'm happy for you. He's the only one who knows and you found him.'

'I need to talk to you. What time can you come by my office?'

'I hope I won't have to repay all your visits to me. Let's not see it that way,' she said laughing. Then she grew serious. 'I suggest neither your office nor mine. Let's meet at my home. At six this evening.'

I asked for her address. 'Number 7, Tobazi Street, in Pefki,' she said. 'It's off Chrysostomou Smyrnis Street, close to the Katsimbali Park.'

I wondered whether I should inform Ghikas and tell him what I'd learned from Kalafatis or whether I should wait till I'd talked to Coralia Yannelis. It was more a question of patience. No matter how many years you've spent on the Force, no matter how experienced you are, as soon as you get wind of some success, you immediately rush to your superior to gloat. It's a kind of impulse that carries you away. I decided to be patient, because the correct thing was to talk first with Yannelis and then go bragging to Ghikas.

How do you fill five hours when you're on tenterhooks? I kept the reporters longer than usual. They stared at me flabbergasted because it was the first time I had ever engaged in chit-chat with them. Sotiropoulos, who suspected something, decided to stay longer, for the benefit of all. He opened up his favourite discussion concerning the suicides and I answered him with a lot of twaddle simply to pass the time. In the end, I felt some remorse and told him to wait another twenty-four hours as I would have more news the following day. He pressed me for details, but I was unshakeable as a rock, and so we went on for a while tossing the ball back and forth. I went down to the cafeteria three times and got three not-so-Greek coffees, a croissant in cellophane and a packet of rusks to settle my stomach.

I reckoned that it would take me three quarters of an hour to reach Pefki. The most reasonable route was to go up Kifissias Avenue and then, at the Ivi building, to turn left into Aghiou Konstantinou Street and that would bring me to Chrysostomou Smyrnis Street. It was Monday afternoon in summer, the shops and offices were closed and I didn't meet any traffic. I arrived a quarter of an hour early and drove round the block twice in order to arrive exactly on time. The bell at 7 Tobazi Street bore the name Coralia Yannelis. I wondered whether Skouloudis was dead or whether he had simply been struck off by the living. Her flat was a penthouse on the fifth floor.

She opened the door herself. She had the same smile and was wearing one of the same outfits that I'd seen on her at the offices of Balkan Prospect.

'Come in,' she said, leading me to a spacious sitting room that spilled over onto a balcony with the awnings lowered and with a variety of plants, mostly saplings, in large pots. In the wall on the right, there was a closed sliding door. The faint sound of a TV could be heard from the other side.

'Please have a seat,' she said, pointing to an armchair that was facing the park. 'Can I get you something?'

'No, thank you.'

She sat down on the sofa opposite me. She seemed to be trying to give the impression that she had invited me for coffee and a chat, but she found it difficult to conceal her anxiety completely.

'So where shall we begin? With Minas Logaras?'

She laughed. 'There is no Minas Logaras, as I'm sure you've realised.' She suddenly became serious. 'No, we ought to begin with my father's arrest.'

I let her start in her own good time. Now that I was sitting opposite her, I felt more relaxed. I was in no hurry and I waited.

'They arrested my father in the spring of '72. They woke us up one night at around two a.m., grabbed hold of my father and began hitting him and dragging him towards the door.' She halted and said without any emotion, as if simply stating a fact: 'That was the last time I saw my father, Inspector.' She let out a sigh and remained silent for a moment. 'Throughout his life, my father was involved in movements and revolutions. So was my mother. But they wanted to keep their children away from all that. They never talked about it to us, they never explained it to us, they never said anything. They did it to protect us, but also out of fear we would let something slip. And so we grew up in the dark, in an atmosphere of indefinable fear. I'm telling you all this so you'll understand our panic when they came to arrest my father.' She looked at me and said with a slightly ironic smile: 'Anyhow, you're a police officer and I'm sure you know what I mean.'

I knew. Although in my line of work I rarely saw the panic of the innocent. It was usually the panic of the guilty that I saw.

'I was in the final year of high school then. Kimon was in junior school. Our mother had died two years previously. We didn't have anyone, we didn't know anyone. The following morning, I began asking discreetly where those who had been arrested by the soldiers were taken. And so I learned about the Military Police Headquarters. I got together a bag with clothes because my father hadn't had time to take anything with him and I went to the Headquarters. They told me I should see Major Skouloudis. He received me very cordially. He said he would personally see to it that my father got the clothes, that they were holding him for interrogation and that he didn't know when he would be released, but that I shouldn't worry because he was fine in his health, and that if I wanted to know anything or leave anything for my father, I should always go to him.' She stopped again and looked at me. 'Perhaps you've already guessed what I'm about to tell you. When you've lived all your life in fear and in the dark, when you're on your own and with a younger brother and you don't know where to turn and suddenly you meet someone who is friendly to you and seems ready to help you, then that person sooner or later wins you over. But it wasn't only that. I never got any answers from my parents. Skouloudis, however, was always ready with an answer. He answered all my questions. Agreed, a lot of what he told me was make-believe, but frightened, little children are reassured by make-believe, it's as simple as that.' She again let out a sigh. 'Are you sure I can't get you anything?' she asked.

'No, thank you.'

'Then I'll fix myself a drink.'

She got up and went out of the sitting room. I've done countless interrogations in my life and I knew how confessions are extracted: like getting blood out of a stone, with hesitations, long-windedness and pauses. I waited patiently, with the sound of the TV still coming from the adjoining room. Yannelis returned holding a glass of whisky with ice.

'That's why I fell in love and married my husband, Inspector. For the sense of security that he gave me,' she said, sitting down again. 'I was still a minor. I don't know how Yangos managed to get hold of a marriage licence. We got married quietly. I had Kimon with me, Yangos had invited two friends of his. After the marriage, I asked to see my father. Yangos said that it would be bad for me psychologically, but it would also be bad for him because no one looked kindly on his marriage to the daughter of a bomber. So I sat down and wrote my father a long letter. I didn't receive any reply. I wrote to him again. Again there was no reply.'

She paused and took a sip of her whisky. It seemed she wanted to get her breath before moving on to the more difficult stuff. 'The reply came after the fall of the Junta.'

She got up and went over to a cabinet that was on the wall facing the sliding door. She took a folded piece of paper from one of the drawers and handed it to me. I wouldn't have called it a letter. It was more of a note, written on a white sheet of exam paper.

You betrayed me. You married my torturer. From now on, all I want is to hide the shame. Don't ever come near me. You're no longer any child of mine. Kimon will stay with me. You'll never see him again either.

The signature was a capital 'T'. I returned the note to Yannelis.

'I made countless attempts to see him, tried numerous times to phone him, but to no avail. Both my father and my brother cut all ties with me.' She was upset and took a deep breath in order to calm herself. 'When I read the news of his suicide, I managed to find out where he lived and rushed to his home. My brother opened the door. He told me to go away and not to attend the funeral because he would have me thrown out of the church.'

'Didn't you show your husband the note that your father sent you?'

'By the time I received the note, it was my husband's turn to be in prison. They arrested him a week before the first Karamanlis government was sworn in.'

'And afterwards? Didn't you ask him to explain himself?'

She let out a bitter laugh. 'Are you surprised?'

'A little surprised, yes.'

'Come with me,' she said, getting to her feet.

She opened the sliding door and let me go through. I found myself in a smaller room with a sofa, a coffee table and four high-backed chairs against the walls. On the wall facing the sofa there was a TV with an enormous screen. Sitting midway, between the sofa and the TV, was a man in a wheelchair. It was clear at first sight that he had suffered a severe stroke. His left arm was paralysed, his head was resting on his left shoulder and was shaking constantly, while his mouth was twisted to the point of disfiguration. He could only move his right hand, and then with some difficulty.

'This is my husband, Inspector,' I heard her say from behind me. 'Cashiered Infantry Major Yangos Skouloudis. Ol' Yangos as they called him in the Military Police. He was sentenced to fifteen years' detention, suffered three strokes in his despair and was released with irreparable damage to his health. He can't walk or speak and our only communication is by means of these notes.'

She pointed to a basket with notes that was attached to the arm of his wheelchair. A little table, rather like a modern school desk, was fitted to the arm and on it were a notepad and a biro. Evidently, Skouloudis wrote the notes and pushed them into the basket.

'Read them if you want,' Yannelis told me.

The effort Skouloudis had to make to write them was visible to the naked eye. The letters were rounded, compressed and written separately, one by one.

> This slant-eyed girl only makes me tea. I ask her for coffee and she pays no attention. Oh dear, Oh dear.

The second one was a cry of anguish:

> MASHED POTATO! MASHED POTATO! I'M FED UP WITH IT!

'He can't chew,' Yannelis, who was reading over my shoulder, explained. 'All he can eat are soups, purees and at most a little mashed fish.'

The third was an order in a military tone:

> Tell the old bird to take me out for my walk later in the day. She brings me back early and then I suffocate all day.

The last one was a comment:

> I saw *American Yakuza 2*. Everywhere it's the strong who win. We were the only ones who lost. A disgrace!

Yannelis bent over him. 'I have to discuss a few things with the gentleman and then I'll come back. All right, Yangos dear?' she said sweetly.

With the constant shaking of his head, it was difficult to know whether he was giving his assent or ignoring her completely. Yannelis motioned to me to go out with her and she closed the sliding door behind us.

'Three days after his arrest, a friend came by the house and gave me an address and a key. The address was in Liossia. I found a two-roomed flat full of files. Yangos kept copies of all the interrogations he carried out with documents, reports and photographs. Among them, I found my father's file and the files of Jason Favieros, Loukas Stefanakos and Apostolos Vakirtzis. That's how I found out about the "Che" organisation. After they'd burned the archives of the Military Police in Keratsini, these were the only records to remain,' she added with a smile.

'And where are they now?'

'Let me finish. While he was in prison, I began to realise the size of the network that Yangos had set up over the years. From time to time, various people came knocking at my door, bringing me information in the hope that they would help "the Major". One day, during his visiting hours, I told him in sign-coded language that various people kept coming and bringing me gifts for him. He understood immediately and said sharply: "Don't even touch them." Till one day, someone came with information that interested me personally. He told me that Yannelis and his group had begun their activities again. They had dissolved the Che Independent Resistance Organisation and, in its place, had founded the October 8th Revolutionary Organisation ...'

The name reminded me of something. 'Weren't they the ones who planted the bombs in local bank branches?'

'Yes. And two in the Stock Exchange that didn't go off. Che Guevara was killed on October 8th, 1967. The man who brought me the information was extremely methodical. He had discovered their safe house and had photos of them coming and going. He had even succeeded in getting into the safe house using a skeleton key and had taken photos inside. Yangos had told me not to touch them, but I kept them. Apart from my father, all the others made their living in respectable professions. Jason had started a small construction business, Loukas had entered politics and Vakirtzis had started making a name for himself in journalism. As time went by, their careers took off and, dazzled as they were by success, they forgot about the revolution, till they wrote it off completely. By the mid-eighties, my father had remained alone, betrayed by his daughter and by his former comrades.

She went into the kitchen and came back with another glass of whisky. She took a sip, closed her eyes and tried to put her thoughts in some order.

'The idea of revenge came to me after my father's suicide. I convinced myself that it was they who had pushed him to commit suicide and not me. My reasoning was very simple. If he was going to commit suicide because of me, he would have done it much earlier. He committed suicide in the early nineties because he saw how his former comrades had become big names in the system they once wanted to overthrow. The collapse of the communist regimes was just the *coup de grâce.*' She held the glass between her palms and gazed at it. 'I know, you'll tell me that I see it like that because it suits me. Perhaps you're right. I'm tormented by that doubt too. Whatever the case, I wanted to vent the anger that had accumulated within me. They had cashiered Yangos, the little money I had saved went to the lawyers and I had to find work. At the same time, I was studying business management and computer programming in the evenings. When I made my decision to exact revenge, I submitted an application to Favieros's company using my name Coralia Athanassios Yannelis. My father had hidden his shame as he had told me and had never told anyone that I had married the torturer, Yangos Skouloudis. Yangos, on the other hand, had forbidden me to appear at the trial. So I was certain that Favieros didn't know the truth. And, sure enough, after a few days, he called me to his office, satisfied himself that I was Thanos Yannelis's daughter and hired me. I was good at my job and quickly climbed the ladder. In my free time, I wrote the biographies of the three men. I had Yangos's huge archive together with all the information that the various do-gooders had brought me. When I had finished the three biographies, I put the plan into action.'

'You'd already sent the first biography to the publisher?'

'Yes. I chose a small, unknown publisher so as not to run any risks. Then, via email, I began sending Favieros copies of the documents I had in my possession. Each day, I sent something more, without any comment. The information automatically deleted itself the following day and was replaced by more information.'

I recalled one of Stefanakos's notes about someone who had information and whose demands were outrageous. It wasn't Vakirtzis, as I had thought, but Logaras, in other words, Coralia Yannelis.

'And how did they react?'

For the first time, she allowed herself a spontaneous burst of laughter. 'Favieros sent me a curt message: "How much?" Stefanakos was more diplomatic. He wrote: "I don't know what you want, but I'm willing to discuss it". And Vakirtzis replied bluntly: "Name your price, you bastard". I replied to all of them in the same way. "What I want is for you to commit suicide in public and I'll take care of your reputations with a eulogistic biography. If you don't do it, I'll bring everything out into the open and I'll destroy you and your family". Then I sent them the biographies in order to convince them I meant business.'

'Why in public, Mrs Yannelis? That question has been bothering me since the first day.'

'I know. You've mentioned it time and time again,' she replied with a smile. 'Because my father hanged himself and remained hanging there for three days till he started to smell. They had to die before everyone's eyes. Of course, on the other hand, I was offering them the possibility of a heroic exit which would be accompanied by their biography. You realise what would have happened if I had revealed that these businessmen, politicians and journalists had been planting bombs in banks and the Stock Exchange in the early eighties? It would have meant not only their end, but also of their wives and brothers, who were the shop windows for their businesses. All three of them had grown used to the high life, they were big names and couldn't stand the thought of ruin, exposure and prison. They preferred the solution that I offered them.'

'And how did you know that Vakirtzis would commit suicide on the same day that you sent me his biography?'

'I knew that every year he threw a big party on his name day. I made it a condition. I told him that either he committed suicide then or the deal was off.'

So now all the pieces were there before me: the common secret from the past, Logaras and his biographies, the hypotheses I had made that had been correct up to a point, but that hadn't got me anywhere. There was just one question I had left.

'Why me, Mrs Yannelis? Why did you choose me?'

She stared at me and laughed. 'Because you were the only one who wanted to find out the truth. That made an impression on me from your first visit. No one else was interested. They wanted to take care of the funeral, put the unpleasant event behind them and move on. You were the only one. And something else, that I've already mentioned to you twice today.'

'What?'

'I think you understand. I don't know why but I honestly do.'

'Perhaps I do understand, but that doesn't change the fact that it is an indictable offence. Incitement to commit suicide is a crime and is punishable. You'll have to come with me to Headquarters to make an official statement.'

She laughed. 'Come now, Inspector. How are you going to make the charge stick? You have no tangible evidence other than the print-out of a biography written by someone called Minas Logaras.'

'Perhaps, but I'll find something.'

'You won't find anything, I can promise you. I destroyed the part of the archives that didn't interest me years ago. The other day when you received the Che T-shirt, I burned the rest. There's not even one document left, Inspector. Apart from my father's note. Other people have photos of their fathers to remember them by; all I have is a piece of paper in which mine renounces me.' Her bitterness was only momentary, she immediately recovered. 'So how will you make the charge stick, Inspector? And where will you find a public prosecutor to indict me?'

She was right. I wouldn't. That's why she had been playing cat and mouse with me. She knew that I wouldn't be able to touch her.

'Those three men deceived both my father and my husband, Inspector. My father would never have had anything to do with them if he had known they would become businessmen. He hated businessmen. And my husband would never have tortured them if he'd known that they would become businessmen. He admired businessmen; he swore by Onassis and Bodosakis. The one was found hanged and stinking, the other did fifteen years in prison and from being a torturer became the one tortured. I'm not trying to whitewash anyone, not even myself, but those three had to pay. The frightened little girl beat them in the end.' It was the first time I discerned a hint of pride in her voice.

She got to her feet to indicate to me that our conversation was over. I wanted to say something to her, but nothing came to mind. Evidently, she saw it in my face because when we reached the front door, she said:

'Tomorrow, you'll go to your office and I'll go to mine. I'll continue to do all I can to make the companies I manage make a profit; I'll go on working with Mr Zamanis, Mrs Stathatos, and Mrs Favieros and no one will ever know that I sent the friend of the one and the husbands of the other two to their deaths. But I wanted someone else to know, apart from me. I'm glad it's you, believe me. Whatever you may think of me, I'm glad it's you.'

She opened the door for me to leave. I stood in the doorway, hoping that I would think of something to say, but I couldn't. I could neither revile nor reproach her, but nor could I shake her hand. I simply turned and left.

I got into the Mirafiori, but I didn't have the energy to start up the engine. I tried to put my thoughts into some order, but it wasn't easy. I would have to tell Ghikas everything, just as it happened, without concealing anything. The same applied to the Minister. Neither of them would be overly distraught because we couldn't touch Yannelis. On the contrary, they'd be overjoyed because the suicides had stopped and the case would be forgotten without anything coming out into the open. And Ghikas had an additional reason to be happy: because the next day he would have Koula back working for him.

Did Favieros, Stefanakos and Vakirtzis deserve to die? I couldn't say. Did Coralia Yannelis deserve to stand in the dock? I couldn't say that either. So what was left? The three winners: Andreadis, Kalafatis and Yannelis. Along with Ghikas and the Minister. And from what Zissis and Andreadis had said, I was one of the winners, too. Perhaps they were right. After all, I'd managed to get my old job back and my standing with Ghikas and the Minister had gone up a few notches …

I'm not an ungrateful person, but how is it that in the end I always feel like a twerp?